D1479232

The Plough's Share

The Plough's Share

David Richards

thistledown press

Library and Archives Canada Cataloguing in Publication

Richards, David, 1953-
    The plough's share / written by David Richards.

ISBN 1-894345-73-8

    1. Barr Colony(Alta. and Sask.)--Fiction. I. Title.

PS8585.I173P56 2004   C813'.54   C2004-904339-0

Cover photograph (ACCN 4467) courtesy of Saskatoon Public Library —
Local History Room
Author photo: Della Kowalchuk

Cover and book design by Jackie Forrie
Typeset by Thistledown Press
Printed and bound in Canada on acid-free paper

Thistledown Press Ltd.
633 Main Street, Saskatoon, Saskatchewan, S7H 0J8
www.thistledown.sk.ca

Thistledown Press gratefully acknowledges the financial assistance of the Canada Council for the Arts, the Saskatchewan Arts Board, and the Government of Canada through the Book Publishing Industry Development Program for its publishing program.

*To Art & Violet Richards, Albert & Maria Selinger —
homesteaders — and their children, Ross & Kae*

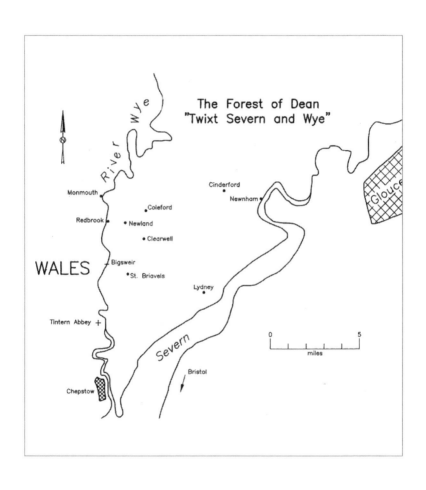

The Forest of Dean
"Twixt Severn and Wye"

River Wye

Monmouth

Cinderford
Newnham

Coleford

Redbrook
Newland

Clearwell

WALES

Bigsweir
St. Briavels

Lydney

Tintern Abbey +

Glouce

Severn

Bristol

Chepstow

0   5
miles

Revelations

CHAPTER 1

The Forest — Gloucestershire — 1898

Hobnails on wet cobblestones — scratching and skidding. The heavy boots marked his hurried progress along the high road. He glanced to his left every few seconds, searching the western skyline for the oak, but a low-lying mist and the remnants of night obscured the hilltop. He paused for a proper look. The first light of false dawn tinted the eastern sky behind him but his oak tree remained obstinately invisible on the west ridge. Damn and blast and damn it all again! He wanted free of this wretched village. The oak was his mark to turn off the roadway and strike across country. If he travelled too far north and missed his way then he'd just have to come back. For the hundredth time he touched the small envelope tucked in his waistcoat pocket. A summons — finally — from this rural dungeon. He hitched his haversack around to the small of his back and peered up, straining for . . . there! A black silhouette against the brightening sky. A few more yards down the road he found the stile that lifted him over a stone wall and dropped him into ankle deep, stinking muck on the other side.

He scarcely noticed and little cared. With luck, this would be the last time he'd have farm boots on his feet or farm manure on his boots. He strode along the path that soon began to rise up the hillside. He dug his toes in and climbed like an alpinist, pushing with his thighs — stabbing his walking stick uphill and pulling forward. Damp grass on the verge of the path splattered his canvas gaiters. His breath came in small puffs and he welcomed it, sucking in the morning air. The last rural air he'd ever breathe. He leaned into the hill, eager for the top.

Then he was up, out of the valley and atop the ridge. Gasping happily he paused to look back. His landmark, the Newland Oak reputed to be one thousand years old, was now clearly visible just a short way down the crest. Below, a single church tower poked through the valley mist. All Saints — The Cathedral of the Forest.

He spat, then regretted it. Already he was behaving like a yokel. God what a place, its grip on him seemed palpable. The village, the whole Forest, was aggressively primitive, determined to take delight in its backwardness. The Newland Oak — really nothing more than an old oak tree. The cathedral just a village church. Yet the Forest dwellers insisted on the aggrandizement of the unremarkable to justify their perverse sense of superiority. He smirked. They would fall over gawping if ever they saw a real cathedral like his beloved Gloucester. Well, they could stay wallowing in their tiny vanities, it was of no further consequence.

The fog blanket rippled and began to flow around the church spire like river water around a half submerged rock. A moment later the breeze crept up the hillside and fanned his face. Then it died, the fog settled calm again. Now a high, rushing sound, hissing like the dry cackle of an old woman's voice, coursed up the hillside. The hairs on the back of his neck tingled. Unnaturally warm wind whipped past his face, stirring bits of grass up into the sky. Yet the fog bank remained unruffled.

The wind increased until it tugged at his cap, flapped his coat tails. Dry and hard edged it swirled back and forth over the hilltop shoving him roughly. For a moment he fancied it was saying something. A wild gust shouted the word — Jack — and tore his cap loose. He scrambled down from the crest to retrieve it. The wind flew over the ridge and into his back, pushing him back towards Newland. He was suddenly frightened. Of what? The wind? It rolled downhill, hit the fog and tore gaps in the white bank, revealing half the church, the Ostrich pub, and a cottage on the high road. It wanted him to turn back, surely . . .

"Damn!" He swore loudly to hear his own voice, stop the superstitious rubbish filling his head. He turned and left Newland behind. Walking swiftly he reached the bottom of the mile-long reverse slope where it met the road. The air was calm in Redbrook valley, and clear, no fog. He laughed, touched the envelope and turned left for the village. There his mother and surely, please God, his deliverance from the Forest of Dean awaited him.

The chief feature commending Redbrook to Jack was its proximity to the River Wye and the fact that the Monmouth-Coleford railway passed through it. A short run up the Wye valley to Monmouth, then change trains for Gloucester and he could be home in a few hours. A whistle blew from the grey, industrial pile that marked the Tinplate Works south of town. The Wye valley was lovely but the Foresters managed to blight it with their smoking factory.

He found the narrow street marked by St. Saviour's church and sped past a block of crumbling houses before turning uphill. The climb was steep and soon only the occasional overgrown cottage marked his way. Why must his aunt live in the back of beyond — surely one of those council slabs would suit her best. The unpleasant thought died as he rounded a tall hedge and saw Offa's Rose. Until this moment he'd supposed the name to be a pretentious Forest exaggeration. Clearly he'd been wrong.

Auntie Vi had carved a thin slice of heaven and served it to herself in the guise of Offa's Rose. A view that excluded most of Redbrook below, gave north and south through the green-leafed hills that overlooked the Wye. A waist-high drystone wall enclosed a quarter-acre plot and a two-story stone cottage. Its spotless white trim wore a green vest of climbing vine. The front garden sported a small sea of floral delight. Crocuses, daffodils and narcissus were first evident, then as he inspected more closely, the various colours revealed pansies, snapdragons and carnations. Banked strips of delicate white bells hovered over lily of the valley while the jasmine and chrysanthemums — not yet in bloom — smiled neatly throughout, waiting their turn.

Jack paused, breathing deeply. This lovely place must be a good sign — a first reward. His headlong rush out of Newland was over. He walked carefully around the perimeter of the wall to the back garden. No ash pile or tip here. Instead apple and plum trees, neatly pruned and just off bloom. Gooseberries growing against the far wall and strawberry plants spaced out from them. Then rows of good things breaking through the vegetable garden topsoil — carrots, onions, and lettuce — he was certain of those. Clearly the work of a gardener. The thought that his "forest aunt" — Violet — could afford to pay even the few shillings of a gardener's wage surprised him.

It made him suddenly conscious of his dirty boots and gaiters. He consulted his watch, only quarter past eight. He couldn't simply crash into the house dripping muck like a farm oaf fresh from morning chores, his mother would scarcely be out of her bed. He hurried to the back gate, let himself quietly into the garden and sat on a small bench under the apple trees. Effectively screened from the house he stripped off the boots, gaiters and heavy socks. Opening his haversack he retrieved some decent hose and a pair of shoes — soft brown leather, thin soles, and neat stitching. He had polished them last night in a state of anticipation and wriggled his toes in delight. The past months had not been a complete waste. They had taught him to appreciate the simple, finer things that he'd never much considered before.

The odious boots and gaiters were tucked under the bench. Aunt Vi's gardener could have them. Shrugging off his overcoat, he fastidiously brushed every inch of his jacket and trousers. Then he made a final adjustment to his tie, passed a comb through his hair and sat again, crossing his legs with his coat folded upon his lap. The transformation from bumpkin to gentleman was complete.

At ten o'clock Jack Thornton presented himself at the front door of Offa's Rose. Two raps on the knocker brought a young woman in servant's uniform. She stood arms akimbo in the door and grinned widely at the sight of him, but made no move to let him in. There were precious few gentle folk in the Forest and she was likely unaccustomed to any but his aunt's rough manners.

"Oo be it?" an old lady's voice cracked from inside.

When he made eye contact the maid blushed and stepped back in some confusion, half closing the door.

"It look like a young gent!" she hissed. "Vi, Vi! It be a young gent — 'ere at ours!"

"This is my 'ouse, b'aint ours!" came his aunt's rebuke. "And you'll not be using my Christian name again lest you feel like losing your position!"

"But I think it be a boy-chap gentleman!"

"Then it's likely Jack — early an all. Let him in ye sawney thing."

The door opened and to Jack's immense satisfaction the girl dipped respectfully toward him.

"Missus says to please come in, zur."

She took his haversack with another unabashed grin. He walked slowly through the tiny hall into the parlour. His aunt, buried in layers of dark clothing sat opposite the door, a long, red nose, ruddy cheeks, and eyes darting like a bird's greeted him.

"Jackie!" she clapped her hands. "It's been a right long time. Come to your Aunty."

The "Jackie" might have rankled six months ago but not now. Nothing could dampen his spirits this day. He crossed the room with studied calm, took both her wiry hands in his, bent from the waist and pecked them.

"Aunt Violet, a pleasure."

"Vi's good enough for me, Jack. No airs in the Forest, eh lad?" She patted the settee and he sat. "Your Mam will be down soonest."

Jack sank into the comfortable cushions, an involuntary sigh escaped him.

"You have a lovely place here Aunt . . . ah, Vi. The garden is wonderful. I had no idea you were such a green thumb."

"I'm not." She shot him a sideways glance. "It was your Uncle Billy's passion. I just keep it up in memory of him."

"Really?" Jack couldn't hide the surprise in his voice. "Billy did all this? That's rare in Forest men."

She leaned from her chair and took one of his hands. "Colliers and miners by necessity are our men. That doesn't make them anything less than clerks and Vicars 'n' such."

She held his eye steadily. "I see Forest work has roughed your paw and browned your face. It's a good start but it hasn't knocked the snob out of you. That will come in time. Though I doubt you'll ever be a true Forester."

He pulled his hand free, conscious of the calluses and chapped skin. "I should hope not Aunt," he said more sharply than he intended. "And once I get back to the firm I shall not be even a clerk much longer, I trust."

She cackled and wagged a finger at him. "Thee dusn't know all, boy-chap. But I'll attend your mam, she can explain. Wyn! Lazy girl. Bring us a bit o' taye and some o' they tarts," she screeched.

A beam of sunlight slanted through the lattice window, tracing diamond shadows onto the rug near his foot. The river valley presented itself like a landscape painting framed in the window.

"Never tire of that view." Vi murmured. "Why live anywhere but on the banks of the Wye," she chuckled softly. "That was my Billy's line."

Jack nodded. The Wye valley really couldn't be considered as part of the Forest. It could be accepted as something special, and beautiful. He rose and crossed to the window, flipping the top latch free. "May I Aunty?"

"Of course," she said.

He opened the bottom latch and pushed the metal frame. It swung open easily. Sunlight on the front flowers scented the air that wafted in. He inhaled the aroma and blinked peacefully in the bright light.

"Come sit again, Jack. Tell me how that son of mine is behaving. I'm surprised the Vicar hasn't sacked him by now."

He returned to the settee and reluctantly called his cousin to mind. Charles Cordey — ex miner — ex soldier — part farmer — part fraud and full-blooded scoundrel. A familiar sensation of distaste rose at the back of his mouth. Then it rapidly subsided in the flower-air filling the parlour. He was free of Charlie Cordey. What concern were Cordey's petty little swindles and seductions? His aunt need not know the truth.

"The Vicar seems very happy with him. Claims the farm is at its best now that Charles is managing it."

The bird eyes raked him, unblinking.

"Are you . . . lying to me, Jack?"

He started at the blunt and perceptive question.

"No Aunt, those are the Vicar's words." Defending Charlie Cordey shouldn't have been so easy but the man was an efficient farmer, despite all his vices.

15

"Aye," she smiled. "I don't doubt Charlie has the Vicar fooled. A naive and trusting man as I remember. Amazing he has climbed so high in the church. It's rare for a true Christian to even take to the cloth — much less succeed at it."

"Oh Aunt." Jack stiffened at her Forest insubordination. "He is a gentleman. Of course he's a Christian. Who ever heard of an ordained minister . . . "

"Ha!" She cut him short. "You've a lot to learn, Jack. A long road to walk. Don't lecture me on the church."

Jack refused her eyes and glanced out the window. Why on earth was he arguing something like church appointments with his aunt? Might as well debate it with the cat.

"Where's that girl with the taye! Wyn! WYYN!"

Jack winced. "Anyway, the Newland church is scarcely the definition of a high position."

"The Cathedral in the Forest?" His aunt's voice betrayed genuine surprise. "I should hope a cathedral appointment is a much sought post."

He gritted his teeth. "Yes Aunt."

"WYYYYN! We're gasping in here!"

The girl entered the room with long gliding steps, holding a large copper tray cautiously before her.

"'Bout time," Vi snapped.

"Didn't want to spill anything missus," Wyn replied casting a frank eye over Jack and leering when he acknowledged her.

"Table, Jack, oot." Vi motioned toward a low occasional table beneath the window. Jack fetched it and set it before his aunt. Wyn, bending stiff kneed to set the tray down, managed to brush her bottom against his hip as he backed clear.

"Thank you so very much, I'm sure," Wyn purred. Jack retreated rapidly to the settee.

"Is that blue on your lips?" Vi asked. "It is by God. You've eaten one of my blueberry tarts you sneaking glutton."

Wyn blushed and wiped quickly at the corner of her mouth. "Never! I never stole so much as a crumb, even though I'm nearly starved on what you . . . "

"Out! Leave us and save the lies!"

Wyn fled the room feigning tears of outrage to cover her humiliation in front of a visiting gentleman.

"Really, Aunt." Jack frowned. "Why do you stand for such insolence from that girl? She's lacking even the smallest notion of her position!"

"Wyn?" Vi laughed. "I love the silly little rabbit! She's scarcely house broken, true enough, but what would she get up to if I didn't employ her? Besides, she is excellent company and works like a pit horse."

Jack shrugged by way of reply. Again, what point in discussing domestic arrangements in a Forest cottage — even one as lovely as Offa's Rose?

"Oh, Jack. It is you. I heard the commotion at the door and hurried down. You look wonderful. Come here, come to me my Johnny. He's wonderful isn't he Vi? He is, just wonderful and so brown and strong . . . "

Jack managed to stem the flow by quickly crossing the parlour and embracing his mother. Tall where Vi was stunted, and soft where Vi was rough, his mother did match her sister in all things verbal. Her habit of non-stop chattering had been a source of some discomfort to him, but not any longer. Another backhand benefit of months in the Forest dungeon — his mother's natter now sounded as lovely to him as a warbler's song.

He held her, and for a long moment she seemed to almost cling to him. "Oh, Jackie," she whispered in a tiny quaver. It was all coming right. She wanted him back as desperately as he wanted to come back. The last shreds of his exile fell away. He was as good as home. It was all here in his arms, embodied by his mother. She had finally made it right. Gloucester, the firm, decent clothes, honourable work, his friends, and his commission in the volunteer battalion but most of all her, his mother, and home. Tears of relief stung his eyes surprising him — relief at what? He found his own voice quivering "It's all going to be fine, Mother. It will be good again."

"Give him air, Gladys!" Vi's harsh command drove between them. "And sit for some taye before it stews. The boy must be starving."

"Have you eaten, Jack?" his mother thrust him out at arm's length. Sunlight fell bright on her face revealing a woman suddenly older than his mother. Thin streaks of grey striped her mass of chestnut hair. Her dark brown eyes — his own colour — were black- shadowed beneath and grew deep crows' feet at the corners. They flickered at him nervously — or perhaps just tired.

He shook his head, and murmured, "Mother, please, not Jack, John . . . I'm not a boy any more."

"Oh, John then. Here, sit. I'll be mother," she busied herself with milk and sugar. "These tarts are marvellous, blueberry jam in heavenly pastry. No fresh blueberries yet, of course, but the jam is absolutely delicious. Is that enough milk, dear? Should I stir the tea? How long has it been steeping? You shouldn't have waited for me."

She looked up from the fussing and smiled — a wide-eyed smile that dimpled her cheeks and warmed him. Jack brushed a strand of hair from his forehead and surreptitiously dabbed the corner of his eye as he accepted his teacup and a tart. It was delicious — even the tea tasted better. His mother and Vi spoke in a simultaneous babble. His mother lavishing praise on Jack's rugged appearance and Vi salting it with the opinion that he needed another good few months as a farm worker to straighten him out. Maybe even a trip down the coal pits.

Jack smiled, ate, drank, and watched the sunlight creep across the carpet and over his shoes. Bliss. True bliss — until now only a word used by poets. First the firm, of course. He'd have to work hard but a year or even less should see him back in the way of a management position. With his father's estate settled, there might even be enough capital for him to make a small investment, nudge the partners along toward an earlier appointment. He finished a tart and passed his cup to his mother for a refill. Next was his lieutenancy in the Second Volunteer Battalion. He could sit his final examination for certification in late June. Just in time for summer manoeuvres. Would the firm release him for the training? That might be tricky — have to test the waters.

The women had fallen silent and were staring at him.

"Well?" his mother asked.

"Sorry, I was daydreaming, Mother."

Vi shot a knowing glance at her sister, who had reddened.

"How did you enjoy your time at Newland?"

"As you found in my letters, Mother," he replied. "I did not enjoy. In fact the whole vile Forest ordeal could scarcely rise to be called tedious. It was — "

Vi glared at him.

"Ah . . . naturally there were some advantages." He smiled an apology at his aunt. "Principal among them, the rough life and outdoor work have given me a greater appreciation for Gloucester and proper employment."

Vi sniffed loudly

"Yet it seems now to have been an unnecessary exile?" he prompted. "I trust there were, in the end, no difficulties in settling father's estate?"

His mother smiled but her lips were compressed, the cheerful dimples of a few moments earlier were gone. She studied her teacup closely.

"Father's estate is clear for release? Or not?"

"Oh yes, cleared," his mother said quickly, eyes half closed, chin jutting forward defiantly. "Never fear on that point my son. Your father was a fine and honest man. Of course, once lies and rumour take root, well, it's difficult to . . . um, uproot." She finished lamely, reaching for the teapot even though all the cups were full.

The subtly delivered blow made Jack's hand twitch, rattling cup and saucer. All was not right. The Newland oak, Offa's Rose, the flower garden lattice sun on his shoes, the tea and tarts, his mother's embrace. An elaborate succession of false signposts conspiring to bring him not home, but to the edge of a cliff whose existence he had refused to acknowledge. His mother's grey streaks and sad eyes; Vi's abuse of the clergy; these were the true waymarkers.

He swivelled to look at Vi. She flushed and her eyes shot down into her lap, refusing to meet him. He wondered if it was the first time in her life that she had ever acknowledged the sensation of embarrassment. But it confirmed his mother's message. He was seized with a reckless desire to know the worst, all of it now, and have it over.

"Was there scandal? With the Dean?"

His mother held the teapot like a royal orb, a grimace frozen on her mouth, eyes staring.

"Mother? Please? Is that why you've met me here rather than call me to Gloucester?" The thought he'd held hard in his subconscious now strolled forth and announced itself. "There was scandal. The estate is small . . . inadequate? You're here to live with ah . . . live here? I'm not to go home?"

He checked his rush of questions. Despair crept into him at the lack of his mother's intervention. How much farther could he go? Vi sat still and calm, but as yet unable to meet his eyes. The only sound was the clicking of his cup against the uneven surface of its saucer. He gripped them in both hands and drew a breath.

"You're saying, Mother, that the Dean made trouble against Father?" He pushed his voice to a stern tone. "Did the Dean somehow shift his misdeeds onto Father's plate? For God's sake, Mother! A dead man can't defend himself but his widow and son must . . . our duty to him. We can't — "

"*No!*" Vi's head snapped up. Her blush was gone and her bright eyes held him. "Tell him, Gladys. Tell all, my girl. Thee cosn't protect him, but mustn't torture him neither."

The teapot descended slowly to the table. his mother worked her lips but they only produced a thin mewing sound and a rapid flutter of eyelashes.

"Gladdy . . . come now," Vi, almost gentle, coaxed her. "The lad deserves telling."

"There will not be any charges," his mother started bravely. "And there would not be charges even if he still were alive. He was not a thief."

The denial struck only slightly less hard than a conviction. "The Reverend Wallace Thornton, B.A., M.A., assistant Dean and senior member of the chapter of Gloucester Cathedral is not and never was a thief." No comfort in that thought.

"Your father made some investments on the advice of others whom he trusted. These investments proved to be . . . unwise." She frowned like a disapproving schoolteacher. "In fact, his only fault was to trust incompetent men with his money. Money earmarked to help you with your commission and business interests. Now it seems his reputation is to be tarnished and we are punished because a man of God trusted his fellow man."

Even for his mother, this was an astonishing evasion of reality. "Mother!" Jack smiled despite the sick twist in his stomach. "We didn't go from Gloucester to the backwoods because of a poor investment. Just tell me."

"I thought I had," her shoulders sagged, eyes darting away as she regained the teapot, overfilling her cup. "All quite ridiculous and really, dear, inexplicable, but your father was not a thief. It seems to me the lawyer and brokers might well look to that label but it is we who are left without a penny."

"Penniless . . . literally?" Jack croaked. "And my commission with the Volunteers?"

"Gone, Jackie . . . John," his mother waved a hand as though it were merely her favourite doily lost in the laundry, but her lips trembled violently. "All quite gone. But not exactly penniless. I have moved here at Violet's kind request and will manage to live free of her charity."

"At least you're safe; that's something." Jack spoke more to himself, his mind racing to collate his options — make a plan. Like the little Dutch boy he desperately sought to save the dike, jamming a finger first into one leak, then another. "I'll visit the solicitors myself, see what can be salvaged from the estate — get my position back at the firm and look to my salary. I can live frugally 'til I'm on my feet again. Commission doesn't have to be lost, just deferred to next year's exams."

"No, Jack." Vi stopped his ramble. "B'ain't no return for you or Gladys. Your feythur did quomp Gloucester for you once an all. Gladys, bring him the papers while I have a talk with him."

His mother rose and suddenly the tears came. Great streams flooding down her cheeks. Neither sob nor wail, just silent weeping. She walked through the sunbeam and disappeared down the hall.

"I'll strip the varnish off it for you, Jack, though I take no pleasure in it," Vi said with relish. "Because there's nought to be gained by leaving you with a false hope."

She sipped her tea and settled back. "Soon after your Feythur died the church solicitors told your Mam that they had a claim against his estate. Wallace's replacement — the new mon, Proctor — had discovered a gurt pile of money missing from the Cathedral building fund. Nay, "discovered" be too harsh," she hastened to soften her tone. "But I'd aim that was why you hurried off to Newland after the funeral — just in case things turned rasty.

Jack stood involuntarily, "But that was my father's wish! Just before he died — a deathbed wish as it turned out. Had I known of the missing money I'd never have run . . . that is, I'd not have left Mother . . . "

His words died. It was too much, a coward protesting his innocence.

"Thee did not know about the church's money," Vi paused, then raised her eyebrows to make the statement a question.

"Of course not. Father was scarcely capable of speech after the stroke. He said he was at odds with the Dean; that there might be scandal but wouldn't say why. That it would be best if I was physically gone, so gossip would be less likely to attach to me. But I thought it was the Dean who had, you know, created some irregularity, certainly not Father."

Vi spread her hands palms outward. "He foresaw it, the coming trouble — hoped to protect 'is boy," she shrugged, "a very little hope. I'd expect he was that desperate. Doost thee want the details before Gladys comes back?"

He sat back down and nodded.

"Proctor found a promissory note signed by your feythur. No attempt to hide the missing money but no approval from Dean, chapter ner Bishop neither," she nodded significantly. "He'd

23

invested the money figuring to return it in six months, along with the church interest. 'E thought 'e could triple the church rate from his scheme, then keep the extra."

She paused, but Jack was held speechless by her beady gaze.

"Investments failed, lost half the money. He returned what was left, then comes the stroke, then this Proctor crayture sniffin' about for the missing money. Much confusion and prideful struttin' from the high clergy but in the end the Bishop's solicitors sold Wallace and your Mam's wum, furniture and other such goods, repaid the rest of the note. But nay talk o' fraud. There is enough left, as your mam says, for her to stay clear of my charity."

"Is it really that bad? Is it all down to Father? The newspaper, my friends," Jack found himself standing again. "Surely there would have been some mention of Reverend Thornton's disgrace. I read the paper, wrote regularly to my friends, and there was nothing. I nearly came home many times, and would have except for Mother's insistence that I stay here."

"Never thought why she wouldn't have 'ee back, then?

Vi watched him carefully, daring him to lie. "Never figured why your Feythur sent you away if it was the Dean oo be the bad 'un?"

"Yes, I wondered, Vi. I tried not to but, of course, I did. My friends over time became less enthusiastic in their writing. I became afraid to read the newspaper. I was suspicious and . . . afraid." This came out in the small voice of a boy at confession. He coughed to clear it. "I've hidden here, in the Forest, afraid of what Mother might be facing, yet too cowardly to go home and find the truth, I suppose. The dying wish was convenient. But Mother's note . . . "

He touched his waistcoat as he had done in Newland with such hope.

"Thee yud told 'ee it had come right." She tapped her head, then placed her palm over her heart. "But 'ere, thee must 'ave knowed."

"Well, as I said, nothing in the news and nothing really from my friends — our society. Yes I thought it was safe."

"I'll not judge your courage past," Vi said. She glared fiercely at him. "But make no mistake, this 'society' in Gloucester has done with thee and Gladys. This blow be yours to take and take well — your mother is near beat senseless by this last six months. Thou cosn't be nesh, for her sake."

The sun still shone on the carpet. The blueberry jam still tasted good on his tongue, even though he was a self confessed poltroon and the son of a disgraced minister. Funny that. You'd think a cloud would have intervened or the jam gone bitter.

"So he was a thief — really," Jack murmured in a voice that didn't seem much to care.

"Ha!" Vi lunged forward and slapped his knee. "Never, never! He did naught more than most men in his position have done and a lot less than others. If his scheme had worked not Dean nor Bishop auld care one wit! Instead of helping others, he helped himself! 'E be guilty of greed but no worse than any of 'em. His only sin was bad luck and a worse investment."

Gladys, red eyed but composed, swept into the room and passed him a small, leather briefcase. She retreated to the windowsill and perched, watching him. Jack opened it and began to scan the documents inside. Like a punch-drunk boxer who hasn't yet fallen down, he took the successive blows, not stoically, but in a stunned daze.

There were Bishop's letters, auction invoices, solicitors statements of account — even an overdue mess bill from the Second Battalion Volunteers — all confirming that his employment was gone, commission denied, and his home sold. Then there was a two-day-old newspaper, front page, small article but with bold typeface in the title: "Former Member of Cathedral Chapter Investigated." His father's name. The "irregular" use of funds. All monies recovered. No charges. And finally the statement from the bishop's secretary, to bandage it all over: " . . . our Christian duty to forgive a momentary lapse in a previously unblemished character. His grace has extended his sympathy to Mr. Thornton's widow and son. He considers the matter to be at an end."

Jack stopped reading.

"Your letters, these last six months, Mother," he struggled to keep his voice neutral. "They mentioned none of this. I had no idea it had gone so far, so wrong. But I suspected and was too frightened to face those suspicions. I'm sorry."

"I had hopes, John," she pleaded as though he'd accused her of some villainy she must explain. " I hoped you could come home, take up your work, carry on like always. I didn't want to . . . I couldn't give you such a disappointment." She pointed to the newspaper. "Until now — until the end."

"Thank you," he rose, took her hands, kissing each one in turn. "Thank you, my love. I ran once, I will not run again. You must consider yourself free of any further burden as regards myself or . . . Father."

"Well said, boy-chap," Vi muttered, but he didn't acknowledge her.

"Come walk with me, Mother," Jack kept one of her hands and led her to the front door. She offered no resistance, following him out the gate and around to the bench in the garden.

"I'm so sorry, John, so very — "

"No, Mother, hush," he squeezed her hand. "You have nothing to apologize for. It was Father's ridiculous money scheme. It was I who hid in the Forest. Now we seem destined to stay in the Forest — as though we've been suddenly caught in a net — trapped below our station."

She tried to smile but it failed, puckering her mouth like an old woman.

"Time, Mother," he suddenly realized he needed her smile and fought for it. "Just a few more months. I'll save my wages from Newland and go to Bristol — maybe London — get a position then I'll send for you. I won't have you here long. Just a little time and I'll come to your rescue. Can you be brave a little longer?"

Four hours ago, in a different lifetime, he had been the son — hoping to go home to his mother. Now he was a man, offering refuge to a defeated woman, aged well beyond his mother.

"Vi and Offa's Rose suit me, John," she said, rewarding him with a warm, dimpled smile. "This is my home now. I'll bide here — you go forward my boy. Do great things but don't do them for my sake. Make your own name."

"Offa's Rose is fine, temporarily I agree. But you deserve better and I'll give it you."

"No, you have misunderstood," his mother shook her head. "I want to be here. I owe it to Vi. She must be allowed to save me. I have owed a debt for twenty years and now I mean to repay."

"Debt? But she said you had some money . . . "

Her back stiffened. "It is a debt from before you were born. Sister to sister. I will stay with her now as long as we both live. And I am happy — indeed grateful for the chance to do so."

"How much is owed? How came we to be in Uncle Billy's debt for twenty years — is that what Father needed money for?"

"No, not at all." She raised her hands, palms outward. "It is not between your father and Bill. It is owed strictly from me to Vi. Leave it alone. Go back to Newland, think about your future. Save your wages, then go on with your life wherever you want, just not Gloucester."

He began to protest, but she cut him short. "Please, John. All I want now is peace. You can visit me here every Sunday!" She straightened his tie and smoothed his lapels. "Won't that be lovely? Peace is what I crave above all now. Can you give me that?"

CHAPTER 2

Past noon, which meant Charlie Cordey would be in the pub. Jack hesitated — the Vicarage and solitude or the Ostrich and more hard truths. He'd walked the long way back, following the Wye then cutting cross-country to Newland. He'd set himself a fast pace and now arrived breathless and sweating, back where he'd started at dawn. He was calm, depressed, in the mood for disappointment. He stepped into the pub and paused to let his eyes adjust to the dim light.

Cordey sat uncharacteristically alone at a small bench near the room's one large window. Dark curly hair, broad open face, with a broken nose that seemed to suit his rough charm, he was the first among patrons of the Ostrich. He pulled at a glass of ale then rummaged in the bread and cheese on a plate resting on his lap.

"Jack, just in time for lunch. Come on, I've saved you a spot." Cordey patted the bench.

Jack sat to avoid direct eye contact. Charlie's expectant grin and quick eyes had already pricked him.

"Saved me a spot? When I had no plan to return?"

"Knew you'd be back. Just couldn't be certain you'd come see me first so I established my picquet here at the window." He chuckled, "You know, observe without being observed — light infantry like."

"Well, my plans have changed, temporarily, as it so happens," Jack conceded.

"As it so happens! That's good, Jack lad, keep up the act, you'll fool most here," Charlie nudged him, "but not me. Best have a pint, you look tired out. Care for some cheese? You'll need something in you 'cause we're tacklin the troughs this afternoon while it's dry and warm."

He waved toward the bar, "Sally, my sweet, a pint for young Jack; he's gasping."

Jack shrugged, forcing a smile. "Act? What are you on about now? I've decided not to go back to Gloucester until after harvest, that's all. Really quite simple. Mother and I discussed how I'd best be placed as regards the firm and the regiment . . . "

"I'll stop you right there, you young pup," Charlie cut in hard and low-voiced. "I know about Gloucester Cathedral, the Dean and the money Uncle Wal got stitched for. I was going to do you a favour by not telling this lot . . . "

Sally approached with the beer and paused for her usual flirt with Charlie, but he sent her off with a curt, "Thanks, Sal."

Jack accepted the glass taking two long swallows. God Almighty, how could Cordey be so far ahead of him? What a fool he'd been to expect a clean escape from this place.

"I was going to keep mum," Charlie continued, "but, by Christ, don't play the gent with me anymore, sonny, or your father will be village gossip before sundown."

Jack of yesterday would have stormed out but today he stayed on the bench. Charlie bloody Cordey and Aunt bloody Vi knew about his father's disgrace while he, like an infant, had hidden, sheltered by his mother. It galled him and it humbled him but it also aroused a perverse determination. It did present a dark opportunity to prove at least to Cordey that he was not a boy. He would take this clear faced now, like a man. In fact, he would come straight to his point and ask for the final blow before Charlie could feed it to him with a sneer.

"I'll behave as a gentleman if I choose," he replied and sipped his beer. "If I'm guilty of taking on airs I then apologize, for that is not the manner of a true gentleman. Besides, my father's situation is now published news, your threat means nothing."

Charlie snorted, glancing out the window.

"I do have a question that I should like a straight answer for. I'll ask it plain . . . what is the debt my mother owes your family, please? I would look towards discharging it as soon as possible."

Cordey's head whipped around to face him.

"Debt?"

"Mother is staying with Aunt Vi, she says because of a debt originating before my time. She refused to tell me anymore. I'll only ask the amount, I'm not particularly interested in the details that gave rise . . . "

"Good, because you'll not get them from me," Charlie's demeanour had transformed. For an instant the brassy, bluff exterior faded and his voice fell quiet, almost soft. "There's no need for you to be involved. As to the circumstances, well, your mother is right. It's between Mam and she, naught for you to be concerned over."

Charlie drained his glass, rose and jammed his cap on his head. Sally waved him goodbye but he ignored her and made for the door. Jack, slightly dazed at having scored a blow when he expected to receive one, could only sip his beer and speculate on the vast amount he did not know about his own family.

An old miner sporting startling blue scars and a badly bent back plopped himself down on the vacant seat.

"Thee be from oover," he declared, tapping Jack with the stub of a grubby clay pipe.

"Over?" Jack snapped, irritated at the intrusion.

"Aye, oover t'bridge on Severn what takes the road to Gloucester. You be a foreigner."

"I'm from Gloucester, yes, hardly a foreigner."

The old codger bristled up at this. "Jolter knows a foreigner. I'm born in the hundred o' St. Briavels. I'm a free-miner and dug iron in this Forest my whole life — never been 'oover' myself, so we knows a foreigner, don't we?"

Jack stood and looked down. "Never been out of the Forest, once? Your whole life? Poor old bones."

"Doosn't thee fret for I," he wheezed, half rising in challenge. "I bain't tired o'round 'ere yet."

Jack offered his unfinished pint and the wreck lost interest in the debate. Jack made his escape to the satisfied, smacking sounds of the ancient miner guzzling ale.

● ● ●

The Vicar's stable seemed to be a source of unending labour. Jack stamped on his spade, driving it down sharply beside the trough. Better to have knocked the place flat and build new rather than repairing first this bit, then that piece. He heaved on the handle and pried the last chunk of hard, dried manure away from the trough.

"Right, here's the crowbar, see if we can shift the bugger." Charlie passed him the iron bar then knelt and thrust his shoulder against the trough. Jack hammered the bar under the bottom plank and lifted, his shoulders creaking with the effort. They were rewarded by a splintering snap as the plank popped loose and the whole trough crashed over.

"Christ be praised, that's the last of 'em," Charlie wheezed. Jack stood puffing, oddly pleased with their little success. He and Cordey worked well together. And, he had to admit, there were skills to be learned from Charlie. Two men in two days had

demolished the old fences and troughs and levelled the stable yard
bare. Neither had mentioned his father or the debt.

"I'll get the barrow," he offered, and crossed the yard to the
stable. Its dark interior was a cool relief from the sunburned yard.
It was a barn really, not a stable, only one horse — not fit for riding.
The rest of the building had been refitted last winter by Charlie
and him to accommodate a milk cow, pigs and the ubiquitous
sheep that the Vicar seemed to love so dearly but insisted on letting
run loose. He scarcely noticed the thick smell of the animals, so
overpowering only six months ago.

"Charles! Charles Cordey, a moment please." Jack recognised
the voice and paused. It was the Vicar's niece from London, another
foreigner from "oover", and a lovely foreigner at that.

"Miss?"

"My uncle has said that I may have the trap to go into Coleford
this afternoon."

Jack crept back to the doorway and stood to one side, peering
through a gap in the boards. Emma Wilson's profile was just visible.

"All right, miss, I'll have Bobbi harnessed and ready for you."

She turned and rubbed the bridge of her nose, which was a
trifle long and freckled. Not a classic beauty, Jack thought, but he
nonetheless held his eye resolutely to the opening, studying the
dark hair, long white neck and graceful body. A twinge of guilt at
spying on her was greatly outweighed by the pleasure of examining
her without restriction.

"Uncle can't drive today so you will have to; I'm to visit the
Mitchells and stay for tea."

"Oh, aye." Jack heard the disapproval in Charlie's voice. "If it's
calling for tea then you must be driven. Vicar won't mind me
interrupting the yardwork, I suppose, to drive you to tea."

Jack's face flushed at the insolence but Emma merely tilted her head back a fraction and gazed down her nose, a tiny smile on her lips.

"Don't smile at the peasant," Jack whispered to himself.

"Seems to me the yard is nearly clear. Uncle says the men will be here to begin placing the cobblestones soon, but if you're too busy I'm certain Jack could drive."

Jack's morale took flight. An afternoon drive with the delightful Emma!

"Right you are, miss. Only remains to haul this trough to the burning pit. I'll leave young Jack to do that so I can clean myself up a bit to drive you."

"That's better!" She beamed at her victory. "We shall leave at two o'clock."

Jack contrived to be in the yard lethargically dismantling the last of the trough and loading it on the barrow at two o'clock. Charlie lounged beside the trap, shining, clean shoes, best tweed vest, laundered shirt with a red neckerchief tied at a jaunty angle. Freshly shaved as well by the look of it. The Vicar and his niece emerged from the house. Charlie doffed his cap.

"I say, Charlie, yard looks terrific. Be wonderful to have it paved properly, eh?"

"Yes, Vicar," Charlie nodded deferentially. "Make a world of difference, especially this winter."

"Well, you've made a good job of it, you and young Jack." The Vicar, bald with a wispy grey-haired fringe, was a wiry, active man with sharp eyes. "Tricky getting those old troughs out I'll wager? I'd have had a go myself but for these interminable deanery meetings all week."

"We could have used you, sir," Charlie smiled. The Vicar started toward the stable.

"Well, I fully intend to be on hand when — "

"Uncle?" Emma called him back. "It's past two and we really should be going."

"Ah, yes, of course, let's have you up then." He supported her as she stepped up into the trap.

"Oh, I nearly forgot the book!" Emma turned to look for Jack. "Jack Thornton, here, I have your book."

Her tone was nearly the same one she used to call her dogs for a treat and Jack tried hard not to run like a faithful beagle. The Vicar read the cover.

"*A Pair of Blue Eyes*?" He gave Jack an embarrassed glance. "Hardy, eh? A bit sentimental for a man's reading . . . I'd have thought."

"Oh Uncle, it's perfectly well-written literature. Since Jack isn't leaving us after all," she hung there for a second and Jack pulsed with embarrassment. "I thought he would enjoy this. He loved the *Trumpet Major*, didn't you ?"

"Ah, well, yes, I confess I did find it interesting." He avoided the Vicar's eye.

"These young ones and their novels. What a business, eh Charlie?"

"Not my cuppa, Vicar. I'm reading a history of the Glosters — my old Sixty-first Foot. Colonel Smith published a few copies last year." He shot Emma a quick grin, missed by the Vicar.

"Excellent choice, Charlie, well done. Perhaps you can instruct my niece in some of our county regiment's history. Serve her better than this Hardy fellow I'd say."

"Now, Uncle," she pretended to scold, "Jack has told me that he is an officer with the Glosters and you give him no credit for it." Emma's eyes slid curiously to Jack.

"Ah, well, I *was* an ensign, Miss Wilson," Jack said, cheeks glowing red. "But only with the Second Volunteer Battalion — not regular army." He forced himself to the full truth of it. "And not even an ensign anymore. Thanks ever so for the loan — book, that is."

Emma's expression of curiosity faded to sympathy . . . or apathy? Then she looked away. Jack took the book.

"Never mind, perhaps one day you'll gain your commission," the Vicar interjected with forced cheerfulness. "Now off you go. Bye, my dear."

Emma allowed Jack a smile and a pretty little wave goodbye.

"So what would you like to know about my old regiment, miss?" Charlie stepped up on a wheel spoke and vaulted into the front of the trap, cane brandished like a sword. He tapped the horse. "Walk on, Bobbi, up now, girl."

"Start with this curious hat badge business, Charlie. Do all the soldiers really have two?"

"Oh yes, one in front, t'other in back, on account of our fightin' the Frogs back to back in Egypt."

Their voices faded, the Vicar made for the stable but Jack stood, book in hand, very much aware that it was Emma's book from Emma's hands. Her words floated back to him, "Oh, Charlie, one in front and one behind at the same time . . . it seems so extravagant!" And she laughed casually, familiar and comfortable. Too familiar for a farm employee. Jack bristled at the sound of it. Would they share a secret joke about his lost commission? She may have read the newspaper article — know about his father. He had to assume the Vicar was aware of the scandal, but he'd not gossip to her surely. The Vicar was a decent old stick and much too practical to gossip, wasn't he? The same couldn't be said about Charlie despite his promise in the pub.

"Jack, lad," the Vicar called. "Let's have a look at your burning pit before I get back to work."

• • •

35

The warmth of the day had gone, leaving behind cooled air that glowed yellow in the setting sun. The two-storey addition at the rear of the Vicar's house faced west, its lower-floor kitchen was shut down and dark, but the upper-floor windows were thrown open. In one of these Jack Thornton sat, back propped against the dormer wall, one leg dangling over the sill, achieving the best peace he could find in the Forest of Dean.

A Pair of Blue Eyes held him in thrall. Each turn of the page immersed him deeper into the story until he reached a point where he was aware of only the sun's horizontal rays warming his cheek, the soft air passing his face, and Thomas Hardy's characters performing for him.

"Son of a bitch!"

Charlie Cordey stamped up the last of the steps to their room and banged the door open. He flung his cap against the wall and aimed a kick at his bed frame making it jump. "Son of a goddamn bitch!"

Jack closed his book but did not move from his window perch. Evenings usually found Charlie enthroned at the Ostrich, charming pints out of his friends. His early return was a disappointing interruption of Jack's solitude. But seeing Charlie defeated and angry was some compensation.

"Trouble at the Ostrich, my older cousin?"

Charlie picked up his hat then threw it again. "Never got to the goddamned Ostrich, did I? Might as well have been there guzzling for all the good I accomplished . . . "

He seemed to catch himself, making an almost physical effort to control his anger.

"Anyway, no point cryin' over spilt milk, eh?" He attempted a laugh.

Jack's interest was piqued. "Then trouble on the trip to Mitchell's was it?" Perhaps coarse Charlie had soured Emma. He tried to keep his hopes in check.

"No, cousin," Charlie relaxed and flopped on his bed. "That was a delightful little expedition — pretty company and good conversation all round. Very satisfactory."

"Well, why the temper then?" Jack probed, disappointed that the drive to Mitchells had gone so well.

"Personal matter, doesn't concern you — silly little thing really. Don't know why it got so far under my skin, Jack." He forced a cold smile warning Jack to go no farther.

"Fine, but best lay off the cursing or Vicar will hear."

"You weren't with us lambing this year. You should hear the Vicar when one of his precious ewes has a breach or worse, a stillborn lamb. He won't use the Lord's name in vain — true — but hello!" Charlie laughed fondly. "He used about every other oath that man's invented. Besides, that's part of my job here, didn't you know?"

"To swear?"

"Gawn! Jack, you're a babe sometimes, aren't you," Charlie scoffed but was clearly happy to shift the conversation onto Jack's naïveté. "I'm the man with the bark still on. I've soldiered in India and sweated in the iron mines and I work for him, see?"

Jack shook his head no, then regretted it.

"Oh, come on! Surely you see it! He spends his time writing sermons, having tea with parish ladies, poncing around doing lily-white good deeds but he needs to be a man sometimes. That's what I do Jack! I work and sweat and swear for him and pretend to be his pal — but not too familiar like — so he can think he's a blue-scarred boy from the Forest of Dean. A badger running his ship and workin' alongside o' me." Jack looked for Charlie Cordey, the familiar Forester, but he was gone. And in his place stood revealed a complex villain. Months sharing the same loft, table and work, Cordey had fooled him as easily as though he was a child, while he had not the tiniest secret free of Cordey.

"Why, he even knows about the farm books, Jack! You thought yourself the clever clerk, I'll wager — when you discovered me skimming from the hay sales and fiddling the feed accounts." Charlie rose from the bed, in full flight of confession now and crossed to the window, his face defiant, proud.

"He knows about them — all the petty lifts. It suits him to wag his head and think what a rascal he's got hold of. So long as it's only a few quid he doesn't care. His farm makes a profit like damn few Forest holdings and that's because I manage the place for him. He wants me to be a sharp — a flash lad on the fly — so long as I play Jolter for appearances sake."

Villain, yes — but good at it — like everything else he did.

"And Emma?" Jack couldn't stop himself. "Do you deceive her?" Then a sudden revelation, born of his earlier fear that Emma was too familiar. "Or do you both deceive him, my God, are you and she — ?"

Charlie stepped back as though from a cliff edge. "*No!*"

He turned away to conceal his face for a moment. "Not her — or me — nothing there. Don't be too quick, young 'un. Watch where you tread."

Jack knew not what to say, or think. He stared down at his book, the words a meaningless blur. The suspicion of Charlie and Emma now firmly planted, he'd not be able to think of anything else.

A moment later Charlie retrieved his cap and clomped down the stairs. "Going to the Ostrich, don't wait up, dear!"

• • •

"Heigh heave-ho, lads!" the Vicar sang as he and Charlie and Jack dug in their heels lurching backward, straining at the end of a rope that ran up through two pulleys rigged from the stable loft-beam and down to a pallet of stones in the builder's cart. The pallet rose slowly clear.

The Vicar shouted "Clear man!" and the driver moved his team forward to pull free of the pallet.

"Steady as she goes and down gently, boys," Vicar Wilson singing again with a spirit rarely heard in his hymns. They allowed their feet to skid slowly forward and the pallet settled beside the previous dozen already offloaded.

"Cut along now, boy, and tell your boss he can start work tomorrow as he promised!"

The young carter tugged his cap brim, "I'll tells 'im, Vicar. But he don't take orders from me."

"Blast your smart answer, you young pup," the Vicar shouted. "We've done his heavy work, the yard is clear and level, and we've even offloaded his materials! There'd better be no excuse or delay, by heaven, or he'll hear from me directly!"

The young man whipped up his team and left with an empty wagon clatter.

"Well, lads," the Vicar smiled and mopped his sweating red face. "A good day's work, I'd say. I've asked Emma to bring us a pitcher of cider. We'll sup in the stable, don't want our grime in the house."

"After the way you drove us today, Vicar," Charlie smiled, "I could take a whole pitcher myself."

"Gawn wi' you!" The Vicar beamed, clapping him on the shoulder. "I heard you come in from the Ostrich last night. I'll wager you've had your fill of ale."

"Vicar!" Charlie protested with mock offense. "I scarce touched a glass last night."

"Don't believe a word this rascal says, Jack." The Vicar winked at Jack. "I heard you singing that Bombay love song of yours, and thou were peart, Charlie Cordey — perhaps market peart."

They made their way into the stable where each sat on a hay bale. Jack smiled and laughed at the appropriate places as the Vicar ragged Charlie about his songs and boozing. But the truth was, he'd never seen Charlie as drunk or as maudlin-depressed as the last few nights. It had started the night he'd come back from driving Emma for tea. A lover's quarrel cured by drink?

Emma appeared in the doorway. She held a white, ceramic jug in one hand and three tin mugs clutched in her other fist.

"Here she is! A thirsty working man's salvation," the Vicar piped. "Forest Cider — the best there is. This is pure, from styre apples. Pour my girl, don't hesitate. Sing her your song, Charlie!"

A moment's panic flicked across Charlie's face.

"A'hm that dry, Vicar, I don't think I could. Besides, not my place to sing for Miss Emma."

"Oh, I don't mind," Emma chimed in. "How could I take offence at an honest Christian's song? You may sing."

This last was spoken as a command that cut briefly through the levity. Jack stiffened, sensing the tension between Emma and Charlie.

"I'll sing then, if he's too shy!" The Vicar, oblivious to the feelings just passed, broke forth in his tenor.

> *Give your love,*
> *and never count the cost.*
> *Lose your heart,*
> *and never call it lost!*

He stopped, eyes casting toward Charlie, "*Um dee dum, dee dumble umble um* — confound it, I've forgotten the words, help me!"

"My purse and my fortune," Emma's clear voice picked up the tune,

I'd glad give to you,

Her eyes went boldly to Charlie.

But first my love,
I'll call your heart from you.

"Well done girl! Now let's be at the refreshments." The Vicar clapped and roared with delight. Charlie applauded, shifting uncomfortably and unable to meet her eye.

Emma poured for each of them. She was behaving as though she was their friend rather than their mistress. Jack searched her face for some clue as to what had just happened, but she refused him.

"Where did you learn that song, my dear? You sang it just right."

"Oh, Charlie taught me all about soldiers' Bombay love songs . . . " she giggled. Charlie burst into a violent, hacking cough, spraying cider down his front. " . . . on our way to Mitchells the other day. Remember," she arched one eyebrow at her uncle, "you insisted he instruct me on the practical history of our famous country regiment?"

Charlie's coughing reached a higher crescendo. Jack watched closely, surely this was a good sign. The brute must have offended her, put her off. Not that Emma should have needed "putting off". How could she have any feelings at all for the Charlie Cordeys of this world? True, he was sly and had sufficient cunning to trick her friendship away, but he couldn't sustain it or turn it to love. It was repulsive to even think it, yet think it he had. Brooded on it, in fact, for these last three days but now . . . well, here was capital evidence of Charlie sent packing. The cider and the idle song showed her indifference as a clear contrast to Cordey's discomfort, and his restless boozing. Jack took a long draught and, suddenly cheerful, entered into the Vicar's spirit.

"Is it really a song from the regiment's history, miss? Never heard it myself."

"Oh my yes, Jack." She beamed at him. "Almost as famous as the badge back *and* front. Our Glosters are apparently quite sentimental. I've grown partial to the song but it seems to disagree with Charlie just now!"

Charlie, spluttering to be excused, hurried from the stable and engaged in a retching series of coughs outside.

"Dear, dear," the Vicar smirked. "Poor chap sounds like he's going to drown." He took a long, satisfied pull at his mug then held it out to her for a refill. "I'll be ready for supper tonight. What has Mrs. Toomey got for us?"

"Why chicken, Uncle, you remember, surely. We will take half of it with us, cold, tomorrow to Tintern."

Vicar Wilson's face lost some of its cheer. "Tintern Abbey, tomorrow? Really, was it tomorrow?"

"Oh Uncle! You've forgotten. Don't say we can't go, please!" she pleaded, topping up his cider. "I've been waiting all week for this picnic. The Mitchells are meeting us and the weather is fine, and you've promised repeatedly that I might visit the abbey but we've never — "

"I know but my builder is coming tomorrow — to start paving the yard. I simply have to be here," he protested. "Why don't you go anyway? The Mitchells can pick you up — and Mrs. Mitchell is a formidable chaperone so I've got no need to be there."

"I wanted you to come," she pouted.

"You and Jennie Mitchell don't need an old muffin like me boring you — I'm just deadwood on a trip like that."

She sighed, shrugging agreement. Charlie, recovered but, red faced, returned to the stable.

"Here now!" The Vicar brightened. "Charlie can drive you again."

"Oh no, Uncle," she said. Jack noted the strength in her refusal. "I mean . . . could you spare him?"

"I'd serve best if I was here, to help you with the paving," Charlie rescued her but with no conviction. Clearly he'd have liked another chance to be alone with Emma, repair the damage if he could. Jack, quite pleased with the turn of events, cleared his throat expectantly.

The Vicar snapped up his cue. "Well, young Jack, then, he'll drive you."

"Of course, John," she shot Charlie a quick glance. "We can talk about Mr. Hardy's books to pass the time."

She'd called him John, not Jack, not his labouring name. For the first time since he'd been to see his mother and Aunt Vi, he felt that life could be tolerated. The icing on the cake was Cordey's expression of defeat, the mentor surpassed by his protégé.

CHAPTER 3

The trap was light and well-sprung; Bobbi moved them at a smart pace. Jack was content to be in Emma's company on a fine morning; he deferred to her quiet mood, waiting for her to initiate conversation. No bull-at-a-gate tactics *á la* Cordey. She would appreciate a gentleman's good-natured company, he felt certain. He was a year her senior and, in reality, her social equal. He would act accordingly.

They travelled west to intersect the river road that followed the Wye south from Monmouth to Chepstow. The trees thinned as they approached the junction and a glitter of sun on water appeared. Jack eased the trap around a milk cart stopped squarely in the crossroad, then turned them south. The village of Redbrook squatted on the riverbank not a quarter-mile ahead; Jack instinctively searched the heights above the rooftops but Offa's Rose was buried in the foliage. His mother buried alive in Offa's Rose, His father buried in Gloucester, and his happy future buried with them.

"How far from Redbrook 'til the abbey?" Emma asked.

"Eight and a half — nine miles. All of it hard by the river and as pretty a drive as you can imagine. Tintern should be lovely on a day such as this. The ivy will be luxurious," he ventured, omitting the "Miss Emma".

"You sound as though you're a frequent visitor," she said, as though he shouldn't be familiar with such places.

"Only twice," he replied. "My parents and I took the train to Monmouth, then a boat down to the abbey. You get a different perspective from the water."

"I can't see why," she replied, vaguely nettled.

"Well, you're clear of the trees. You can capture the whole valley with a glance. I read Wordsworth's poem for my mother on our last trip. It was lovely for her to be gazing up into the actual hills that inspired his words."

He glanced back over his shoulder to catch her staring at him, a curious wrinkle on her brow. She didn't look away so neither did he.

"How odd. I've had a sensation just now, rather like a half-remembered dream or . . . what is it? *Déjà vu!*"

"Reminds you of a previous visit?"

"Oh no," she waved a dismissive hand. "I've never been to Tintern Abbey. I meant it's so odd to hear you, a farm worker, speaking of Wordsworth and boat trips to picnic at the abbey. The picture is of a common man yet the voice is of a gentleman — you see, so unlikely yet familiar at the same time."

Jack turned away, pretending to adjust the reins. Was that an insult — or a compliment — or a simple casual observation? He decided it was too risky to follow up, he didn't want her shutting him off as a servant. He'd need a new tack.

"Rather like Hardy's novel, *A Pair of Blue Eyes*," she drawled. "Two lovers joined then separated because of class divisions. His protagonist, low born yet educated and working in a gentleman's profession, is first uplifted by the love of the Vicar's daughter then rejected because of his parentage. While you, John," she paused, tugging thoughtfully at her bonnet ribbons, "you were born well enough, and going up as a clerk and a militia officer before you were brought low — driver for the Vicar's niece."

Surely this was sympathy for his cause, not just idle curiosity, and he leapt to reinforce it. "I agree, absolutely! The injustice of my being forced below my station simply because my father died before he could give me a decent inheritance." He stopped. Did she know of the scandal? He'd promised himself never to shy from it again, but the familiar weakness tempted him. "It is an unpleasant pill to swallow, I can tell you."

Emma gazed at him, noncommittal now, as though trying to decide if he was a victim or simply a boy with a grievance. He felt the urge to explain more but feared it would seem like petty croaking. He turned to face Bobbi again, allowing a long silence to settle between them. The traffic was thin and they meandered south by the river without another word for three more miles.

"Here's Bigsweir Bridge, then." Jack broke the quiet. She did not respond. He looked back. She was partly reclined against the side of the trap watching the river. "We cross here to the west bank," he tried again but she continued to ignore him. "Some say the prettiest bank . . . west bank, that is." His voice trailed off lamely.

"Your mother, though," Emma spoke loudly. He twitched with surprise but did not turn again — he had to resist his puppy dog impulse to lap at her feet.

"Forest born, I understand?"

"Yes, her father was a mine owner, a man of not inconsiderable business affairs," he replied and immediately kicked himself for trying too hard again. My God, she drew the boast from him, it wasn't his nature but he couldn't stop himself.

"Ah, now here's a question. Charlie says his grandfather — thus yours as well — was a butty man. Is that the same as a mine owner?"

"Technically not . . . an owner," Jack squirmed. "But hardly a butty man! I should think Charlie would have given Grandfather his due as a business man."

"You Forest folk do have a prickly sense of class," she said, her voice inquisitive again. "Butty man better than a free-miner and free-miner . . . what is it? 'Born within the Hundred of St. Briavels' better than a company man who, of course, is better than anyone *not* bearing the famous blue scars!" She laughed, as one would at a joke's punch line. He being the joke, his pretension the punch line.

"I'm not Forest folk," he shot back, anger and pride suddenly in control. "I'd never been to the beastly Forest of Dean 'til Father died, and I'll be gone as soon as I can save some money. A year ago we'd have been sharing this picnic and Charlie Cordey would have driven me!" He reared around, glaring, daring her to call him a Forest oaf again.

"Oh dear," she batted her eyes in mock distress. "I've trodden on toes. I sometimes despair of my own society. You know, I always thought it would be a relief to be working class and not have to . . . " She coloured self consciously, twisting away from him. She breathed deeply, her long neck arching back. "I suppose that a Vicar's son can look a Vicar's niece in the eye. Your mother had education, I'm told, and your father was hardly a curate. A year ago we would have been on a par . . . of sorts. Not that any of it really is my concern."

Uncertain whether that was an apology or a rebuke, Jack stared hard at her until she looked up, unblinking and inscrutable, green eyes almost hypnotic.

"Charlie says you're in that betwixt and between world," she continued calmly. "A gentleman ranker he said, and I believe he's got it right. How does one manage such a station, I wonder?"

She lolled back and returned her attention to the Wye. Jack accepted this as a truce and flicked Bobbi's reins. So he had been a subject of discussion. Surely not at Charlie's instigation; she must have enquired. Gentleman ranker — one who must regain his social class through a feat of bravery. No more puppy at her beck and call, but a wronged gentleman gamely fighting back from an undeserved blow. Not bad at all, he mused.

• • •

Bobbi's coat showed slick near the collar and breech when they re-entered the sunlight on the last turn before the abbey. Jack swore quietly; he'd not meant to work her so hard, but the image of himself and Emma reclining over a picnic on the lawns of Tintern had dragged him forward. Now he'd have to fuss over Bobbi's water and bait to make sure she didn't get a chill, or the grease, or some other of the thousand maladies horses seemed to attract.

A familiar jab of apprehension struck him. He had been an infrequent and unskilled horseman — living in Gloucester they had walked or taken cabs. Over the last few months he'd learned to harness Bobbi, although never just right — too tight — too slack — causing sores or cracks or rubs. His driving skill was also suspect. He'd once almost snapped the shafts driving out of a deep rut — much to Charlie's hysterical, shrieking horror. Another time he'd forgotten to chain lock the wheels leaving Bobbi to wander a half a mile down the Scatterford lane before the Vicar, frantically racing cross-country, caught her.

He clucked for her to slow down, which she did with an indignant toss of her head as though to say "too late now." They followed the Wye's sweeping turn out of its narrow high banks toward a wide, valley floor. The gable end of the abbey nave appeared, thrusting above a screen of trees.

"There's the west front," he called over his shoulder, "we'll be in the village presently."

"Oh John," Emma's voice came from close behind him. "It's lovely here, slow down. I want to study it first, from a distance."

She knelt on her seat, one hand on his shoulder for support, her scent palpable. He pulled Bobbi to a halt. The soaring pile of stone, its bare tip pushing above a cover of spring-green ivy, immediately spoke to him of a different world. His old world of cathedrals and pleasing prospects.

"That's the nave entry, you can see the north transept to the left, nearer the river."

She didn't answer but he could feel her breath on his neck.

"Beyond that is where the chapter house, infirmary, and dormitories were supposedly situated, according to the survey done by that Brakspear chap," he continued in his guidebook voice, very conscious of her hand squeezing ever so slightly on his shoulder.

"If I had to paint a picture of the word 'romantic'," she murmured, "this would be it."

"Romantic, ah yes, it is." Caught off stride, Jack tried to switch from science to romance. "Wordsworth said no poem was ever composed under circumstances more pleasant."

"Are you sure?"

"About what?"

"Did Wordsworth really say that, about this place?"

"Oh yes, or something pretty close to it. The gist, you know."

Her hand pulled his shoulder around until his face was but inches from hers. She studied him for a long moment with her unblinking green eyes. "How very, very odd it seems that you should quote Wordsworth."

"Ahoy! You lot!" A powerful male voice thrust between them. "Drive that cart or park it clear of the road!" A large brake clipping along behind a matched team of greys approached from the rear.

Philip Mitchell stood in the front waving his cap, and Jennie Mitchell's face peered from the back seats.

"Mind your manners, Phil Mitchell," Emma retorted gaily. She shifted back onto her seat with a terse, "Drive on, Jack."

At least two dozen vehicles were parked close to the nave. The open ground between the nave and the river swarmed with locals hawking everything from souvenirs to sausages. Jack carefully worked Bobbi through the pedestrians toward a wide space of turf well clear of the other carriages. Philip Mitchell clattered past him, snapping at the yokels to clear a path, then expertly wheeled his team up between two parked carriages.

"Let's stop near the Mitchells!" Emma called.

He ignored her, concentrating on two young girls with flower baskets, rushing towards Bobbi.

"Get off there," he bellowed, "you'll spook her!"

His own nerves translated themselves down the reins and Bobbi suddenly attempted a series of sidesteps, wrenching the trap with her.

"Woot, Bobbi. Woot, girl, that's my girl," he cooed to her and she straightened out. They rounded the west end, cleared the hawkers, and drove slowly toward the open area.

"Oh stop here, then, and let me out," Emma snapped impatiently. "You can park where you like. We'll be at the crossing for lunch in two hours. Bring the basket then." She opened the small door, dabbed one foot on the step and leaped, skirts held up, to the ground. She strode toward the Mitchells. He stared after her. Her words slowly brought comprehension. He was not part of her picnic. Not that he or Charlie sat the Vicar's table at home, their place was the kitchen, but he'd thought here, somehow, after his declaration of misfortune this morning that she would accept him. She linked arms with Jennie and joined the Mitchell family as it made for the west front, talking and laughing at once — no backward glance for her gentleman ranker. He only allowed Bobbi a small drink of water to start, petrified that he'd give her a chill. She took it quietly and he stroked her neck, feeling under the damp collar.

"Not so bad eh, Bobbi? I'll give you a good brushing when we get home if you promise not to break out in sores."

He checked the chain brake twice, then went for more water. Phil Mitchell was standing beside Bobbi when he returned.

"Ah, Charlie . . . oh no, wait. It's not Charlie," he said, twitching his moustache. "You are Miss Emma Wilson's man aren't you . . . or have I got the wrong rig?"

"This is the Wilson's," Jack replied, setting the bucket in front of Bobbi. "I'm John Thornton, we met last month."

"Yes, I suppose so," his face showed no recognition. "Well no matter, Miss Wilson has asked me to tell you there's been a change in plan. The crossing is packed, children and all sorts whipping about. So bring her basket to the grass beyond the east end of the abbey."

Jack nodded.

"You understand?" Mitchell peered at him. "Do you know where that is? That is the west end, just so," he gestured as though speaking to a simpleton.

"Yes, I know," Jack cut him short. "The presbytery gable is the east end, I'll bring the basket there."

"Oh, well done," Mitchell turned to leave, nodding at the horse. "Not too much water eh, Charlie. It's a warm day."

He let Bobbi finish two-thirds of the bucket, then pulled her nosebag from under the driver's seat. He flicked water into it then pressed his thumb into the mixture of oats and chaff. "Dusty bait snack's worse 'n no bait at all," he quoted Charlie. Bobbi rolled her eyes, so he held the open bag up for her inspection. "Will that suit

Miss Bobbi or should Jack fetch something more to her bloody liking?"

She sneezed and turned her head. He dutifully added more water, "Beg your pardon, miss. But I'se a Forest lad, sees? No sense enough to dampen a horse's luncheon afore serving it, like, goddamn me to hell for it."

"Pity he doesn't speak to *me* like that!" Emma's voice, behind him. A giggle, then Jennie Mitchell, "Perhaps Bobbi is more of a lady than you."

He fitted the nosebag and turned, face throbbing crimson. "Pardon my language, I didn't hear your approach."

"I should think it's Bobbi who deserves the apology!" Emma replied. Jennie half crumpled, suppressing her laughter.

"Mr. Mitchell already delivered the message — about the change in lunch," Jack said.

"Good, but we've come for my parasol, I find the sun too bright and I forgot to ask Philip to fetch it."

He climbed quickly into the trap, found the parasol and leaped down, anxious for the encounter to end.

"Anything else?"

"No, thank you. Lunch in an hour at the east gable will be fine."

"But he hasn't apologized to dear Bobbi yet!" Jennie protested.

Emma laughed and turned to leave but Jennie stopped her. "Em! Wait! Let's see if you can get him to apologize. I so loved the way he talked to her. Make him apologize!"

Emma looked clinically from Jennie, to Jack, to the horse.

"Well, our Mr. Thornton is a gentleman of sorts," she said, considering the proposal. "And I don't see why Bobbi should be cursed without some expression of remorse . . . "

"Oh goody!" Jennie clapped her hands. "Now you must do it, Jack. Go on, your duty awaits."

He could have played up and made the joke. He might have even turned the situation to his advantage. "Please, Miss Bobbi, accept my most equine expression of apology for having offended . . . " the words were there. Then a flourished bow and bit of cheek for Jennie. Yes, it would have worked well. But Emma's complete lack of expression, her calculated assessment of his position held him in check.

"Well, Jack?" A thin-lipped smile crept onto Emma's face. The warm, green eyes, so frank and plain only minutes earlier were hard now. "You're not going to shirk your duty as a . . . gentleman?"

"Oh yes, and he must speak like a Forest man." Jennie lowered her voice, "Jolter am wery sorry, he am," sending herself into a renewed fit of sniggering.

The hair on Jack's neck tingled, lifting in anger. "Why do you mock me? What have I done to deserve this?"

"Oh, he *is* prickly, and almost rude!" Jennie squealed. "Clearly no gentleman."

"Aye," Emma's back stiffened and she cocked her head, the full figure of a society miss. "Therefore, Bobbi shall take no offense at his language. Come, let's catch Philip up."

Jack stood, trembling with a racing mix of emotions. Rage? Shame? Fear? That he should prove himself incapable of coping with the likes of Jennie Mitchell galled him. And Emma, play acting her station above him just for Jennie's sake. His grand notion of being a gentleman ranker seemed soiled, frayed, almost ridiculous. He swore at Bobbi, damned if he'd spend the day with her, and struck off for the dining hall ruins. He crossed it quickly and hurried along the cloister walk to dart into the north transept. His feet sped him to the centre of the cathedral — the crossing of the four great arms of the church — nave, transepts and presbytery. North, south, east and west.

A throng of children swept squealing past him, playing tag up and down the four arms but he scarcely noticed them. He craned his neck back, staring up at the symmetry of the crossing and felt for his father's hand. How many times had they stood hand in hand in Gloucester Cathedral — his father's beloved cathedral — gazing up into the perfection? He was for a moment his father's little boy again, at a time when all was good and everything possible.

Tintern's roofless crossing was strangely reassuring. A cloud, white and round, drifted through the blue square above him. Someone nearby began to recite the Lord's Prayer. Very softly, the voice kept cadence with the cloud's passage:

"Our Father, which art in heaven."

His father a thief? No. Father in heaven.

"Hallowed be thy name. Thy kingdom come. Thy will be done on earth as it is in heaven."

Was it his father's will — God's will — that he should be friendless, alone, an object fit only for labour, for contempt?

"Give us this day, our daily bread."

The chant grew loud, demanding bread. Startled, he realized it was his own voice. He looked around to discover two children staring at him. They were local village waifs carrying baskets of flowers. The same girls who had spooked Bobbi.

"Forgive us our trespasses, as we forgive those who trespass against us," said the littlest one, without blinking. "And lead us not into temptation, but deliver us from evil," she said solemnly. "Should always finish a prayer — once started, sir."

He bought a white carnation from her and slid it through a buttonhole on his coat. He stayed in the centre of the crossing, unwilling to break the spell with his father. A father dead months before his son truly mourned his passing. Jack was suddenly ashamed. Eight months railing against his lack of inheritance, against rural drudgery, then against loss of position and rank. Not a true tear shed nor a real prayer spoken — until now. Even now he had not wept for his father. Even now a flower girl had to finish his prayer for him. He looked up again at the blue-sky crossing and heedless of those gawping nearby he recommenced, "Our Father, which art in heaven."

He finished the prayer and carefully dried his eyes. He would bide a while here with his newfound peace, studying the church from its heart.

His eye was carefully following the fragments of delicate stone tracery still present in the great east window. A heavy flow of ivy covered the lower part of the opening. But its arched apex was clear and invited speculation on how it might have looked five hundred years ago, facing east, during sunrise. The east window — presbytery — east lawn — lunch. He checked his watch, astonished to find over an hour and a quarter had passed. He was late. Off like a hare he went, dodging back through cloister and dining hall. A stranger was stroking Bobbi, talking to her. The trap was a good dozen yards from where he'd left it and Bobbi was jittery. He ran to her side, aware of the turf torn up where she had dragged the chained trap.

"What's wrong Bobbi?" He joined the stranger in stroking her.

"Aw's left t' nosebag on her for over an hour is what's wrong," the stranger said. A small, dapper man of fifty, he cast Jack a disapproving glance. "Some horses will nay bother. Others won't stand it. Finished her bait and she wants shot of t' damn thing." He dropped the canvas bag at Jack's feet.

"Oh, I, ah, lost track of time I suppose."

"She were shaking 'er head like a terrier shakin' a rat — fair dragged your cart into the drink in a few more minutes if I hadn't come along."

He paused to whisper in Bobbi's ear. "You're better now, my girl? Naught to fuss over, ye silly daft bitch."

"Thank you very much." Jack put his hand out. "I'm very grateful for your intervention."

The stranger ignored it, hawked, and spat near Jack's boot. "Yer welcome, boy."

Jack inspected her minutely for injury and breathed a heavy sigh of relief to see her harness and hide were intact. Then he pulled the picnic basket from the back of the trap and ran for the east lawn.

The Mitchells were seated at a large cloth spread over the grass. They sipped wine from long glasses. Empty dishes lay in their appointed places, awaiting food. Emma was halfway between them and Jack, striding at a furious pace toward him. He jogged up puffing his apology.

"Don't you dare make an excuse to me, you petty creature," she snapped, turning on her heel. "Bring the lunch, everyone is already sufficiently inconvenienced."

"But I am truly . . . "

She stopped and faced him, angry red spots on each cheek. "Jennie and I indulge a tiny pleasantry at your expense so you choose to repay us by ruining our picnic? It is the act of a spoiled schoolboy." Her anger was out of proportion to the crime. She seemed to sense this and took a large breath, exhaling slowly. She regained her middle class *sang froid* and shot him a condescending glance. "If I thought you worthy of even a workingman's position, I'd have words for you, Jack Thornton. But since you've shown yourself to be a child, I'll treat you as one. Now bring the hamper and be quiet."

Mrs. Mitchell gave him a foul look, the rest of the Mitchells ignored his presence. He set the wicker panier down, opened it and stepped back. Emma quickly began unpacking but did not dismiss him, leaving him to stand awkwardly behind her.

"It will taste all the better for waiting," Jennie said. "I confess my appetite is now quite sharp whereas before I was indifferent to lunch."

"Thank you," Emma replied formally, carefully arranging the chicken on a large platter.

"Oh Em, don't be so stiff," Jennie coaxed. "What difference does it make? Don't let it give you a bad humour to spoil this fine meal Mrs. Toomey has prepared."

Jennie looked up at Jack. "I expect he was reading poetry — perhaps Wordsworth — to Miss Bobbi and her charms quite made him forget the time of day."

Emma laughed and the tension broke. Jack, perspiring freely, smiled his gratitude at Jennie who scowled in reply.

"Why be sad when we can be jolly?" She raised her glass. "A toast to a captivating lady . . . oh, I say, Em. Here comes Mr. Halket. He, of the brownest eyes, we met in the nave. How do I look?"

They turned as one to inspect a young, well-dressed man approaching from the abbey. He stopped short of the picnic cloth, tipped his hat and bowed slightly. "Miss Mitchell," he smiled bright teeth at her, "and Miss Wilson. I trust you enjoy your meal?"

"Oh yes, Mr. Halket," Jennie oozed. "Allow me to introduce my mother, father and brother Philip. This is Mr. Halket from Gloucester. He very gallantly assisted me down from a pile of stones that I shouldn't have climbed."

The elder Mitchells engaged him in small talk for a moment. Mr. Mitchell's attention strayed to the uneaten food, Mrs. Mitchell cast a wary eye from Halket to Emma.

"But I interrupt!" Halket caught the hint. "Delighted to see you again Miss Mitchell, Miss Wilson enjoy your lunch."

He walked around the cloth brushing past Jack, then halted abruptly, turning to stare.

"Johnny Thornton? By heavens it is!" He grasped Jack's hand and began to pump it. "How extraordinary! Are you with the Mitchells?"

Jack had been inching away from the picnic the minute his old comrade from the Gloucester Volunteer Battalion had appeared. But now he was trapped.

"No, not really. Ah, Miss Wilson . . . um, actually."

"But you're not eating? What are you standing about like a china sentry for? I almost missed you — "

Halket stopped. His eye took in Jack's clothing at a glance. He let Jack's hand go and stepped back.

"I heard about your father, old boy," he murmured. "Bad luck all round. Gather you're not coming back to the regiment?"

Jack shook his head, unable to compose a reply, wondering if "bad luck" referred to his father's death, or disgrace. Disgrace, of course, death wouldn't upset Jimmy H. Now at a loss for words and clearly embarrassed, Halket turned to face the Mitchells. They were watching like an audience at a play, waiting for him to conjure up an explanation as to why he appeared to be pals with the farm help. The sky-blue crossing and his father's recent embrace came back to Jack, calming him. "Thank you, sir," he tipped his cap, "for asking after my father." To Emma, "I'll return for the basket, miss, in — "

"An hour," she finished the order. "That will be all for now, Jack."

"Very good, miss," he turned, caught Halket's eye and walked back toward the trap. He was mildly astonished to find he was looking forward to his bread, cheese and cider in Bobbi's company. Perhaps he *would* quote her Wordsworth — not such a bad idea after all.

"The fever of the world," he called loudly. "Hath hung upon the beatings of my heart — How oft, in spirit, have I turned to thee." Bobbi whinnied as he drew near. "Not you, daft horse, the river. Now listen. O sylvan Wye! Thou wanderer through the woods. How often has my spirit turned to thee!"

• • •

Bobbi, of course, was not mollified by poetry. She retaliated just after they turned off the Monmouth road toward Newland that evening on the return trip. Part way through the narrow valley opposite Knockall's Inclosure, she went lame. Jack leaped down and immediately fitted the chain brake so the cart would anchor them. Emma, dozing under a blanket, awoke. "What now?"

They were the first words spoken since leaving Tintern.

"Horse is lame, I think." He ran his hand down Bobbi's flank to her right foreleg, then slid it down to the hoof as he'd seen Charlie do.

"You think? Can't you tell?"

He tugged and her foot shot up, clipping his shin. He couldn't see anything in the dusk light, but the shoe wobbled to his touch. Damn, probably a result of her hysterics over the nosebag.

"Shoe's loose."

"Well . . . tighten it and let's be away."

He let the hoof go and she touched it gingerly to earth.

"Can't do that here, its practically dark."

"Can't? Or don't know how? There's a hammer in the box — I've seen Charlie use it," her voice jabbed him.

"Don't know how then," he replied, defeated again. Charlie would have done the job deftly and quickly with a saucy comment to make Emma laugh. Jack just wiggled the shoe.

"What's to be done?"

"Well, she can't pull the trap without risking real injury so I'll unharness her and we'll have to walk home. Get the cart tomorrow when . . . "

"Walk! How far! Where are we?"

"Only about a mile. We're past Redbrook."

Jack ran his hands inside the shaft. It was dark enough now that he had to feel for the buckles and clips. Emma stamped past him and around the bend in the road. He leaned his head against the horse's warm ribs, resuming his search for the releases. She nickered, but let him stay.

CHAPTER 4

Untouched since spring, the Wilson hayfield stood tall and thick in the late July sun. Bounded by dry stonewall and holly hedge, it was a perfectly square enclosure of green seated at the foot of High Meadow Hill. This field wore a thick layer of soil and consequently a heavier growth of hay than most of its neighbours — farther north, the Severn-Wye limestone bed carried a threadbare coat of earth. Even so, Vicar Wilson's field had just now finished producing its one and only hay crop.

Four men, twisting in half circles, scythes outstretched, moved like clockwork cogs. They cut parallel lanes through the field, shuffling around it each day from predawn to noon, then evening until dark, paring it down, whittling it to nothing. Charlie scythed well — an even, rhythmic stroke. His blade but two inches above the earth flew level and smoothly through the grass depositing a straight windrow to his left. The hired miner from the village was jerky — not a twisting dancer, but a scything mechanic. Nevertheless, he moved well and his windrow paralleled Charlie's nicely. Through dint of hard work he maintained his position three yards off Charlie's rear flank. Jack had improved greatly over the week. He left a stubble that waved up to four inches of wasted grass then down to a quarter inch from the earth and a dented blade. His windrow was a snake. But he no longer lagged far behind and he perspired freely from the work, not profusely from clumsy hacking.

But the Vicar, my God. The Vicar scythed as other men painted, or sang, or danced. The Vicar did not stroke. His upper body simply twisted back and forth, swinging as a pendulum on a clock — no apogee could be seen — merely a fluid flood and ebb. The scythe moved through the grass leaving a perfect carpet of one-inch stubble over mounds and down dips. He laid each cut of tall grass exactly upon the end of his previous cut — an arrow straight windrow. He simply strode through the grass mowing as he went, leaving even Charlie behind.

"Whet, boys, *whet!*" His command brought them to a halt.

Jack jabbed the tip of his blade in the ground to steady it, pulled on a heavy leather gauntlet, and laid his stone against the blade. He paused to get his breath, checked the alignment, then stroked the blade. "Once each side, twice each side, three times and shining," he sang to himself. Except his blade only shone for three-quarters of its length. Concentrate, hold the stone evenly. "Once each side, twice each side, three times and shining."

And it did. A clean bright streak one-quarter inch wide down the full length of his blade. He grinned with simple delight.

"Thank God for good weather, let us make hay," the Vicar sang out for the hundredth time since dawn and they began cutting again.

Jack's newly-sharpened blade hissed through the grass toppling the stocks in perfect succession. A scent of fresh-cut green filled his nose. He breathed it in and out, tasting it. A large bead of sweat collected at the end of his eyebrow. It ran in a flash flood past his eye, across his cheek, and into the corner of his mouth. He licked. It salted the grass-green flavour on his tongue. Nothing came to him. No thoughts or ideas. His mind was quietly closed for the morning so that he could occupy himself with mowing. Being the last mower, he was nearest the village children Charlie had hired to do the tedding. They, too, worked quietly. Stoop, gather an armful of grass from the windrow, stand up, spread it to the next windrow, stoop, gather an armful of grass. Only children, eleven or twelve years old, yet they moved like men and women accustomed to hard labour. Their pace was solid and efficient. No wasted effort or idle chatter to disturb their work. They left a wide wake of cut grass spread evenly over the stubble to dry.

Jack had broken his reverie to look back at them, once, and was rewarded with a clang of scythe blade on rock. That dent had taken him twenty minutes of painstaking work with the peening hammer to correct. Now his eyes never flickered from their task and it gave him peace reminiscent of the crossing at Tintern Abbey. He cut, whetted, and perspired for another hour until the Vicar called break. He looked up as though waking from a solid sleep and discovered he was hungry. The lunch was stacked in baskets under the shade of a chestnut tree that grew in the corner of the field nearest them. Jack carefully laid his scythe so the razor edged blade was well into the tall grass. No Forester would dare trample unmown hay, so it would be safe there.

Emma waited beside the lunch, brandishing a large tin of cider.

The sight of her, even covered by a heavy linen piny and large straw hat, still affected Jack. Not the silly yearning of the morning they'd driven to Tintern. He'd found his station at Tintern and it was beneath her. In the intervening two and a half months he'd discovered it was happily beneath her. The murky world of gentleman ranker had been altogether too difficult to inhabit. He needed order and a measure of peace. As a child and young man he'd found it as a Vicar's son. Now he'd found it again as a Vicar's labourer. In a year or so he'd have enough money for Bristol or even London where he could climb back into a clerk's position, gradually move up, and call himself John again. He had plans, he had youth and he had the bright-blue square above Tintern's crossing. It was all he would need.

Yet there was Emma, pouring cider for the children — hard brew for eleven year olds, apparently acceptable to Foresters. Emma not to yearn for, but Emma to be what . . . admired? No. Dreamed of? Not in his present situation. She had been civil to him since the abbey, but only as befitted a young woman of charity and decorum; she'd offered no friendship. She still flirted to and fro with Charlie — often almost playing the coquette — like a cat with a doomed mouse; other times as a younger sister. She sent Charlie by turns cheerful, boozily maudlin or stuffy and angry.

A strand of hair slipped across her face. She finished pouring the miner's cider then swept the hair back behind her ear, smoothing it into place. Jack followed the simple motion, treating himself to her broad, smooth forehead, soft cheek, and delicate ear as one might study a painting or a sculpture. She looked up for his cup and caught his gaze before he could avert it. She frowned but he felt no embarrassment. He would watch her as he chose, never to discomfort her but neither as a sneak or a voyeur. He put his cup forward, she filled it, and he lifted his hat.

"Thank you, cider is very welcome today, Miss Emma."

She turned to the children and served them as naturally as though she was their mother, not as a Lady doing charity for the poor. He moved to the base of the tree where the men sat around a food basket.

"We'll finish today if we can hold the pace," the Vicar said. "And a fine pace we've set. My thanks to all for your efforts lads; we've really done well. Four men, twenty acres, four days. Better than an acre per day per man and that's not bad."

"Specially if you reckon we're not really four mowers," Charlie bit into a quarter loaf of bread.

"Eh?"

"Three mowers and an apprentice." He inclined his head toward Jack.

"A week ago I'll grant you apprentice." The Vicar winked at Jack. "But this young man has made great strides. He'll cut his acre today I'll wager."

"And t' Vicar cuts like a angel — makes hay for two men, says I," the miner spoke up. He consumed bread, cheese, and cider in heroic quantities, seeming to speak while swallowing. He was a small taciturn man made of wire and gristle.

"Like an angel?" Charlie said, incredulous. "Well, there's praise for you, Vicar, especially coming from one who I'd ha' thought to be unacquainted with the notion."

The miner's sallow cheeks reddened but he didn't break stride with the food. "Sez the kettle, callin' the pot black."

"Well said!" Emma joined them, kneeling between the Vicar and Charlie. "If an angel ever mowed hay, it would be indistinguishable from you, Uncle."

Charlie forced a smile. "Miners! Breathing that coal dust makes 'em cheeky, Jack. Don't ever you go down the pits, eh?"

Jack shook his head. "I don't know about angels but I'd bet our Vicar could have been a model for Levin."

"Oh, Jack, come now!" The Vicar laughed, enjoying the attention of his workers.

"Levin?" Charlie gnawed a piece of cheese. "Sounds like a Jew — don't know any Jew mower myself."

"From *Anna Karenina*. Tolstoy's book. Levin was a Russian landowner who used to mow alongside his peasants." Jack paused, suddenly conscious of the gaping stares from Charlie and the miner — acutely aware that lectures on Russian literature in a hayfield were not the done thing. Emma's eyebrows arched inquisitively and a smile tugged at the corners of her mouth.

"A angel," the miner grunted.

"Exactly!" Jack cried, relieved at the intervention.

"Oh, get away with your angels!" Charlie snapped. "Coal dust has addled your brain."

"Oh aye," a largish piece of bread vanished as the miner spoke. "I mind your Feythur in the collieries — he was never addled. An' yerself was underneath as a young 'un. Thee bist too good for us now, Charley Cordey?"

Charlie's riposte was stilled at this. He lay back on one elbow and sipped his cup. "I was underground nearly three years, the old Bannut is right," he said quietly. "Then I ran to the army and never been under again. They say army life is hard but, ah, it's sweet peace compared to the coal face."

The miner, content with his victory, began sifting the basket for leftovers. Jack finished his lunch and knelt beside Emma for a refill of cider.

"You've not borrowed a novel from me in months, Jack. I thought perhaps you'd forgotten how to read?" she said with the curious half-smile still on her lips.

"Didn't seem right anymore." Jack was cautious, was she mistress or fellow book lover? "Bothering you for books — not really my place."

"You seem to be thriving in "your place" as you call it, yet here you are discoursing on Tolstoy. Hardly "your place" to do that!" She studied him for a second and her voice mellowed. "How many mowers delve into the depths of *Anna Karenina,* I wonder."

"Emma!" The Vicar's egalitarian hackles bristled. "Leave the young man alone. A mower can quote Tolstoy if a Vicar can mow — or his niece serve them lunch, I daresay."

"It's all right, Mr. Wilson, I've taken no offense and I'm certain none was intended." Jack was pleased with himself. Talk of his place as a labourer would have made him grit his teeth only weeks ago. But now her barbs held no sting, if indeed they were barbs at all.

"Of course no offense was intended, Uncle. I am merely commenting on a rare circumstance, namely, a man who makes his living as a farm worker is not often a student of Tolstoy or Wordsworth." She put both hands on her hips like an MP debating in the house. "It is a phenomenon to be remarked upon, how could it be considered rude?"

Charlie gave a large snort and tipped his hat down over his eyes.

"Our Jack has had the benefit of a sound education and he should not be ashamed to use it," the Vicar spoke in his sermon voice. Jack cringed inwardly. Wilson's habit of defending the common folk still embarrassed him, especially since he was "common" now himself.

"Any Christian should be happy to see the day when all men, be they miners, farmers, or weavers have the benefit of decent schooling."

"Oh Uncle, this has gone all out of proportion to my simple observation. He may borrow as many of my books as he likes. In fact, I shall insist on it — so there." She smiled woodenly at Jack. "I've just finished *Far From the Madding Crowd*. Have you read it?"

"No."

"Ah well, it's only our humble Thomas Hardy again, I'm afraid. I can't seem to get enough of him for some reason. Call for it this evening."

"If it's not inconvenient to you, miss," Jack tried his Forest twang.

"I've just said you may have the book," she snapped. "If it was inconvenient, I'd not have offered."

Jack allowed himself a small grin. In the Forest of Dean lunchtime debating society it appeared that the mower-miner team had triumphed.

"Then I'll come round later, and thank you very much, Miss Emma. It is most kind of you."

The Vicar laughed aloud. Emma shot him a nasty look. Charlie chuckled from beneath his cap.

"Perhaps I'll ride around to all the fields and mines, flinging books at anyone I see." She flipped Charlie's hat off his face. "And you, Charlie Cordey, will be my first victim. Let's say Voltaire — in French, mind — none of this English translation fakery."

Charlie snatched his hat back and pointed it at Jack. "See now youngster! See what trouble you've stirred up?"

"Well then, Charlie, fight back!" the Vicar crowed. "If you must read her books, she must mow your hay."

"Now there's a thought," Charlie extended his hands, palms upward. "Cast your gaze on these calloused flippers. There's my education — a university degree in good, honest work."

Emma jumped to her feet, clasped his hands and pulled him up. "Well then, professor Cordey. I shall have my first lesson, right now if you please."

Charlie looked to the Vicar for permission.

"If you're willing to risk your blade on my niece's attempt at mowing," the Vicar was suddenly serious, "then I suppose it would be . . . ah, make sure she doesn't cut herself, Charlie."

They left for the cutting lanes, Emma chattering like a robin and Charlie laughing in good humour. The miner stretched out and was snoring in less than thirty seconds. The children knelt in a circle playing a game with two sticks and some pebbles. The Vicar stood, eyes following Emma and Cordey. He removed his cap and scratched his fringe of hair anxiously. "Don't overdo it now, Emma . . . Charlie," he shouted. They seemed not to hear.

"You mustn't mind her, Jack," the Vicar said. "A young woman scarcely a year from London is unlikely to appreciate the unique society we Foresters have evolved. In time she will adjust."

Jack waited for more, but it was not forthcoming. He knew Emma was the daughter of the Vicar's brother — a senior man at Whitehall, and that she was here for two reasons. The country air for her health, and to manage the widowed Vicar's household. Both obvious fabrications since she was robust as a pit pony, and the Vicar's wife had died eight years earlier and he'd easily coped with Mrs Toomey and a part-time cleaner for seven of those years. Nobody questioned the real reasons for her presence in the Forest, anymore than they questioned the reasons for his own employment on the Wilson farm.

"Been a bit of a change for me too," he ventured, hoping to nudge the Vicar down Emma's path. "I've learned to float with the tide rather than swim against it."

The Vicar winked. "I watched you swim with some determination against it, my boy. I knew your father, although only professionally and at some distance. Were you aware of that?"

"No," Jack was startled. "I didn't realize."

"Not close acquaintances mind, but I was sorry to hear of his death. So when Charlie asked for you as his new assistant, I agreed. But with some trepidation, I must say."

Jack had hoped for illumination on Emma, but now it seemed his dirty laundry was about to be aired. The Vicar surely knew about his father's fall from grace.

"Trepidation?"

"Not an easy transition for a young man with education, business prospects, social connections and . . . uncalloused hands." He smiled. "Didn't know if you would stick it. I'm glad to see you've decided to swim with the tide."

"Not much sense in doing otherwise," Jack replied cautiously. "My father's legacy was adequate for Mother, but his financial affairs at his death — "

"Are none of my business," Vicar Wilson finished the sentence. "I'm not prying, Jack. I'm just happy to see that you've settled."

Suddenly Jack wanted to talk about the loan at Gloucester Cathedral, justify it and clean it. Here was a man who wouldn't judge him. He wanted to tell the Vicar about the crossing at Tintern — confess his shame at not honouring his father's memory. But he couldn't do that without stepping back into his personae as a young gentleman. If he reopened his expectations of business, commissions, and status then he'd risk reopening the pretensions and anger that Tintern had boxed up. So he put his battered straw hat on his head and touched the brim.

"Thank you, sir. I'm obliged."

"Not at all. Now I believe I'll follow the example of our man with the blue scars and have a quick nap."

He loosened his dog collar and curled up against the chestnut's trunk. Jack hopped the drystone wall and walked to a point where a tall hedge continued as the field boundary. Farther down the hayfield, Charlie and Emma were engaged in an animated discussion of the scythe. They did not notice his approach on the opposite side of the wall. He continued on for another two dozen yards until he was well shielded by the hedge, then unbuttoned his flies. His stream spattered against holly leaves and he stepped back quickly, fastidious, even in work clothes that Bobbi had liberally doused only the day before.

"Charlie!" Emma's voice carried clearly from the hayfield on the other side of the hedge. "Stop fussing so, I'm not a china doll. Just show me how the stroke should be done," she commanded.

Jack's hand twitched involuntarily. Her voice seemed to go not to his ears, but to his open trousers. He was instantly conscious of being as intimately exposed to her as it was possible for a man to be. John would have blushed, but Jack found himself exploring the sensation, marvelling at it.

"Your uncle will see! What's the matter with you!" Charlie spoke, now frustrated, yet waiting to be coaxed to do something. "He watches us closely, you know that."

"Oh nonsense, we have our backs turned to him. At this distance he can only see you and me . . . scything." She said the last word with a giggle.

"Then that's what we'll do. No more funny business. Now get hold of the nibs and move the snath out from your body."

"Come closer and show me. Help me take the first few cuts, then I'll go on my own."

There was no reply from Charlie.

"Oh do help me. I promise — no funny business."

Jack buttoned up and without premeditation, moved quietly down the hedge to an opening where a stile cut through. He peered through the gap between hedge and stile. Emma faced him about ten yards distant. She held the scythe handles and was drawing the blade back. Charlie stood behind her, arms around her so he could hold the snath and guide her movement. Charlie swung Emma and the scythe smoothly in one fluid motion, dropping a neat semicircle of grass. He swung back for a second stroke. Emma suddenly bent, throwing her head and shoulders forward. Her bottom was propelled into Charlie. She took a quick step back and ground herself against him.

"Damn it, Emma! You promised!" Charlie stumbled, the scythe whipped wildly through the grass but he did not let go.

She pulled the scythe in and performed a rapid two-step that pushed her body tight against him. She looked back over her shoulder, straw hat flapped in his face, a strand of the chestnut hair blowing loose. Jack tried not to think that it was the same colour as his mother's hair.

"You don't want this?" A low chuckle from her throat. "Truly, Mr. Cordey?" She rotated her hips. This time Charlie gave a convulsive thrust forward to meet her. She sighed.

"Ain't proper. Like animals in a farmyard," he protested without conviction.

Jack had never in his life seen anything like this. Never. He had kissed and been kissed with some passion. He had even held a girl's breast for several heart-stopping moments during an unchaperoned game of Blind Man's Bluff played in a half-lit parlour. He had seen French postcards and thought he understood the mechanics of lovemaking. But a respectable woman, gluing herself to a man — never mind a man of much lower class — in such a determinedly lewd fashion — for her gratification — never. The thought, the sight, at once repelled, startled, and attracted him. He stared helpless, scarcely able to keep his mouth from dropping open.

"It's not unnatural. It's very commonplace in nature. Jennie Mitchell and I sneaked out to their stable last autumn. A man brought a stud to serve Mr. Mitchell's mare. And this is what they did. Of course, they didn't have all these clothes getting in the way."

She worked herself slowly against him, still half turned, watching his face. His eyelids drooped.

"But they are farm animals — not human," he murmured. "It's not natural for humans."

Jack pulled back from the gap — his breath coming hard and quick. His fingers and toes had grown strangely cold as though in shock. He began to walk rapidly away from the stile, but Emma's low moan stopped him. It was worse than his worst fears. His naive terror had been Charlie holding Emma's hand, stealing a kiss, whispering cheeky soldier's limericks, winning her heart. His wildest, dark fantasy had never considered them to be rutting animals. And most shocking of all, Charlie was clearly not the seducer. She whinnied like a horse and Charlie laughed. A short, grunting laugh. Jack found himself back at the stile, watching, reaching to readjust his trousers to accommodate his physical turmoil, unable to control the carnal fever that flooded his mind. Charlie the master craftsman at work again: his left hand gripped her waist and his mouth gnawed at the side of her neck. Her head was thrown far back, eyes tight shut, red tongue darting out to lick her lips.

"Tonigh,t Charlie — come for me tonight, please," she spoke loudly in a guttural tone.

"No, we can't." He pushed free of her with an effort. "No more, Emma."

"Halloooo!" The Vicar called from the far end of the field. "Thank God for fine weather! Let us make hay!"

Jack threw himself away from the stile, ran to the end of the greenery, then scuttled bent over beneath the dry, stone wall, muttering the Lord's Prayer and trying desperately to clear the image from his eyes. Emma writhing against Charlie — it was burned into his retina like a photographer's flash powder. He reached the tree, unseen by Vicar Wilson, rounded it and climbed the wall on the other side.

"Jack, I missed you. Where did you get to?"

"Ah . . . call of nature." Jack struggled to catch his breath. He was forced to rearrange his trousers again while the Vicar turned to herd the children back into the field. He followed them to where Emma worked, proudly swinging the scythe. Charlie stood conspicuously well clear of her, fiddling with his belt buckle.

"Nothing to it, Uncle," she cried taking one last cut then grounding the blade and leaning on the handle. "These nibs need some adjustment, of course, but the snath suits me just fine."

"Oh aye — you've got the terminology down pat, Miss Clever Clogs," her uncle replied. "Let's see the results."

He examined her lane. "Well, well, three or four good cuts. I'll be bound but what in heaven's name happened here?"

He pointed to a mangled quarter circle of grass.

"Oh that was Charlie's fault," she said, patting the scythe handle and grinning broadly. "He's not much of a professor. He should stick to training horses, really."

They cut until the worst heat of the day struck, then returned to their previous day's cuttings to rake and stack through the afternoon. Back to cutting after tea, they finished mowing the last acre before sunset. Jack had to work for another hour by lantern in the stable, peening four large dents from his blade. He'd been so rattled that he'd been lucky not to slice his leg off.

He was relieved to find the novel sitting beside his plate in the kitchen and equally relieved to see Charlie's dirty dishes in the sink. He needed a quiet meal alone to consider his discovery. Emma not only loved Charlie, she lusted for him. It was much for Jack to think on.

• • •

There was no moon. Both windows were open and a fresh breeze stirred the black room. Jack lay on top of his blankets, letting the cool air run over him. He knew Charlie was awake. He had to be. Thinking of a refused appointment with Emma, a meeting which had promised erotic manoeuvres beyond imagination. How could any man not be overwhelmed with such thoughts? For that matter, how could any man resist such a temptation? Yet Charlie had. Jack knew he could not have resisted. His pathetic veneer as a "gentle" man had been stripped away in seconds, reducing him to a panting pig. What did he know of love? His romantic notions had been crushed under a hammer of lust. His self-loathing was matched only by his desire to rerun that hayfield scene over and over in his mind's eye. Emma's body — gyrating, her tongue, neck, low-pitched moans —

He shut the scene off with an effort and turned his thoughts toward Emma as a puzzle. He'd worked out a theory but it needed confirmation.

"Charlie?" he ventured into the darkness.

"What."

"Why was Emma sent here from London? I mean really, not the health and housekeeper business."

No reply.

"Do you know? The true reason I mean?"

"Yes, Jack, I do."

"Tell me."

"It's none of your business." The tone was final. "She asked me the same question about you — why did your father die poor? Why didn't you stay in Gloucester? Why don't you go to Bristol or London?"

"She did? She asked about me? Did you tell her?"

"Yes, she did ask and no, I didn't tell her." Charlie's voice was calm, almost fatherly. "None of her business, neither."

Jack waited, deliberating, wording his next approach carefully. He couldn't let it rest here. There had to be a reason why Emma could love Charlie.

"It's because she loves men, in the biblical sense, I mean. Because she liked men too much and caused a scandal in London?"

"Go to hell with your biblical sense!" Charlie barked. "Say that again and I'll smash your face." Jack, for the first time in his eighteen years, saw the world as a truly wicked place full of unsavoury secrets. Fathers not to be trusted with money, mothers bound by hidden debts, and young women — lambs in appearance — but slavering seductresses underneath. And most unexpected, Charles Cordey rascals who fought against the lamb's seduction.

It fired him with an unreasoning jealousy. He should have been horrified, disgusted by her behaviour, her duplicity. Yet he wasn't. He was still drawn to her and not just by lust. Her strength in the hayfield encounter, her domination of Charlie somehow counted for more than her lack of modesty. At Tintern, all he had truly desired was her approval. Now, after this bout of introspection, he discovered that he needed her love. He'd fallen in love with an entirely unsuitable woman who scorned him. Could this simply be the result of months of exposure to the coarse Forest environment?

CHAPTER 5

The England that lies between the Severn and Wye rivers is not the soft forelock tugging England of Kent or Hampshire, or even the rest of Gloucestershire. It is hard, feisty, and only productive after a battle has been fought. Colliers and miners must wrench their coal and iron from her. Foresters cut, drag, strip, and saw their timber. Even the sheep run free and roughshod over anything not protected by fences. The early summer of 1898, wet and cold true to form, had only yielded its usual single crop of hay — and that, late. But the Forest of Dean very uncharacteristically mellowed in late summer. And, for those few souls who possessed the low land, the skill and the daring to grow wheat and barley were rewarded. Three hot, dry weeks in August took the tall, milky-soft plants, stood them up straight, and hardened the kernels to perfection. It was a crop to put all else — sheep, pigs, and orchard — in its shadow. It was a crop rarely given to Forest farmers. Vicar Wilson, which is to say Charlie Cordey, had twenty-two acres in wheat and nearly forty in barley. Except for the hay meadows, it was every acre the Vicar leased. Nothing lay fallow.

Mr. Wilson had been thrilled as an agriculturalist to achieve such a crop — even to the point of hiring a photographer from Coleford to come take his picture standing in chest-high wheat. Charlie had been thrilled as a counter of pounds, shillings, and pence. He was convinced the barley would go malting grade and fetch top price. When a profit emerged from the farm operation, the Vicar traditionally paid handsome bonuses from it. This year

Charlie stood to earn his whole year's wages over again in the corn bonus alone — if the crop could be harvested without damage.

Both men were like expectant fathers, darting out to the fields twice a day, rolling heads of wheat between palms, chewing the kernels to test hardness. They dithered and ponced about trying to decide if the grain was ready for harvest — yes — no, better wait a couple more days. A heavy thunderstorm complete with hail had shot up the Severn, missing Newland by two miles. It produced a furious prayer from the Vicar and caused Charlie to watch the skies for a week, greying at the slightest hint of cumulus cloud. Jack discovered that the bonus system worked for him as well. Rather like Royal Navy prize money — the lion's share to Charlie, but a good-sized payout for himself. Calculations of bushels per acre and price per bushel and bonus percentages wrought visions of London. And, if he admitted it, pride in a hard job well done lurked not far beneath the surface.

Finally the barley was ready, the wheat not far behind. Jack thought himself prepared after all his labour from shearing and haying seasons. In fact, he discovered that he'd never actually worked before, not compared to harvest time when a prime crop stood in the balance. Charlie had pronounced Jack unfit to scythe anything other than grass, but the Vicar demurred. He was unwilling to risk a lengthy harvest that could run into foul weather. Charlie backed down and every cutter was drafted into service. Two binders and a stooker were hired for each cutter; a few shillings in extra wages was deemed well worth the return.

Each morning, Charlie, Jack, the old miner, and the Vicar stand in a single brave rank on the edge of the uncut barley. Razor-sharp scythes with large basket hoops attached are held at their sides. Four spartans, facing the hordes. Charlie and the Vicar advance to reconnoitre for dew, then retire to wait. The precious sunlight penetrates at a better angle and the grain begins to dry. The scouts venture forth and this time they nod. The attack commences. First the Vicar, scything and depositing perfect bundles of barley to his left. Two yards behind him Charlie starts, then the miner, then Jack. The grain is soon dropping into four swaths and upon these descend the binders. Mostly village women whose quick hands snatch up a cut bundle, whip a straw around the stalks, secure it, then drop the bound sheaf. The next bundle up nearly before the sheaf hits ground. Finally comes the rear rank, the boys and unskilled men. They retrieve the sheaves, stand them on end, stalks down, heads up, like poles on a wigwam, wedged together into upright pyramids. The battle rages all day till a shower or darkness calls a halt.

The Vicar's flock of harvest toilers grew up to twenty in number at times . Mrs. Toomey and Emma lugged heroic quantities of food to the fields, and often stayed to stook behind the Reverend for a few hours. Likewise, the two Mitchell boys volunteered to work. Tall, strapping lads, they struggled to keep up with the scrawny village women. There is no point in hurrying such labour. A harvester who cuts fast in the morning will stagger to a near stop by midday. Anyone running to pick up sheaves one day will be crippled the next. A steady pace was understood by all save the Mitchell boys, who learned their lesson quickly. But that steady pace did not cease. An urgency, unknown in haying, drove them and bonded them. The Vicar performed his cleric duties, but at a minimum. Evensong times grew later, corresponding with the amount of cutting time left in the sun. Two Sunday morning sermons were cobbled together in an exhausted rush the night before. Social calls ceased, and only those on death's door received visits from Reverend Wilson.

The fifteenth day of harvest dawned warm and calm. They faced their last field of wheat. It was going to be safe. The wheat had been cut, bound, and stooked two days earlier, only six men remained on the Wilson harvest crew. The two Mitchell lads, one driving Bobbi in the Vicar's cart, the other driving a Mitchell horse in a borrowed cart, were in their element. Riding, not walking — driving, not working. Jack and the miner forked sheaves onto a cart where they were sorted and packed by the Vicar. A full cart would leave for the Vicarage for Charlie to unload while the second cart was filled. Charlie had insisted on building the ricks. He carefully constructed the corn mountains so they could withstand strong winds then covered them with huge waterproof rick-cloths each night.

The carts filled and emptied, cycling back and forth, only pausing for an occasional sparing drink for the hot horses. Even Bobbi, the undisputed queen of the stable was treated no better than a toiling navvy. In her cart at dawn, out at dusk, and precious few kind words. She was in a sullen mood. Strangely, she seemed to pout for everyone but Jack. This was discovered the third day of harvest when Bobbi, sidestepping and stamping, had received a good blast from Charlie. Jack had come to help and, the instant he laid his hand on her, she calmed. Then only Jack put Bobbi in and out of her shafts. The Vicar, betrayed, was jealous until Emma made a joke of it. She claimed Bobbi was sweet on Jack because he made Emma walk home from Tintern so that Bobbi needn't pull the trap. And so the last day of harvest ended. Two ricks of prime barley and one of excellent wheat, their conical peaks tarped down tight, stood neatly beside the stable, waiting for the thresher. Only one task remained. Mrs. Toomey's harvest dinner.

• • •

Jack and Charlie performed their evening ritual early today. Every foot of fencing that surrounded the grain was checked. No animal could approach to sample the sheaves. The rick cloths were examined, the tie downs twanged for tight security. Then all was double-checked.

"See, it's a blessing and a curse, Jack," Professor Cordey was lecturing again. "We Foresters can run our ship free on crown grass, so we can cut our hay meadows to feed horses and such with enough left over for cash sale. But then we have to go to the trouble of fencing every damn bit of forage or the sheep will have it."

"I thought raw grain was bad for sheep?" Jack spoke without thinking, then instantly regretted it. Any encouragement simply prolonged the lesson.

"It is bad for 'em but the daft buggers would eat rusty nails if you let 'em. More trouble than they're worth, I sez. And mutton tasting like greasy — "

"But the Vicar loves his sheep so no point in thinking you can get rid," Jack deftly cut off the sheep debate.

"Aye, but pigs, especially the Gloucester Old Spots, that's a smart go. Tough, don't take up much space, good eating and always a market for them." He patted the side of a rick. "But they'll not see a kernel of this crop. We'll buy a bit of mouldy Monmouth corn to make our swill. That's my secret, see? Make a lot of a few good products and buy what you need cheap. Most farmers here try to raise everything from milk cows to apples on a few acres. They end up with nothing to sell and not enough to eat.

Jack tugged a tie down rope. "This is a cash rick, I know. You've told me your profit secret before. Can we go now?"

Charlie laughed, punching his shoulder. Jack laughed with him, unable to suppress a mixture of camaraderie and pride at this sign of acceptance from Charlie. They made their way to the house to change and wash. For a moment Jack considered wearing his suit and good shoes. He decided, no, that day would come, but not now, not for a Forest meal — even Mrs. Toomey's harvest supper. They walked around the Vicarage to the west lawn where they had positioned three long tables earlier in the day.

"What the hell is this?" Charlie stopped at the edge of the lawn. "Has she gone silly? Who ever saw the like?"

Jack understood at a glance. Bathsheba Everdene's shearing dinner — straight out of Hardy's novel. He kept quiet, feeling Charlie's exasperation grow tense. The tall, dining-room windows were open onto the lawn. One of the trestle tables actually protruded from a window. Half the table was inside the dining room, the other half ran over the sill and extended onto the lawn where its legs were levelled by blocks of wood. The remaining two tables were laid end to end with the first one forming a single, long eating surface that pierced the house like a harpoon. A gaggle of villagers, freshly paid their harvest wages by a beaming Vicar, now clustered around him as he poured ale. They were easy and happy in his company, as he was in theirs. A separate, small table, near the windows, was laid with white linen and crystal. Here stood Philip and Jennie Mitchell, a large farmer with his wife, and a curate from the new church in Coleford. Emma dispensed sherry and tinkling laughter to them. Jack went immediately to the ale keg. Charlie veered close to the dining room, then joined him.

"Eight places set indoors — good china — best tablecloth," he reported like an army scout. "Quality," he nodded at the sherry table, "dine inside, rest of us grub it outside. She just doesn't understand the Forest. This ain't London."

Jack counted heads quickly. "Seven quality and eight seats," he said, nudging Charlie. "Looks like you're the eighth bit of quality."

"Me?"

"Farm manager must be next in line."

Charlie glanced down at his clothes, tugged at the frayed shirt cuffs, then tucked them back up inside his matted, tweed coatsleeves. Next to his one suit, Charlie was wearing his best: yellow waistcoat, silk handkerchief knotted at his neck, clean corduroy trousers tucked into well-shone but equally well-worn riding boots. In fact, the same actual articles as Philip Mitchell, but Mitchell was dressed haphazardly casual, and cut a stylish figure several notches above Charlie Cordey at his best.

"She can't be serious. I've only sat the Vicar's table a half-dozen times, and never since she's come."

"It's the Vicar's work, I'll wager," Jack replied. "He'll want to show you off. Your crop is probably the best one around this year and the Vicar knows it."

"I can't be seated with that lot. I've come to enjoy myself tonight, not worry about which bloody knife to butter my bread with."

"Charlie!" Emma waved to them. "At last! Come here, there's someone you have to meet."

Jack turned away but Charlie's powerful hand locked onto his arm above the elbow and propelled him toward the sherry. "It's you'll be sittin in for me, my boy," he whispered. "Play along."

"This is Mr. and Mrs. Norris from Cross Farm." Emma forced a smile, a look of desperation strained her face. She shoved a glass into Charlie's fist. "Mr. Charles Cordey, our manager."

Norris resembled a Gloucester One Spot in a poorly tailored suit. His red face, rough hands, and uneasy manner marked him as an unwilling head table member. His wife, however, revelled in the role. Overdressed and sallow, she barely acknowledged Charlie before pitching into Emma with the details of a recent scandal.

"Saw your ricks comin' in," Norris grunted.

"Aye." Charlie replied, sipping the sherry and casting a sidelong glance at the ale.

"Vicar's claiming a pretty high yield."

Charlie glanced at Jack. "How'd we figure?"

Jack, very happy to play the yokel, merely shrugged his shoulders. "High."

"Vicar says thirty," Norris continued.

"More like forty, forty-five," Charlie countered.

Norris and Cordey exchanged a long, hard stare.

"I might believe thirty, any more is pretty rare, even in barley."

"Aye." Charlie replied, swallowing his sherry. Now the two men stared into their empty glasses, fidgeting. Jack began a series of small sidesteps, edging toward the laughing, happy crowd around the Vicar. Charlie's hand shot out like a striking cobra, caught his arm, and pulled him back.

"Jack, here, is new to farming. But he's bright and taken to the scythe tolerably well. He can tell you about our crop whilst I get some ale."

Norris smacked his lips and gazed at the beer keg. He shot a nervous glance over his shoulder at his wife, winked, and whispered, "I believe I'll join you, Mr. Cordey."

The three men began to amble away from the sherry party and nearly escaped before Mrs. Norris' sharp voice pinioned her husband.

"Mr. Norris! Gerald!"

Norris stopped with a long sigh.

"You'll be interested to meet the Mitchells, I'm sure."

Norris turned, but Charlie and Jack accelerated away. Just as they reached the ale, Reverend Wilson spotted them. "Ah, Charlie and Jack!"

He passed a glass of beer to Jack then took Charlie's arm. "I've insisted that you sit by me tonight. Want you to back me up on our crop. Norris is here — met him, have you? Excellent man — what he doesn't know about farming simply isn't worth knowing.

Wife's a bit tart but a grand Forest woman at heart. She did eight years as a housemaid in Cheltenham before she snagged old Norris."

Jack drew long and with satisfied relish at his ale, watching them go. Jennie Mitchell was talking to Emma. Emma searched the labour crowd then pointed directly to Jack. Jennie pressed a small handkerchief to her lips and appeared to be laughing. Jack turned his hand up and examined it — brown and hard as bark. Large veins connected it to a thickening wrist. He smiled. John Thornton had changed. The ale tasted fine and he liked the power of his grip. He had no desire to trade wit with Jennie or Phil. He'd earned his keep as a harvester and, by God, somehow that wasn't such a bad thing. He looked up and caught Jennie's eye. He kissed his fingertips, blew in her direction and grinned. She whirled around, showing her back, and he grinned even more broadly. Jack could blow her a kiss, but John could not. One day she'd call him John Thornton and offer him sherry. But he wasn't concerned when that day might come.

The early September sun carried summer's warmth but its setting brought the first cool evening air of autumn. The supper was called, grace was said and they set to the feast. Mrs. Toomey's meal, while not *haute cuisine*, was excellent plain cooking and in sufficient quantity that even the scything miner was eventually filled and content. Jack, seated between two village women who had bound sheaves, was initially ignored by them. They applied themselves to a single minded, furious attack upon the food. Lean, hard female versions of the miners; they ate with manners, but spared little time for proper pleasantries. Even when the meal ended they seemed strangely lost for conversation.

"Lovely meal," Jack tried.

"Oh, aye, Mrs. Toomey cooks well enough, eh, Liz?"

"Well enough," Liz said, "considering she has a barn full of fine food to cook up in t' first place, Maude."

"Like to see what she'd produce on a collier's wage," Maude agreed.

"An oo's idea were this? Man — 'oman — man — 'oman? I didn't come to no harvest supper to be stuck next my old man all night." Liz cuffed her husband who seemed no happier seated next to her.

"Men at one table, women at t'other. Always works best that way," Maude confirmed, tossing her head towards Mr. Maude, a man Jack recognized as having done stooking between his shifts in the mine. By way of answer, Maude's husband pulled a pipe from his pocket, charged it with very black, shaggy bits of tobacco, lit it and blew a cloud of smoke in her face.

"Send your foul smoke elsewhere," she coughed for effect.

He tapped his glass with the pipe stem. "Fetch us a drop of ale in here, old girl, and I'll overlook your cheek."

"Me? Fetch for you? 'Tis *my* harvest supper. If you had any manners about you, then, you'd be fetching to me," Maude indicated her own glass. "And I'll have cider, if you please."

He laughed and tapped his pipe on his mug again.

Liz planted her elbow firmly in Jack's ribs, manoeuvred him back, and leaned across to squawk, "Wastin' your breath, Maudy. No Forest woman ever gave birth to a gentleman!"

This seemed to find general agreement from all within hearing: women laughing; men perversely proud of the fact. Liz removed her elbow from Jack's side to acknowledge her audience. Unwilling to relinquish the floor, she dropped her hand onto his shoulder.

"Here's the proof, sitting at my side ladies. Young master Jack is a man of Gloucester city. He would fetch a lady a glass of cider, wouldn't ee, Jack?"

"O'course he would!" Maude, on cue, slung one arm around Jack's shoulders and presented him with her glass. "Show these Foresters how it's done."

Jack, acutely conscious of both women pressed tightly against him, even more conscious of the hard stares from their men nearby, was trapped, speechless. Trying to think of a neutral reply, he could only force a grin resembling the rictus on a corpse.

"Ah, you darling boy." Liz crowed. "He's blushing!" She clamped his neck in her powerful grip, pulled him over, and planted a loud kiss on his cheek. Jack redoubled his blush until his face throbbed crimson. It was the best thing he could have done. The men immediately leaped to his rescue.

"Give over 'oman, he bain't have an old ewe gnawing at him!" Liz's husband.

"You'll smother the lad! Leave him be — bullies!" Maude's husband.

Jack broke free and quickly scooped up all five glasses. "That's two ciders and three ales, then."

His return a few moments later was greeted with approbation from the ladies and good-natured jeers from the men. Maude and Liz clinked glasses with him. "Here's to Gentleman Jack," Maude declared the toast. Jack looked down the table length. The Vicar, at its head, was in deep discussion with Norris and Charlie. Charlie seemed to be making a heavy point — doubtless about free-grazing sheep and selling hay. Emma, on the Vicar's right, was listening to Phil Mitchell, but her eyes were drawn to the loud commotion surrounding Jack. The women drank their toast and this time both delivered a crushing kiss, left and right, creating a chorus of squeals from the other women present. Emma smiled. Jack raised his ale when the noise subsided.

"To the ladies of the harvest. If not for the former, we would never accomplish the latter."

The woman drank to their own toast while the men booed and hissed. Jack glanced to Emma. She nodded, then looked away. The men applied themselves to ale and pipes and cross-table conversation, but the women were unwilling to let the moment pass. Liz, elbowing Jack out of the way again, leaned across to Maude.

"He is lovely, isn't he?" She said in a low voice.

"I got eyes, don't I?" Maude squeezed Jack's arm. "Young and fresh. Nay like our old sticks."

"Master Jack is just what us need, Maudy. What say we share 'im?"

"I beg your pardon, ladies," Jack flexed his elbows outwards breaking the huddle. "But the object of your discussion *is*, in fact, present. I'm not an item of produce, you know — not a loaf to be shared out."

"Speaks lovely, even," Maude sighed.

"You two are impossible," Jack laughed.

"Wouldn't be the first time it's happened," Liz hissed, her demeanour suddenly turned gossip serious.

"You be talking about our Sir Charles and his Fanny?"

"Aye, there bist a gentleman who can do his duty!"

Both women dissolved into sniggering, low-pitched laughter.

"Are you referring to *the* Sir Charles Dilke? The MP?" Jack asked, astounded these two had any knowledge of someone like Dilke.

"Ain't you heard of what Sir Charles got up to with his pretty friend Fanny? Oh, about seven or eight years ago?"

"I know he was prominent in the Cabinet, then gave up his seat. You're saying he was caught being unfaithful to his wife? Some scandal? If so, I never heard of it in Gloucester." Jack tried to hide his irritation at such unpleasant gossip. But after the hayfield, he was not as quick to discount it as he once would have been.

"Couldn't say he was *caught* cheating, really." Liz adopted a thoughtful pose.

"No, *caught* be the wrong word, altogether," Maude said. "Since Sir Charles and Lady Dilke and little Fanny all shared the same bed, nobody *caught* nobody else."

"Good God!" Jack lowered his voice to a whisper and bobbed his head down close to theirs. "I've never heard of such a thing!"

They sniggered again.

"You're teasing me!" Jack, suddenly angry, drew back.

"Don't be a muntle! We wouldn't make up something like that," Maude tugged his sleeve and he rejoined them.

"You are saying that Dilke, his wife, and this girl actually had concurrent . . . ah . . . relations?"

"Don't know if they got around to doin' concurrents, whatever that is," Liz said earnestly. "But they all three of 'em performed the deed together, at the same time, like."

Maude, Liz and Jack sat quietly now in a frozen tableau. Jack wrestling to comprehend what he'd just been told, the other two savouring it as the best gossip in a century. The forbidden image of Emma in the hayfield forced its way into Jack's thoughts and mingled with the breathtaking notion of two women and a man in bed. He became conscious of Liz's hand resting lightly on his knee and Maude's shoulder pressed warmly against his. His eyes flickered to their faces and he realized that neither woman was likely older than thirty. Children, hard work, and years of poor diet had left their mark, but here were two very healthy women and himself, together. Unthinkable proximity and unthinkable conversation anywhere else but somehow, here in the rebellious Forest of Dean, almost . . . well, he could see how Dilke may have fallen from his morals.

Liz tweaked his knee.

Jack bolted upright, waking from the trance and broke the spell. Both women flushed and seemed to find urgent topics of discussion with others around the table.

The Vicar eventually rose to speak. He was brief, hearty, and applauded. It being a small farm and consequently a small supper, there was no dance, but a singing and verse tradition had been established in past years. To this end Maude's husband produced a violin and transformed himself into a fiddler. The Vicar went first with a fine tenor rendition of "Am I a Soldier of the Cross?" The violin carried him so well that Jack suspected the two of rehearsal. Liz and her husband sang "The Maid of Tottenham". They were joined in the fifth verse by all the harvesters bawling in unison:

> *I took her to the under grove among the grass so green*
> *The fair maid spread her legs so wide*
> *That I fell in between*
> *Such tying of a garter you have but seldom seen*
> *And we both jogged on together, my boys*
> *Sing fal the dal diddle all day.*

The Vicar, suppressing a grin, pretended not to hear the offending verse. Emma actually started to sing along, then stopped abruptly. Mrs. Norris and the Coleford man contented themselves with stern glares at the west end of the table. Emma replied sweetly with "Barbara Allen". Jack sat rapt as she sang about Barbara Allen's suitor.

> *He sent her letters with his man,*
> *she read them small and moving.*

Emma paused ever so briefly and fixed Charlie with a steady gaze.

No better shall ye be,
Ye'll not *have Barbara Allen.*

Charlie missed the look entirely, guzzling at his pint. She flicked her eyes down the table and connected briefly with Jack. His heart leapt with the old Tintern hope. Surely this was a message that Charlie would never have her love, no matter how ardently his suit was pressed. Charlie, bellicose with ale and cider, leapt over the table and through the dining-room window, escaping Norris at last. He then sang every verse of "British Grenadiers" and "Soldiers of the Queen". Neither song was really suited to the fiddle, so he was a cappella for "Soldiers of the Queen". This fired the harvesters who then belted out "Goodbye Dolly Grey" *en masse.*

A colossal, three-dimensional moon rose in the east and glowed bright orange as it caught the final, high rays of the sun, already gone down in the west. Darkness pressed in on the Vicarage. A half-dozen lanterns were produced and arranged in a circle around the fiddler. Glasses were recharged. Jennie Mitchell sang a beautiful version of the "Minstrel Boy". The moon climbed as her backdrop and the lantern light illuminated her chin, cheeks, and forehead leaving her eyes in black shadows. This drew everyone in close to the pool of light surrounding the violinist's grass stage. The wiry old miner, carrying his own weight in food and ale continued the mood with a long and surprisingly loquacious ghost story, set in the Clearwell mine. The huddle tightened and even Liz snuggled close to her man. The Norris' and the curate sat primly upon chairs but the Vicar, Emma, and the Mitchells sat on the grass closest to the lanterns, much like campers around a bonfire.

Jack alone was set back from the crowd. Genuinely fearful of Liz and Maude and cautious of the "quality", he lounged several paces out in the darkness. He could observe without being observed and, hopefully, not be asked to sing or recite. One of the harvest women sang a love song in wavering degrees of competence. Then Philip Mitchell, in a strong, confident baritone, did Gilbert and Sullivan's "The Pirate King", complete with hornpipe dance. Emboldened by Philip's example and nearly two quarts of Tanglefoot cider, Maude lurched onto centre stage and began to recite:

> *We are the Jovial Foresters*
> *Sir Charles shall be our man*
> *We'll send him back to parliament . . .*

Mr. Maude, realizing that this was perhaps too bold even for a freedom-loving Forest congregation, dropped his fiddle and strode quickly to her side, embraced her, and silenced her with a kiss.

"Come now, Maude, my girl," he said loudly, "let's not get ourselves cyawpsin tonight."

As he bore her offstage she managed one last encore yodel, "That there verse uz for me and Lizzy's Gentleman Jack!"

Had he been on his feet rather than reclining, Jack might have made a clean escape. As it was, the party turned on him before he could be afoot. Charlie led the pack, baying for a song from the "Nesh Gloucester boy". Hustled into the circle of light, he stood limp with stage fright, desperately wishing he'd drunk more ale for courage. The shining faces crowded up to the lanterns expectantly and with an obvious lack of patience. He glanced to the Vicar but there was no reprieve.

"Come now, Jack," the Vicar coaxed. "Swim with the tide, boy — just a short song, if you like — a Gloucester song, eh?"

The Vicar's words conjured Tintern and the urchin who said the Lord's Prayer for him — then his father's presence and its peaceful surge — then his mother, sweet and chattering and lonely in Offa's Rose — then, finally, Gloucester Cathedral's stained glass sunlight pouring over its choir. Suddenly he was singing, the fiddler catching up skilfully, a song the choir had performed only a month before his father's death.

> *Now the day is over,*
> *Night is drawing nigh.*
> *Shadows of the evening*
> *Steal across the sky . . .*

The spirits working within Jack lifted his performance beyond himself. He turned to face the harvest moon and it pulled the verse from him.

> *Jesus gave the weary*
> *Calm and sweet repose.*

His father's hand was in his again. He closed his eyes and it seemed that it was his father singing — alive and with his old power. Free of the place and company, he sang on to the end.

> *Now the day is over, now the day is done.*

Silence. He opened his eyes to the moon, very conscious that he stood alone, the assembled Foresters at his back.

"Aaaw, yer so bloody lovely, Jack, my sweet," Liz bawled like a lost calf. Applause, whistles and more applause poured from possibly the toughest audience in the United Kingdom. Jennie Mitchell dabbed her eyes and Maude, weeping shamelessly, blubbered about her sweet boy. Jack, the mood over, fled quickly to his place beyond the scrum. The Vicar quieted them, ensured everyone had filled their glasses, then dragged them to their feet for "Auld Lang Syne". Charlie bellowed for a toast to Mrs. Toomey, then a toast to the Vicar, then to the Queen. He led them all in "God Save the Queen" at which point he fell over, drunk, and the party broke up.

Philip, Norris, and the curate hoisted Charlie up and dumped him across Jack's shoulders before taking their leave. Jack, doubled over, knees and back creaking under the strain, shuffled toward the rear of the Vicarage. He stumbled badly just as he rounded the house and was grateful to see Mrs. Toomey lighting the door with a lantern. She swung it open for him and he sped past using a last burst of energy to climb the stairs. The lantern followed him. He tripped over the doorsill, fell to his knees, and launched Charlie toward his bed, missing by several inches. Charlie, limp on the floor, began to snore gently.

"Thank you, Mrs. Toomey," he gasped, struggling upright. "You've saved the day."

"Do I look like Mrs. Toomey? Truly, Jack?" Emma raised the lantern until its light shone full on her face.

Truly, she did not. Her eyes, bright from cider and the flickering light, held him. Emma in his dark bedroom of fevered dreams and fantasies. Emma in the flesh — not Emma of those imaginings. A wild array of thoughts chased through Jack's mind, smashing into each other, merging and then careening away. Emma in the hayfield whinnying with lust — Lizzy pinching his knee — Vi's maid brushing against him — Wordsworth — the Wye — Charlie maudlin drunk — Charlie pulling back in the hayfield — Dilke and Dilke and Fanny together — Charlie and Emma and Jack together now.

She walked slowly past him and prodded Charlie with her toe. His deep breathing did not falter. She turned and smiled.

"Here we are, then, the three of us."

Had she read his mind? He was still panting from the stair climb; he felt like some kind of beast.

"You were very popular with the women tonight, Jack. A side of you that I've never seen."

He sweated, tried to control his heavy breathing, and failed.

"What were you up to?"

"Nothing, really. It was them, mostly."

"Do you mind me asking?" She stepped closer to him. Her face shone, she was perspiring, too.

"No, I don't mind," he lied.

"Well? What then? Why would two stern Forest miners' women propose a toast to Gentleman Jack, then kiss him? *Two* women! At the same time! Quite a coup for a quiet young man who only recently "found his place" and renounced all claims to gentleman rank."

"Just play — teasing me because I blushed — then I fetched them some cider — they were tweaking their husbands, I suppose."

She examined him, like a buyer looking at a horse and shook her head. "More to it than a blush, I think." He smelled her now, so close, scrutinizing him and demanding a better answer. Not perfume or bath salt, but a warm smell, like Bobbi standing in a hot sun.

"Well, they told me an outrageous piece of gossip concerning Sir Charles Dilke, the MP. I'm sure it was a joke designed to embarrass me. I didn't believe . . . "

"You mean about Dilke and Fanny?"

"Why, yes. Are you saying it's true? I mean, are you actually familiar with the story?"

"Last year, Uncle and I were in Cinderford for a fête." She spoke quickly with little of her upper-class reserve — not much different than Maude alive with gossip. "Sir Charles and Lady Dilke attended, also. When they arrived, a pack of village louts began chanting "Where's Fanny — where's Fanny?" Sir Charles stood up to them, shouted them down, and they loved him for it. Uncle wouldn't tell me what it was about, but Charlie did."

She stopped herself, walked to Jack's bed, set the lantern on the floor, and perched on the edge of his mattress.

"Seems a woman named Crawford and Sir Charles became lovers before his first wife died. Crawford didn't last long but she told anyone who would listen, including the London newspapers, about the affair. She also insisted that a second woman, Fanny, joined them in their lovemaking — a threesome, Charlie called it."

"Maude got it wrong," Jack said quietly. "She said it was Sir Charles and Lady Dilke and Fanny — not this Crawford woman."

"In fact, she got the whole thing wrong. Dilke was innocent. Isn't that awful?" She laughed, an easy laugh that encouraged him to join it.

"But why did anyone believe such a fabrication? He lost his cabinet posting and his reputation because of a fairy tale?"

"Oh, no fairy tale. Crawford and Fanny were part of a threesome, all that is true. But it was with a rival politician. Their story was very plausible. The Foresters want to believe it, you see, they take pride in it." She waved a pale hand in the lantern light. "They don't have our class — *my* class rules to follow. Dilke will never lose his seat. They love him for being a rascal, even though he isn't one!"

"Doesn't work like that anywhere else. A bad reputation is a blight — an irrevocable blight." Jack thought of Gloucester and its opinion of the Thornton family.

"Mmm," Emma folded her hands in her lap. "Speaking of reputations, I shouldn't be here alone with you, should I?"

Jack started at this. "You only came to help me with Charlie — nobody would construe that as wrong, surely."

"But I didn't come to help you with Charlie." She paused for a long sideways stare out the window, as though uncertain whether to stay or go. "I came to ask you questions."

Jack looked toward Charlie, who continued to lie like an overfed pig. His heart began to thump and he cursed himself for a frightened virgin.

"Me? But Charlie is your . . . ah, your interest, surely."

"Charlie interests me, true. But not tonight."

Jack stepped back involuntarily, unable to bring himself to look at her, certain her unblinking green eyes were now upon him.

"Charlie loves you," he stammered, defending by offence.

"I know. But I don't love him." She said it so honestly, as a matter of fact, that Jack looked up and finally met her gaze. "I've never loved any man." She passed the back of her hand across her forehead and it came away slick with sweat. Suddenly she was a young girl, not in control. "I think I'm incapable of it. Love, that is."

It was the truth. Jack thought of her expression when she sang Barbara Allen. But he also thought of her in the hay meadow with Charlie. The contradiction was too great to reconcile.

"You must love Charlie!"

"No, I must not." She stamped her foot. "Why do you say so?"

"Because, well, no reason except I assumed — "

"I'm not here for Charlie. I want to ask questions of Jack Thornton." She drew a deep breath. "May I?"

He nodded yes because he had no choice, like a child submitting to a teacher's interrogation. Yet the teacher now reverted to the uncertain girl.

"When you sang tonight — it was more than just a harvest song." The toe of her boot tapped nervously against the lantern case, flickering the light. "I felt it, and others also. What was inside you? What were you feeling?"

The question was preposterous. Nobody had ever asked about his personal emotions. Nobody asked anybody about their personal emotions. She studied her boot, light wavering back and forth across her face.

"I know it's very, um, well, rude to ask such a question. But here, in the Forest, they do things that aren't done and — " The tapping stopped. She slowly raised her face up to him.

"My father," he said. "Gloucester Cathedral. My mother at Redbrook. And a little girl who said the Lord's Prayer for me when I couldn't say it for myself. Father, mostly, is what I sang about. It was like . . . as though he was here tonight, holding my hand."

"Good Lord," Emma murmured. She examined him again, as though looking for a physical manifestation of these thoughts. He submitted to her frank stare.

"Now you want to know why I had to leave Gloucester. Charlie told me you asked. You want to know my father's blight," he said, ready to tell her everything and not caring if she knew or if she gossiped it to the Mitchells.

"Yes. I was going to ask you just that. But not now." She stood and picked up her light. "In fact, I think I feel ashamed. I hoped to discover your dark secret so that I could feel better — about myself." She swayed, as though dizzy. "Now I see that isn't possible."

She walked past him, then stopped in the doorway and half turned. "Funny thing is, Jack, I don't remember feeling ashamed of myself for anything I've ever done. Embarrassed or regretful, yes, but not shame." She smiled. "Perhaps there is hope for me after all."

She disappeared and the room fell dark. Jack made no move to light a candle. His eyes adjusted to the moonlight. Charlie lay as a snoring shadow on the floor.

"She is everything I thought I disliked, Charlie. Aloof, self absorbed, even promiscuous." He tapped Charlie with the toe of this boot and Charlie replied with a slobbery snort. The perfect partner for the conversation Jack felt compelled to have.

"She's not even truly pretty — not enough to blind me anyway. So why can't I escape her? And you, Cordey, the dedicated workingman's man. Her class and her type disgust you. Why are you tilting at her windmill? You've had your physical victory, but that's not a tenth of your feelings for her."

Jack knelt beside Charlie, pulled a blanket off the bed, and draped it over him.

"Am I in love with her? Can that happen without one actually making a conscious decision? I always thought I'd take a bride. But she seems to have taken me, and she doesn't even know it."

Jack kicked his boots off and settled on his bed, taking great care to lie next to the spot she had occupied.

CHAPTER 6

Night soil. Odd name for excrement; or better, excremental slop. Why not just call it muck? Or dung? Muck was much more accurate and dung certainly more evocative. Night soil could almost be thought a romantic word. Jack finished the entry Charlie had dictated for the journal.

> *December 19, 1898.*
> *Fine day to start but very wet afternoon. Brought load of night soil down from Scatterford. Second load brought from Inwood. Turned night soil into dung pile. Carted dung and night soil onto 10 acres of pasture.*

His hand was still summer brown, fingers thickened and dotted by a myriad of tiny scars and nicks that came from farm work. Fingernails were short, cracked, and never properly clean. Yet despite its hardened transformation to a labourer's mitt, his hand still produced near-perfect script. More than a year since his father's death. More than a year since he'd earned a city clerk's living. He laid the pen down, and passed the journal to Charlie.

"Good. Looks like more of the same today."

Jack wrinkled his nose involuntarily. He couldn't seem to adjust to this one job. Casting manure on the hay meadows was nothing, but night soil was something else altogether.

"Aye, needn't look so sour, Jack. We may have to shovel shit all winter but, come harvest time, that soil pays for itself ten times over. Your squit bonus — "

"My undeserved harvest bonus," Jack cut in, reciting Charlie's oft-repeated complaint, "was grown in the best fertilized fields to be found between Wye and Severn."

"Well then, my boy! Let's be off to our smelly duties."

The entry for today would read "very wet, all day." Mercifully they were hauling the last of the night soil because the dung clamp was nearly gone and they needed to mix the two — night soil was never spread neat on the fields. There would be another round of the dirty business in February before ploughing began, but Jack calculated he'd be in London before then. Half his bonus, a very generous percentage of the profits, had been paid when the first lot of threshed barley was sold in November. It had gone malting quality as Charlie predicted. They would finish threshing the rest of the barley and the wheat by mid-January for sale soon after, when prices would be best. The second portion of his bonus would be at least as much as the first.

Charlie, ankle deep in the wet dung, cheerfully sang an India song as he worked. He claimed turning manure in a cold, soaking, English rain was superior to marching through the blazing heat of heathen India, so count your blessings. Jack mentally recalculated his earnings then compared it to his two primary expenditures. First, he would repay the mysterious debt his mother owed Aunt Vi. Then, depending on what was left over, he would make for London or Bristol. The debt couldn't be too severe; surely the women exaggerated. How much could his father have borrowed from a Forest miner? Bristol was cheaper to live, but fewer opportunities. London more expensive, but limitless opportunity. He wanted London if Vi's debt left him enough to afford it. London offered other attractions above Bristol. Emma's parents were coming for

Christmas. There was, according to Mrs. Toomey, an agreement that Emma would be returning home with them. Her "health" now sufficiently restored.

Charlie was, by turns, relieved and depressed at this news. Since the hayfield encounter, Jack had learned to read the signs of their couplings quite accurately. Charlie invariably guilty and morose; Emma almost flighty — silly, after they had been together. Jack had joined them as an invisible member of their tryst. He observed closely, noting how often the two lovers would simultaneously disappear for an afternoon or evening on concocted errands. Like a seedy voyeur he followed Charlie one evening, shortly after the harvest supper, and saw him meet Emma at a small hut in the woods on the hilltop east of Newland. He heard them murmur, thrash, and call out wildly — but stopped short of actually peeping in at them.

Disgusted with himself, angry at Emma, jealous when he had no claim to jealousy, and refilled with an unreasoning lust, he'd resolved to ignore them. That resolve crumbled and, within a week, he'd begun watching again. But there'd been nothing to watch. Emma had no more physical trysts with Charlie in the next three months and her social encounters never went beyond the demands of normal courtesy. That a change had occurred, there could be no doubt. What it meant for him, he couldn't fathom. Why had she stopped meeting Charlie? She said she didn't love him; was she ashamed of her inability to love?

He moved Bobbi forward a few feet, climbed into the cart, and pushed a hump of night soil onto the next section of the dung heap. He jumped off the cart and landed with a splat. Then they began turning the soil over, mixing it evenly with the dung. He worked just hard enough that his body heat offset the cold rain. If Emma returned to London in January, and he could establish himself there by the end of February, then he could legitimately call upon her. Although content with their social segregation now, he knew in his heart that he'd be drawn to her in London. He would transform from Jack, the night soil carter, to John Thornton, city man with prospects. City man with a deep need to be with Emma, to taste her passions rather than watch them. Love her rather than serve her, discover if she could love him. Is that what she was trying to tell him after the harvest supper? That she might love him as her equal one day?

A wind gust drove cold water down his neck. He redoubled his shovelling efforts, putting Emma from his mind.

• • •

The last Sunday before Christmas there came a frost hard enough to freeze mud and turn the rain to snow. Jack woke that morning to a fresh, white Newland. A backdrop of low, grey clouds made each snowflake distinct as it fell soft and wet to coat the village. He attended to his chores in the stable, returned to the kitchen for a bowl of porridge, then galloped upstairs making as much noise as possible for the benefit of Charlie's hangover. Cordey merely burrowed deeper into his blankets and shot a halfhearted curse in Jack's direction. Jack dragged a large zinc tub to the centre of their room and made two trips to the kitchen pump, two buckets per trip, to fill the tub half full. He then retrieved Mrs. Toomey's largest copper kettle from where it boiled on the stove and emptied it, steaming, into the tub. With soap, razor, and towel arranged neatly on a stool nearby, he stripped and, with great satisfaction, lowered himself into the hot water.

"Oh, thank God for this bath."

Cordey's head popped out from beneath the bedclothes.

"A hot tub — just what the doctor ordered." He raised himself up. "Much obliged, Jack, you can have it after I've done."

Jack, deadly earnest, replied, "You will have to fight me for this bath, Charlie Cordey. And I will fight hard."

Charlie flopped back down. "Well, at least leave it warm for me." He farted loudly.

Jack scrubbed his skin until it glowed pink, then dressed slowly for church. Today, for the first time, he wore his suit. Shirt, collar, hose, all were applied carefully. The celluloid collar, loose the last time he'd worn a tie, was now snug on his neck. He luxuriated in the cut of his trousers, how they hung clean, pressed, and straight from the suspenders. The waistband, snug the last time he'd worn them, was now loose. He wiggled his toes inside his shoes, so light, soft, and civilized. Leaving Charlie still shivering in the bath, trying to staunch a shaving cut, Jack descended to the kitchen where Mrs. Toomey waited.

"Oh, Jack, love." Her eyes widened. "That suit does you proud. I wonder but you'll not want to be seen with the likes of me."

The oversized pinney, cotton skirt and dust cap were gone, replaced by a strikingly-cut, blue, velvet dress with lace collar and waves of hair upswept to a broad-brimmed hat. A bright-eyed face, free of flour and oven heat, smiled at him. Jack suddenly thought that the long deceased Mr. Toomey had been a lucky man.

Jack put his hat on and adjusted it to angle over his right eye. He opened the door, and proffered his arm.

"If I may have the honour, Mrs. Toomey," he murmured.

She actually blushed. "Oh, Jack, stop it." She clamped his arm to her like a train coupler, and they began the short walk to the church.

Newland church was, in fact, as pretty as any English country church in or out of the Forest of Dean. Snow had drifted across the great east windows, painting the tracery white. The porch roof joined the higher south aisle which, in turn, stepped up to the nave and above all sat the west tower with its four pinnacles. The roofs of All Saints Church were like the shoulders of a glacier-capped mountain rising toward the peak. Still refusing to refer to it as "the Cathedral", Jack, nonetheless, had developed a fondness for it. He had come to enjoy the perverse Forest insolence that occurred even here, inside the church. There was a beautifully-incised, brass slab, well over 300 years, old depicting a lady and knight. But there, between knight and lady, somebody had skilfully cut the image of a miner: pick, work clothes, hod, Nellie clenched in mouth, working his free-miner rights and not the least bit concerned by the proximity of aristocracy.

Jack and Mrs. Toomey sat in the nave, close to the northeast-ernmost arch where he could glance across to the Miner's Brass. It pleased him to know the miner was there, labourer near lord, it suited his situation. The Wilsons arrived moments before the service was due to begin. Emma's father and mother marched confidently to the head of the nave and turned to scan the front row for their places. It took some time for them to realize that there were no empty seats and an embarrassingly long time for them to accept the situation. The Vicar's brother, a senior government man from London, could have expected this courtesy in any English country church. This being a Forest church, no such pecking order was respected. Jack smiled sympathetically as the Wilsons, now bewildered, began casting about for any empty harbour. Only now did they realize that Emma had deserted them to sit in the south aisle. They beat an unceremonious retreat and joined her. A hurried conversation ensued. The serious, even pained senior Wilsons' expressions were in sharp contrast to Emma's broad grin. A grin that turned to a stifled laugh when Charlie Cordey rushed through the porch and plopped himself, none too gently, next to Mrs. Wilson.

There was a small choir composed mostly of miners who sang as beautifully as their Welsh cousins across the Wye — but only

someone wishing a "smack in the chops" as Charlie said, would
ever suggest they were Welshmen. The Foresters generally were less
struck with religion than most people but they filled the Cathedral
of the Forest regularly to hear Henry Wilson's sermons. The Vicar
preached as simply and with the same joy that he lived and they
loved him for it.

But Jack was distracted and could not seem to stay connected
to the homily, recalling his days as a boy chorister in Gloucester,
when he had trouble finding a note. The more the Master stared
at him, the more restless he became and, consequently, the farther
the note receded from his voice. Somebody was staring at him.
He stole surreptitious glances left and right, but saw nothing
suspicious. The Vicar finally relinquished his pulpit and they stood
to sing a hymn before the preparation of the gifts. Jack contrived
to drop his hymnal and twisted artlessly around to retrieve it. A
pair of green eyes lanced through the congregation and struck him.
Emma. Staring at him. The hymnal clattered to the floor again
and Mrs. Toomey gave him a strained look. He sang like a braying
donkey and simply could not wipe the smile off his face.

• • •

Mrs. Toomey, Charlie, and Jack were appointed to attend the
Vicar's drawing room at two PM to receive their Christmas gifts.
As he and Charlie shuffled into the room, Jack experienced a clear
vision of the Thornton's cook and maid in Gloucester doing the
same shuffle. How proud he'd been to pass them their gifts — his
mother seated by the tree handing up the presents — his father
offering a single glass of sherry and stilted conversation. So English,
so right and proper. But Vicar Wilson was not the typical English
master, of course. He ushered them into the room, made proper
introductions to Emma's parents, and seated them comfortably on

chairs before the fire. Then, like a crazed Fezziwig, he darted about heaving another log on the fire — no coal for a Christmas fire — refilling their glasses from the smoking bowl of bishop, starting conversations, making jokes and,without warning, launching into carols. "Here We Come a Wassailing" was first and caught them completely by surprise but Emma and Charlie quickly joined in. Mrs. Toomey and Jack cautiously followed with the Wilsons, bewildered again, finally humming along.

The Vicar was not to be denied. Sunday or no he was hosting a Christmas party. Two more carols and several glasses of punch later found Mrs. Wilson laughing loudly at Emma's rendition of the Bombay soldiers' songs Charlie had taught her. Even Charlie talked easily of lambing and haying and harvest to Mr. Wilson, and Mr. Wilson even listened with genuine interest. The Vicar and Mrs. Toomey then wheeled teacarts and trays in from the kitchen. The Vicar arranged them along the east window and, with a flourish, whipped the teatowels clear to reveal the feast. Meat pies, pickles, chicken, sweet bread, and sliced goose breast. And from the Forest: Broadoak Salmon, Styre apple jelly, Gloucestershire Khaki Campbell duck, and cold ham from the revered Gloucester Old Spot complete with a Blaisdon plum sauce. A tray of fresh wine glasses arrived with French and German bottles soon uncorked and flowing. Then fruitcake, tarts, cheese, nuts, port, and cigars deliberately smoked in the presence of the ladies while Emma played the piano and the Wilson brothers sang the daylight into dusk.

Finally, an hour before the evening service would call him away, the Vicar arranged three chairs next to the Christmas tree. Toomey, Cordey, and Thornton were seated while the rest stood by the tree. Mrs. Wilson, no longer awkward, first thanked Mrs. Toomey for the meal then shook her hand and held forth a large box crowned with ribbons and bows. Vicar Wilson clasped Charlie's hand in both his and shook it warmly.

"The very best to you, Charlie Cordey. The very best."

He drew a long wooden case from beneath the tree. It was made of polished mahogany and opened with a well-oiled click. Fitted into the velvet-lined interior was the stock and barrel of a twelve-bore shotgun. He presented it to Charlie.

"Your Purdy . . . " Charlie gasped.

"*Your* Purdy, now." The Vicar said.

"I can't . . . it's too much . . . not your Purdy." Charlie's slick veneer was stripped clean away. He sat, stunned.

"Take it, man, before I drop it."

Charlie took the case in his hands like a father with his first child. "It's too much . . . I can't . . . " he repeated.

"That's what Edgar said." The Vicar nodded at his discomfited brother. "I have no son, no nephew. Edgar can't use it. I can't hit a damn thing with it any more, it's collecting dust, take it and Merry Christmas."

Jack would have bet his bonus that Charles Cordey was as close to tears as he'd ever come in his life.

"Thanks, I . . . ah . . . thanks, Reverend Wilson," Charlie croaked.

Emma bent under the tree, her cream dress rustling. She picked up a small package and walked toward Jack. He started to rise, but she motioned him down. She stopped directly before him. Her eyes, green as the brooch on her high collar, held him.

"For you, Jack, a very Merry Christmas."

"Happy Christmas, young Jack," the Vicar echoed.

Jack took the package. Books by the feel of it, wrapped in tissue paper. He opened it carefully and found three pocket size novels — Thomas Hardy of course. All three bound in red leather.

Emma's slim hand appeared before his eyes. He took it and,for one reckless moment, considered kissing it.

"Thank you, Miss Emma. I love . . . I enjoy these stories immensely. I look forward to reading them."

That night, while Charlie stripped, oiled, and lovingly reassembled his shotgun, Jack retrieved his Hardy novels. Opening the cover of *The Mayor of Casterbridge,* he was crestfallen to find no inscription. Not even "Jack, Xmas '98." Three books, then — nothing more than a Christmas gift. He flipped to the title page and there, in a feminine hand was written:

For Gentleman Jack. With fond gratitude for opening her eyes. From ELW.

Careful lest Charlie should see, Jack slipped the book under his pillow and slept.

• • •

Jack's three days at Offa's Rose, Christmas Eve to Boxing Day, were bearable, but only because he spent them with his mother. Aunt Vi was prickly as ever. The maid Wyn was bold and familiar. Christmas services at St. Savior's in Redbrook were dull and he found himself wishing he could have attended Vicar Wilson's sermon in the Newland church. Vi boycotted church on the principle that they were rich men's sinecures and Charlie, home only for Christmas day, stayed back to keep her company. Jack was grateful to have his mother to himself for at least part of the day.

After church, Jack took his mother for a long, slow walk along the banks of the Wye to admire the snow on the surrounding rooftops. He reminded her of his harvest bonus and used it to broach the subject of the Thornton-Cordey debt again. She refused to discuss it, much less name the value owed. He coaxed and demanded, but to no avail. Finally he told her that he simply could not continue on to Bristol or London until he'd seen the debt paid. She called his bluff by stating that it was her debt, she would pay it in her way, and he must stay clear of the whole issue. They returned to Offa's Rose with him none the wiser. His only remaining option was Vi. Dreading the encounter but determined to clear the debt obstacle, he waited until she was alone. Wyn was off to visit her own family for the afternoon, his mother was napping in her room, and Vi was knitting in the sitting room.

The clouds of the last forty-eight hours had broken up and sun cut through the window. The latticework shadows cast on the carpet reminded him of his visit in the spring, when he'd learned of his father's scandal and the debt. Vi prized plain talk and honesty so he started straight in on her.

"Vi, I've come to ask you a direct question," he began. "I hope for a direct answer."

"Well thee dusn't hear but a direct answer from me, Jackie." She smiled confidently at him. Her bent fingers manoeuvred the needles quickly, not breaking stride.

"It concerns the debt my mother owes you."

The knitting stopped abruptly.

"Debt?" Her sharp eyes searched him.

"Twenty — more than twenty years ago — she said she borrowed from you. Has been in your debt ever since."

Vi, uncharacteristically silent, only nodded.

"I need to know what is owed — I can calculate the interest if necessary. I mean to pay it and have it clear."

"Your mam was wrong to speak of that . . . debt, as she calls it." She recommenced knitting. "Chunt a debt neither — least not as it concerns thee, young Jack."

"Oh yes it does," he said firmly. "The Thornton name may not be worth much anymore, but I intend to work my way forward, to improve myself. I can't do that until I know my slate is clean."

"Your name is worth whatever thee make it, Jack. Thee cosn't buy it back squeaky clean from Violet Cordey."

"So you intend to refuse me. Hold it over my head." He felt the bitterness, submerged these last months, creep up his gut. "No matter what I do in the future you can crow about how the Cordeys are still owed. This is some kind of . . . I don't know, social power. Your sister and nephew have fallen and, by heaven, you'll keep us down. Is that it?"

He'd touched her. The needles stopped again and she glared at him. "Don't be a gurt muntle. Now be quiet young pup — we'll talk no more of this."

"No, Aunt Vi. No more young pup — whipped pup. I'll have this answer and I'll pay this debt. I have money that I earned myself, with these," he held his hands up. "I'm going to clear the Thorntons here and now."

She smiled and the twinkle returned to her eye. "Well said, Jackie. Well said. A year in the Forest has done you a world o' good. But this debt is past your reach. Ask your mam, she may explain — not I."

"I have asked her — and Charlie. They're like clams. You're the key here — you're the creditor. Now Vi, let's stop this game and . . . "

"You asked Charlie?" she interrupted.

"Yes, of course. Why not?"

"Not Charlie." Her face glowed. Hard, bitter anger edged her voice. "Thee bist thy feythur's son — I can see that. Proud and cruel. It does you no credit. We see a dip mommuck now, Jack, leave it and never speak to my son about this again. *Never.*"

The insult to his father snatched Jack's control clean away.

"And are you your son's mother? Bully, coward, and fornicator? Spitting on your betters when they're low and licking their boots when they're not? I'll leave half my present fortune on the bed in

111

my room and go this evening. You can keep it, burn it, give it to Wyn, or your precious son. But I consider the debt paid as of today."

He turned on his heel to leave, already sick that he'd failed. She'd beaten him and would cackle over it later when her temper cooled.

"Wait! I'll tell you then, John Thornton. I'll tell of this debt and you can regret the day you forced me to it."

He turned. She motioned for him to sit and he did, his anger dissolving rapidly. She picked up her knitting and began work. He could hear air rasping in and out her lungs. Eventually she seemed to breath more easily.

"Your mother, Gladys. She owes me three children."

Her fingers began the flickering movements of a human loom. She did not look up.

"Three children . . . " he coaxed.

"Yes, three. Exactly three. A babe of seven months, a two year old, and a sprack little boy of four."

He forced himself to sit back, not take the bait and be made to look a fool again. The knitting accelerated to a blurring whiz of near-mechanical efficiency. She did not meet his eye, nor did she seem even interested in the subject. Yet she was. Aside from flying fingers she was as rigid as an iceberg — he felt the cold.

"Let them die, if Billy won't take the pledge," she said. Her voice lost its Forest accent and even its stubborn Forest words.

"Pledge?"

"I had four children. Charlie was oldest at six when the dysentery came twenty-two years ago. I started boiling their water, but too late, see. The bug was in their guts already. Charlie was strong — the others were too small."

The needles clashed at a frenzied pace, like a tap dancer on opium. The sweater grew before his eyes.

"Pledge?" he repeated, still unable to make sense of it, but now frightened by what was to come.

"The others died. One, two, three on a Friday, Saturday, Sunday. All dead before the first one got buried."

He shifted uncomfortably.

"Pledge? What kind of pledge, Vi?"

The whispering needles stopped. The silence was profound, as though a pile driver had suddenly ceased pounding. Her eyes came up and fixed him, unblinking flint.

"A bit of medicine, some skim milk, and a decent plate of food would have saved my babies. We had none and could afford none. I went to your mother and asked for money. She asked your father. She stood by his reply."

A tear started from each eye and began its journey down her granite face. Her voice did not waver.

"If Billy would stay out of the pub, you'd have money for laudanum, milk, and vegetables. Let Billy come to the Reverend Thornton and solemnly vow to never drink again . . . "

She paused and drew a deep breath.

"*The pledge!*" she grunted as though punched. "My Billy," she went on quietly again, "was not a drunkard. He spent no money on ale when my babies were sick. He sold his watch and my bits of china — got us two days-worth of laudanum for four patients — not enough o'course."

Jack defended by instinct and spoke without thinking, "So why not take the pledge, then?"

For a moment her control wavered and he thought she might attack him — her face a mask of rage.

"You're not a man yet, are you, Jack? You will be one day. Some fellows never are, they stay children always, but you'll be a man one day, I wager. See, Billy was a man. He was willing to take the pledge but I wouldn't let him. I stopped him. My sister had the money or she could have talked your father around. But she stood by her man. She was willing to make my children's lives equal to a pledge won! A pledge marker that her husband could use for his career. 'I've cured a sinner! Praise the Lord, but praise me first!'"

Jack's newfound love for his father shrivelled at this. He tried to reinvent it, to think of the peace he found in the crossing at Tintern Abbey, but it slipped away from him.

"So, no money — no medicine?"

"Right-O, Jack." She smiled, horribly. "Your parents' cruelty and my . . . I don't know, my pride, I suppose, killed them." Tears ran to the corners of her mouth and she licked them. "All dead one, two, three. Billy never drank so much as a glass of weak cider for the rest of his life. And I never let him inside me again. No more children for us."

She wept now. Quietly, and almost without emotion.

"Funny," she hiccoughed and smiled again. "With only Charlie to feed and the price of coal gone up, we prospered. Offa's Rose was bought for us by three little, dead children. We could never have afforded it with four mouths to feed, see? That's why all the flowers. I live in a cemetery, a funeral parlour, Jack."

She laughed loud and hard.

"And I'll be goddamned if I'll let your mother escape it. She will live in this coffin with me 'til I'm gone."

She resumed knitting, paused to wipe her face and looked up to him again.

"Probably am already — damned that is," she chuckled. "You go now, Jack. Take your money and go away. You may visit next Sunday, as always, if you choose."

Jack left. London and Emma were beyond his reach now. His father, Vi, his mother, and three dead children held him in the Forest of Dean. How long would they hold him? Maybe forever.

CHAPTER 7

Jack from oover t' Severn bridge was not yet welcome at the Ostrich, but neither was he unwelcome. He drank his pint, spoke when spoken to, and went home. His initial forays to the pub had brought hard stares and "where's Charlie?" But a year in the Forest and the Vicar's patronage and a softening of Charlie's attitude had changed the local men. Of course he was not, and never would be, a Forest man. He'd been born away and he hadn't spent five minutes underground. He could be tolerated because the Vicar and Charlie tolerated him and they were good men. But that was the limit; no Gloucester toff would ever be welcome in the Ostrich. Jack reflected on this social dilemma as he strode through the October rain toward the Ostrich. He reached inside his jacket and touched the envelope. If his plan worked, he would soon be clear of the Ostrich stigma; clear of the Charlie-Emma-Jack quagmire; clear of the debt that held him and his mother prisoner; clear of his father's ghost and, perhaps, the recipient of Emma's affection.

The letter, of course, was the key. He'd watched and waited ten anxious days for its arrival. As Charlie dreaded the letter, so Jack longed for it.

Jack had spread manure in February 1899 in a depressed daze, content to wallow in night soil because it suited his life. His life! Hi father, a professional Christian, letting little children die for the want of a few pounds. The same man who lost his reputation, and his son's reputation trying to make a few pounds in a deal scarcely better than a swindle. And yet the very man whose spirit had come to him, giving him peace at Tintern Abbey and, again, at the harvest dinner. His father and mother together saddling him with a debt that seemed impossible to pay. A debt he could not ignore because he'd hidden from scandal once and he'd not abandon his mother again. Then, his mother, living in a flowered, beautiful prison cell with an old harpy as her jailer. And he, Jack, breaking his back hauling night soil and manure through the rain to slop onto his master's fields.

He'd harrowed behind Charlie's ploughing in March, his mood unaltered. But April brought sunshine and seeding. His spirit awoke with the spring flowers. He'd begun to count his money and search for an escape — an honourable escape. Emma had not departed for London, nobody was certain why she stayed on in the Forest. She and Charlie had become friendly, and she spent more time in his company now. But Jack thought she was fond of Charlie as an older brother. Her attention seemed to cheer Cordey greatly — he had obvious hopes of winning her — but Jack remembered the night of the harvest supper. He had begun borrowing books from her again, mostly Dickens now. He'd thought to escort Emma to London as an excuse to leave Newland, but that was flimsy and she hadn't gone to London. So he stayed for haying. Then he tried to pry his mother loose from Offa's Rose, hoping to take her to London, but she clung to Vi like grim death. So he stayed for harvest. Finally, he simply resolved to walk away from it all, but his nerve failed and the end of September found him slumping toward depression and night soil, again.

Then salvation, from a people he'd barely heard of. The Boer farmers of Transvaal and the Orange Free State in Africa in the early autumn of 1899 decided to spit in Great Britain's eye. Britain ordered ten thousand men from India to South Africa, much to Charlie's delight. Dutch farmers versus British soldiers was a farce to be sure — but a farce requiring thousands of horses eating tons of oats. And oats was what they had grown this year, the prices were already shooting up. Their 1899 yield was only two thirds the size of the 1898 crop but prices were sky high and Charlie Cordey stood to earn a handsome profit. Enough money for his own land, his own house and, perhaps, a wife to keep it.

Then the Boers had done the unthinkable only ten days ago. The fools had mobilized, threatened an ultimatum and got ready to fight. Still a farce but now a deadly farce and Lord Salisbury called up his reserves. Thirty thousand men were to be called back to the colours. One of those men was Charlie Cordey, with six months left in his reserve term. Charlie was furious, then outraged, then drunk, cursing his rotten luck. But no call-up notice surfaced that first week and he began to think himself safe. Surely they'd call up men with at least one year's service left? What would be the point in pulling a man in only to discharge him six months later?

Jack immediately saw the opportunity, but the Army had to recall Charlie to active service if his plan was to work. The letter had been special delivered this very evening to the Vicarage by a courier from Coleford. Jack had intercepted the courier, signed off the receipt, and now stepped through the Ostrich front door. Conversation slowed, he was inspected, then ignored. Charlie, standing beside Sue with a fresh pint, hardly glanced in his direction. Jack drew the paper and approached from behind Sue. He caught Charlie's eye and flashed the notice up so Charlie could see ARMY RESERVE on the letterhead. Then he retired to a small bench flanking the bar. Charlie joined him in an instant, snatching the envelope up and tearing it open.

Army Form D.463
ARMY RESERVE
Notice to join the Army for Permanent Service

117

Name: C.R. CordeyRank: Pte.
Regimental Number, 10742 — The Gloucestershire Regiment
You are hereby required to join the DEPOT at Bristol with the least possible delay. Should you not . . .

"Goddamn them to hell," he murmured. A long sigh and he read it again. "The bastards couldn't leave me be, Jack."

"You're for South Africa, then?"

"Aye," another long sigh and a strong pull at his pint. "Six bloody months left. Eleven and a half years out of twelve complete, only six months and I'd have been clear. Blast them!"

Presented with a similar civilian problem Charlie would have slipped past it like a seal sliding off a rock. But the mere army stamp seemed to drain all the flash from him. He was once again Private Cordey, bound to do as other men bid. And, Jack thought, all the more likely to snap at any plan he might present.

"There is a way to win clear, you know," Jack began, watching Charlie carefully. His pitch must match the man's mood, work with it.

"No there isn't," Charlie snuffled at his ale. "You don't know the army, the real army. Come and go from the volunteers all you like, but there's no escaping the genuine article."

"The newspapers said reserve men would be fifty percent of the regimental strength — that's four to five hundred men, yes?"

Charlie nodded.

"Five hundred men reporting to Horfield barracks in two days. They have to be medically inspected, kitted, assigned companies, and sent on to the regiment. That's a lot of men, a lot of confusion and chaos to sort out."

Charlie's head rose like a trout inspecting a fly.

"I reckon that's all true, so what?"

Jack drew breath and plunged in. "You never saw this call-up notice, Charlie. I intercepted the courier, my name's on his receipt. I stole it and took your place." He snatched the telegram back.

"I report to Horfield barracks as Charlie Cordey. In the confusion nobody will notice or care. Private Cordey was called up and he attended — your name is stroked off the list. I know enough drill to pass for a reservist who hasn't seen a parade square in five years.

"Never work!" Charlie snapped, but his eyes had narrowed and he was thinking hard. "A soft toff like you will be spotted — "

"Look at my hands, my face," Jack grinned. "I look like a labourer and I stink like a pig cot."

"What will the Vicar say? He'll come after you, or your mother will."

"I've written them both letters for you to deliver once I'm gone. I've told them I'm joining as a volunteer gentleman ranker. If they come after me, they'll be looking for John Thornton and the army will have no record of me — 'cause I'll be Charlie Cordey! Besides, I'm twenty now and nineteen is the limit for active service, they have no legal grounds to chase me."

Charlie smiled craftily. "The regiment won't be taking volunteers but the Vicar and your mam's not to understand the difference between reserve and volunteer. They might buy it."

"They'll have to." Jack took Charlie's pint and sipped from it in triumph.

"Nah," Charlie retrieved his drink. "What about my old mates? They'll come to look for me and find you, then the game's up."

"Really?" Jack shifted his gaze away. "When I tell your old pals that Charlie's pulled a fast one and dodged the guardhouse one last time — you think they'll peach? Turn their old comrade in when he's only got six months — "

"*No!* By God not a one of 'em!" Charlie wanted this now, but he was still wary. "If they catch you, the worst they'll do is chuck you out, but me," he shook his head grimly, "it'll be two years in the glasshouse."

"You forget," Jack folded the letter and replaced it in his pocket. "You never received a call-up notice — no proof you ever saw it. I hooked your old pay book and certificates from the drawer in our room, where I've seen them many times. How were you to know I'd done these awful things? You thought I'd gone to volunteer, just like the Vicar and Mother. I fooled all of you, eh?"

"You'd still sing, if they caught you," Charlie said.

"No I wouldn't. For three very good reasons. First, Britain doesn't punish men for lying to join the army and fight for her. I'd be a patriotic, if overzealous, Briton and subject to minimal punishment — chucked out, as you said."

Charlie shrugged. "Maybe your nerve wouldn't hold if they threatened worse."

"Second," Jack continued. "If I betrayed you then any chance you had with Emma would be destroyed. While I don't care much for you, I'd not take a chance on her happiness. If you are really what she wants."

Charlie straightened, bristling like a bantam rooster. "Why, you little shit! Me and Emma are none of your — "

"Quiet!" Jack snapped, staring Cordey hard in the eye. The hairs on the back of his neck prickled. He leaned across the table, anxious to hit out, ready to fight, two years of anger flooding him.

"Third, this repays the debt. I take your place in the firing line. I take your chance. You tell your mother the truth about my going. If I'm killed, then the Cordeys will know why and leave my parents in peace. If I survive, well, it's no more than your own survival when you were a child. Either way I'm free of you and the bloody Forest of bloody Dean!"

Charlie's angry face turned to a sneering smile. "Deal." He held out his hand. "I never saw such balls on a Gloucester city poodle before."

Jack took the hand and shook to seal the contract.

"Now, listen here," Charlie hitched closer to Jack. "You keep yourself quiet when you get to Horfield depot. Stay well clear of the officers, they're more dangerous than the Boers will ever be. You were nearly an officer yourself so I shouldn't trust you, but I must."

"What do you mean keep quiet?"

"Oh Lor'." Charlie sipped his beer. "All right, here it is spelled out for you. The soldiers are like . . . ah, normal men. The officers are interfering swine always looking to make a soldier's life miserable, right? If you come to an officer's attention you'll be discovered. So stick with the middle of the pack. Do what the other men do, think what they think, eat what they eat, keep yer eyes open and yer mouth shut."

"I'm not a total fool. Of course I'll steer clear of authority."

"I know you!" Charlie hissed. "You've got some crazy notion that you're a gentleman ranker. Well you're *not*, chuck it out of your head. I don't want to hear that Charlie Cordey tried to win a Victoria Cross."

• • •

The first two days at Horfield barracks had indeed been chaotic. Jack was shoved past a corporal who never even glanced up while he received, stamped and noted Jack's papers. A sergeant reminded him that he was still under his oath of allegiance while a harried doctor performed a lightning medical examination. They slept on hard, wood floors curled in blankets the first night, and washed with icy water in open ablution sheds the next day, then stood in endless lines to receive their khaki field dress, Wolseley helmets, and one meal of boiled pork.

The morning of the third day the muddle miraculously disappeared. Regimental Sergeant Major Trevelyan arrived on the early train from the battalion at Aldershot. By nine o'clock that morning he had four hundred thirty-seven reservists quivering at attention on the vast parade square. His shrieking voice echoed and re-echoed from the grey, stone barracks as for two hours he drilled them single-handed until sweat ran down their backs. He then deftly formed them into four companies, gave them each a colour sergeant as mother hen, and stood back. Rifles, blankets, puttees, cap badges, webbing, and all the absent minutia appeared. It was issued in an orderly fashion and they did a ten-mile route march before supper, just to break in their boots.

• • •

The blisters were nearly the size of plums, but thank God, only on his left foot. Jack eased the heavy boot from his foot and lay back on his cot. The long, stone barrack room, whitewashed and lined with two rows of beds, was just beginning to warm. That is, the coal fire at the far end of the room had managed to thaw some of the frigid air. Only an hour earlier he'd been sweating freely at the end of the forced march. Now he shivered, except for his left foot that throbbed hot. The rest of the section worked industriously on their feet, and he suddenly realized that he was the only one not tending to his sores. He must fit in. "Do what they do," he whispered Charlie's motto, "think what they think." As an ensign he'd worn properly fitted boots, privately purchased. As a private he must somehow come to terms with the hobnailed horrors he'd been issued. The technique seemed simple. Clean needle, lance the blister, squeeze the fluid, wrap it tight, and roll a fresh, wool sock over it. The man next to him, Billy Webster, an Irishman from Bristol, had a bloody mess on one foot. Yet he hardly twitched as he cut away the loose flap of skin and washed the blood clear.

"The man's a criminal, by Jazus," he muttered glancing at Jack's foot. "Ten miles first day and me sitting on my arse in a shop these last three years never walking farther than the pub."

"That man be our RSM, Paddy, and I'll ask you to show some respect for the son of a bitch, if you don't mind," a voice with a thin Forest accent called from the end of the room.

"Saints be with me, just Billy's luck to be stuck in a section full of Forest yokels." He limped to the end of his bed. "Be there any civilized men from Bristol here?"

"You rasty Mick! I'll give . . . "

"You can kiss old jolter's ass . . . "

The roar of good-natured insults and one flying boot were Billy's answer. He glanced sidelong at Jack.

"Here's the quiet one, brown as a Forest turd, for certain, but no mouth on him?"

Jack smiled and put his hand out. "Charlie Cordey, Newland now but Gloucester mostly."

Billy shook. "Aye, well, Gloucester's not much but it's the best we can hope for, I suppose."

They fell into an easy conversation as they worked on their feet. Billy talked freely about his various women in Bristol and twice mentioned his wife. Jack spoke of the Vicar's farm and thought of Emma. The Vicar would have explained his departure by now. She would see that he had saved Charlie so that nothing stood in their path now, should she really want Cordey. She must be completely free to make her decision. But would she see Jack as a gentleman making a heroic gesture, or a fool? Was he manipulating her or being chivalrous — he wasn't certain himself.

"Here's the yokels!" A huge voice bellowed from the stairwell. "Where's that Bombay whorehouse hussar, Charlie Cordey?"

Jack instinctively ducked. Two men barged into the room. Both in their late twenties, one was a tall, lean private, the other a short, stocky lance corporal.

"Present yourself, Private Cordey!" the tall one roared, eyes casting round the room, lighting briefly on Jack then moving away. The other men in the section looked expectantly at Jack.

"He's not here," the short corporal said. "This is the Forest platoon, ain't it boys?" He asked his question of Billy Webster.

"Except for one Bristol Irishman, bein' myself, yes this is the Foresters' home Corp."

"We're after Charlie Cordey, a Forest mole . . . "

"Well, you're looking at him. That be he," the man across from Jack pointed. "I be George Grigg from Cinderford, this here is Frank Wills from St. Briavels an' that's Charlie Cordey o' Newland."

"Like hell he is," the private snorted. "Crazy yokels! That's not Private Cordey of the Sixty-first of Foot what served in Poona, Bombay, and Nasirabad with Eight Company. What a daft bunch of coal heavers."

Frank rose, as did George. "We're Forest men here, and proud of it. You'll take that back or we'll take her back the hard way." Several other men began to move toward the door and Billy rolled up his sleeves. The Foresters were all shorter than even the corporal — about half the size of the tall soldier. Jack had prepared for this moment and, in the Ostrich, he'd been quite confident of himself. But now, seconds away from sparking a barrack room brawl, he shrivelled timidly. The tall soldier spat, stamped his huge boots and raised his fists.

"Come ahead, ye pit ponies, might as well start off as we mean to go on. I ain't apologizing to no Forest hick this side of Afriky."

"That's enough! Put 'em down," the corporal barked at his companion. " And you lot, stand fast!" He grinned. "Christ, we've only been in camp three days and you're already scrapping. God help the Boers, eh?"

The Forest men stood quiet.

"Come on, boys," the corporal coaxed. "No harm done and no hard feelings. Charlie's a Forester and he was also our best chum when he left the colours in Devonport five years ago. But this object here," he walked to Jack's bedside, "ain't Charlie Cordey."

He put his hand on Jack's shoulder and examined him closely. "Why he's no more a reserve man with six years service than my mother!" he exclaimed. "I'll kiss my own arse if this boy is reached two decades."

"Well truth is, Corp," George shrugged, "we only met him ourselves yesterday. Me and Frank and the lads, we were all Light Bob's in the Sixty-first and Billy the Irish was Three Company. We don't know aught about old Eight Company men."

All eyes now swivelled onto Jack. He stood, his carefully prepared explanation completely vanished from his memory, and blurted out his plea for clemency.

"Charlie's got a woman and a farm and he wasn't too keen on giving them up for six months service. I'm a volunteer who wants to go to Africa. We swapped places. He said his old mates would understand — not drop him in the fire."

They goggled at him, incredulous.

"And for my part," he put his hand out to George. "I'm a farm worker from Newland. Name's Jack Thornton. I'm determined to do my duty as a soldier. I'm hoping you'll take me in and leave Charlie out."

George stared at his hand, but did not move. The room stayed silent. Finally the tall soldier elbowed his way through the men and grabbed Jack's hand, pumping it.

"Balls of cast iron that Charlie Cordey." He whooped and pumped Jack's hand again. "The bastard's slipped his cable and I say good on you, Charlie Cordey."

The corporal touched his stripes self-consciously. "Blast you." Then he smiled. "Officially, I never heard a word of tonight's little surprise. And don't call me on it for I'll not give up my hooks for you, boy."

George Grigg stepped up and took Jack's hand. "We'll not betray a fellow Forester, am I right, lads?"

The others murmured their assent. "But you," he squeezed Jack's fingers until they tingled, "let us down once, and we'll eat you alive."

"Praise to Mary and her sweet son, Jesus," Billy laughed. "But isn't this better than a night at the Bristol Music Hall. The Forest of Dean has now got its official issue Irishman. I'm with you boys, body and soul."

· · ·

The grey rock pile of Horfield barracks lay just on the north edge of Bristol. An open plain dotted with farm buildings surrounded the barracks. A long column of reserve men of the Second Battalion, Gloucester Regiment, formerly her Majesty's Sixty-first Foot, snaked back toward the barracks after a wearing route march. The late autumn sun was setting in their eyes. Jack Thornton concentrated on two simple things. First, he resolved to keep his chin up, physically never let his head droop. Second, he willed his left foot forward, deliberately throwing it out a full pace, even though it shot pain up his leg each time it landed. The Forest men marching around him were also hurting, but as old Light Infantry they refused to acknowledge fatigue or pain. Jack was pledged to stay with them until he dropped. Billy Webster was visibly hobbling, shoulders down and head hanging, but he kept the pace. His chattering wit had dried up two miles back but now that the barracks were in view he regained some life.

"How's the hooves, Charlie-Jack?"

Jack grunted, afraid if he opened his mouth, he'd whine.

"Well I never thought I'd say this," Billy puffed. "But I'll be glad of a cup o' English tea, a lump o' English pork and an army blanket tonight".

"Gawn," George scoffed. "A stroll like this is nothing for the Light Infantry. Tea and bed indeed! Should do another five miles now that we're properly warmed up."

Grigg was Forest iron. Jack knew the man's leg was game from their first march two days earlier, but his step was brisk and his face calm. A shouted command from the head of the column floated back, repeated by each company in succession. The troops obediently wheeled through a gap in the fence on their right and moved onto a large pasture.

"Ah me, it will be the hill, then," Billy groaned. "I'd sooner have the five miles Georgie."

The colour sergeants led their men into line formation and halted them. A small knot of horsemen stood atop a low ridge three hundred yards distant. The companies were stacked one behind the other, in line, facing the ridge. Four horsemen broke from the group and cantered down to the first company. A major, a captain and two lieutenants divided the company into three platoons. Jack's company, being second in the column, was stood easy to wait their turn. He was relieved to see the leading company advance in a simulated attack. One platoon leading as a firing line, the other two following in support and reserve. He'd practised this at volunteer camp several times as an officer, it should be a simple drill to follow in the ranks. As the "attack" reached the base of the ridge the men halted, fixed bayoncts, then charged up and over with a cheer. The four officers rode back. A dark, very tall, young lieutenant walked his horse to Jack's platoon.

"Who have we here, then?" he called to them.

"Forest men, mostly, sir," the sergeant replied.

The lieutenant smiled. "Not afraid of hard work then, Sar'nt."

"Old Light Bob's of the Sixty-first, sir, and miners to boot. Hardest men in the battalion," the sergeant replied with a small laugh.

"Right then, lads!" The lieutenant stood in his stirrups. "Let's see you get to the top first, eh?"

They advanced in quick time over the pasture. The young officer and sergeant bellowed constantly for proper spacing, sharper volleys, straighter lines. Jack found himself panting as they approached the hill. The old soldiers were much quicker with their rifles. They came from the trail, to the shoulder, simulated a volley, worked the bolts, and were back down at the trail in half the time he managed it. He felt clumsy, the Lee Metford heavy and awkward in his sweating palms. Then new commands came rapidly. Halt — order arms — prepare to fix bayonets — bayonets — present. Jack took two tries to get his bayonet locked and was the last man up, much to the shrieking indignation of the colour sergeant who cursed him as a clumsy oaf. All three platoons were then rapidly manoeuvred to form a long, double line facing up the ridge, which looked more like a cliff up close.

"Right, Glosters!" The major called, putting his horse to the hill. "Up and go!"

"Slashaaaaa's!"

Jack took up the Slashers cheer and pounded up the slope, determined to be in the lead.

He ran out of breath halfway up. Men stumbled and gasped beside him, lunging upwards, bayoneted rifles thrust forward. His blistered foot sent flaming spears up his leg and his stomach began to cramp as he sucked in huge mouthfuls of air. Sweat poured from him, a cold, unhealthy perspiration. He clenched his teeth, breath whistling fiercely now, and flung himself upward. The Irishman, grunting with pain, scrambled just ahead and Jack surged to catch him. Then Webster went down. Jack reached instinctively, hooked Billy's webbing, and forced himself to keep running. Billy retched loudly, gained his feet, then vomited and stumbled to his knees again. Jack's hand seemed to have spasmed. He couldn't shake it free of the straps so he dragged Webster like a dead pig, holding his own rifle forward with his free hand. As they neared the top, the rest of the section began to pull away from them. A wild glance to his right revealed the tall lieutenant, looking down from his horse, straight at Jack and the puking Irishman.

Stay clear of the officers — dangerous swine, Charlie's words came back. Strength born partly of pride, partly of fear swept Jack upward. His mouth flopped open releasing an inarticulate bellow — he hoisted Bill over his shoulder like a sack of grain and sprinted for the top. He felt the racking cramps hit his stomach and it began to heave. His legs were gone, dead wood, yet he kept flinging them forward. He and Bill burst through the line of Foresters. He topped the hill, hurled Webster to the ground, reeled sideways toward two mounted officers and flopped face down, retching and spewing, into the grass. Moments later he was joined by the rest of the company — many as sick as he, the others bent over — gasping for air.

"Form *up*! You're supposed to be soldiers!" The colour sergeant strode through them. "Form ranks! It looks like a ruddy circus up here!"

Jack levered himself up onto all fours and was rewarded with a tremendous thump on his buttocks that sent him flying onto his face.

"Get up! On your feet!" The colour sergeant roared. "By God, I never thought I'd see a Gloster lying down in an attack! Up, by heavens, or I'll kick your arse off this hill then kick it back up again."

Jack, trembling and ill, regained his knees, and leaned on his rifle. A pair of powerful hands seized him from behind and shot him to his feet, steadying him as he wobbled.

"Stand fast, boy," George muttered in his ear. "Chin up."

Frank formed on his left, propping him up and straightening his helmet. The colour sergeant moved on down the company front, bawling and thrusting the men into line. Jack's stomach finally unclenched itself, and he drew in a ragged breath. The young lieutenant was conferring with the other horsemen, one of whom held a watch in his hand. They all laughed at something the watchman said, then the lieutenant rode back to the Foresters.

"Well done, the Forest of Dean!" he smiled. "Adjutant says fastest up from both companies so far — by a fair margin." His eyes ran down the ranks, stopping at Jack.

"We may not be the prettiest regiment in the British army." He stared at the lumpy stain on Jack's tunic and a ripple of laughter went through the ranks. "But if Lord Roberts asks us to take a hill away from Johnny Boer, well, do you know . . . " he winked at Jack. "I think we've got the men to do it."

• • •

Jack shivered as a cold wind whistled through the darkening ablution hut. His tunic and undershirt soaked in a bucket while he washed the stink of dried vomit from his face and chest. The rest of the company was at their supper and, although his belly ached with emptiness, he dared not feed it yet. He scrubbed the clothes, rinsed, and scrubbed again, then climbed slowly back up to his barrack room. An envelope lay on his cot. It bore Emma's handwriting. He carefully hung his tunic to dry, then retrieved the letter, turning it over slowly in his hands, savouring the feel of it. He resisted the urge to smell it, but he traced his fingertips over the lettering — her hand so close to him. It was addressed to Pte. C. Cordey, but it felt as though she was reaching for him. The rest of the section sat at a long trestle table at the other end of the room wolfing down their meal. They took no notice of Jack.

October 14, 1899
Dear Jack,

I hope this finds you before your regiment embarks for Africa. Uncle Henry informed me of your departure but was unable to explain your decision. Charlie was scarcely more forthright, although he eventually told me of your plan to restore your former status by battlefield heroics. He used the term Gentleman Ranker and it wounded me. The very words I spoke to you on the picnic to Tintern. Perhaps it is vanity on my part but I feel certain there is a connection between my actions that day and your scheme to take Charlie's place in the Glosters. I told you flippantly, once, that I despair of my own class, but I was earnest. Some may see risking your life to regain my class as a romantic gallantry, but life has taught me to think differently.

I am a person who looks for reality in life, not romantic gestures. Do you remember the harvest dinner last year? I was touched by the love you showed when you sang. That was true and it affected me profoundly. I resolved then to study you and your behaviour as a true gentleman — regardless of wealth or position. I have been your student this past year. The more I watched you, the more I realized where my future happiness would lie. It has been a long path for me. I still harbour some

uncertainties but I believe that one day our two paths will join,
if you wish it as I do.

    Charlie has again pressed a suit on me, as you may have
guessed. He thinks of your departure as a "clearing of the path".
You should never have presumed that I needed your blessing to
accept Charlie. I have always regarded myself as free in such a
decision. Jack, it is not Charlie who takes my interest, but, of
course, you.

    I am praying for your safe return to England but, please,
do not write me. I could not bear a false start by paper and
ink. If we are to share any true feelings then it must begin as
we face each other. I deeply regret not speaking to you earlier,
but my progress to love was slow and painful. I write now to
beg you make no more empty gestures of gallantry, at least not
for my sake. Be guided by your duty and the natural courage
I know you possess.
Waiting for your return,
I am yours, sincerely
Emma

Jack read the letter again, scarcely able to believe it. Emma, his
admirer, his student, and his love. Right under his nose, his
inescapable love, and he'd walked away from it to make . . . what
were her words? "An empty gesture of gallantry." Emma, ignorant
of his mother's debt, had nonetheless proved his mother, Vi, and
Charlie to be right. It wasn't his debt. Never had been. My God,
he could be in Mrs. Toomey's warm kitchen drinking cocoa with
Emma this minute. His Emma!

    Billy, cheerfully gnawing a piece of pork, approached him but
stopped abruptly, grimacing.

"Ah, here we come, my darling," Billy croaked, then released a long rumbling belch reeking of stomach bile. "Oh, tha's much better." He patted his belly. "How's your guts, Jack-Charlie?"

Jack looked up from the letter. "Good, Billy . . . better, but not ready for boiled pork."

"Well, at least try some bread and tea. I'll fetch you some, give us your cup. Least I can do seen as how you saved my life on the hill. Do that in Africa and you'll be getting the VC"

He hobbled away. Jack sat rooted to his cot, slowly folding the letter. "Jack Thornton," he said loudly, his voice echoing down the barrack. "You are the damnedest great fool the Forest of Dean has ever produced."

CHAPTER 8

December 29, 1899. With only two days left in the century the Second Battalion Gloucestershire Regiment was moving house from Salamanca barracks Aldershot, to Capetown South Africa. Men from Six Company heaved quartermaster stores packed in heavy crates onto wagons bound for the railway station. "One, two, three, hup!" George Grigg called. Jack straightened his legs, hoisting his end of the crate up to the wagon bed where Billy Webster shoved it into place. Jack stepped clear, puffing white breath into the winter air. He pushed the Wolseley helmet back, wiped the sweat from his face, and flexed fingers numbed by the cold. Stripped to vest and braces, a thin fog rose from dark patches of perspiration on his chest.

"Sweating and freezing at the same time," George said. "Only the army could master such . . . "

A horse's high pitched whinny — nearly a scream — cut him short. The battalion machine gun section was in a turmoil near the quartermaster store. The horse in question was doing her best to crow hop out of the shafts that held her in the machine gun limber. A hapless soldier clung to her bridle but clearly the horse was making all the decisions. The angry mare was harnessed between the shafts of a small, two-wheeled cart limber. The limber consisted of nothing more than a narrow box mounted on the axle, and a Maxim heavy machine gun bolted across the box and axle. The gun's wide tubular barrel protruded just beyond the wheels, like a stubby cannon. But the gun limber was tipped precariously.

The horse reared, wildly, toppling the soldier and nearly flipped the whole gun upside down. It would have galloped but the machine gun sergeant gamely threw himself at the collar and bridle, digging in his heels. A stunning string of oaths drowned out the horse's desperate neighing.

"Ride 'em, cowboy!" Billy shouted. "Charlie-Jack! Where's you going?"

Jack reached the horse just as she gave the carriage a resounding kick with her hind legs. Her eyes bulged wild and white and for a moment he was back with Bobbi at Tintern abbey. He caught her head as it came up from the kick and put her muzzle in his armpit, his arm over her eyes.

"Husht. Husht, girl," he spoke in her ear.

She shook her head and nearly threw him but he managed to hang on.

"Husht. Hush, you daft bitch! Come now, its fine. Jack's here. Come now, come now, husht."

She pushed her nose hard into his armpit and stopped thrashing. He talked quietly in her ear, softly calling her his best girl and she gradually settled. He slowly uncovered her eyes, still bulging white, but no longer wild.

"Let go," Jack said and the machine gun sergeant gratefully scuttled clear.

"Good girl, sweet girl, there now, that's better, eh? What happened, Sergeant?"

"Brute wouldn't even take the harness, she's still half wild, so we were fighting her from the start."

Her hooves began a quick tap dance, shooting gravel at the sound of the sergeant's voice.

"Hush girl, hush," Jack stroked her. "Maybe best if you lowered your voice for a minute, Sergeant, 'til she's good and calm."

"Calm you want?" the sergeant hissed. "We showed her the shafts and she nearly went berserk. Be quicker to harness the men in! I don't know how we'll get her on the train . . . *if* we can get her to haul the gun to the train, that is."

He gestured to her ribs, "Goddamn beast has gone and injured herself, look at that!"

A small rivulet of blood dripped from under the neck strap above her shoulder, down her side.

"Well there's your trouble, Sarge". Jack nodded at a twisted strap. "Got the buckle warped so the stem's inside out. Like sticking a nail in her neck every time she moves."

"Can you straighten it for us?" The sergeant asked, backing a step farther away from the horse. "She seems to trust you."

Holding the leatherwork loose, Jack unfastened the buckle and inspected the wound. "Not bad as of yet. Just a jab, won't need stitches."

He pulled a handkerchief from his pocket. "Here fetch us a bit of water," he said to the machine gun man who'd been thrown down. The soldier looked to the sergeant, who nodded, and the man sprinted toward the storehouse. Jack talked to the horse and straightened the fixed tug that had twisted the buckle in the first place.

"Oh Lord, not more trouble is it, Sar'nt Miles?" An officer approached from the parade square.

Jack manoeuvred himself closer to the horse, instinctively trying to find shelter. It was the tall, dark, young lieutenant who'd chivvied them up the hill at Bristol. The sergeant stiffened to attention and saluted.

"It's these damned foreign nags, Mr. Wethered. They're shoving them on to us at the last minute, sir. First, they take our good mule and the only men wot knows about these four-legged devils an' transfers 'em to the Mounted Company. So now, I'm short three men. Then they give me this crazy bitch from Canada what was likely raised by red Indians an' never seen a harness nor — "

"All right, Sar'nt Miles," the officer snapped, striding up to the horse and glancing at Jack. "I've heard your complaints and there's nothing to be done. We'll have to cope."

"Beg pardon, sir, for being heated up but this whore's mother . . . "

"Sar'nt *Miles*! Moderate your language man! The colonel's wife is on the square just yonder!"

The sergeant actually staggered with embarrassment. "Sorry, so very sorry, sir. Never saw her there, sir. Wouldn't offend the colonel's wife for all the bloody . . . ruddy tea in China, sir."

The soldier returned with a bucket of water, but stopped short when he saw the officer.

"Carry on Palmer" the lieutenant said. "Let's see if we can shift this gun before the new year turns, eh?"

Jack dipped his handkerchief in the water and began to clean the wound.

"Good girl, there's my Bobbi girl," he said as she flinched at the cold water. "Come now, Bobbi, be a brave girl."

He re-threaded the neck strap through the tug, then wrapped the wet cloth around the buckle and tied it off so it would press against the wound as a bandage. Then he gently let it ride back against the horse. She didn't move. He took her lead and began to walk her. "Woot, Bobbi, Woot," he urged her into a long right hand circle. She followed him easily, nuzzling his neck as they turned. Another officer, with a veiled woman on his arm, walked from the square toward the lieutenant. Jack stopped and checked the bandage, just now conscious that he'd been calling her Bobbi. The curious officer was the colonel, the woman must be his wife. He didn't need this, too many officers and NCOs by a long chalk. He glanced over his shoulder to the wagon where Billy and George stood staring at him. He held the rope out to the other private but the young officer interceded.

"Walk her back here, if you please."

Jack obeyed. "Coom Yeh, Coom Yeh Bobbi." He turned her left, using the Gloucestershire commands, even though she was foreign. He halted in front of the dark lieutenant who bent over to inspect Jack's work.

"Well Joe?" The woman spoke cheerfully. "Will you manage to get your contraption to Africa or not?"

Lieutenant Wethered straightened up and saluted. "Just about, ma'am." He nodded toward Jack. "Looks like we've found somebody that knows a harness from a paving brick at least."

"Are the men standing at attention?" she asked. She carried her head at an acute angle, addressing the question toward the sky.

"Yes dear," the colonel answered. "Stand the men easy, Sar'nt." Miles relaxed and nodded to Jack and the other soldier.

"I could hear him, you know, Joe, all the way over on the square."

Sergeant Miles gasped and racheted himself back to attention.

"My apologies, ma'am," Wethered shot Miles a filthy look. "Soldier's words said in anger. He never realized . . . "

"Not the cursing," she laughed. "The young boy with the Forest accent who calmed the horse down. Husht girl, come now, Bobbi, there's my girl. Woot girl, Coom Yeh. What's his name?"

"His name?" Wethered stammered and turned to Miles. Jack shrivelled.

Miles shook his head. "Six Company man, sir. He just run over and tamed this brute, volunteer like. I don't know his name."

They all turned to Jack.

"Well?" Wethered raised his eyebrows.

"Private Cordey, sir, reservist, Six Company."

"Never!" The woman said. "Reserve man? Sounds like he's ten years old."

"How old are you, Cordey?" Miles barked like a well-trained dog. "Tell the colonel's lady how old you are! Sharp now!"

"Twenty-nine, ma'am," Jack growled as deeply as he could. She laughed, a natural warm laugh. "Oh come, come, really now! What does he look like Joe?"

Wethered's dark face blushed even darker. "Ah, well I'm not much of a hand at describing men actually . . . "

"I'd bet my regiment to a biscuit he's not a day over eighteen, my dear." The colonel inspected Jack closely. "I think you're onto something."

Jack's knees dissolved into water, he stumbled against the horse but she held him up. Why couldn't he have kept his nose out? They were for it now, Charlie and he were going to jail. He saw it in a flash. Charlie was right, his own "officer meddling" led him to interfere and now the colonel and his wife were hunting him like a pack of foxhounds. What was this crazy woman up to? Asking such odd questions from behind that heavy bonnet and veil. He couldn't make out her face. "Bugger off!" he shrieked inside his head. "Mind you own bloody business!"

Lieutenant Wethered stepped closer to Jack. "By heavens, ma'am, I believe I do know this soldier! Do I know you, Private Cordey?"

"No, sir," Jack growled. The woman chuckled again. "Oh, isn't he sweet, such a fierce voice now."

"I do! You're the one who carried a man up the hill at Horfield with the reserve companies . . . ah . . . about two months ago."

Jack, now totally defeated, let his shoulders sag. "Yes sir, you're right about the hill."

"Knew it! Never forget a face!" He turned triumphantly to the colonel.

"Well now," the colonel looked from Jack to the young officer. "He's not a reserve man. No India sun ever burned that face. He's lied about his age and lied about knowing you, Lieutenant Wethered."

Jack stayed on his feet, but not by much. His bravado at the Ostrich — "just chuck me out — I'm a patriotic Briton" was gone. This was the real army, a real Colonel, and he would be going to the glasshouse with Charlie.

"On the other hand, he's a dab hand with horses, he's fit, he looks out for his fellow soldier, and he even volunteers to help in sticky situations."

"I do need three more men in the section, sir," Wethered ventured.

"Well first, find out if Cordey has committed any real crimes before coming to us. I'd wager not, but check. If he's only a minor villain then have Six Company transfer him and two more men to your MG crowd. I'll tell the adjutant."

"Thank you, sir," Wethered saluted the colonel and his wife away.

"I'll see the OC of Six Company directly." He looked at the Quarter Master wagon. "Those two Foresters?"

"Yes, sir. Privates Webster and Grigg," Jack answered, then realized Billy wasn't actually a Forest man. God, he'd told another lie.

"There's your section up to strength then Sar'nt. Carry on and get that gun to the train while I arrange to have these men transferred. They can move their kit in with our mob after the MG is on the train."

"Very good, sir," Miles enthused. "An' thanks for slippin the word into the colonel like that sir. Much appreciated. Can't operate a highly technical section like this whilst three men short as I was a sayin' — "

"Carry on, Sar'nt," Wethered cut him short and strode off toward the battalion orderly room.

Miles turned to Jack, grinning like a new father. "Welcome home Cordey. You're a godsend, I don't mind admitting. Those two pals o' yours know anything about horses? Never mind, you can teach 'em, I reckon."

He bellowed to George and Bill who hastened into their tunics, curiosity plain on Billy's face.

"But Sergeant," Jack asked. "What about my crimes? Aren't you going to investigate, like the colonel said?"

Miles snorted and spat. "Colonel doesn't think you're a villain, good enough for me. An' Mr. Wethered plainly don't care."

"But . . . "

"All right then," Miles sighed. "Private Cordey, atten . . . *shun!*" Jack straightened up.

"This is an official inquest into the background of Private . . . " he looked at Jack.

"Charles."

"Private Charles Cordey. Are you a criminal or other such low form of life as would bring dishonour to this regiment?"

"Well, no, Sergeant."

"Right, inquest closed, stand at ease, Private Cordey. Any other daft questions?"

"Actually, yes, I have another question, Sergeant."

Miles gave him a squint. "Actually, yes? Wot the 'ell kind of talk is that for a private soldier? You some kind of toff hidin' in the ranks? *No!* Never mind, I don't want to know. Colonel and his lady says you're a Gloster then that's what you are."

"That's what I'm wondering," Jack continued. "What about the colonel's wife? She's got a funny way of talking and ears sharp as a fox and why does she speak to ordinary soldiers? What's she doing here at the barracks anyway — no place for ladies I'd have thought."

"Blind o' course!" Palmer blurted out. "Don't you know nothing about this regiment? Colonel Mrs. Lindsall is blind as a bat!"

Sergeant Miles flicked one hand out and cuffed Palmer on the side of the head. "Show some respect, you oaf, or I'll bat you."

Miles nodded to where the colonel and his wife were talking to a group of men near the barracks block.

"Mrs. Lindsall is blind right enough — that's why she hears better 'n a fox and asks funny questions about what you looks like. She also cares about us — the regiment. So she's come today to see us off to battle. No march past in review for her. She knows we're a working man's fighting battalion."

"Aye," Palmer sighed. "And most of the lads love her best 'an all." He neatly dodged Miles' hand and sighed again.

• • •

"Cheer up, Georgie." Billy was in excellent spirits. "I reckon it's a stroke o' luck that Charlie-Jack got us transferred out of a rifle company."

The three men walked rapidly through the streets of Aldershot, already dark in the early, winter night. Billy led, George and Jack followed.

"Machine Gun section — not real soldiers any more, are we? Six Company are real soldiers, what are we? We lug ammunition for Lieutenant Wethered's gadget."

"Aye," Billy stopped and tapped him on the chest. "And where are Six Company right now? Working like navvies at the barracks and where are we? Free on the town for the last night we'll have in England for a long stretch to come."

"Right you are," George quickly agreed. "Let's get off the streets before the provost guard sweeps us up."

They hurried on to a small court off a narrow street. There were brick rowhouses, quiet and mostly well lit, lining the court.

"I don't see a pub anywhere here," Jack complained, nervous that they were out of barracks at all. Technically they were off Six Company strength, and Sergeant Miles didn't want to see them again until reveille, so they were, in theory, free men. And a final pint in a quiet pub especially known to Billy was very tempting.

"More like an inn really, a boarding house, friends of mine." Billy walked confidently to the second house, passed quickly through a brick archway and led them to the back door. He rapped twice and a moment later they were let into a dark hallway. They climbed a dimly lit set of servants' stairs and entered a parlour.

"Ah, Mr. Webster and his companions, at last!" A tall woman, mid-thirties Jack thought, crossed from the fire and offered a hand which Billy dutifully kissed.

"Gents, this is Mrs. Downs and that is her niece, Miss Diana Wells. Ladies, may I present Mr. Grigg and Mr. Cordey."

The young woman perched on a settee nodded at them. A couch near the fire and a small table bearing a single lamp were the only other furniture in the room.

"Please, seat yourselves gentlemen," Mrs. Downs said.

Billy was on the settee in a twinkling, George and Jack made for the couch but Mrs. Downs touched Jack lightly on the sleeve.

"Mr. Cordey, could I ask your assistance? It's my girl's night off so I'm afraid we must serve ourselves . . . "

"Of course, ma'am," Jack bowed slightly. He was relieved. He'd been worried about a raucous night ended by the police dragging Billy home. It seemed like years since he'd been in a civilized house. Mrs. Downs poured sherry for herself and her niece. Jack opened three bottles of dark ale, poured and smelled stout. Mrs. Downs' perfume was powerful in such close proximity, but Jack welcomed it after three months in barracks. He glanced at her and found her staring openly at him. She blushed and uttered a low-pitched laugh. Her eyes were green — green as Emma's — and she wore an emerald broach on her high-neck blouse — like Emma.

"Pardon so direct an inspection Mr. Cordey, but you remind me very much of my own son who's gone for a soldier to India these past three years."

"Surely not! You can't be old enough to have a grown man for a son," Jack said, genuinely surprised.

"Oh," she squeezed his wrist, "you're just lovely, what a compliment."

Jack thought of Maude and Liz.

They drank sherry and stout, the men smoked their pipes in easy conviviality. The women made no protest, in fact they encouraged an informal, relaxed mood. Billy made them laugh with soldiers' stories: Jack carrying him up the Horfield hill; pantomimes of Forest yokels doing drill. Mrs. Downs and Miss Diana were lively and laughing and so feminine that Jack found himself over-playing the gentleman in opposition to George's dour disclaimers. They fed more coal to the fire and the ladies sang for them, arm in arm, Gilbert and Sullivan's "Three Little Maids". They dragooned Billy into acting the part of the third "blossom". Jack was taken by surprise when the men stood to sing and he felt himself unsteady. How many bottles had he drunk? The women applauded their clumsy vocals, then Mrs. Downs once again recruited Jack to hold a tray while she loaded empty bottles on it and led him through to the kitchen.

"I'll bet there's a young woman who'll be crying for Charles Cordey when the Glosters sail," she smiled, emptying the tray.

"Not really," he answered, a quiet belch escaping. "Pardon me."

"Oh I don't believe it," she said. "What's her name?"

"Well, Emma, but she's not really mine. I mean I can't say she — "

"*No!*" Mrs. Downs seized his arm, surprise on her face. "My name is Emma."

"What a coincidence," he replied, suddenly unsteady again. "She even has green eyes like yours."

"Charlie," she slid her hand up and down his arm. "Let's not be so formal. Call me Emma, dear."

"All right, Emma," he agreed. Then pleased with his own wit he said, "I mean Emma dear."

She giggled and leaned against him. "Oh, that's cheeky." She pecked him on the forehead and walked, somewhat unsteadily herself, toward the kitchen door. Jack hurried to her side and offered his arm. She took it and he inhaled her perfume, delighted at the attention of an attractive, older woman.

"Such a perfect gent," she murmured. "Here, one more small detour before we join the others." She opened a door leading off the hall between kitchen and parlour. It was a tiny smoking snug, one overstuffed chaise lounge, a thick carpet, and a side table with a lamp.

Jack turned "but I don't smoke, Emma . . . "

Mrs. Downs was undoing the top buttons of her blouse. Green eyes locked onto his, no demure blush or coy glances. Her hands flew through the buttons, whipped the blouse free of her skirt and dropped it on the floor. Her breasts welled up over the top of a cream corset. Three tiny, pink bows decorated the front. Jack counted them, distracted, unable to focus his thoughts. She darted to him, threw her arms around his neck and kissed him, surprising him with a hard tongue thrust into his mouth, searching frantically for his tongue. He responded. His fingers and toes turned cold, as though he was going into shock.

"Oh God, Charlie," she pulled back, panting for air. Her fingers tugged, expertly unfastening his belt and flies. His trousers dropped to his ankles.

"Emma," he croaked. His own voice seemed to break the spell. "No. I mean, I can't. I've never . . . " He reached for his trousers.

"You *are* a virgin!" She swatted his hands away from the trousers and undid the knot on the corset laces. Then she grappled him for another long kiss. When they broke, her skirt was gone. She turned her back to him.

"Unhook me, love, smartly now."

"I can't. I should leave." His hands disobeyed him and began to flip the hooks free. "I'm a clergyman's son. I have a duty to Emma — "

"I'm Emma, Charlie!" She ground her bottom into his crotch and twisted her neck to his mouth. Her scent fogged him. He licked then bit into the long, white, arc of flesh.

"Jesus, Charlie," one of her hands whipped back behind his head, caught a fistful of hair and rammed his teeth in. "That's good for Emma. Again, Charlie."

Her buttocks churned against him and then she really was Emma and for the next long, mad minutes, he was Charlie. They were in the hayfield. They were in the shed in the Forest of Dean. They were upstairs on the night of the harvest dinner, in his bed. The bed of so many fevered nights of fantasy and longing — now come true. She bent forward, took him in her hand, and he was the stud at Mitchell's — she his mare, neighing with lust. He rammed until they staggered. Then he was on his back on the lounger. She straddled him, lowered herself with a long sigh and began to pump furiously. Her body flew up and down, nearly demented, massaging her own breasts, pulling his hands up to do the same, biting his fingers. Then it was done, with a shout and a small scream.

They lay together, warmly melted into one body for a long time, and dozed. Slowly Jack regained himself. Her back curved long and naked to one cheek, prominent and plump. A heavy thigh lay draped over his own leg. He saw these things as though they were a photograph. They could not be real — not him — not Mrs. Downs. It was awful; it was disgusting. He thought of Emma and cringed at his infidelity. It was wonderful; it was more than, and so different from his own imaginings. It was no worse than Emma had done with Charlie. He loathed himself and was tremendously proud. Then the stout hit his bladder and he had to leave — urgently. He slipped from under Mrs. Downs and threw on his clothes. He paused for one last stare at her white, shining flesh; she opened one eye, winked, then closed it. No chamber pot to hand and the situation now desperate, he relieved himself into the stout bottles in the kitchen, outraged at his own crude behaviour, yet giggling all the same. "Oh please, don't let Miss Diana come to the kitchen now," he sniggered to himself.

He made his way back to the parlour. He would retrieve George and Billy, then make their escape.

"Brass before," Billy's voice came loud, hoarse from the parlour.

"Brass behind," George roared back the reply.

"Never feared a foe of any kind!" They called in unison.

Heavens, drunk and bellowing. Jack smiled as he pushed the door open and stepped into the parlour. Billy stood, nude from the waist down, with his back to the fire. Miss Diana, completely nude, crouched in front of him with her face buried under his belly. George, naked save his undershirt, knelt behind her, thrusting into her. His hard belly made slapping sounds against her bottom.

"Jack-Charlie!" Billy saluted with great exaggeration. "Witness the finest tradition of the Glosters. One in front, t' other in back, just like Egypt when we whipped the Frogs in Ought One."

"'Cept this is a whorehouse," George gasped. "An' that was a battlefield, you daft bog trotter."

"Officer's whorehouse!" Billy corrected him.

• • •

A new year. A new century. The first day of January, 1900, and the Gloucestershire Regiment, nearly one thousand strong, embarked from Liverpool aboard SS *Cymric*. Jack Thornton stood pressed to the railing amidships straining to see the last of England before the light disappeared. It was cold and damp. His hands were numb gripping the rusted steel rail, but he didn't care. Most of the men were below in the cramped and already sour-smelling quarters. The band, the colonel's wife, and all the well wishers were gone from the dockside. Tugs would nudge the *Cymric* out before dawn and when he woke, England would be gone.

Duty and natural courage, she'd said in her letter. He wasn't sure of either any more. Jack was now the best-known private soldier in the entire battalion. The story of Mrs. Lindsall's perceptive discovery that he was masquerading as a reservist had whipped through the barracks that last night in Aldershot. The regiment's regard for her had transferred itself onto him, making him their mascot, their little brother. Then, in Billy's oft repeated phrase, he'd "rogered Mrs. Downs senseless." It had nearly caused a riot. Dozens of soldiers sought them out. They shook Billy's hand and whistled in amazement at his coup. A private soldier with the run of the officers' sporting house. How had he done it? "By good reconnaissance, daring assault, and bold defence of the objective once gained," Billy replied with the straightest of faces.

Naturally Billy never told the truth; it was too mundane. His niece worked in the house and she had told Billy of Mrs. Maisie Downs' appetite for young, virgin soldiers. A bit of negotiation,

148

some play-acting and strong stout had done the trick. But the regiment divided into two camps. There were soldiers who slapped Jack on the back and guffawed, envious. Then there were those who were hurt. They shot him sullen, reproachful looks. He was their little brother — Mrs. Lindsall's dear boy with a Forest accent. How could he leave her company and, the same evening, descend into a drunken orgy with a whore old enough to be his mother? One junior, very pink lieutenant named d'Esterre even gave him a thoroughly angry lecture on morals. Wethered intervened, not bothering to conceal a huge smirk as he sent the young officer away. He referred to d'Esterre later in the mess as a jealous pipsqueak.

Darkness came from Liverpool and settled over the harbour. Hero, mascot, rascal, labourer, gentleman, soldier, clergyman's son, whoremaster Jack Thornton, alias Charlie Cordey, turned from the rail and from England. Surely to God he could do his duty, recover some natural courage and start fresh in Africa. He would return home a clean man to claim his Emma.

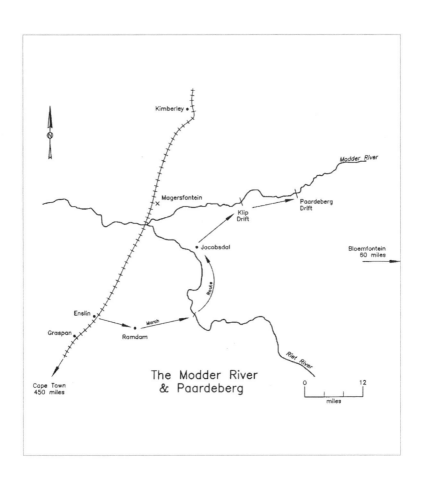

Kimberley

Modder River

Magersfontein

Klip
Drift

Paardeberg
Drift

Jacobsdal

Bloemfontein
60 miles

Route

Enslin

March

Ramdam

Graspan

Riet River

The Modder River
& Paardeberg

Cape Town
450 miles

0   12

miles

Swords

CHAPTER 9

South Africa, 1900

Tunic unbuttoned, head back, mouth hanging open, Sergeant Miles slept. Rivulets of sweat tracked across his face, through his short hair, and snaked into his already dark shirt collar. No other man in the Gloucestershire MG section could sleep. Crammed into third-class passenger carriages for two full days now, they were tortured by an inactivity that was almost worse than the heat and the sand and the dirt outside.

Jack Thornton pulled a piece of bread from his haversack and forced himself to nibble at it. The heat had stolen his appetite their second day at Capetown, and he'd begun to lose weight. George noticed and now insisted that every piece of boiled meat, every scrap of bread, and every drop of tea be consumed. He'd seen heat weaken men in India and knew the consequences. Jack ate methodically, paused to spit a bit of grit onto the floor, then chewed again. Eating was his job, for now. Nothing else was as troublesome, even the stink of soldiers. The smell of close-packed men, sweat-soaked — dried — then soaked again, no longer bothered him. Indeed his revulsion the first day had disappeared and he no longer even noticed the odour. He sipped from his water bottle to soften the dry bread, then chewed again. Brown shrivelled scrub, grey sand and grey rock whipped past the window. Two days on a train on a straight line pointed anywhere in England would put one in an ocean. Yet this scarcely brought them past Africa's south doorstep.

It was an awful place, and it was huge. He touched the square shape of *The Mayor of Casterbridge* where it lay in the haversack. Then he felt for Emma's letter inside his tunic and took comfort from them.

That evening in the chaotic, but blessedly cool, darkness they offloaded at De Aar. Jack fussed over Bobbi's water and bit of feed then suddenly found himself hungry and tired. He slept well, for the first time since leaving the *Cymric* two weeks earlier.

• • •

The Karoo desert was still hot and brown but less monotonous, for a series of ridges had sprouted in the distance and were edging toward the railroad. These were the hills everyone was talking about. The news of Black Week had hit them the minute they landed in Capetown. Buller, the VC, whipped at Colenso — and whipped badly. General Roberts' son killed there. Then General Methuen with his Guards and Highlanders shot to bits in front of kopjes on the Modder River. That's where General Roberts — Bobs — and the Glosters were going to show Johnny Boer a thing or two. Mind, Jack thought, that's probably what the Guards and Highlanders had thought too. Still packed like cattle, the Glosters sat in open trucks now. Jack, face and hands exposed to the sun for seven hours, was burned. He thought of his brown arms and rough hands harvesting in England's August sun, and he realized that there was no such thing as a hot day in an English sun. Not compared to seven hours in an open wooden box under an African desert sun. He'd taken his helmet and tunic off to try to get some relief from the blasting heat, but George and Billy had blasted him for fool. That had been five hours ago. A bare head, shoulders, arms would have been suicide. He saw that now.

Sergeant Miles slept, sweating, propped in a corner of the truck. Miles swore that he could store his sleep. Once they started marching there'd be precious little kip he declared — best stock up now. They would join their brigade — General Knox's Thirteenth — at Belmont for training and acclimatization. Jack gingerly touched his roasting cheeks and patted some water on them. Just exactly what would acclimatizing be? It sounded ominous.

• • •

The battalion was gone. They had marched a mile from the railroad and camped by the time Jack led Bobbi and the machine gun from the train station; now the machine gun section had to catch up. Sergeant Miles halted his men near a small grove of weedy trees that sheltered a newly constructed graveyard. It was quiet after the chaos at the station. Two-score crosses marked fresh graves. Scotsmen dead already. Killed pushing the Boer off one of those steep ridges. Jack wondered if they'd vomited when they reached the top. Bristol seemed easy already. What was a bit of cold rain and a grass-green hill compared to this. A half-dozen highlanders wearing Black Watch kilts rested under the trees. They sported slings and crutches along with pipes and hard smiles.

"Was you wounded here, Jock?" Miles called to them.

"Naw, Magersfonstein up north was our packet," one replied flapping a slinged arm. "Mauser bullet's still got most o' my elbow stuck to it up there."

The other Scots laughed.

"How were the Boers? Good as they say?"

The Jocks stopped laughing.

"Never saw a Boojer — never saw bugger all but sand in our faces. Johnny Boer shot us like cattle in a slaughteryard. He can hit your arse from six hundred yards if you stick half of it above ground."

They fell silent. Finally Miles led them on toward the battalion camp.

"Good luck, Glosters!" A Scottish voice chased them. "Aye, an keep your arse down!"

• • •

For three days they drilled and performed route marches. Route marches were done without the water cart. "Learn to survive off your water bottle, don't count on refills more than once a day." Sergeant Major Trevelyan declared Glosters in India could go two days on one-day's ration.

"See this here?" He shook his bottle at them as they stumbled back into camp, tongues puffy with thirst. "This is Poona water, vintage 1893! Save your water boys, save your water."

The tented accommodation would have suited a brigade but the whole of Six Division had arrived so they packed fifteen or more into ten-man bell tents. Jack and George slept outside with their rubber groundsheets thrown on top to keep the dew off. The groundsheet was a godsend but the rest of their kit was already suffering. Their boots were cracking badly. Jack had to repair his left sole after only the third march. Everywhere they sat or knelt was rock, sand, or scree. The knees and seat of his trousers were already fuzzy and thin. The seventh day they were declared "acclimatized". Their hands and faces had peeled and burned again to near black. They were impervious to the sun now. Lean, able to ration water and thrive on boiled meat served in the noon day sun, they resembled racing dogs.

The Glosters began to draw outpost duty on a series of picquet sites atop the tall kopjes surrounding Belmont. Forty-eight hours of heat and isolation then forty-eight hours in the tents. The lieutenant's long legs powered up the narrow track, the others followed, perspiring in the early-morning sun. Near the top a Two Company rifleman popped up from behind a large rock.

"Halt"

They did.

"Advance one and be recognized."

Wethered walked forward, his rifle slung.

"Password?"

"Saskatchewan," Wethered said.

"That's the one," the sentry smiled. "Is that how it's pronounced sir? We never could get the hang of it. Sas-catch-as-catch-can was it?

"Sas-kat-chew-wan," Wethered spoke slowly.

"It's no good, sir. I can't speak this Dutch-Nigger language."

"It's Canadian actually," Wethered said, waving the section up past him. "Canadian battalion had these posts last week and put their own words on the password list."

"Canadian?" The sentry saluted. "If you says so, sir. Never heard of the like. On our side, are they?"

Wethered ignored him and fell in beside Jack.

"How's Bobbi, Private Cordey?"

Jack stroked her nose. "Tough as these rocks, sir. The Mounted Infantry horses are dropping like flies but Bobbi doesn't seem to mind the heat or short feed."

"Take good care of her, Cordey," Wethered slapped her flank.

"Coincidence, sir," Jack said.

"Eh?"

"I mean Canadian troops here last week and now Bobbi's here and she's Canadian."

Wethered smiled. "She's a Gloster now."

The outpost was perched atop a stony high ridge that had been christened Scots Ridge for the Highlanders who died taking it. They parked Bobbi in a shady cleft short of the summit and manhandled the Maxim gun up the last fifty yards. In the end they carried it like a stretcher, every one of them gasping in the already hot, morning air. They occupied a narrow rock frying pan which the Two Company men gleefully fled. Three shallow scrapes lined the rim of the outpost. Each scrape had low, stone walls built up on two sides and the men, following their predecessor's example, stretched blankets over the walls to create some shade. Lieutenant Wethered, Sergeant Miles, and Wethered's batman occupied the forward hovel along with the Maxim. The remaining six men were split — four to the large shelter and two to a small one. The Forest sanger held Jack, George and Billy Webster. Their fourth was Palmer, the man Bobbi had thrown back at Aldershot.

Jack climbed down to check Bobbi, who was snoozing sensibly in her shady patch. He returned to see George and Billy, armed with spades, leaving with the sergeant. Jack squatted under the blanket, set his rifle pointing north and slipped his helmet off.

"What's the sergeant up to?"

"That stink," Palmer wrinkled his nose. "Two dead horses and at least one Boer about eighty yards down the other side there."

The reek was palpable, tasted rather than sniffed. Jack levered himself up and walked forward until he could see the three men picking their way down the slope toward three brown piles of rubbish. He squinted through the shimmering haze. The two large ones became parts of horses, the third was obviously a man, bloated and missing an arm.

"Shellfire — lyddite got 'em."

"Going to bury them in this heat?"

Palmer fanned a swarm of flies from his face. "Two Company — lazy bastards — should have done it already."

Jack retired to the shelter. It was no surprise that Billy and George had drawn the dirty work. Palmer was blond, well built and looked like a soldier. He always seemed to be first in line for food, drink and light duty — last in line for hard graft. He had memorized a wealth of detail about the Maxim's technical components, but Jack suspected he actually understood very little. Palmer never missed an opportunity to deride the Forest yokels, but was smart enough — no, sly enough — to stop short of having to back up his words with his fists. Jack and Bobbi had become a special team which Palmer envied and feared.

The problem was their lack of a corporal. The machine gun section was entitled to one but neither Miles nor Wethered seemed concerned. Palmer wanted the hooks and tried to act like a corporal so his superiors might make it a fact. Jack wondered if he should just tell Palmer that he was not interested in corporalship. He wanted nothing more than to do his duty and go home. He slipped his hand into his grubby haversack and touched the small oilskin package that contained Emma's book. A cloud of black flies erupted from the piece of bread inside the bag. Half of them lighted on his sweat dampened head. Too tired to even grunt with disgust, he shoved the helmet back on and tried not to think where the flies had been before they found his bread.

• • •

George was the only one to have carried his groundsheet up to the outpost, so all four men huddled under it while the night rain lashed them. Spectacular forks of lightning rooted themselves into the Karoo to the south, illuminating the sheets of water that swept over Scots Kopje. The storm was moving southwest to northeast, so the sky due north was relatively clear. The sodden Glosters crouching in the mud under their skimpy shelter gazed north, in the mistaken hope that it was a sign of the storm's departure.

"Now here's the surprising turn of events." Billy's teeth chattered on the 's's. "First, how could this waterless godforsaken desert come up with enough wet for a storm? And second, why isn't the stuff at least warm? By Jesus, the very air was hot as the devil's fart this afternoon yet the rain is cold? Not fair lads — not fair at all."

Jack was past caring. He'd just returned from checking Bobbi's line. She was drinking from a natural-rock pond and seemed quite content to let the rain bathe her. The journey had taken him nearly half an hour — stumbling through the mud, feeling for the path in the dark, orienting himself during the lightening flashes. George had given him his place between Palmer and Billy — the warmest and driest place but, in fact, precious little heat or dry to be had. George then stood in the full fury of the storm, siphoning rainwater off the groundsheet into their water bottles and Bobbi's changa.

"That'll taste right good tomorrow in the heat," he congratulated himself crawling back under cover.

"You're a brick, me George. Ta very much," Billy said, nudging the others.

"Aye, thanks Grigg," Palmer acknowledged. "Still, can't think I'll be thirsty for a long time to come."

"Hey now," George thrust his arm out, pointing north. "There's African lightning for you — like nothing ever seen back home or in India."

Jack peered from under his helmet and a moment later saw it. A broad slash of light, angled from earth to the clouds, but perfectly straight.

"See? It's not crooked and it comes every ten seconds." George pointed again, enthusiastically. "I timed it when I was filling the bottles."

Jack's mind started counting. The strange light appeared three more times, exactly on schedule before he realized what it was.

"Searchlight George," he said. "It's the Kimberley searchlight."

"Where the siege is? All that way off and we can see the light?" Billy asked, somewhat incredulous.

"O' course!" Palmer snapped. "Damned yokels! It's fifty miles off. That's where General Bobs and us are going — Kimberley. Going to lift the siege."

"Bloomin' hell," George murmured. "A light so big you can see it fifty miles away."

"African lightning!" Palmer laughed. "Oh Grigg, did you know the beam's so strong a man can climb up it? All the way to the clouds. You should ask Sergeant Miles if he'll let you climb the Kimberley searchlight when we relieve the town."

"Aaaw, you can't fool old Jolter with that," George drawled. "He knows better. You Bristol boys would let us get halfway up — then turn off the light!"

"No fooling you, Georgie," Billy laughed and dug Palmer in the ribs. "Jolter ain't climbing none of your fancy English light beams."

The next day George's water tasted sweet under the grilling sun. Both men from the other sanger developed severe headaches and, by night fall, were nearly prostrate with fever. But it wasn't heat stroke because their fever worsened overnight. They had to be carried down the next morning. The next train south took them back to the hospital in Capetown. Typhoid, somebody said. Miles called it enteric fever and blasted them for not boiling their water before drinking.

• • •

The gun and limber were slated for one truck, Bobbi for a boxcar, but Wethered let Bobbi ride with them. She was no trouble. They were loaded just after dark and lay in the open truck staring up into the African sky. Jack was beginning to recognize some constellations but couldn't help himself looking north for the dippers and the polestar. The train shuddered, then moved into the night. Two minutes of swaying motion set the machine gun section to snoring. They'd had forty-eight sleepless hours of daytime heat and drenching night rains on the outpost. This was followed by a day of packing and loading and sweating. But now dark, cool, and comfortable, they rocked northward to the Modder, Kimberley, and the front line. For exactly one and one-half hours. Then the train slammed to a halt. Lanterns appeared and raucous voices ripped them from deep sleep.

"Enslin Station! Enslin Station! What mob is this? Hoy there! This Thirteen Brigade? Well, the right train and on time for once . . . I'm damned!"

A short firecracker of a Service Corps major strode along the tracks snapping orders to a gaggle of men behind him.

"Goddamn me — it's the Glosters is it? Good, good. Sar'nt Major, lead the rifle companies to area four, tell 'em to bed down. And take 'em by the hand, mind! Nobody wandering around lost, hear me?"

A light bobbed up beside Jack's head. "What's this? Transport?"

"No sir, Maxim Gun section," Jack replied, groggy and looking for Miles who still slept soundly.

"Maxim Gun! Right then, wheel it off and my boy Smitty will lead you to area four once you find your mule . . . "

A hot little face inched over the edge of the boards, eyes bulging. "Son of a bitch there's a horse on this open truck. Horses go in closed cars for Christ's sake! What the hell are you playing . . . ?"

Jack stumbled to Bobbi's bridle. "She's gentle as a lamb, sir, doesn't need to be boxed."

"Insolent young bastard! Hold your tongue."

The little man vaulted like a gymnast into the truck and raised his light just as Wethered appeared at Jack's side.

"Sorry sir," Wethered saluted. "We'll get her to a box for the next leg north."

The major patted Bobbi's neck. "You're walking now Lieutenant — no harm done I suppose. Right, get this gun and horse off the truck quick as you can. Smitty will get you to your staging . . . "

He whirled around and roared into the night, "*Private Smith!*"

A soldier loomed up near the truck. "Sir?"

"Damned insolent sonuvabitch you are Smitty — where did you disappear to?"

The private sighed audibly.

"Gloster's Maxim — area four — don't get lost."

Then he leaped from the truck, gathered his entourage, and began bullying the occupants of the next truck. Jack harnessed Bobbi into the gun carriage and they moved away from the buildings and lights. Smith led them into the night. They trudged through sand still warm from the daytime heat.

"Now we march, boys," Sergeant Miles spoke as though passing sentence on them. "Yonder Enslin will be your last view of civilization for a while. I reckon."

They walked quietly for a few minutes.

"For some of you," Miles spoke again, thoughtfully. "It may be the last view of civilization ever."

• • •

Of course, area four was not their staging area. The regiment was moved three times during the next day — slept two hours — then arose at 1:30 AM to coffee and marching orders. Then they sat in ranks for four cool night hours. The march commenced just as the sun rose. Jack thought he had never known fatigue such as he experienced during those first dust-filled, plodding miles. Then the full heat of the sun fell upon them and he realized that what had come before was nothing. Nothing at all.

At the fourth mile they walked past the supine figure of Lieutenant d'Esterre. His batman held a coat over the officer's white face to shade it. Half a mile later Palmer dropped to his knees, retched up the water in his belly, and fell half conscious into the gravel. George dragged him clear of the gun, propped Palmer's haversack over his face, poured water from his own bottle onto Palmer's neck, and ran to catch them up. Men, all white faced and semi-conscious littered the trail. Oxfords, Buffs, West Ridings and Glosters. Officers and privates, dropped by the sun, choked by dust. Nobody had water left after six hours. The ten minute breaks meant nothing — just breathing dust while sitting rather than shuffling. They stopped at a farm station called Ramdam. Nine hours — nine miles. Jack knelt beside Bobbi's head at a mud-churned pond. Her slobber floated past his face as he sucked the brown sludge into his mouth and swirled it around his fat tongue.

"Sips, boys, sips," Miles croaked. "Don't make yourselves sick."

Nobody mentioned boiling. There was no fuel for fire and no strength to build one. Oxfords, Buffs, West Ridings and Glosters all jostled at the watering hole. No energy left to fight for water, more like cattle at a trough. The regiment had neither meat nor bread for them but near sunset they got porridge — good, salted oatmeal porridge. Jack Thornton nearly cried when he spooned the first mouthful in. It was smooth and lovely on his throat. It sank firm and filling into his shrivelled belly. He thought of Mrs. Toomey's kitchen — her porridge on early, misty mornings. Tears of regret, of longing, started in the corners of his eyes. It was February 11th. The real Charlie and real Bobbi would be hauling night soil — maybe even ploughing — in cool, rainy England. He gave half his porridge to Canadian Bobbi and she gratefully accepted it. At sunset Jack slept, thinking himself exhausted — not yet fully comprehending the meaning of that word.

They marched at 4:00 AM into the broiling sand of another day. Palmer lay half-draped over the Maxim, scarcely able to propel his legs. Jack's concern for the extra load on Bobbie soon toasted to apathy. A river appeared later in the day complete with water that flowed and only stank a little. Jack drank it but his empty belly would not let him sleep until Foresters from Six Company gave him fresh mutton taken from an "enemy" sheep. He ate and must have slept, for he woke with a gasping jerk in the cool night air. Billy had kicked him in the buttocks croaking, "Walk on Jack Charlie, walk on."

Jack was surprised to find himself in full kit, one hand holding Bobbie's line. He stumbled forward, confused by a light on the horizon to his right. He pulled at his water bottle, mysteriously half empty, and stared right. The sun was rising. It soon washed the sky white and began its work on the soldiers. Jack, missing an entire night's march and most of his water, soon lost the use of his tongue as it dried and swelled in his head. At day's end another river appeared. Jack toppled face first into the tea-coloured liquid letting it flow through his mouth, swallowing trickles. He vomited, drank again sparingly, ate biscuit, fed Bobbi, then slept.

Jack's next fully alert moment came at sunrise when a brief crackle of distant rifle fire ground the column of soldiers to a halt. A troop of guns galloped past them full of martial energy. Moments later the Glosters, Buffs and West Ridings were told to sit down. The unfortunate Oxfordshire boys set off at double time after the guns. Jack slept instantly, head dropped forward on his chest. He registered the thump of the fifteen pounders and another tiny popping of rifle fire behind his closed eyelids. A handful of Boers fled north to tell Cronje the news. The artillery cleaned their guns. The poor beasts of the infantry slept and ate for an entire day near yet another river — pathetically grateful for a respite from the marching.

"Here it is lads, our turn has come," Miles said the next morning. "Mr. Wethered has our orders and he told me to pass 'em on. Cronje's whole army has left Kimberley and it's running east along the Modder. We're going north cross-country for the Modder and cut him off. It will be a forced march, then a hard fight to trap and smash five thousand Boer riflemen at Klip Drift. It will be our battle." Jack looked to Bobbi's harness and feed. She had grown thin, but remained calm and strong. There was little talk now and no bravado. Billy checked his water bottle a dozen times and George hummed a little Forest tune incessantly as they prepared to march. Otherwise, there was no display of emotion.

A battle was not real to them. Not yet. Even the long service India men had little experience of it. George had been shot at from a distance twice by hill bandits on the Northwest Frontier. Billy and Miles, never. Palmer claimed more experience, nobody believed him. But fifteen miles forced march in midday heat was a very real prospect. It frightened Jack more than a poorly imagined battle. He prayed for courage but, really, he was begging God to save him from the heat stroke.

The three rivers of Jack's mostly blacked-out memory in fact had been one, the Riet. He drank its water greedily one last time then they marched with the sun overhead. Then they marched with it on their backs. No track, just a rough plain with occasional gullies to skid down and claw back up. Bobbi, slick and scrabbling up the gully, while all of them, even Sergeant Miles and Lieutenant Wethered, heaved against the gun to help her. It was a working pace that required attention. Step over a rock, through some brush, around an ant hill. The long columns of companies in line ahead stirred up dust clouds that coated the sweating machine gun section bringing up the rear. Small groups of cavalry and mounted infantry rode far in front with compasses held pointing northeast. They still marched as the sun hit the horizon and clung to it for a long, hot moment. The east sky began to soften into a heavy, purple, African night while behind them the west flamed. The sun died and they marched away from its set, into the dark.

Jack reached for his bottle. He had grimly resisted it during the day, taking only rare sips. He'd promised himself a good drink in the dark where the cool air wouldn't sweat it back out of him in minutes. Neither had he relieved himself — both George and Billy swearing that you must hold your piss in daytime heat. Now he did both and smiled with pleasure, as though he'd partaken of great luxury. The sound of a spattering waterfall came from the machine gun limber.

"Aye now, Bobbi, who's a clever girl," Billy called to her. "*she* knows to hold her water 'til night fall . . . unlike others I could mention."

"That's enough from you," Miles shot back quickly. "Holdin' in your pee is like holding in poison. Daft Irishmen and loony Foresters — it ain't natural. Blimey, Webster, all it proves is you're no smarter than a horse."

Billy's answer was to make his own stream, accompanied by a long groan of ecstatic proportions.

When they passed a farmsite at midnight Jack took heart. His head had fallen in a stupor despite his best efforts to hold it up. But farms, sheep, and cattle could only mean the Modder was near.

He smoothed one palm over Bobbi's nose and she puffed her thanks to him through flared nostrils. A half-hour later the horizon straight ahead flashed once, twice, then lit with a ripple of bright sparkles. Moments later, the whump of artillery and snaps of rifle fire reached them. They stopped, but when the men in the rifle companies tried to sit the NCOs shouted them back to their feet. Then they were hurrying, quick step toward the now-constant stutter of rifle fire. Mounted Infantry thundered out of the dark to guide them and the Glosters strode toward Cronje. Quick, hot, blood Jack would have sworn he no longer possessed rushed through him, carrying him forward like a magic drug. The scrabble of a thousand boots over rough country, clinking bayonets, clacking mugs, and rifle slings, these things he heard clearly, as though they were significant.

An invisible twig snapped high overhead. Then a buzz and another snap. Rifle bullets from far to their front, fired high. Jack panted for air although he no longer felt tired. He thought quickly about his duties when the gun went into action. My God, it had seemed so unlikely that they would fight. Surely their job had been to march, suffer, and drag the damn Maxim across Africa — not actually shoot it. Then, suddenly as it started, their battle ended. The column halted. The Buffs edged forward cautiously into the night. Minutes later, two companies of Glosters were sent to their support. The rest of the brigade lay down on their arms to await battle orders that never came. The machine gun section, completely drained now, slept heavily for the rest of the night. Near dawn, the Boer rearguard shook clear of the British and ran east, free.

"Not real soldiers, us," George complained as he sloshed water over his head. "Our regiment is sent in to grab Cronje's tail. But we of the Machine Gun are left on our arses to watch. What we want lads, is to go back to a rifle company."

"To get shot like yon Bristol boys last night?" Billy splashed him. "That's why we should be of the Emma Gee, Georgie. To stay above the lowly slugging."

Jack felt himself inclined to agree with George but did not join the debate. A long column of mounted infantry began to slosh through the Modder downstream of them. They had fought all night and looked terribly haggard. Their horses were nearly used up. As the head of the column reached the north bank it turned east. Palmer rose from the shallows and splashed toward them. His buttocks white as bleached bones, flashed in the sunlight.

"Is that Colonel Hannay's men?" he bellowed.

A drooping mounted soldier lifted his hand and waved.

"Where does Hannay go?" Palmer called.

"To catch Cronje, upstream," came the reply.

"Save some for us!"

The mounted man stood in his stirrups, raised his helmet in the air and waved it. A cheer rolled from the naked Glosters.

"Go *on!* Hannay!" George shouted.

"Hannay — Hannay." Palmer roared.

The others took up his chant, hundreds of desert-hoarse voices croaking Hannay — Hannay and ending with a long huzzah as the last of the column cleared the river. Palmer shot a meaningful glance toward Miles who nodded in return. Jack saw the exchange. Palmer was a leader. He'd started the cheering; he'd lifted their morale, made them feel like warriors again. He'd make a dandy corporal. Once more, Jack was tempted to clear the air — declare his lack of ambition — but it would sound exactly like thwarted ambition.

"Feel better now, George?" he said. "We'll get our turn. When the cavalry pin Cronje down they'll need the infantry for the kill and we've got the biggest rifle in the whole regiment." He deliberately caught Palmer's eye and grinned.

"Aw, the calvery will get the job done whilst we sit bare-arsed in the Modder."

"Cavalry can't fight — not like infantry. They'll need us, tell him Palmer."

Palmer, oblivious to his nudity, swelled up with self importance. "Forest boy's right. Our guards beat the Boer at Graspan, sent him running and the Ninth Lancers were supposed to cut 'em off and finish the job. Cavalry came back well-whipped. Their colonel was so ashamed he topped himself. An' I hear Lord Kitchener's not best pleased with Hannay for losin' the fight with Cronje's rearguard here."

"Been over to Kitchener's tent for a chat on strategy then, have we, Palmer?" Billy smirked.

"Just what I heard," Palmer bristled. "But it makes sense and anyway, a good soldier keeps himself informed."

"A good soldier," Billy flopped back into the river, "keeps himself fed, watered and comfortable and lets the officers ponce about talking strategy. Am I right Jack-Charlie?"

"I believe Palmer," Jack tried to patch Palmer's ego.

George grunted. "I still think we're set for marching all the way back to Coleford without firing a shot. Not proper soldiers, whatever Palmer says."

Palmer looked to Miles and shrugged, indicating the gulf that existed between the oafish private soldiers and their betters. Miles led them back up the bank to where their clothes lay piled like small corpses on a battlefield. The face, neck, and hands of each man were burned near black by the sun but their startling, white bodies produced a delicate, almost fragile contrast to their weather beaten extremities. Jack had a fleeing image of these scrawny porcelain figures standing up to Mauser rifle fire. He glanced toward the Klip Drift farmhouse where the wounded lay in stifling heat. Then he dressed in his ragged khaki and put the image from his mind.

• • •

The cavalry did, in fact, catch the Boers and pinned them miles upstream. But the horsesoldiers couldn't defeat Johnny Boer, much to Palmer's vindicated satisfaction and George Grigg's delight. The Boer army entrenched itself and waited for the British Infantry who duly began their chase at sunrise. Jack and Bobbi quickly fell into their marching routine, picking their way through the rocky scrub, sipping water; holding their pee. Twice in the first five hours their rest stops coincided with small streaks of vegetation creeping out from the river. Bobbi cropped the dusty grass with evident relish and Jack gnawed a biscuit from his haversack.

The pace was a mile per hour; the sun was no more fierce than any other day, and the dust was actually somewhat lessened by the fact that they were the lead brigade in the lead division on the march. Jack and Bobbi fared well. They stayed alert and Jack mentally drilled himself for the coming fight. He must keep Bobbi and the Machine Gun close to Mr. Wethered. who would locate their place in the firing line. Then Jack would unhook the machine gun and take Bobbi twenty yards to the rear of the gun while the officer actually fired it. Palmer fed the ammunition belts into the gun. The other men hauled ammunition boxes and guarded the gun under Sergeant Miles' supervision. When the time came to move on, Jack and Bobbi had to be quick and precise. Regardless of any battle chaos, they must hook into the shafts and be ready to go in less than a minute.

It was then very unfortunate that, in the eighth hour of their best day of marching since Enslin, they let the section down. Jack gave Bobbi her head while he dropped back to check the rapid release attachments on her traces and poles, ensuring all would give way cleanly and quickly when the time came. He jogged back to her head and was coiling in her lead rope when he struck the toe of his boot on a heavy rock and stumbled. His rifle sling slipped off his shoulder and he fell, jamming the muzzle into Bobbi's flank. She sidestepped in surprise, skidding the opposite wheel of the limber into a rocky outcrop she had just moved to avoid. The jagged, anvil-shaped stone caught one spoke at its narrowest point, shearing it clean through. Bobbi, now alarmed, leapt forward smashing another spoke and damaging a third.

"Goddamn and blast!" Miles snarled from behind the gun. "Whoa, you Bitch! Bobbi!"

Jack was up to her head in an instant. "Still Bobbi!" he snapped. She ceased moving and immediately stood fast.

"Dirty bastard," Miles kicked the rock. "Look what's happened. Mr. Wethered! Look at this mess. Jesus Christ, sir . . . "

"All right Sar'nt, I saw it happen. Spare me your description." Palmer materialized at the officer's elbow.

"Shall I get the lads to lift it clear, Sergeant?" He stared across the gun pointedly at Jack. "Before any more damage is done?"

"Get Bobbi out first," Wethered commanded. Jack and Bobbi quickly performed the very drill he had just been mentally rehearsing. He walked her well-clear of the wreck and they stood as helpless and embarrassed observers of the repair operation. Miles and Wethered swiftly inspected the damage and came to the conclusion that one broken spoke could be strapped up but not two and certainly not three. Any further movement over the rough terrain would ruin the wheel and possibly damage the axle. The assessment, on Miles' part, was punctuated with frequent oaths and not a few withering glances in Jack's direction. Palmer repeated these looks. Wethered seemed less perturbed. He pulled George aside and detailed him to run for the adjutant who was riding two hundred yards in advance. George, the proud ex-light infantryman set off at a fast jog. The rest of the men joined Jack and sat in Bobbi's shadow. Jack, somehow feeling he should be receiving a punishment, stood at attention by her head in the sun.

"Aw cut yourself one, Charlie-Jack. Come sit with us. It was an accident," Billy said sympathetically. "Pay no attention to Palmer. He's got his nose shoved so far up Miles' arse even Mr. Wethered's sick o' him."

"No thanks, I'll attend my duty here," Jack said, quietly relieved the others were on his side.

"Attend my duty?" Billy laughed. "What the hell kind of Forest talk is that? You remind me of an officer, standing there like a mad dog in the noonday sun."

Two horsemen cantered toward the gun. George ran by their side, his rifle at the trail, and his face showing scarlet through its nut-brown tan. It was the adjutant and Colonel Lindsall. They conferred with Wethered while Miles and Palmer stood respectfully clear.

"Private Cordey, fetch Bobbi here, quick now," the lieutenant called. Jack's heart sank as he ran Bobbi over to the crippled gun.

"Still Bobbi," he said, stamping his boots to attention and halting simultaneously with her. They both stood recalcitrant and rigid.

"Is she hurt?" Lindsall dismounted and walked to Bobbi's side.

"No, sir, I've checked her. She's fine, sir." Jack held his voice even, staring fiercely to the front. Perspiration poured down his face.

"At ease, Cordey," Lindsall murmured as he ran his hand down Bobbi's side.

Jack stayed at attention.

"Private Cordey *stand at ease!*" Miles squealed. "Are you bloody well deaf or just insubordinate?"

Jack stood at ease, still rigid and not flickering an eye. Bobbi remained at attention.

"He's right. The animal is fine." Lindsall spoke as though they were at an agricultural fair examining livestock. "All is not lost then, Mr. Wethered."

"No sir," Wethered replied. "We can mend it or get a new wheel when the division stores wagons come up."

Jack's heart rate slowed considerably.

"Aye," Lindsall beckoned to the adjutant. "Write a note for Lieutenant Wethered, sign over my name. Make it for any stores necessary for repair."

While the adjutant scribbled the requisition on his message pad, the colonel remounted his own horse.

"Right, Joe. The regiment will likely reach Paardeberg near sundown. We'll bivouac there and be fed into the battleline early tomorrow. You get repaired and come up with the rearguard battalion of Ninth Division — they're about five hours behind us. Then rejoin us at Paardeberg. Get your rest now — march all night if need be. Cronje's laagered at Paardeberg Drift and is standing to fight — your gadget will come in very handy tomorrow I dare say."

Wethered took the note and saluted. Colonel Lindsall walked his horse close to Jack. He extended one hand and scratched Bobbi's ear. "You've done well with your Bobbi," he said, loud enough for Palmer to hear. "She's come a long way from that wild Canadian I first saw at Aldershot."

Bobbi stood at ease. The machine gun section rigged blankets for shade, and tried to sleep until the division wagons came.

• • •

The Boer daredevil, DeWet, and his Commando hit the lightly-defended supply depot on the Riet and destroyed half the food stock of Roberts' Corps. The army would be on half-rations commencing immediately. This distressing news came from the divisional quarter master's men when they passed through late that afternoon. However, spokes, rims, and tools had not been touched by DeWet. Sergeant Miles and George finished repairing the wheel by lantern light just as the last brigade of Ninth Division stumbled past them in the growing dark. The brigade major pointed out the rearguard battalion that was sweeping up all the stragglers from the line of march. They shrugged into their webbing, shouldered rifles, and stood quietly waiting as the dimly-seen line of soldiers approached. From the east came the thump of a cannon — then a series of blasts, one melting into the next, forming a roll of thunder.

"Battle's started," George spat. "And here we sit, just like I said. We've missed it boys."

"Just artillery softening Cronje up," Palmer said with firm authority. "We don't attack 'til tomorrow dawn."

Billy cleared his throat, rolling his eyes.

"And, *yes,* Webster," Palmer snapped. "I did get that from a chat with the colonel. Cordey heard him too."

"Palmer's right," Jack said.

"Palmer's right, Palmer's right! You sound like a parrot Charlie-Jack. I never said he wasn't. This time, anyway."

Lieutenant Wethered approached the rearguard battalion. "Hello! Is this the RCR?"

"Who wants to know?" A tired voice snapped from the dark ranks.

"Lieutenant Wethered, Machine Gun Section of Second Battalion, Gloucestershire Regiment," he replied equably. "We're

Sixth Division, had some damage to repair. We'd like to tag along with you to Paardeberg."

A man veered obliquely from his company toward them.

"I'm Captain Arnold, A Company, RCR. Fall in behind me if you like."

"Much obliged," Wethered waved the gun forward. The captain returned to his company.

"What the devil are RCR? Welshmen?" Billy asked.

"Royal Canadian Regiment," Palmer answered.

"You're full of . . . "

"Palmer's right," Sergeant Miles cut in.

"You mean the 'Sas-catch-as-catch-can' people?"

"The same — Canadians."

"Why, Bobbi's Canadian," Jack said. "This is some kind of . . . I don't know, omen — more than a coincidence."

"What the hell are you on about now, Jack-Charlie?"

Jack rubbed Bobbi's nose. This animal and all these ethereal men, half-visible in the gloom, leave Canada separately, travel thousands of miles across oceans, only to meet up on the Modder River in Africa, in the middle of the night. It was some kind of omen.

CHAPTER 10

Heavy howitzers sited near the river crashed backwards, hurling shells over the river. The RCR, exhausted from their all-night march, sat in the early morning sun, waiting their turn to ford the river. An artillery battery of fifteen pounders was crossing carefully against the swift current, wheels tipping, long cannon snouts canting left, then right, in the frothing water. Mounted troops galloped up and down both banks of the river and rifle fire cracked in noisy tattoos, out of sight, upstream. Major General Smith-Dorrien, commander of the Nineteenth Brigade, and Colonel Otter, commanding officer of the Royal Canadian Regiment stood on the verge of the Modder. Smith-Dorrien, tall, slim and handsome was pointing toward a hill, some distance beyond the north bank. Otter, fiddling with his long moustaches, made occasional notes in a small, black book. Lieutenant Wethered had positioned himself close enough to them to be noticed but not to intrude.

"I hope he can find out where the regiment has gone." George spat into the dust. "I've had enough of this Colonial squit."

Jack had been studying Bobbi's oblong body and large head. Distinctive, he had decided — Canadian — exotic. "Could be worse, George," he said. "These RCRs might come from the wild west. You know, where . . . "

"Lord save me, Jesus," Billy interrupted. "If you mention Bobbi's Canadian home, or the wild west, or it being an omen one more time Jack-Charlie, I swear I'll have you."

Jack let it slide. Still, he couldn't stop glancing at the RCRs with their maple leaf badges on the side of their helmets. His pulled a long-past geography lesson from his memory: five great lakes, Montreal and Halifax — the great Royal Navy port and garrison — the Rocky Mountains, and the great plains. It was all he could muster. Bobbi shifted beside him, creaking her harness as she, too, peered at the foreign troops.

"Hey up — here we go now," Palmer called for their attention. The conference had ended and Wethered managed to catch both men before they left. Smith-Dorrien glanced at the machine gun then pointed east. He and Wethered spoke quietly, Smith-Dorrien shaking his head several times. Finally both men looked to the RCR Colonel who nodded vigorously, for all the world like an Otter breaking surface in a river.

Wethered hurried back to the machine gun "Sar'nt Miles, here now, quickly."

They all crowded in to hear. "Our lot went about five miles east, along the south bank last night. But exactly where they are now seems anyone's guess. The brigade commander wants to keep us with the Canadians until things firm up. They don't have a machine gun and he has attached us to them for the time being."

George groaned and Miles shot him a nasty look.

"I understand, sir. We are under RCR orders, then. Colonel uh . . . what was it . . . Beaver, sir?"

"Otter, Colonel Otter, not Beaver, Sar'nt. Try not to create an inter-colonial incident, eh?"

Wethered smiled at the whole section. "Not to worry. I've obtained permission to go east, find the Glosters, then come back for you once I'm fully in the picture. With luck we'll be back home tonight, but it all depends how far east Thirteen Brigade has deployed and if they're in action already."

"I'm to be on me bloody own then, sir?" Miles did a poor job of disguising his apprehension. "With these here damned colonial troops? Alone with them?"

"Not alone Sar'nt," Wethered ignored Miles' lost-puppy look. "You report to Captain Philips, their adjutant. He'll make sure you're given orders and food. The RCR are being sent over the river. They'll be guarding the drift and trail north for the rest of their brigade when it crosses. Not much chance of anything unpleasant happening."

Miles brightened at this. Wethered took him off to find Captain Philips.

"Colonial baggage guard, by God," George croaked. "A sad fate for a British soldier."

"Not baggage guard," Palmer snapped, clearly as disappointed as George, but unwilling to admit it. "We'll be facing the Boer laager. If they sortie to cut the general's line of march, why they'll meet up with our Maxim and then there will be action."

George sniffed. "If they sortie! Aw knows they're miles off fightin' real soldiers. We're nothing but baggage guards. Ruddy "colonial" baggage guards at that. Paardeberg Poncers — that's us!"

They hovered near the RCR adjutant like lost chicks for less than a half-hour after Wethered departed before he lost his temper with Miles. He shuffled them off to see Colonel Otter which put Miles into a terrible funk at having to address a commanding officer solo. Otter, not unkind, escorted them back to A Company and Captain Arnold, who quite happily assumed command, allocated them a bivouac area and sent for rations.

"Not so bad, boys." Jack paused in his attack on the beef a taciturn young Canadian had delivered to them. "Snooze for a couple of hours before it's too hot, cross the river, and rest. Beats chasing all over the south bank of the Modder with Mr. Wethered looking for a lost regiment."

"*We're* the one's as is lost!" George, pride mortally wounded by the Canadian adjutant's indifference, refused to be mollified. "These toy soldiers should be kissing our feet — real British soldiers to stiffen 'em up like! But they hardly know what to do with us."

"Got a point there, Grigg," Palmer said. "Half-trained colonials can't be expected to understand the proper tactical employment of a section like us. We're wasted here."

"Well now, this is desperate." Billy winked at Jack. "Palmer agreeing with George Grigg. What the devil's next?"

"I'm going to try to talk to some of them," Jack said, defiantly. "Pretty decent of them to share their food with us seeing as how it's half rations already. After all, they're really British, same as us."

"*That* is traitor talk!" George pointed a shaking finger at him. "These is colonial tripe — wouldn't call 'em Royal Canadian Regiment would they — be Royal British Regiment if they was . . . "

"Shut it," Miles cut them off, nodding at a Canadian sergeant who was striding toward them.

"NCO in charge?"

Miles stood, slowly munching the last of his bread.

"Sergeant Tom Kerslake," the Canadian extended his hand. Miles, clearly abashed at such intimacy, hesitated, inspecting his opposite number. The Canadian was sunburned black, lean and dirt stained as themselves. His uniform was patched at knee and elbow, but he sported a trim moustache, clear eyes, and his bearing was confident. Miles finally shook hands, gingerly.

"Sergeant Miles," he said gruffly. "Second Battalion Gloucestershire Regiment — the old Sixty-first Foot."

Kerslake dipped into his haversack and produced a long tin flask. "Thought you boys might like a touch of this, before we go into action."

He unscrewed the lid. Miles conjured his cup with the deftness of a magician and held it out expectantly.

"Action you say, Kerslake?"

Dark rum splashed into the mug and was instantly thrown back with a great smacking of lips.

"Aye. Captain Arnold told me to pass the word. Be ready to cross the river in thirty minutes. We'll swing east and attack toward Cronje's laager."

"Attack!" Palmer, now filling his own cup from the flask, squinted hard at the Canadian. "You mean mount guard on the track," he said, a thick streak of condescension in his voice.

Kerslake returned the stare. "No, Private, I do not mean guard duty. The DCLI are baggage guard. We attack up the North Bank. The Highland Brigade on the south bank are pinned down — that's their musketry you hear. We're to pull Johnny Boer off their back."

Miles gulped audibly and recharged his mug, taking Jack's ration. "My gun? Part of the assault is it?"

"Captain Arnold says you're to stick to him like shit to a blanket. A Company is leading the assault and he intends to use your gun the first chance he gets."

"Cornwalls is baggage guard?" George chuckled. "Good job for 'em — not much in the line o' sojers there — DCLI, Duke of Cornwall's Luggage Infantry! You can count on us. man and boy." He slapped Jack's back. "Front line is where Glosters do their best work, Sar'nt Kerslake."

Kerslake laughed, walking to the gun limber.

"Maxim heavy machine gun, .303 calibre, two-hundred-fifty rounds per minute, accurate out to one thousand one hundred yards, water cooled, gas recoil," Palmer rattled it off. "We can have her in action in under a minute."

The Canadian ran his hand down Bobbi's side. "She looks familiar," he said. "Long back and jug head. Just like my uncle raises back home. Selling a lot of western-bred horses to the British army."

"Western bred?" Jack said, shoving an elbow into Billy's side. "We knew she was Canadian stock, but didn't know she came from the Rockies."

Kerslake shook his head. "No mountains — prairie where he ranches."

"But out west for certain?" Jack slapped Bobbi's rump and squinted at Webster.

"I'd bet on it."

"Jesus Christ Almighty," Billy grinned. "Like an omen."

"Be a shame to lose her," the Canadian frowned.

"What's that? Lose her?" Jack bristled. "She's not going anywhere. I keep her in good shape — tough as old boots, she is."

Kerslake scratched Bobbi's ear. "I mean if we lock up with the Boer, she'll be a hard target to miss. Apparently these Dutchmen can hit a man at eight hundred yards with their Mausers."

• • •

The Guards and Highlanders had gone in at Magersfonstein as a tight column and had been slaughtered. The RCR lines speckled the width of the plain that extended north of the Modder very well spaced out. The Gloucestershire machine gun detachment of a horse, a limber, and five men clustered around it presented the very best target on that flat plain.

"Right lads, I'm buggered, but there it is. I'll have to operate this damn gun. Can't think why Mr. Wethered had to go off like that. I can *fix* the Christly weapon with my eyes closed — but firing it, well, that's officer's job."

He glared around at them, daring a contradiction. They plodded toward a line of treetops protruding from the distant river bed. The Modder swung north in a sharp bend about a mile farther on to present itself across their front. Although the noise of rifle fire was loud from that direction, no bullets came their way.

"Buggered, I am," Miles said. "What kind of battlefield is this? Empty as a whorehouse on Sunday goddamn morning."

Jack squinted down the long line of RCRs. A few anthills, some boulders and thorn bushes broke their advance, but nothing else appeared in the shimmering morning heat.

"I'm buggered. Let's make sure we're clear now, damn you all. If we come into action Cordey does quick release and takes Bobbi back one hundred yards, just to be safe. I start hosing that tree line with .303 and Palmer feeds. Grigg, Webster keep us one open box and another standing ready."

He licked his lips and wiped sweat from his eyes.

"Buggered," he muttered. "All right, if I'm hit, who takes over the gun?"

"Me, Sergeant!" Palmer sounded much too eager.

"An' who takes Palmer's place feeding this son of a bitch if Palmer cops one?"

"Ireland steps into the breech," Billy said. "And on behalf of the Emerald Isle may I say it will be an honour to step over yon Palmer's twitching English body and . . . "

"Shut it, Webster. Damn, I'm buggered right well, boys."

The cackle of rifle fire slowed, then died out. A Company and its adopted machine gun arrived at the edge of a long, flat, gradual slope that led down to the riverbend now about a half-mile distant. A straggling firing line composed of prone, kilted soldiers appeared four hundred yards directly ahead.

"Highlanders on the north bank!" Capt. Arnold paused, fumbling for his field glasses. The company slowed. He waved them on. "Keep going RCR, keep — "

A thousand tiny thunder claps sounded, drowning his voice. Jack instinctively looked up at the sky. Then the Mauser rounds arrived. Snapping overhead, cracking and splashing off rocks, thumping heavy and deadly into the sand. The RCR lengthened their stride, hurrying.

"*Steady boys — steady,*" Arnold bellowed. The sergeants repeated his call and the line regained its order.

Jack's head whipped left, then right, searching for Boers, looking for soldiers to fall. But none of these things were to be seen. The RCR walked forward, the Mauser fire crescendoed into a steady, rushing sound, like river rapids, and the green trees beckoned. Sand sprouted miniature volcanoes here, there, all around them. A high-pitched 'wang' startled Bobbi. He calmed her and glanced at the bright, metallic smear of a Mauser bullet on the iron axle band. He felt nothing but a vague apprehension. It was noisy; it was confusing; was this a battle then? It was like waiting for a summer storm to break. They made another hundred yards before the Boers finally calculated the range correctly. Hell opened its gates and the RCR stepped through. Four bullets hit as fast as Jack could count them. One crashed through the chest and out the back of the RCR directly before the gun. He fell without a murmur, like a deflated balloon. One skinned Bobbi's front-left shoulder, gouging it red. She flinched, wild eyed, ready to bolt. Jack ran his hand down her neck, calling her his good girl. Two struck the Maxim with awful, spanging sounds.

"Action front, down boys." Arnold waved his men into a firing line. RCRs went down, impossible to differentiate between those knocked down and those taking cover.

"Open on that treeline if you please, Sergeant Miles."

Arnold stood calmly pointing to their target, trees — not Boers. Horrible sounds hissed, snapped and rippled the very air they breathed. Jack swung the gun around and unhitched Bobbi in an instant. His stomach was clenched in awful anticipation. Any second now. "Now, Now, Now," he muttered, waiting for his bullet.

He and Bobbi walked to the rear. Her wound was light, but he could not think clearly about it. His whole body cringed and his brain spasmed in the rifle storm. Palmer and Miles' voices came clear and steady as they loaded, then cocked. A long, rolling hammer of Maxim gunfire erupted. Jack swivelled, the vignette imprinted itself onto his mind. Miles, perched on the limber, counting his bursts. The gun vibrating, spewing smoking, empty brass casings into the hot African sun. Palmer feeding the belt almost reverently into the gun's maw. Billy and George kneeling in the dirt, an open ammo box between them. Arnold, field glasses trained on the treeline, speaking to the Glosters, even though they couldn't hear him.

Then it ended. A whooshing squall of Mauser steel jacketed lead enveloped them. Arnold dropped, squirming on his back, clawing desperately at his belly. Miles' helmet flipped backward, pouring blood onto his shoulders. He stayed upright, hands on the gun handles until another bullet whipped his arm back dislodging the body, which slid smoothly onto the trail. Palmer's right knee caved in. He shrieked and rolled under the limber. Billy and George threw themselves flat. Bobbi took a deep gouge along her right buttock and without further ado, she jerked the line out of Jack's hand and fled at a gallop. Jack screamed for her. A loud 'pock' sound filled his ears and blood filled his mouth. He lay down, spitting a bright, white tooth onto the sand, where a small pond of his blood was gathering.

The Mausers eased up for a moment. He rolled onto his side, supporting his head in one hand. His knees curled up instinctively to the fetal position and he lay like a young, sleeping child while blood poured from his mouth. He fished the molar out of the red pool and held it before his eyes. There was a large chip missing, otherwise it was intact. He thought of the tooth fairy and tucked it into his tunic breast pocket. In a minute, the blood flow slowed to a trickle that he occasionally spat out. Pain flowed in to take its place, but not wicked pain. His tongue found the hole in his lower jaw where his tooth had been, but oddly, the rest of his teeth were firm. For that matter his tongue, bathed in blood, was moist and supple, nearly a relief from the hot day. He smiled at the thought, and knife cuts of pain stabbed his face. He gingerly tapped his jawline with one finger and felt its tip slide though a wet hole into his mouth. He pulled it out, disgusted. "Jack-Charlie! Are you dead, son?"

Jack raised his head an inch, "No!" He winced and dribbled a fresh mouthful of gore onto the sand.

"Then get up here with us. You're sticking out like a turd on a tabletop."

He began crawling, dragging his rifle and spitting as he inched over the rocky ground.

"Go Right! Your Right!"

George now, yelling directions. Jack scuttled right like a crab and found a long, rock outcrop perhaps ten inches high that gave shelter. He slithered along this until he reached the two surviving Glosters, ensconced in a small depression.

"Jesus, boy, are you sure you're not dead?" Billy's eyes stared wide and white out of a filthy, strained face.

Jack motioned with his finger to indicate the hole in his face. Then showed them his tooth.

"You're a lucky sod," George quickly inspected his mouth. "A bit higher and it 'ould have tore your head off, like Miles."

They all three glanced toward the derelict machine gun. Miles' red-soaked body lay draped on the trail. Had he known? Is that why he had been nervous? The Boers still whipped rounds into the limber. Miles' corpse had been hit again. George produced a mildly-filthy bandage — part of an old puttee — and wrapped it around Jack's jaw and head. He soaked it with water from his bottle and placed Jack's helmet back to hold the bandage secure. Then he took Jack's head in his own large palms and cradled it.

Jack curled up beside George, thinking of his mother and her tenderness during his boyhood illnesses. The wet bandage and George's warm hands were a balm. The bleeding stopped and the pain eased. He felt strangely content.

Billy called for Palmer, who lay beneath the gun and Miles' dripping body. Palmer called back in a voice warbling with pain that his kneecap had been blown completely off. Billy urged him to get clear of the gun limber, calling it a Mauser magnet. Palmer began crawling on his good side but must have been disoriented for he went toward the rear, open slope. A hail of Boer bullets pummelled the Maxim in response to Palmer's movement.

"He's killed," Billy said. Jack stayed cupped in George's hands, unwilling to look.

"No, by God, he's not! They missed him, but he's going to crawl right through the clear spot there. Palmer! Palmer you daft bastard — go left man — move left!"

The air hissed with bullets that thumped and splashed into the ground.

"He must have gone doolali." Billy gave up shouting and instead commentated like a horserace announcer.

"He's quarter way. He's behind a boulder. Now he's in the open again, they'll kill him there. He's still going. Mary, Joseph, and Jesus he's *still* going and they haven't laid a glove on him. He's got pluck — for an Englishman and a toad eater, that is. By God, he's almost out — another few yards and he'll be over that little ridge. Go on, boy, go on!"

Billy's voice became urgent; hope and unfamiliar respect filled it. He began to bellow. "*Go on Palmer. Crawl you English son of a bitch. They can't touch you. Go, boy, go on.*"

Jack propped himself up and searched the open plain. Palmer, nearly a hundred yards to the rear, coiled then straightened, propelling his body over the rough ground like a caterpillar. Earth fountained all around him, one leg dragged, floppy and red. Soon the men huddled nearby began to shout their encouragement. For long, tense seconds Palmer struggled through the rifle fire. RCR voices and Billy cheered him on. Jack found his jaw aching terribly then realized he was gritting his teeth, muttering encouragement. Palmer hove into full clear view on the rim of the rising ground. He paused, waved one arm to them, then rolled swiftly out of sight to safety. Jack lay back, putting his head in George's hands.

"Well done! Up the Glosters!" a Canadian voice roared. "Three cheers for the Gloucestershire Regiment. Hip Hip."

The cheers rolled down the Canadian line. Strangely, the Boer rifles fell quiet. Jack, weak and without proper rest for nearly a day, promptly fell asleep. He breathed through his nose, for the fierce African sun quickly congealed, then hardened, the heavy smear of blood that sealed his lips.

• • •

Shellfire! Jack's eyes snapped open and he tensed, waiting for the explosion. Nothing. Another roar of gunfire from the laager but no shells burst. The sun was gone. Wind pushed cool air past him. He lay on his side, blinking at the heavy, dark clouds scudding overhead. Thunder rumbled again. He tried to speak, but his lips were glued shut. He felt the crusted blood and began picking at it, claustrophobic, almost panicking at the thought that his mouth was locked. Drops spattered, steaming off the still hot rocks that lined their shallow shelter. Then rain, ice cold and driving hard engulfed him. He turned his face upward and tasted the rehydrated blood as it released his lips and flowed into his mouth.

"Give us your bottle, Jack."

George sat upright, in the curtain of rain. He held his rubber sheet between outstretched arms. Billy tipped one end into a crease that funnelled the rainwater into his water bottle. They replenished two bottles before the Mausers began searching for them. George dropped flat again. An angry Billy shouldered his Lee Metford and shot back into the grey rain. He worked the bolt like a journeyman weaver at a loom and emptied his magazine in a few seconds. He dropped down, breathing heavily.

"Probably killed five Boojers just now." He tapped George. "Try it. It's a tonic."

George propped himself up on elbows and delivered his rounds at a steady, aimed rate of fire. He rolled onto his back and grinned at them. "Up the Glosters, eh lads?"

The desultory Boer fire suddenly accelerated. Jack peered from under his dripping helmet rim. Just fifty yards distant, four men ran crouched over toward the machine gun. One of them carried a stretcher. They reached Captain Arnold, threw his unconscious body on it, and began lumbering to safety. One bearer fell, clutching his leg; his partner took both rear handles and they kept going. The front right man fell; his partner took both front handles and they kept going. The remaining front man was then cut down just short of cover. The lone survivor, a tiny man, hoisted Arnold across his shoulders and scurried, ant-like, to safety not ten paces from the spot where Palmer had escaped. No further rescues were attempted. Jack, Billy and George, shivering cold, now lay in an icewater bath.

"Still not fair. Should be warm rain." Billy said. "An' look here. This shit is turning to mud. Sand should stay clean. But not African sand — oh no, it's hot blazing burn-your-arse sand in the sunlight but bog Irish muck in the rain."

George draped his rubber sheet over them and they spooned up against one another to stay warm.

• • •

The late afternoon sun felt good. Jack, helmet off, lay sprawled like a dog in it. Their wallow had drained quickly after the storm. Even smeared with thin mud, he actually felt clean. Scoured by the rain and now dried by the sun, he had transformed from animal back to human. His jaw ached but the tooth was cleanly extracted and the bleeding stopped. The cold rain had reduced the swelling. Surely they'd be withdrawn once darkness came. Just sit tight and it would end. They would survive and be rested and doctored. Nobody could ask more of them. Even the Boers were scarcely shooting now.

"Better clean 'em lads." George spoke, contradicting his thoughts. "They'll rust certain and jam when we needs 'em most."

Jack waited for Billy's rebuttal but it never came. Instead they fished oil bottles and pull throughs and cloth from their haversacks. Resting on their elbows they drew their rifles clear of the mud. Bolts out, swabbed with oil, barrels run through a half-dozen times, then bolts back in. The Lee Metfords gleamed and clicked smoothly as the shiny brass .303 rounds were pushed back into magazines. It seemed a shame to lay the rifles back down in the mud so they propped the muzzles on rocks.

"What I'd give for a chance to stand up, stretch, and get a cuppa," Billy mused, shifting to his other side, scrabbling pebbles out from under his hip.

Jack felt no such urge, except for the tea. He was content to lie back — amazed by the thought that a thousand men similarly hugging the earth, surrounded him and they faced a thousand more, five hundred yards away. Yet the three of them were in a perfect solitude. The rim of earth a few inches above them. The open, rain-washed sky overhead. A brief vista of ground rising behind them, dotted with the untidy heaps of two dead men and the battered machine gun still carrying Sergeant Miles. The wounded stretcher-bearers had crawled to shelter behind a boulder, leaving the open killing ground in sole possession of the dead. This was their universe. The entire British army, Cronje's five thousand, artillery, wagons, ox trains, tents — all gone. Vanished and perhaps vanished forever. A sudden burst of Boer fire disturbed his reverie. The rounds flew high above them, seeking targets well to the rear. More stretcher-bearers? A relief? A string of bayonet tips appeared over Palmer's ridge. These were followed by the rifles, then heads, then bodies of British soldiers marching purposefully into the growing fire. They began to drop, slapped down by the relentless Mausers. Then, like the mounted infantry, like the Highlanders, like the Canadians, they went down, first on hands and knees, then on bellies, crawling into the singing rain of bullets. Two sweat-streaked men burrowed in beside Jack.

"Are you crazy?" Billy demanded, grudgingly making room for them. "Did none of our military geniuses think to tell you that the Boojer holds onto yon river like a Scotchman holds on to tuppence?"

The men, wearing the same wild eyes that the Glosters had worn that morning, simply shook their heads.

"What regiment?"

"Duke of Cornwall's Light Infantry," one of them gasped. "Told us we'd storm the river with the bayonet. Over in a few minutes."

"Cornwalls?" George exclaimed. "You're supposed to be the baggage guards!"

"I bloomin' well wish we still were," the soldier replied. "How long you been here?"

"Six hours." George replied without hesitation.

Jack was stunned. Miles dead six hours? Not six days? Was it only this morning he and Bobbi had crossed the Modder? Only this morning he wondered what a battlefield looked like?

"Well, did you at least bring us some tea?" Billy asked.

The DCLI's were still too Mauser-stunned to see the joke. They exchanged blank stares.

"Cornwalls!" A stentorian voice raised up over the sound of the Boer rifles, above the whole battlefield. "*British soldiers!*" it roared again.

Two men, swords and pistols drawn, walked calmly across the open ground.

"Colonel Aldworth, and the adjutant," a DCLI said.

The Colonel stopped amid the flying bullets and gazed around him.

"*Cornwalls . . . up!*" he screamed.

The two DCLI's stood, as did their comrades. The colonel raised his sword.

"*Charge!*"

He ran for the river. The Cornwalls ran cheering after him. They drew the Canadians out of the ground. Bayonets appeared, clicked, and the RCR, howling, ran forward with the Cornwalls. George stood, fixed his bayonet, and stared down.

"The colonel said British soldiers. That's us. Let's go."

Jack staggered upright, dizzy and weak, but got the bayonet snapped into place. Bullets once more took his breath away. His gut clenched in an awful spasm again. Blood and bile from his belly retched up into his mouth. He spat it out.

The three Glosters charged; two bellowing the word "slashers" to shout down their fear; one probing the hole in his cheek with his tongue and wondering where the next hole would be.

• • •

"Damned Cornwalls. Not an ounce of brain between all three hundred of 'em."

George was the first to come out of the shock of their second failed assault of the day. Colonel Aldworth's bullet-riddled body lay stiffening a hundred yards short of the Boer trees, his faithful adjutant just behind him, dead. The rest of the survivors once more scrabbled into the earth, seeking shelter measured in inches of rock or shallow folds of the earth. One such fold held the three Glosters, Sergeant Kerslake, a Highlander and another very quiet RCR. They were now enfiladed from a previously unknown Boer trench in a donga that extended out of the river to their left. They lay with their faces pressed to the earth while angry Mausers cross-cut the air inches above them.

"Hey," Billy giggled. "Ever hear the one about the Scotchman, the Englishman and the Irishman?"

The Scot forced himself to laugh. The English lay silent, staring at the mud before their eyes.

"Seen yur! Seen yur! Ady, Ady mwa." The voice, high-pitched with pain and despair came from nearby.

The Highlander grimaced. "What the hell is that! What's he squealing?"

"Mandew! Mandew! Oh mareejee, mareejeeuss, jowsuf."

"Sounds like a Kaffir." Billy shifted and peered over the edge of their tiny dip. "No, he's in khaki, about twenty yards to our left. Looks like he's got one in the lung. Poor bastard's kicking like a shot dog."

"Seen yur!"

"A white man?" George asked.

"White as me," Billy replied.

"And who says Irishman are white?" The Highlander snapped.

Jack raised his head fractionally until his eyes could just scan the ground. The man's helmet lay nearby. A maple leaf badge was fastened to the side.

"One of yourth, thergeant Kerthlake," he lisped. His cheeks had puffed up and the bandage restricted his jaw.

"Mandew! Mandew!"

"He must be E or F company. Frenchman," Kerslake answered but kept his face firmly pressed to the earth.

"Frenchman!" The Scot grunted. "Good God, worse than Irish!"

"That's enough now, Jock." Billy's voice had lost its sense of humour. "Boys who ponce about in dresses ought to be more polite."

"Seen yur!"

"*Shut up* you! Hey, wee froggie — die like a man, d'ye ken!" the Scot's voice shrieked. He was near the end of his tether. Jack could smell it on him. The Highlander had been at Belmont, then Magersfontien, now Paardeberg. Three battles playing the human target in a Boer shooting gallery and never laid eyes on an enemy yet.

"A French company. Ith that from Montreal, then thergeant?" Tom tried to change their direction.

"Or Quebec City we're recruited from all parts of the country."

"Can you shut yon shilpit's whining? He's driving me crazy."

193

Kerslake nudged the RCR beside Jack. "What's he saying Luc?"

The quiet soldier lifted his head. His hair and eyes were startling black. He stared into Jack's eyes.

"He's Catholic, he's praying. Oh Lord, oh Lord, save me. My God, help me. Mary, Joseph and Jesus help me."

"You're French?" Jack said to the stone face. He shook his head.

"He's half-breed, from the Saskatchewan territory. Half French half Cree — Indian," Kerslake explained. "Don't call him a Frenchman — he'll scalp you."

Jack was mesmerized by the black eyes only inches from him. Plains red Indian — half anyway.

One dark eye winked, slowly and solemnly.

"Seen yur, Mandew."

"Here now," Billy sang out. "I'll pray for you my son! Bill Webster won't let another true Catholic go without a prayer. Even if he is a Frog."

"Lamb of God!" he roared.

Billy peered over Jack's back at the RCR. "Translate will you?" he whispered. The dark face showed no expression, eyes unblinking. Then he shouted out the French words.

"Who takes away the sins of the world," Billy continued.

Luc finished the prayer for Billy.

A weak bubbling voice called back.

"Merci, mon frere. Merci."

He was quiet now. They all fell silent, listening to the angry Mausers snapping at them, searching for their shrinking bodies. George unfixed his bayonet and began cutting the dirt beneath him, then throwing it up in front and to the left. They followed suit, scratching down, each inch descended added to their safety. A half-hour later the Frenchman called again. His voice was firm and calm.

"Adieu. Maman. Adieu."

They dug down nearly a foot. Then they lay waiting for nightfall.

• • •

An hour after sunset Father O'Leary, the RCR chaplain, was delighted to discover a brother Irish catholic in Private Webster. He took Billy with him as a helper, tending to the wounded who were too badly hurt to move. The Boers had gone with the sun. The tiny man who had carried Arnold through the hail of rifle fire turned out to be Dr. Fiset, the RCR medical officer. He gathered the walking wounded, including Jack, and led them a mile to the rear to his tented treatment room. Palmer lay on some straw outside the tent, unconscious, his leg swathed in bandages. The bandages were swathed in flies. Jack found a blanket, lay down beside him and slept.

• • •

"You're next, chum."

Somebody kicked Jack's foot. He sat up slowly in the pre-dawn light. A heavy set Canadian corporal stood over him. The corporal wore a red cross on a white armband.

"Next?"

"Sawbones will see you, go get in that line."

Jack retrieved his rifle and pulled himself up, using it as a cane. He felt weak, absolutely spent. Palmer was gone. The corporal snatched the rifle away, Jack staggered, sending him an angry glare.

"No weapons in the treatment room." The corporal worked the bolt, ejecting the ammunition. "Come see me after you're done and you can have it back."

Jack joined a short queue of battered men sitting outside the tent. Arms, legs, heads in filthy bandages but moving unaided. Adjacent to them was a line of bodies, perhaps fifteen or twenty, he didn't count them. They were covered with blankets or scraps of canvas, only their hobnailed boots and putteed legs protruded. One of them must have been Miles. "I'm buggered lads." Jack turned away, saddened.

It was the tiny RCR doctor who eventually treated him. He bustled around Jack with efficient energy but a face sagging with exhaustion. He spoke very little beyond saying: "mmm,", "bandage off,", "swab it." An orderly tore Jack's puttee bandage clear, ripping hard scabs from his face. Before Jack could defend himself the man scrubbed his face with a cotton cloth soaked in iodine.

"Thun of a bitch! Thtop! Thtop!" His cheeks jolted with burning pain and he stumbled away.

Dr. Fiset turned an angry face to him. "Behave yourself, Private. It's only a touch of . . . well, I'm damned, look at that will you?"

His anger turned to astonishment. He approached Jack and touched his chin, gently swivelling Jack's head side to side. "You had your mouth open when you were shot, am I right?"

Jack nodded.

"Hit your tongue?"

Jack shook his head, then fished the tooth out from his pocket. Fiset pried his mouth open and peered inside.

"A million to one shot — now I've seen everything. In one cheek, clipped the tooth free, then out the other cheek slick as you like."

He and the orderly became quite animated — discussing trajectory angles and timings. They gave Jack another thorough swabbing inside and out. It took all his remaining willpower to submit to this without twitching. Dr. Fiset stitched him as rapidly as Vi had worked her knitting needles and slapped a light bandage in place.

"That's it. Three stitches inside, four outside on each cheek. Lots of tea, get some rest, light duty, and report back to me or your own medical officer tomorrow. *Next!*"

Jack retrieved his rifle, and received a mug of tea and a biscuit. He soaked the biscuit, gnawing tiny slivers off, then swallowing them. He glanced at the dead men and at the crowds of RCRs reforming their companies nearby. The living and the dead. He could not see the battlefield; he did not know where the surviving Glosters were or even where he should report. Captain Arnold, if still alive, would be no help. A horse picket-line had been established at the edge of the RCR camp. A long backed, big headed horse stood second in from the picket. Her head was in a nose bag.

Bobbi.

He could have wept. His Bobbi was safe. He was safe. It was all right. He went to her.

CHAPTER 11

"You can have your light duty tomorrow. We're going to get our gun today and you're bringing that mule." George said it matter of fact as though it was quite logical. "Will that borrowed mule take Bobbi's harness?"

"It's good enough for a short trip," Jack admitted.

"How is Bobbi?"

"Could be worse, wounds are superficial. She should be back in harness in eight or nine days."

"Eh? Super . . . what-the-hell . . . fishing?"

"Light wounds — superficial."

"Why not say so then." George spat and muttered something about officers' language.

Billy was more unconscious than asleep after his night with Father O'Leary. George left him undisturbed. He and Jack set off westward toward the battlefield, retracing their attack of yesterday.

"Look there," George pointed toward the machine gun, small in the distance. "Are those dogs at the gun?"

Three or four animals circled the machine gun but Jack could not make a clear identification. He shrugged. The empty plain gradually transformed itself into an old battlefield. A ripped tunic, a scrap of cloth, empty casings, a smashed rifle, and undistinguishable garbage littered here and there. The spoor thickened as they approached the gun, until the ground looked like a trash tip. A carpet of flies and ants swarmed on the spot where one of the dead had lain, the sand still dark.

Jack stopped, staring at the mess. The body must have kept the rain from washing the blood clear. He kicked sand over the stain thinking it deserved a burial. George tugged his sleeve and they walked on to the gun. The rain had washed most traces of Sergeant Miles' sad ending off the shafts and carriage, but a portion of one shaft sported a large, dark patch and this wood was partially chewed. Miles' helmet, with the tip of the front brim smashed in by the Mauser, lay several feet away. It too had tooth marks and tears in the red-stained, linen cover. George retrieved the badge off the back. The white,metal sphinx was bent and a tip of the brass wreath was snapped clean off where the bullet had exited. A wolf like howl erupted from the trees by the river but was cut short by a series of sharp, yapping barks. Two jackals emerged from the woods, trotted quickly across an opening, then disappeared back into the trees.

"Where were we?" Jack asked, suddenly disoriented by the thought of what the brutes had been scavenging. He looked to the right of the gun, then backward. "Where is that ridge Palmer crawled over? Where is that rock ledge we lay behind? They're gone!"

George had raised his rifle, but too late for a shot at the jackals. He lowered it and gazed at Jack, then the chewed helmet. He shook himself and only at length seemed to comprehend Jack's question. "Lookee here, this ground is flat as piss on a plate. Where did we hide out?"

They moved instinctively, like a search party, scanning the ground. "Here!"

George kicked at a small rocky ledge raised only a few inches above the sand. They followed it toward the river until it disappeared. They followed it back and this time found the muddy depression that had saved their lives. Nothing at all, really. Several long gouges streaked the earth in front of it. One shattered rock lay nearby.

"That's our battlefield, George. A scuff in the desert. Once we take the gun away we'll never find it again. This place was life and death less than twenty-four hours ago."

"Aye. May be just as well. Hell of a day, Jack. Best over and done. Let's shift the gun. I don't like it here."

George's tone snapped Jack out of his maudlin thoughts. He looked swiftly at the river. Would Boers have filtered back into their old position, or the jackals? They fitted the shafts of the battered gun into the mule's harness and hurried away.

• • •

The gun jacket was creased and the mount had been damaged in two places. The carriage and axel sported a dozen gouges and bullet holes. But the Maxim could be brought back to life. Billy supervised the repair work in the cooler evening in A Company's bivouac. The RCR had rebuilt themselves; shelters rigged, weapons cleaned, and the wounded transported. Food had been eaten, the half-ration pittance disappearing in a few bites. They rested. A Company was low, their well-respected Arnold had died from his wound, never regaining full consciousness. Jack, George, and Billy had divided up Miles' few pieces of kit before the burial. Jack got a good belt, George swapped bayonets with the dead man — George's tip broken while digging their trench during the battle. Billy took a thick, cotton shirt and cut it into patches for his trousers. The three Glosters had attended the burial of Miles and nineteen RCRs. Father O'Leary committed them "to the keeping of God's angels" in a brief, but gentle, eulogy. It had taken Jack all the way back to Tintern Abbey and the moment he'd first truly felt his father's passing. Now, handing tools to Billy, the thought returned to him. It disturbed him. At his moment of death, walking, crawling, charging, then cowering through the Boer fire, he'd not once thought of home, or his parents, or even Emma. The dying Frenchman had bid farewell to his mother yet it had not even brought his own mother to mind.

Was he such a coward? Was he thinking only of his own skin? He worked mentally through the battle. The tableau of the machine gun going into action was clear. The belly-twisting fear anticipating a bullet was easily retrieved. But what of his thoughts? George, Billy, Miles, Palmer. These men were his thoughts. They had become his family; they had replaced Emma and his mother. He studied them. George, the real corporal, stolid and rocklike, lifting the Maxim barrel while Billy adjusted the elevation slide. Billy, ragged, scrawny but smiling as he sang a tune he was composing in memory of the battle:

Where are ye Dick Aldworth, with your brave charge making?
The glory you made . . .

He paused, cocking his head, searching for a better word. "No, I've got it.

The glory you cut will be a long time fading.
Ye gallant Cornwall man, wit no fear o' the foe;
Where are ye Dick Aldworth? Oh, where did ye go?
You've gone straight to hell, you Briton true blue.
But why Dicky Aldworth did you take us too?

"Mind your manners." A young voice, accustomed to authority, cut the mood short. Lieutenant d'Esterre stood behind them, hands on hips, surveying their work. Patched, browned, thin and hard-eyed, d'Esterre was a far cry from the pink, young man who had been so outraged — and jealous — of Jack's affair with Mrs. Downs. The three privates brought themselves to attention. The officer glanced at each face in turn, pausing to examine the bandage wrapped around Jack's head. He showed no sign of recognition.

"This is the Sixty-first Maxim?"

"It is, sir." Billy spoke for them.

"Where is Sar'nt Mills?"

"Beg pardon, but it's Sar'nt Miles, sir. Not, uh, Mills."

"Very well, Miles — Mills, what of it. Where is he?"

"Dead sir, buried him this morning near that grove of trees."

"Dead?" d'Esterre examined Jack's face again then looked at the battered machine gun. "You were doing baggage guard — according to Lieutenant Wethered. How dead? And what happened to this man's face? And where is the rest of the section? The machine gun section should muster seven men here."

"Miles dead by Boer bullet through the forehead, sir." Billy spoke as though he was reporting football scores. "Another, different like, Boer bullet through both Cordey's cheeks. Palmer, with another different Boer bullet through the knee. And two men gone down sick back on the rail line at Belmont. Ain't seen them in ages."

Billy paused for a second, frowning, then continued. "So that's one dead, one badly wounded, one lightly wounded, two sick, and two men present and correct, sir."

D'Esterre gave Billy a very hard stare. He passed George's bland, blank face and alighted on Jack. "You, are you Irish?"

"No, sir."

"Right, explain to me — in plain English — what has happened to the Second Battalion Gloucestershire Maxim section since Lieutenant Wethered last saw it."

Jack recounted their story. D'Esterre seemed to lose interest after he heard of the failed Cornwall charge. He interrupted.

"All right Private, let's get to the Maxim. Is it serviceable?"

"Not quite, sir. But we should have it repaired by tomorrow. We were going to test fire it tomorrow afternoon."

"And your mule — how badly is it hurt? Can it tow the gun?"

"Vet says she'll be fit in nine days, sir." Jack was careful not to use the word superficial nor to correct him on Bobbi's bloodlines.

"Nine days, damn. I'll go see the brigade major's man. We'll swap our beast for one of theirs that's fit. Make sure the gun is ready to move when I return — you can finish repairs tomorrow at our bivouac."

He strode off.

"You lot, stand at *ease!*" Billy snapped the order when the officer was out of hearing. George laughed, but Jack scarcely heard the joke.

Bobbi — swapped for a mule. His attachment to her was suddenly a palpable thing, about to be cut. Why had he named her Bobbi back at Aldershot? Because he could pretend she was the Vicar's Bobbi and the Vicar was Emma's uncle and Charlie's boss and right now Charlie would be in the warm Ostrich sipping his pint and watching the cold rain come down while Mrs. Toomey made a delicious . . . Bobbi was Canadian but she was also England. His throat constricted, he found himself staring at the horse lines. He began walking to them.

"Jack!" George's voice caught him. "Help us with the gun."

He ignored them.

"Jack, where are you going?"

"See how Bobbi is doing."

"Come on, boy-o," Billy shouted. "Don't be an arse."

Jack stopped; turned to them.

"She's a bloomin' horse, Jack," George said in the same firm voice that had led them through the worst of the marching and the battle. "She's not your sister. Leave it."

Jack looked back over his shoulder, searching for the long back and big head, but couldn't see her. He returned to the gun and helped them reassemble it. It was nearly dark when Lieutenant d'Esterre finally returned. They stood to: rifles, packs, helmets all very correct. George thought d'Esterre might inspect their kit before leaving.

"Not a four-legged creature of any kind to be had," the young officer said abruptly. "The mounted infantry have ridden that lot nearly to death. I had to fight just to keep our nag from being taken. Apparently, even with two bullet holes in her, she's in the best condition of any animal in the lines."

"No mules then, sir?" Billy's voice was neutral and his smirk went unnoticed in the dim light.

"Quarter master won't trade a mule for a horse! Apparently five horses die for every mule. Won't have a horse at any cost!"

He faced Jack. "Why didn't you tell me we had a horse in the section? Damn it, what a pickle this is."

Jack might have grinned but for his stitches. The officer walked to the gun as though he was about to kick it, but mastered himself and exhaled a long audible breath.

"Change of plan, then. You, with the bandages. What's your name?"

"Private Cordey, sir."

"Acting Corporal Cordey now."

Jack could not help looking to George. Grigg shook his head slowly and gave Jack a half-wink.

"I'm talking to you, Corporal! Do me the courtesy of paying attention. In the absence of Sergeant Miles you will be section NCO and responsible for this lot over the next few days."

"Yes, sir?"

"You at least appear to understand the spoken word." D'Esterre glanced significantly at Billy.

"We are presently in a siege operation. Lines won't change much over the next few days, although we could have used you yesterday, by heavens."

"Regiment in action yesterday, sir?" George broke his strict rule of silence in the face of all officers. "Mr. Wethered all right, sir? How did we do?"

D'Esterre relented a degree and seemed to see them as fellow soldiers for the first time. "Yes, ah . . . stand easy."

They drew near him.

"DeWet got men onto a Kopje about three miles east of here — on the south bank. Looked like Cronje was going to use it as an escape route. We and the Buffs went straight in to take it back. Buffs and half our companies were pinned down. But about a hundred Glosters on the right made a bayonet charge. Pushed the Boer off his hill. Great day for the regiment. Great day."

George, nearly bursting with pride, couldn't restrain himself. "Aw knew it, zur. Knew the lads uld give Boojer a bloody nose if aw got the chance."

"Cost us though," the young officer looked past them. "Five dead, twenty wounded. Lieutenant Wethered went in, by the way — joined the assault companies on the final charge — and made it in one piece. Colonel Lindsall was shot through the lungs, ah . . . may . . . or, ah, may not survive the wound."

Two images flashed before Jack's eyes. The kindly blind woman . . . "Who is the boy with the lovely Forest accent?" The Frenchman, shot through the lungs.

"Right," d'Esterre slapped the Maxim barrel. "'Nough said about all that. Mr. Wethered is assistant adjutant for now while the regiment sorts out. I'm returning tonight, myself. But you three will stay with the gun until your animal is fit — no longer than necessary, mind. If you can swap horses earlier, do so and come soon as you can. Then you follow the south bank eastward to our

Kopje — they call it Kitchener's Kopje now. We'll be camped directly before it. Do you understand me, Corporal?"

"Re-cross to south bank in eight days, or less sir. Move through our support lines three miles to the eastward," he pointed east. "Soon as we reach Thirteen Brigade lines, I shall obtain specific directions to the Glosters' bivouac area, sir."

"Well done, Corporal," d'Esterre didn't bother to hide the surprise in his voice. "Do I know you? Were you in my company at some time?"

"No, sir."

"I'm off then," he turned to leave. George nudged Jack, making eating and drinking motions.

"Ah, sir, a moment please," Jack said. "How do we draw rations? We were attached to the Canadians but they leave for outpost duty on Gun Hill tomorrow.

"It's all arranged," d'Esterre was cold and hard again. He slowed but didn't look back. "You draw from whichever regiment takes the Canadians' place. Different battalions will rotate through here every two days."

They unpacked their kit and rigged their groundsheets over the gun carriage.

"I trust this is to the corporal's liking." Billy bowed and then laid their blankets out under the bivvy.

"Very much to the corporal's liking." Jack scrambled in. George followed, still smiling and shaking his head. "Aw knew the lads would fight well. Up the Glosters. Up the Glosters."

Thunder shook the air and a lightning bolt flashed nearby. Billy crawled into the shelter, shoving the other two to make room. They rolled into their blankets as the first rain drops spattered the gun tarp above them.

"One's in love with his bloody regiment. The other's in love with his bloody horse. And they say the Irish are daft. God save me."

• • •

A half-dozen Shropshire Light Infantry were detailed to help with the gun test the next day. They ran the carriage out a half-mile east of the camp. Billy then proceeded to display a natural genius with the Maxim. He put perfect bursts of fire onto ant hills and shrubs eight hundred yards out and farther with pinpoint accuracy. The Shropshire officer was so impressed that he reported it to his CO. Shortly thereafter, Corporal Cordey and the Second Glosters Maxim section were deployed a short distance behind the siege trenches being dug west of Cronje's laager. They dug in their gun, made a nice underground hut, and proceeded to pump several hundred rounds per day into Cronje's trenches, over a thousand yards away. They became the object of not a little attention. Each successive battalion, Shropshire, Gordon Highlanders, DCLI, dragged their own Maxim out to compete. But none had Billy Webster's unerring knack for choosing targets, elevation and windage, and he became the brigade novelty — private soldier, master of an officer's job. Billy's head swelled to the point where he began to refer to himself, grand-dangerously, as "Machine Gun Webster".

• • •

Colonel Otter's visit, upon the return of the RCR from their outpost duty, was taken easily in stride by Private Webster. Jack, pleased with Bobbi's healing wounds had just this, their seventh day, gone to exercise her in harness. George was away boiling

drinking water from the foetid Modder, so it fell to Private Webster
to receive the colonel's interview. The RCRs were to go into the
siege trenches tonight. They would leave those trenches at 2 AM
and advance by stealth in two long lines on the Boer trenches.
When the Boers opened fire the first line would lie down to provide
cover. The second line, armed with shovels, would dig a new trench
that would dominate Cronje's laager and provide the base to cave
in Cronje's west flank. The question was: "Given a section of men
to tow the Maxim, could it be quietly got into position on the right
of the line to fire in enfilade down Cronje's pits?"

The answer: "Sir, I can fire this weapon accurately at any target,
even an enfilade. And at close range, I'll hit it for certain. All I need
is Sergeant Kerslake's boys to carry me there."

Otter, bristling at the Irish impudence snapped back. "Do you
know what enfilade means, Private?"

"No, sir, sorry sir, no disrespect intended . . . "

"Then shut your mouth, man, and go fetch your corporal."

George, thrilled by the prospect of decisive action, agreed to
the proposal and Jack relayed their confirmation that the job could
be done.

• • •

After midnight they finished the last of their coffee issue. The
RCRs hoisted the shafts of the gun limber and on Sergeant
Kerslake's touch, they wheeled it up to the start line. George had
ladled grease onto the axle and hubs, every loose item had been
tied down or was packed by the Glosters. The Maxim rolled silently
into place behind H Company, Nova Scotia men, on the extreme
right of the Canadian line. A light breeze wafted from the laager.
It carried the reek of putrefied animals, open sewage and burned
wood. It also carried the chilling bark and howl of jackals,

208

interspersed with the eerie giggle of hyenas — drawn to the feast. Seven days of lyddite high-explosive shellfire had killed every animal and smashed every wagon above ground in Cronje's camp. Seven days of African sun and rain had turned the offal and wreckage into a stinking mess, coagulated over several acres of the north bank — upstream from where the British drew their water. George skimmed one to two inches of brown foaming scum off of their water every time he boiled it.

Jack noted the breeze but like so much in his soldier's life now, he'd learned to adapt to it. The first day he'd nearly retched from the ever-present stench. Now, it was just another part of the battle. He sat, leaning against the gun wheel, staring upward. African nights were nearly always clear, the air dry, and soldiers spent most of the night awake. The array of stars seemed to come lower and brighter as he observed them. They were the one part of Africa that he still found wondrous. Sleep shouldn't be a problem this time. Seven days in their comfortable shelter, even on half rations, had returned a rude sort of fitness to the Glosters — hungry, lean, but strong. Jack tried not to look east, tried not to recall the sound and feel of the Mauser storm, tried not to think of the billiard table they must cross before a thousand Boers who were well dug in and waiting for them. Even in the total dark, Cronje's men would put a sheet of lead a foot high over the entire field if they heard so much as a fart from the British lines.

Billy's "Ode to Colonel Aldworth" came humming from the right. George shifted every few minutes, checking his water, checking his rifle, rewrapping a puttee. Jack, feeling their nerves, continued his ritual of picking out constellations, slowly, star by star, drawing mental lines to connect the Cross, the Southern Crown. Sergeant Kerslake walked around the gun, triple and quadruple checking his men — touching them, noting their positions, making them wakeful. Then he drew near the Glosters.

"We go in a moment," he said quietly. "Before we do, I want each of you to have something."

Kerslake's rough hand touched Jack's arm and slid down to his palm. He pressed a cool metallic disk into it and folded Jack's fingers over it. Jack held it before his face but couldn't see it. He ran his forefinger over the disk like a blind man. Three letters — VRI — stood out from the surface.

"What is it, Sarge?" Billy's whisper came.

"Hat badge," Jack said too loudly. "RCR hat badge."

"As far as we are concerned, you boys are RCRs tonight. You'll not stand alone," Kerslake coughed self-consciously. "I promise you."

"Tha's right decent, Sarge," Billy replied. "An' same goes for us."

"We bist brothers now, Sergeant," George said earnestly.

They each sealed the deal with a long pull at Kerslake's rum flask.

The rifle companies rose with what seemed like a tremendous clatter of boots and loose webbing. A stiffening anticipation seized Jack's gut and held it tight for a minute, but the Boers were calm, their Mausers silent. Jack allowed himself to imagine the attack had been cancelled. At that precise moment the RCRs stepped off into the dark. Each man in the front line extended his left arm and took hold of the straps from the adjacent man's webbing. Bayonet-tipped rifles were at the trail in their right hands. Like a wavering string of small school children crossing streets on an outing, they disappeared into the night. The second line slung their rifles, hefted picks and shovels and followed. Kerslake nudged his men and the Maxim set forth, Jack and his two Glosters holding onto the carriage so there was no chance of being separated in the dark. Jack stared at the ground, counting each pace. Five hundred yards to the Boer lines, about a thousand steps. Each hundred paces he extended a finger from his fist. Each time a finger popped out, his gut clenched a bit tighter. By the halfway point he was breathing hard. His lungs seemed to have no ability to inhale, his jaw ached terribly and he couldn't unclench his teeth.

He refused to look up, certain he'd see a bullet flash from the night. Six fingers. A bullet coming straight into his face, smashing through his teeth to make good on the first missed shot that had only punctured his chops. Seven fingers. Three-quarters of the way, he calculated, one hundred fifty yards from the Mauser muzzles. Who would survive? Kerslake? George? Billy? Jack-Charlie Cordey? Had Miles known it was coming? If you didn't know did that mean it wasn't coming for you? Eight fingers. Jesus, Mary, and Joseph and Billy the Catholic would they get right into the Boer pits? Only a few yards now and it would be bayonets.

"Crack." A Mauser shot in the night.

Six hundred Canadians and three Gloucestershire men held their breath. They came to a halt, instinctively crouching.

"Crack," a second shot. Then a Dutch voice bellowed like a lion, warning his fellows of the attack, followed immediately by an unseen Canadian shout.

"*Go in — bayonets, boys. Charge RCR.*"

The command was drowned in a volcanic eruption of rifle fire from the Boer trenches. The dark was split by a livid streak of muzzle flash that covered their entire front. The first volley was high, but only by inches. The RCR front line surged forward, the second line dropped to their knees and began hacking wildly at the ground. Within seconds, the Boers had dropped their aim and bullets zipped through the Canadian lines.

"Eight hundred and six paces," Jack said loudly as they whipped the Maxim around. Kerslake's men were already digging, Billy and George rigged the gun. Jack flipped the first ammo box open, and fed the belt to George. Billy loaded and cocked. Then, with the experience of their first battle fresh in mind, he lay down.

"Down lads," he said. "We open fire when we got our hole dug and not before. I'm not going to keep Miles company if I can help it."

Jack heard him clearly, even though the night was now a chaos of orders, shouts, screams from the first wounded Nova Scotians and overall, the ceaseless drumming of the Mausers from their sparkling firing line. Jack flopped, slapping his cheek against the ground scarce noticing the pain. A new noise took the night: the RCR front line began a rapid return fire. Disoriented infantrymen had been nearly useless against an invisible enemy during the daylight battle but, at night, they had the Boer muzzle flashes to guide their aim. Within minutes the defenders' fire began to slacken. The Canadians, with fewer targets, slowed their shooting until a descending lull settled over the battlefield.

"Corporal Cordey," Kerslake's voice came from the dark pit where his men dug like frantic badgers.

"Here, Sergeant."

Kerslake crawled out of the night to Jack's side. "We seem to have stopped in the upper part of a shallow ravine that leads into the Modder," Kerslake breathed heavily. "The lads have dug the pit about two feet. If we roll the gun forward into the pit, I reckon your muzzle will just clear the top of the ravine. We should measure it."

"Billy, let's have a look."

Holding Kerslake's webbing they followed him forward. The ground dropped perceptibly to the pit, which the men were hacking with picks and shovels. Billy and Jack stood in the bottom of the excavation while Kerslake crawled up the Boer side of the ravine and waved his arms. They could just discern the movement in the gloom.

"Jesus, yes!" Billy exclaimed. "No deeper, stop digging!"

They eased the gun forward, and Billy mounted behind the handles. George checked his belt feed.

"Retire! Bring back the wounded."

A clear English voice rang through the lull. It came from the far left and prompted a clattering sound of men moving to follow the order. Then came Colonel Otter's voice, angry and pleading at the same time. *"Who gave that order? Stand fast RCR! That is an unauthorized —"*

It was drowned out by a furious renewal of Boer musketry. Shouts and counter orders burbled about the rifle fire. The left of the line was crumbling. Some of the Nova Scotians were standing, wavering with indecision. Nobody wanted to be left alone and enfiladed mere yards from the enemy trench at daybreak. Jack stood, half closing the ammo box.

The H Company commander screamed a furious order. *"Stand fast. Blast it! Steady Nova Scotia!"*

Kerslake slapped Billy on the shoulder. "It's now or never." His voice was unnaturally cheerful. "Open fire and the lads will hold," he shouted.

Jack knelt, flipped the box open and gave George slack on the belt. The Maxim began pounding. Billy's third burst virtually extinguished the nearest section of Boer rifle fire. "Where are ye now, Dicky Aldworth?" Billy called into the night. Jack's body lost some of his tension. He readied a second box. "Up the Glosters!" Billy began working a farther piece of the enemy line. H Company instantly rallied and added their rifle fire to Billy's stream. The Mausers tried to concentrate on the Maxim, but Billy was quick to return their fire in double dose. He ripped their line to shreds and the Nova Scotians devoured the pieces. The Boers fell off to infrequent and poorly-aimed volleys and soon even these tailed to sporadic single shots. The Maxim fell silent, no target worthy of its power. Billy crawled off the trail, a wicked, white-tooth grin visible on his dark face.

"Showed those Boojers where the Irishman shit in the woods."

His voice was wild and fierce. It gave Jack a sensation of courage such as he'd never felt before. The RCR were on top of the Mausers now. It was victory. Not dancing in the streets, flag waving, singing victory. That would be for the civilians at home.

"By God, you did so, Private Webster. Well done." Kerslake's reply was the extent of their celebration. They all set to with pick and shovel to expand the pit and build embankments to close off the open sides of the ravine.

• • •

"Well, well, Johnny Boojer," Jack said. "You are well and truly buggered."

He lay near the edge of the ravine, in front of the Maxim, with Kerslake and the H Company commander. The thin glow of false dawn was just exposing the ground before him. Half the Boer trench lay slightly lower and to the left of the RCR firing line. Enemy riflemen were easily visible, moving along its length.

"We'll soon have 'em out of there and running," the officer, peering through unnecessary binoculars agreed. "We'll open on them, then you join in," he said to Jack. "That way your gunner won't draw all their fire."

It was done in less than twenty minutes. The Boer could scarcely raise a single Mauser over his parapet without taking an awful risk. Billy's two-inch tap bursts fed perfectly spaced swarms of .303 rounds onto the trenches. The two remaining RCR companies fired a terrific amount of ammunition at targets seen and unseen. All the tensions and fears of that day spent trapped under the Mausers was released. It poured out their rifle barrels with a cleansing revenge. The four left-flank companies that had retreated in the night now returned in section rushes, firing as they came. The catcalls from the Nova Scotians were more punishing than the feeble Mausers. Just as the Canadian firing line reconstituted itself a white flag popped out of the Boer trenches, waving with jerky motions.

"What the hell?" George laid his hand on Billy's arm. "They're not running?"

Another white rag, then another, then a half-dozen blossomed from the silent enemy line. Canadian officers bellowed for cease fire.

"Surely the Boojers aren't quitting? Surrender?" George disapproved. One fought or one retreated, but surrender was beyond his tactical scope. The white rags now spread eastward across the entire laager. Cronje was finished. There were no British cheers, but Jack imagined he heard a long, collective sigh from thousands of weary soldiers. Silence like a heavy snowfall settled over the acres of shattered stinking battlefield. Then a hymn. Starting low and distant in the centre of the laager it spread, swelling upward and out. Five thousand Dutch voices singing devoutly and with tremendous power. They crawled from their pits and bomb shelters, walking slowly like choristers to a large, burning caravan on the north edge of the laager.

"Israel's children going into exile," Jack said, staring at the throng of Boers — mesmerized by the flowing power of the hymn.

"Hail Mary, full of grace, the Lord is with thee."

Jack turned to see if Billy was mocking them. He was not. His eyes were shut tight and he made the sign of the cross.

"Blessed art thou among women and blessed is the fruit of thy womb, Jesus.

Holy Mary, Mother of God, pray for us sinners,

Now, and at the hour of our death."

Jack closed his own eyes. The open sky above the crossing at Tintern came to him. A little girl said the Lord's Prayer inside his head. He opened his hand and there, for a moment, was his father.

The British army moved as a slow flood tide up to the Boer sangers, then over and into the shattered laager. A dozen enemy riflemen sat cross-legged near their trench while others tended a wounded man nearby. Jack was drawn to them, fascinated by the anomalies they portrayed. Heavily-bearded, dark-eyed, sombre men. But two were not men. They were smooth faced with almost feminine features — boys of no more than fifteen years. Two more were grey and wrinkled, with hard, sharp eyes. They displayed no interest in Jack, nor their wounded comrade with multiple bullet wounds in the legs — Maxim almost for certain. They sang their hymn, hunched over like medieval peasants. Everything about them was "slouch". Sagging wide-brimmed hats, sack-like jackets, baggy trousers, stained, patched and filthy — except their weapons. The Mausers were gleaming, oiled, spotless. Leather ammunition bandoleers burnished and neat. These pious serfs were the killers who had shot the cream of the British army to pieces at Magers, sniped stretcher-bearers, and withstood a hellish siege for over a week.

Jack was suddenly embarrassed. They weren't animals in the zoo. He knew not what they truly were. No longer his enemy, they were an enigma. He wanted clear of their stinking laager — away from them.

CHAPTER 12

The plain became progressively grassy and temperate with each day's easterly march. Rain fell frequently. Farms covered the land, neat treed homesteads provided occasional fresh meat to augment the starving British rations. For the mounted infantry and cavalry, the water and grass came too late. Their dead and injured horses paved the line of march. But Bobbi ate the green grass, passed prodigious gales of foul wind, and gained strength if not weight.

Men visited the "Forest Gun" to inspect Jack's bruised face and see the livid weals of the million-to-one shot. A private from Three Company actually offered to buy his tooth. The whole army knew of General Roberts' praise for the RCR attack that breached the enemy laager. Bobbi's Canadian heritage and hardy constitution became objects of discussion. Wethered confirmed Jack as corporal and even ordered him to nail one of the RCR badges to the gun limber. The machine gun section's heroics were an antidote to the loss of Colonel Lindsall who had been evacuated, half-dead, back to Cape Town.

Cronje's army was gone south to POW camps. The British army chased DeWet, confident of victory. But the Boer seemed to have lost his stomach for stand-up battles and he melted away from successive defensive lines after brief fights. Rumours of a good tented camp at Bloemfontien with full rations and rest swirled through the marching ranks. But nobody believed DeWet and Kruger would leave it undefended. Then General Roberts and a few hundred mounted infantry took it without firing a shot. Billy christened the town "Bobsfontien". That same afternoon, Jack developed a headache that became so severe it made him vomit at the end of the day's march. By sunset his eyes fluttered from the pounding agony behind in his skull. He put it down to an infection from his wound and it faded enough to let him sleep that night. He awoke before dawn, drenched in a feverish sweat. His whole body throbbed, hot and aching.

The last day's march into camp at Bloemfontien was short and started late but Jack couldn't do it. George laid him on the gun shafts and Bobbi pulled him. The headache and fever made the diagnosis easy. Every one of them had seen it a dozen times already, but neither Billy nor George would speak the word and Jack refused to admit it. A decent night's rest in the section bell tent at Bobsfontien and fresh-boiled water helped. But at morning parade, Lieutenant d'Esterre took one look at Jack's swaying, sweating body, touched his face and said, "Enteric. Private Webster, get him to the hospital double quick."

The order cut through Jack's misery. Enteric fever, not a hissing Mauser would take him. He felt it in his aching joints, in the hot sweat surging down his body. The fever was his enemy — as real as the singing Boers. More real, because they had been defeated, enteric had not.

"I'm buggered, George."

"Not. Just going for a rest in the hospital, you lucky sod."

"Buggered, just like Miles." Jack heard his own voice as though it was Miles speaking. "Where is my book? Emma gave it me. Make sure she gets it back . . . "

"Shut it, Jack-Charlie." Billy had one arm, George the other as they marched him toward town. "You keep your bloomin' officer's book so you can read while you're layin about in nice, white hospital sheets."

"And don't figure you're skipping the march to Pretoria, lad," George joined Billy's charade. "We're coming to get you — I'm not taking care of that nag. She's your responsibility."

"Whatever happens, Jack-Charlie, promise me this," Billy said solemnly, "no frigging yourself in front of the nurses."

That night on a cot in the Raadzaal hotel, now hospital, he gained another degree of raging fever. There were no nurses but it was clean and quiet and airy. For two days Jack ate bits of boiled beef and drank water to replace his sweat, thankful that he could rest his body that ached so terribly in all its joints. Sleeping was his main occupation. Each day he glowed hotter as the fever dug in, but his fear faded. Perhaps he wasn't buggered, he seemed to be holding his own.

"Last bowel movement?" The doctor materialized at his bedside.

"Oh," Jack struggled to reconstruct his time. It had been soon after Billy and George had delivered him. "I suppose nearly three days, sir."

The doctor peeled back the blanket and pushed on Jack's stomach. It was taut as a block of wood and protruded above his rib cage. Jack glared at it, suddenly alarmed. Lord, he was filling with his own filth. The doctor took his temperature, and looked at the card attached to the cot.

"One hundred and two," he said. He cast an appraising eye on Jack's belly and lifted his shirt.

"Ah yes, the rose spots! Rash is prominent."

He turned to the orderly taking notes. "Right, then. Corporal Cordey: serious enteric case; approaching crisis, about six days I should think. We'll need this bed for officers soon, so let's have him shifted now, before he begins diarrhea. Find a space anywhere in Ten general's west tents."

He moved on to the next cot. Jack gently probed his gut. He felt the pink rash on his chest and to nobody in particular he said, "I am buggered, then."

The next morning he was ordered out of the Raadzaal. He dressed laboriously. Bending to put on his boots produced agony in his distended belly. Wrapping his calves in puttees was a major effort that left him dizzy. The orderly led him from the hotel toward a huge cluster of bell tents on the edge of town, a half-mile distant. The morning sun was weak but it burned like a flare in Jack's watering eyes, forcing him to squint. The orderly was accustomed to enteric men; he stopped to let Jack rest every two hundred yards and eventually they arrived at the tent lines. The orderly entered a square tent for instructions. He reappeared with a medical corps warrant officer who sported extravagantly-waxed, walrus moustaches.

"Treatment card," the warrant officer snapped.

Jack passed him the card.

"Get your heels together and pull your chin up. You're still a soldier no matter how sick. I've seen worse, my boy. Now, then, sick parade every morning eight o'clock. Stand by your tent, belts and helmets."

Jack came to attention, very conscious of the sharp pain it produced in his neck and upper spine. The warrant read his card, moustache twitching as he mouthed the words.

"Ah, near crisis, I see." He glanced disapprovingly at Jack as though this was a great inconvenience in the efficient operation of the hospital. "Stand at ease, Corporal Cordey. You're excused sick parade until you're past the crisis — assuming you survive it, of course."

He wrote a section and tent number on the card then sent them on their way. They passed through a half-dozen, long rows of bell tents and stopped at one on the outer edge of the hospital camp.

"You're in luck, by jove." The orderly pointed to a six-foot-high burlap screen erected just beyond Jack's tent. "Latrine's next door. Handy when you start the shits."

He preceded Jack into the tent. It was dim and stifling hot, heavy with the smell of canvas and foul, body odours. A thin, trampled layer of dirty straw covered the floor. Seven men lay on their ground sheets, feet to the centre pole, heads radiating to the circumference of the canvas walls. Jack spread his rubber sheet in an open space, covered it with his blanket and sat down, too exhausted to fully comprehend the bleakness of his new ward.

"Morning inspection for bed cases," the orderly said, "kit must be folded and piled at the foot of your bed . . . "

"Bed?" Jack shifted gingerly on the hard ground, sliding his bedding into a hip hollow that must have been dug by the previous patient.

" . . . helmet on top, facing front. Boots laced and placed toes out before the kit. Sar'nt Major is fussy," the orderly finished laconically. "Here's a tip, Gloster. Strip to shirt, trousers and stockings. You're allowed out to the latrine in that so leave your tunic, hat, boots and belts alone. Then you don't have to keep sorting your gear for inspection."

He left. Jack did as he had suggested, carefully folding his clothes and arranging his haversack. He removed Emma's Christmas gift and slipped it under his blanket. Before he'd finished, one of the men darted from the tent, fumbling with his flies, quietly cursing. Three others lay curled on their sides, sleeping. Two more were dozing but restless, muttering short, low grunts, twitching. The last, seventh man, lay flat on his back, nearest the door. His skin was pallid but looked as though someone had rouged his cheeks. His trousers were damp — obviously just washed — and it was he that stank so badly. Feeble from the journey, Jack lay back. His hips and shoulders found grooves in the earth. For this small mercy, his aching body was grateful. He thought about reading some Hardy but found himself falling asleep.

The three convalescent men in Jack's tent stood to sick parade the next morning without the least bit of conversation. The two twitchers seemed scarcely conscious and the man with diarrhea stayed sleeping. There was no comradery. There were no introductions. Each man conserved his energy to face the enteric. Jack felt no urge to break this condition. His fever burned worse than ever. He was desperately weak and completely apathetic of his fellow sufferers. After nearly forty minutes, the warrant officer arrived with his team of orderlies. He quickly inspected the three convalescents then poked his head inside the tent. His eyes darted to their kit arrangements, searching for infractions. At this very instant the "rouged man" released a long, wheezing groan. His body bubbled; Jack leaned up on one elbow to see what could cause such a sound. Blood, streaked yellow, pooled beneath the wretched soldier.

The warrant knelt and picked up the man's wrist, feeling for a pulse. He repeated the search on the man's neck, than called for two orderlies. They wrapped the "rouge man" in his ground sheet and carried his shrouded body outside. It's smell wafted through the tent. The warrant officer collected his treatment card. A quarter of an hour later a cape cart and donkey appeared. Soldiers loaded the corpse onto the cart where three others already lay. The night's dead. Somehow, horror though it had been, Miles' end seemed better in comparison to this process of men rotting to death. That afternoon Jack's bowels began to explode. Amazed at his hidden strength, he ran to the latrine with time to spare. His return to the tent, stocking feet stumbling down the gravelled path, was much slower.

Two convalescents departed the next day and one relapsed into a deep fever. The twitchers passed their crisis successfully. They lay bright-eyed and weak, but relieved. They had passed the trial. Jack and the other diarrhea man ran alternating laps to the latrines. Jack was entirely successful at this for two full days. The other man failed thrice and had the added work of washing his pants. A new patient joined them but, because his fever was just beginning, he was relatively strong. He tried conversation but Jack could not muster the energy to reply. He was now to the point where he couldn't find three consecutive hours sleep without his bowels interfering.

"I'm buggered."

The words came to him every time he thought of the "rouge man". He dreamed but little. His few waking hours not spent hunched and shuddering over the rough latrine planks were used for quiet contemplation. He found that he could concentrate on one simple thing, and bring it to life: Emma's face under a straw hat; or Vi's flower bed; or a passage from *The Mayor of Casterbridge*.

One evening of late summer . . . a young man and woman, the latter carrying a child, were approaching the large village of Weydon-Priors on foot. He treasured these moments of release from the racking diarrhea and sweating fever.

He returned to the tent from the latrine one night and found his aches were greatly diminished. He actually snuggled into his blanket and felt cool. Rain tapped gently on the canvas above him and his mind flushed its misery away. He stared into the dark and there, in his mind's eye, was Newland church — Cathedral of the Forest — frosted white with Christmas snow. He watched Emma and her parents enter the church. She was lovely, more lovely than he'd ever remembered her. Then they were seated before the Vicar's fireplace and she gave him his Christmas present. He reached out into the dark tent, knowing she wasn't there, of course, but indulging the fantasy, he took it. He unwrapped it and began to read. Good old Hardy. Excellent Hardy. England. Sturdy folk, stories of love and loss, honesty and vanity. The simple joys of rural life. Emma read to him. Her voice clear and sweet. He read to her until his voice was dry and his throat sore. She brought him a glass of cool water. It was clean and fresh. He drank eagerly.

"Thank you, Emma my dear. Thank you, Emma my love."

"'Ee's orf 'is blinkin' 'ead," Emma said, frowning. Her voice was no longer sweet, but rough and uncaring. He reached for the book and began to read again, glancing nervously at her.

"Oo is this bleedin' man?" she said. His Emma, but not his perhaps? A terrible fear seized him and tears flooded his eyes.

"It's me, Emma! Jack, not Charlie. Don't be angry. I'm Jack, *not* Charlie. You love me!"

She smiled and took the book. She read, her voice sweet and feminine again.

• • •

He awoke but only one eye would open, the other was crusted over with dried mucus. How long had he slept — the whole night apparently. Without a bowel movement? He felt his backside, expecting to find a pea-soup mess, but his trousers were dry. The diarrhea had ended or slowed dramatically, yet he'd had no crisis. Would he be spared the twitching, fever-ravaged delirium of the "typhoid state"? He pulled back the blanket and sat up, met a swirling wave of disorientation, and fell back with a thump.

"Lover boy's alive!" A new man sitting beside Jack called to an orderly who was standing outside the tent. He entered and laughed, not unkindly.

"Well, my sweet, don't you look like death's last embrace." He knelt by Jack's head, poured water from Jack's bottle over a grubby hanky, and swabbed the crusted eye until it flickered open.

"Lover boy?" Jack croaked, shocked at the weak mew that had replaced his own voice. His tongue was thick, heavily coated with a sludge he had to chew and swallow.

"You've been callin' me 'Emma dear' for two days, you blinkin' barstid," the orderly said good-naturedly. "Beggin' me to read a Hardy and then asking for a kiss."

He propped Jack up for a sip of water. "When your crisis went into its second day, everyone figured you'd pop yer clogs. I took shilling bets at five to one, then eight to one. Told 'em my sweetheart wouldn't desert me, and damned if you didn't. You just won me fifty-seven shillings, Cordey — good on you."

Jack tilted his head, looking for his latrine partner. He lay still, pallid, with rouged cheeks. The orderly followed his gaze.

"Pal of yours?"

Jack shook his head. He scarcely remembered anything about the man except that he had red hair. His buttocks were covered in curly red fuzz that had rippled as the man shook with diarrhoea on the plank next to him. What . . . two days ago now, apparently.

"Cavalryman — Inniskillings. 'E's rode his last 'orse." The orderly shook his head. "Be dead before tomorrow's done. Still, cheer up dearie, you've beat it. Another week or so and you'll be up an' about."

Shattered in body but no longer in spirit, Jack felt hope return. He was unable to move the tiniest amount without panting from the exertion. Washing his cloudy eye was a major task. A half-dozen orderlies visited him, checked his card, then left cursing to pay their gambling losses. A doctor took his temperature, back down to 101 from 104, and pronounced him lucky to be alive. He noted two weeks of further "bed" rest on the treatment card, then added one more word: invalid. A series of sharp, itchy spots had appeared on Jack's armpits and groin. He pointed these out to the doctor, fearing a relapse, a return of the rose spots. The doctor smiled, not rose spots. The straw in their tent should have been changed, the doctor mused, but hardly any point now that it was lousy. Lice wouldn't be got rid of now they'd found a home.

"Not buggered, then," Jack said to himself, smiling. Invalid meant unfit for further service. He would be going home.

• • •

He leaned against the railing at the ship's waist. Still twenty pounds underweight, he needed the railing if he was to stand for any length of time. But he wanted this view. He memorized it. The bay was calm, dotted with transport ships, sitting on the flat, metallic water like toys on a pond. Table Mountain reared above them, glowing in the sunset. Above it soared a range of pink, billowing cumulous clouds that might have jumped there from a Constable painting. The ships were bringing horses and yeomanry and volunteers. The new war had started even before Bobs marched into Pretoria last week. Jack's war was over. He already felt it slipping away. No more infantry fixing bayonets and charging the wicked Mausers or thumping artillery. It was all mounted men dashing across the landscape ambushing each other. He wondered if any of his old friends from the Gloucester Volunteer Battalion were right now waiting to disembark.

The new war was turning "nasty", "ungentlemanly", according to the newspapers he'd read while waiting in the transit camp at Sea Point. The incoming volunteers he'd met complained strongly about cramming fifteen to a tent and getting only boiled beef and that only once a day. They'd probed him about his facial scars. They wanted to know about Paardeberg and tactics and the high

226

explosive effects of lyddite. He tried to tell them about Miles' head and lying in the mud helpless as worms under the Mauser rain, but soon realized that he couldn't explain those experiences. They didn't want to hear it. He did tell them about boiling water and enteric but they had no interest in disease. They would fight and prevail — or die valiantly — galloping over the veldt. They would be the hard warriors. They would not croak as putrid rouge men in a dirty tent.

So he relented. He showed them his tooth; talked of Colonel Aldworth's heroic death; advised them to ask for Canadian horses; contrasted the Lee Metford versus the Mauser, and agreed that they would make excellent warriors who would soon teach DeWet and Botha a lesson. Then he sought and maintained the company of other wounded invalids going home.

The new men would learn their lessons from DeWet and Botha and Africa itself; he could not be their teacher.

There were plenty of empty return ships so the assembled crowd of sick and crippled were soon manifested and boarded on the RMSS *Guelph*. She'd brought nine hundred Connaught Rangers out and was taking five hundred broken men home. Palmer was on board the *Guelph*. His shattered knee had nearly healed when gangrene invaded and they had lopped the leg off at mid thigh. He forced a friendly "comrades-in-arms" style with Jack, but it cost him. He was terrified of going home a cripple. His trade as warehouseman on the Bristol docks had been lopped off with his leg. He was angry about Jack's corporal stripes. Then he was bitter when Jack blundered, saying he didn't care about the damned hooks. Each time he greeted Jack, he had to swallow fear, anger, and bitterness. Jack stayed clear of him.

But that would all end with the ebb tide tonight. Just as it had begun with the ebb tide at Liverpool, nearly six months earlier. Right now he would memorize Table Bay. He would pray for Billy,

George, Palmer and Wethered. He would stroke Canadian Bobbi's nose in his imagination. He would feel the Mauser bullet in his mouth and be proud that he went four weeks with the enteric and never shit his pants once. Tomorrow morning he would remove Emma's creased, dirt-glazed letter from his tunic pocket and study it like the new testament. He would read Hardy on deck in the sea air. He would eat the good, plentiful food the sailors provided. He would stifle his own mounting fear of going home. Africa, war, hardship had become facile. Survive the day was no longer good enough. He had to leave Jack-Charlie Cordey in Table Bay and go home to become John Thornton.

CHAPTER 13

England — 1900

His mother, Wyn, and even Vi swarmed over him with food, non-stop conversation and nursing excesses. The first two weeks home he absorbed every morsel, every word, every caress. He sat for hours in the garden, breathing the flowered air in the English, July sun. Compared to the Karoo sun, it was nothing but a warm, friendly light. It scarcely touched his rough, brown hide. He couldn't get enough green: woods of oak, hazel, chestnut, pine; bright grass; shrubs, all thick luxuriant and close — so comforting after the brown empty wastes of Africa. Thoughts lodged in his head and stuck there, unmoving for hours. One whole afternoon he contemplated the fact that he'd experienced two summers in the space of the last seven months. He spent hours looking at a picture of Emma that the Vicar gave him. She was in London, unaware of his return. The wise Reverend Wilson simply gave him the photo and a slip of paper with her address. He said no more of her.

The Vicar was a relief from the hovering women. He prattled about hay crops — bad this year — oat crops — worse this year and Bobbi, who had kicked the living daylights out of a new trap she didn't like. He asked nothing about Jack's South Africa. He ranted about the general election, called it the "Khaki Election", and the insane jingoism that gripped the country. Some Liberal MPs had formed an anti-war cell in the House of Commons; how he admired them. He was a staunch Liberal, following the tradition of the Gladstone virtues and he deplored the imperialists like Haldane and Asquith. He called them "Limps" — liberal imperialists — and swore they would break the party. Then he hastened to add that he had equal sympathy for the poor soldiers forced to fight Cecil Rhodes' private war. Jack made no comment and the Vicar was instantly embarrassed, assuming he'd given offence. So Jack showed him his tooth and told him of the million-to-one shot. The Vicar cheered up and departed without offering Jack his old job back — which was also a great relief.

Vi and his mother pretended Jack's attempt to clear their "debt" never happened. They wanted him safely imprisoned on the Vicar's farm. The Vicar knew Jack was for London and for Emma. But even he did not know of Jack's fears. Charlie did. Charlie smelled it five minutes after they met in the Ostrich. Nearly smothered at Offa's Rose by the end of July and restored physically, Jack walked to Newland in the early afternoon. It was his first real attempt to confront his fears of the future. They drank more pints than Jack could count, yet he stayed moderately sober. He told Charlie about the machine gun section and Canadian Bobbi. Charlie listened to the enteric story, commenting tersely that he'd suffered dysentery in India — damning the army medical corps. Charlie asked about the empty battlefields where death was a whistling, unseen bullet. And, in the end, when he lay in his old bed over Mrs. Toomey's kitchen that night, Charlie finally said what Jack had prayed for.

"Thornton," Charlie's voice came out of the darkness, hoarse. "She wants you. And I can't have her."

• • •

Jack moved to small lodgings in Chepstow in August. He started work as a temporary recording and correspondence clerk for Sir Harold Brakspear. It was a low, cleric job, no responsibility, merely an assistant to the senior clerk. The original man had gone for drink and been dismissed; Jack would take his place until the summer restoration survey was wrapped up. Jack reacquired his writing hand quickly and by mid October when the contract ended, he'd made a strong impression. Perhaps he'd only looked good because his predecessor was so dismal, but it produced a solid reference from Sir Harold himself and a glowing one from the senior. It allayed his fear of reinventing himself as a middle-class city man — he was competent.

The war was winnowing thousands of bored young men out of their jobs and into the yeomanry and volunteer mounted infantry, now in great demand in Africa. As a result, clerk positions were available and well-paid in London. He applied to two positions and received replies within a fortnight. Based on Vicar Wilson's and Brakspear's references, he could have the position at an export-import firm in Lombard Street at nine pound, six shillings per week or, based on the references and subject to an interview and civil service examination, he could start at the Colonial Office at six pound, ten shillings per week. His commerce background, and the extra money, drew him to the private firm on Lombard. Then he thought of Emma's father, prominent at Whitehall, and he let the Colonial Office prestige sway him. He'd try there first. It only took two days to settle his affairs. He paid a last visit to his mother and arranged for his savings to be forwarded by draft to London. His final pay from the army had still not arrived. When it did, it would be made out to Charles Cordey. Charlie agreed to cash it and give half to Jack's mother, the other half forwarded to Jack's London account. Jack felt not the tiniest flicker of apprehension with these arrangements. Charlie was a flash lad with feed bills and petty cash, but he'd not touch a penny of Jack's Africa money. That was certain.

• • •

An Englishman born and bred, Jack Thornton had never been to London. Its size shocked him. A penny street map purchased at the station in Reading unfolded into a distressingly large puzzle. It took him twenty minutes to find the Colonial Office address, even though it was near Whitehall and St. James Park which were prominent on the map. Then lodgings — what would it cost to live in such a place? Where would one live? His initial confidence in going to London was shaken. He'd trekked across Africa on half-rations, had his face shot and survived enteric — surely he'd find a place to live. He dug into his valise and retrieved both his Gloster Sphinx and the RCR badge. He put them in his waistcoat pockets as touchstones. Now, a plan of attack. He began studying the map, measuring distances, and marking his route. He left most of his luggage at Paddington Station and set off in the early afternoon, map in one hand, small valise in the other. His plan was to set course directly for the Colonial Offices. Cutting southeast through Hyde Park, past Buckingham Palace, and across St. James Park he would strike them at King Charles Street. No more than three miles. In cool, dry, October weather it would be less than an hour's march. It took him nearly two hours. Not because he became lost or misjudged the distance, but because he couldn't stop himself from pausing to gawk at the swells riding the Row, or the Palace, or just the mass of people. People of all dress, class, and shade of character. Carriages, cabs, drays, omnibuses without numbers rushing and rumbling like a flooding river.

Having finally arrived at the quadrangle of government buildings he permitted himself a smug grin. "John Thornton," he said out loud. "Colonial Office." By heavens, it sounded well, but not quite right. "Jack Thornton," he said again, "Colonial Office." That was better, Jack it was. He circled the buildings via Whitehall and Downing Street to fix the place in his mind. Main objective reached, he now struck off northward in search of a modest hotel or boarding house. He would take temporary lodgings for a week. This would allow him to buy some decent clothes tomorrow, interview the next day and, if successful, be within a short walk of his new job. Then he could take advice from other clerks for more permanent rooms.

Up Whitehall, the famous city rolled past him. Horse Guards, the Banqueting House, Trafalgar Square, Leicester Square. Each place name so familiar, yet so new and exciting. The theatres in Leicester Square, the Empire and the Alhambra — Emma had talked with great excitement about seeing *The Pirates of Penzance* there. They were quiet now in mid afternoon, but think of the excitement this evening and every evening. He grinned, thrilled with the thought that one day soon he might escort Emma to the theatre. He crossed to Piccadilly and looked west, imagining he could see Chelsea, see Emma. A loudly cursing drayman bellowed to clear the street and Jack leapt off the pavement as the Burton Ale cart rumbled past. What would she think if she knew he was here, two miles from her house? Following this thought, he walked west then turned right up a broad street with hotel signs. They were a little too grand. He continued past them and turned right again. Gerrard Street was sheltered from the continuous thunder of Piccadilly. The first hotel seemed just the thing.

Quality Rooms — Modest Rates, the painted first floor window declared. He entered and was immediately confronted by a wood and glass cage with a metal wicket. It housed an older man with a long, dark beard who smoked a pipe and was immersed in a newspaper.

"Excuse me, but I'd like to enquire of a room."

The pipe puffed more quickly and a pair of apathetic, liquid-brown eyes peered over the paper.

"Little early, aren't you?"

"Well, ah, early?" Jack missed the man's meaning. "Are your rooms not made up yet?"

The rheumy eyes peered past Jack, looking for something. "Half a crown an hour's the rate."

"Hour? But I'll need at least two or three nights."

The eyelids fluttered, the eyes developed an amused crinkle. "Made of steel are ye then, sir? Figure you're up to that course?"

Jack's dumfounded expression elicited a cackling laugh, the pipe was removed and the paper set down.

"Where's your lady, sir? She must be a real trotter."

"Lady? Why, I'm alone of course. Listen, what the devil are you . . . "

Jack stopped himself, flushed a throbbing shade of red, and made a closer inspection of the lobby. "Good Lord," he muttered. "Lady . . . hourly rates, this is a . . . "

"Don't be disrespectful, now!" The man was enjoying himself. "What goes on in our rooms is none of management's business. No girls actually reside here, see? We run a good establishment. Decent food and good wine with the utmost of discreet service is our motto."

Jack fled, all his new-found, worldly confidence badly battered. Not even half a day in London and he'd visited a knocking shop. In the end, he found a real room off Great Portland Street nearly back to Paddington. Exhausted from the long day, he settled for sausages and a pint in a public house, and paid a boy with a cart to fetch his bags from the station. That night he climbed to the top floor and gazed south from the landing window. London, shining in a late October moon. Emma. His future. It was good enough for his first day back in the world.

• • •

"Swinglehurst," the smart, blond young man strode across the anteroom, hand extended. "Edmund, actually. The old chap must have been well in his cups when he came up with that. Why not Edward, I ask?"

"I'm Thornton." Jack shook. "Here to apply for the vacancy in the office of the Under Secretary . . . "

"Yes, of course you are. You'll be working with me, I'll show you the ropes."

"Well I haven't done my interview or examination yet, so that might be a trifle premature."

Swinglehurst was taken aback. "Interview? Exam? Good heavens, laddie, mere formalities."

Jack knew the civil service interviews and examinations were arduous and fickle. Still, it was nice of Swinglehurst to try to put him at ease.

Edmund was now staring openly at his face. "What are these craters in your cheeks — surely not your wound? At Paardeberg?"

"Shot through and through — Mauser five hundred yards," Jack recited this short litany. It pleased the curious and usually ended the "wound" conversation. "How did you know I'd been wounded at Paardeberg?"

"Read your application o' course. Pinched it from the guvnor's desk whilst he was out of the office. He said we had a wounded Gloster officer enquiring and I wanted to get a sense of you before I bagged you for our crib."

"See here now — "

"Oh huff and puff later," Swinglehurst punched him on the shoulder. "We've been short-staffed for three months now. I'm supposed to have two assistant clerks and I have none. Not a decent chap to be had. All gone to the stockbroker firms, or insurance thingies, or to Africa. In the present climate and government we

hire any returned hero from the veldt — some right duds too —
but when I saw your papers I said *that's* the one for us!"

He guided Jack across the room to a closed door while he
explained this outrageous behaviour. Edmund rapped twice on the
door and ushered Jack in.

A man of about forty years, elegantly dressed and peering from
under immensely bushy eyebrows watched them enter.

"Thornton, sir." Edmund bowed slightly, in earnest or mocking
Jack couldn't tell. He inclined his head, following suit.

The heavy eyebrows raised in query.

"The Gloster officer, wounded at Paardeberg —"

"Actually," Jack cleared his throat. "Sir, I was wounded at
Paardeberg but . . ." He faltered. But what? I was a corporal
because my sergeant got his head blown off and the real corporal,
an illiterate Forest miner, was too smart to take the hooks? What
good would that do him? Losing this job over an army rank that
was now gone. What difference corporal or major general.

"But I was invalided because of enteric. The, ah, wound was a
comparative trifle."

The eyebrows raised again as if to say, "be quiet and get on with
it." Edmund did.

"Knew you'd want to interview immediately, sir. Take action
promptly as you always remind us."

The eyebrows lowered into a frown.

"As I was saying: Thornton; wounded at Paardeberg; three years
experience as senior clerk in a Gloucester firm; agriculture
management experience; assistant to Sir Harold Brakspear at
Tintern. Excellent references, I understand."

Edmund paused, beaming at his superior. "Thornton's father,
sadly deceased, M.A., chapter man of Gloucester Cathedral.
Mother from the Cordey's of Gloucestershire, prominent in
mining."

Jack winced at that. Charlie's description of grandfather as a butty man simply wouldn't have done. Still, 'prominent in mining' sounded awfully like a straight lie when spoken out loud. The eyebrows flickered. A clock ticked. Was he supposed to speak? He glanced to Swinglehurst for a clue. Edmund shook his head ever so slightly. Eventually the older man rose, rounded the desk and inspected him.

"Lapels," he said, flipping the collar of Jack's suit coat. "Carry on, Swinglehurst."

He returned to his desk. Edmund tugged Jack's sleeve and they exited.

"Mining, eh?" Edmund arched his own eyebrow. "That was the tricky bit. Still, McKennitt's happy with it, so there." He rubbed his hands together. "Interview complete. Now let's get the examination done and we'll away for early luncheon."

"That was Mr. McKennitt? Jack grabbed his new partner's coattail, stopping his rush down an adjoining corridor. "That was my interview?"

"Yes, old boy. Gruelling, I know, but you've come through it now, so buck up, eh?"

"You're not serious?"

The bland face sobered. Edmund tapped Jack on the chest with his forefinger. "Deadly earnest. Here's how it will work. We go back to our office. I help you write your examination, if you need me that is. You score high to please the old feller back there. Then you work like a cart horse to clear our backlog. Then I get my social life back. I haven't been clear of this beastly place, except to sleep, for near on a fortnight. You really can do the job can't you? I won't be carrying you, will I?"

"Well, yes, I can do the work, but . . . "

The happy grin flourished on Edmund's face again. "All's well then! Lunch will be quick today. We'll have to get you some decent togs. Nearly sank your interview with that outfit. Salesman saw you coming a mile off. Shoes are good, but the rest . . . "

Jack clutched self-consciously at his tie, straightening it. This fellow looked at him as he once regarded an old man in the Ostrich.

"Where'd you buy that kit?"

"Regent Street, yesterday," Jack replied.

"Off the rack?

"Yes.

"Got the receipt?"

"Yes," Jack touched his wallet.

"Excellent! We'll nip over, return that shocking disaster, tick off the shop chappie, and bully him into a decent suit at half the price."

Swinglehurst swept off, hailing another young man in the corridor. "Jimmy! Here, look what I've got! A Thornton! War hero to be sure. He's galloped in to reinforce my beleaguered outpost. Just in the nick of time, I can tell you."

• • •

Edmund and Jack worked very hard indeed for the next six days to clear the office backlog. No church, no Emma, no dining, no evening entertainments and precious little chit chat. On the seventh day they rested, briefly. Edmund unashamedly reviewed Jack's finances and decided what would best suit for accommodations, then moved him into rooms on the second floor of a very respectable and comfortable house in Hampstead. He showed Jack which train to catch — but "don't let the guvnor catch you on an omnibus between the station and Whitehall or there would be hell to pay." The suit had been a near run thing. Riding an omni with the common herd, well! Safest to walk or take a cab. They tidied up work on Friday, and Saturday, at noon, they departed for a proper break. Edmund claimed he would not sleep until Monday

— he had a shocking load of fun to be got through. Jack, nervous as a cat, found his unfamiliar way back to Hampstead and peered fearfully at his rug as he opened the door to his rooms.

An envelope addressed in Emma's hand lay on the floor. He'd written last night, mailed early this morning, and waited on pins and needles all day. He opened. She was delighted with a row of exclamation marks. He was to come for tea today — no possible excuse would be accepted.

CHAPTER 14

Even Jack, new to London, sensed the change after he passed westbound through Sloane Square. Chelsea was splendid, but not as splendid as Belgravia. The Wilson house, three stories of white-stone solid respectability, could not be considered grand. He stood outside, looking up, trying to guess which window was Emma's room. Emma's bedroom, where she undressed each night. That notion lingered much longer than it should have. He drew a huge breath of cool air, tasting the early-evening fog, to clear his head. The door was painted navy blue, the brass pull knob had a W engraved on it. He swallowed this, his last fear, and rang.

"Good afternoon." A man answered the door — tall, slim, imperious — butler or footman? Jack had no notion.

"Good day, I'm calling on Miss Emma Wilson."

The servant swung the door open and ushered Jack into a black and white tiled entry hall strewn with potted ferns. He extended his hand.

"Shall I pass your card on to Miss Wilson, sir?"

"Card?"

The man's face was stone but he paused just a heartbeat longer than necessary to convey his disapproval.

"No card then, sir?"

Jack shook his head.

"Who shall I say is calling, sir?"

"Jack, ah, Jack Thornton, that is." Damn this London bully and damn me for acting like an oaf, he thought. "She's expecting me."

"Very good, sir."

The servant glided across the tiles to a double set of mahogany doors. He knocked, entered, and reappeared a moment later to take Jack's hat and coat. Jack followed him through the doors. Mrs. Wilson perched on a settee. Mr. Wilson stood, back to the fireplace with a young man. The room was warm, cheerfully lit, and inhabited by a scrum of overstuffed leather furniture. These things registered somewhere in the back of his mind, but not consciously because, in that instant, Emma took him physically and mentally. Green eyes, open wide and locked on his. The curve of freckled cheek; slender neck sheathed in high, lace collar; clear, wide forehead with hair swept back from it. Her lips were parted slightly, unlike his own mouth that gaped. She was seated beside her mother. He might have leaped over the couch or vaulted the wingback chair. He wasn't aware of his own movements, but he appeared in front of her. The genesis of a grin hooked the corners of her mouth but she froze it. Her eyes had not left his. Had she blinked he might have fallen down. Otherwise, she retained the pose of a young lady waiting for tea in the morning room. Jack clapped his mouth shut with an effort. They stared at each other.

"I say, are you quite well, Thornton?" Mr. Wilson's voice hovered on the edge of indignation. Jack should have greeted Mrs. Wilson, shaken Mr.'s hand, acknowledged the stranger. He should still do these things, but for the moment, he could not. Emma looked away, releasing him from the hypnosis.

"Mr. Thornton. How lovely. You remember my mother?"

He lurched through the formalities, learning the young man's name, then forgetting it instantly. He managed to trip over the furniture twice and nearly swore. It was as though a corner of the room had caught fire and he was not permitted to acknowledge the flames roasting his face.

" . . . Colonial Office rather desperate straights these days, vacancies occurring by the hour?"

Blast, he'd been peeking at Emma again. What was the question? Vacancies.

"Yes. Short-handed. I've only been there a week and up to my bloody neck in it already, sir."

The young man smirked. Wilson puffed his cheeks. Mrs. Wilson looked coyly into the carpet. Emma's grin broke loose for a moment before she reined it in. What was so funny? What now?

"Ladies present, Thornton, moderate your language," Wilson murmured.

Jack ran his last words back through his mind. Oh Lord! What was wrong with him?

"Mrs. Wilson, Miss Wilson," he yelped. "I'm so very sorry. I can't think what came over me. Perhaps it's the residue of the army — no excuse — so sorry."

"County Regiment?" the young man said, as though this explained coarse behaviour.

"Glosters — Second Battalion. Old Sixty-first Foot. Went out to Africa in January."

"Of course." He tipped his eyes down his nose. "How come you're back to England so soon?"

"Invalided out — rather bad case of enteric. But I've been lucky enough to recover fully."

"Enteric?" The man turned toward Emma and Mrs. Wilson. "Tommy doesn't know any better, of course, but I'd have thought," he turned back to face Jack, "the officers would drink clean or boiled water."

Mr. Wilson came in like a terrier down a rat hole. "Oh, Jack went out as a private soldier, Mr. Warden." He smiled.

Warden, that was the name. Warden glanced significantly at Emma. "Not yeomanry volunteer but an actual infantry soldier . . . County Regiment."

Jack, finally aware of how badly he was faring, could only answer, "Yes."

"Mr. Warden is going next month. Volunteer mounted company from the Fusiliers — top-notch men from the city — crack outfit." Mr. Wilson bored in. "Warden accepted a position as ensign, but I'm certain he'll climb higher." He looked from Warden to Emma and back to Warden. "We shall miss him when he goes."

"Well, service is the thing, as far as I'm concerned." Warden coughed politely. "Give the Boer a right good hiding, put him back in line. Clear it up smartish, that's the ticket. Of course, mounted men," he paused to glance at Jack's infantryman feet, "intelligent and capable of independent action are what's required."

"Do you agree, Jack?" Mr. Wilson again.

"Absolutely. War's changed since Paardeberg." He paused on "Paardeberg". "We simply marched in, shot it out with Johnny Boer and took our chances. Much more complex now. Apparently, it's all ambush and raid. Ride into a Boer farm at night, burn out the women and children, then dash away. Definitely a job for intelligent, independent mounted volunteers."

Warden chewed his lower lip as though it was a beefsteak. Mr. Wilson mottled his face an angry shade of red but, unwilling to admit a setback, rather lamely tried the enteric gambit again.

"Glosters were at Paardeberg — famous victory — heard all about it, of course. PM made a speech in the house, especially singled out the Canadian volunteers for the final push. I suppose, enteric and all, you were too sick to see much of the victory?"

Jack hesitated, pondering this opportunity. He could crush right now, of course. The machine gun section he had commanded, well, George actually, had been critical to the famous Canadian success. But how would it sound? Like bragging — implausible — a lie or extreme boast. He'd already offended enough for one day.

"No, sir. Actually I went sick at Bloemfontien after Paardeberg. Modder water got me, should have been more careful with the boiling."

Warden beamed with self-satisfaction, inclining his head toward Emma, who frowned again.

"Then you did see action, Mr. Thornton?" Emma asked. "You must have fought at Paardeberg." His fire in the corner burned brightly for him.

"Well, yes. We spent a couple of uncomfortable hours playing targets for Cronje's practise." He smiled his gratitude at her and nearly went back into his green-eye trance.

"Oh, I say!" Emma rose and walked to Jack's side, examining his face. He smelled her powder, then a swirl of delicate perfume. He counted the freckles on the bridge of her nose.

" . . . fever caused it?"

Blast! He'd done it again. Fever caused what? They watched him expectantly. Emma edged closer, concern on her face, one finger poised over the scar on his left cheek. The wounds!

"Ah, there you mean?" He touched both marks.

"Why! There are two! How extraordinary, like dimples," she laughed. He laughed and inhaled her scent.

"No, not fever. Fever doesn't leave scars like that. This was a Mauser. We were under heavy fire. Sergeant shot through the forehead, dead. Loader's knee blown off." He found himself speaking honestly, without his usual reserve. He wanted to tell her everything he knew. "I was calling for my horse when a Boer shot me. The lads called it a million-to-one shot — through and through — from five hundred yards out. Knocked out one tooth, ventilated my chops, but not much else."

"Jack!" Emma touched his face. He nearly swooned. "How awful, it must have hurt horribly."

"Bled like a broken tap. Spitting blood like a fountain but otherwise not too — "

"Mr. Thornton, please!" Wilson was gesturing toward his wife who was pretending to be shocked but was actually on the edge of her seat, listening intently. Warden, however, looked genuinely peaky.

"Sorry." Jack pushed his face against Emma's fingertips. Her eyes sparkled with surprise for an instant. Then she withdrew her hand and returned to her seat. Warden recovered his colour but fell quiet.

"Lily Hampton's son was at Colenso." Mrs. Wilson, quite animated now, spoke up. "Not wounded . . . " disappointment crept into her voice. "But he sent her home a souvenir. From one of the Mausers we hear so much about — an empty casing with her initial carved into the brass."

"Well Jack," Emma said with feigned displeasure. "Here you are in person and not a single souvenir for us."

"But I do have something for you." He whipped the RCR badge from his waistcoat hurrying toward her, then he stopped, conscious that he'd blundered yet again. "Well, nothing, really," he palmed the badge. "Best not, perhaps. No right really, to bring you presents . . . "

"I should say not, young man." Mrs. Wilson snapped. "That may be acceptable in the Dean Forest but in London, strangers do *not* give respectable young women — "

"Mama, I must have it." She was so bright, so alive, so awfully real and desirable. A blooming flower in a winter garden. "Jack's not a stranger — you can't tease me like that!"

He looked to Mrs. Wilson.

"I suppose, so long as it's just a trifle."

He gave Emma the badge.

"It's lovely. What regiment?"

"Royal Canadian Regiment. I was with them, actually at Paardeberg when I was wounded. Rather a long, complicated story, I'm afraid."

Mrs. Wilson looked at him, not unkindly. A conquering hero might be tolerated.

"One of their sergeants gave it to me as a sort of thank you. Now I give it to you." He said this much too earnestly. Emma grinned broadly, rose, and planted a kiss on each wounded cheek. This time he did swoon, stumbling against a footstool and nearly wiping a row of china figurines from the side table. Mr. Wilson blanched and cast a frightened look to his wife.

• • •

When the tea came, it might as well have been undiluted army rum, for Jack was intoxicated. Emma contrived to have him sit beside her on the settee — Mr. Wilson contrived to have Warden sit on Emma's other side. Warden held the conversation and was, as best Jack could remember, quite witty and at times even entertaining. Jack either seemed too stunned to answer simple questions or else discomfited everyone with honest answers. Emma's mother stole occasional glances at him, at his wounds, more particularly, as though they compensated for his lack of grace. Her father cut him dead. Jack's war record — wounded with the wildly popular colonial troops in Britain's one clear victory — was a direct affront to Mr. Warden. Warden was a junior at Whitehall serving under Wilson. He was obviously to be matched with Emma — a safe match. Jack was supposed to have made Warden look good, not leer at his daughter. Jack saw these things quite clearly later when he sobered up, but for the moment they were well beyond his fuddled mind. His hip was less than two inches from Emma's. He measured it with his eye, carefully, so he could recall it and hug it to himself later. Every breath he took was her scent. The hair drawn back from her face, her voice — deep for a society woman, her gurgling laugh, but especially her spirit swamped him. He was sitting much too close to the fire and she burned him to a crisp.

Tea consumed, Warden rose to take his leave. Jack shook hands and wished him luck. A long, very awkward silence settled into the morning room after Warden's departure. A maid cleared the tea dishes. Mr. Wilson consulted his watch twice, tapping it — then holding it close to his ear the second time. Mrs. Wilson said, quite loudly, that she should have a short nap before dinner. Jack stood stupidly by the mantelpiece, eyes flickering toward Emma, completely oblivious to the hints. She, alone, possessed the social courage to tell him to leave but she did not use it. Instead, she admired the RCR badge, wondering to nobody in particular if she could have it cleaned and mounted as a brooch. Eventually Mrs. Wilson let loose a sigh so long and powerful that it ruffled a nearby fern leaf. Emma relented.

"I suppose you must be on your way, Mr. Thornton, plans for your evening and all," she said.

"Oh no. No rush at all," he replied. "Thanks for asking, though."

"Mr. Thornton," Emma laughed. "It wasn't a question. It's time for you to go."

The Wilsons, at once horrified and relieved by their daughter's bluntness, practically threw him out of the morning room as they shook his hand and thanked him for dropping in. He must say hello to Vicar Wilson when he returned to Gloucestershire. He was returning to Gloucestershire wasn't he?

• • •

He was on the pavement, eastbound on Fulham Road before he noticed the rain slanting through the lamplight. All was black, glistening, and November-cold. His face was wet, his hat brim poured a half-cup of water down his coat front when he looked at his wet feet. He seemed to regain consciousness and instantly cringed. Physically. He hunched over, punched with embarrassment at the recollection of his behaviour at tea. A small bench circled beneath the nearest lamppost. He shuffled to it and sat, elbows on thighs, hands hanging limp between his knees.

Was there anything to salvage? No, on clear reflection, nothing. His position at the Colonial Office and his service in Africa had been his only two social cards worth playing. The one he'd squandered with an oath. The other he'd used to embarrass Wilson. But Emma's eyes had sparkled when he'd pushed against her fingertips. She'd sheltered him during tea. Because she wanted to or because she felt it her duty? She'd done these things because she wanted to.

He sat up, startled by this conclusion. There it was, plain, he couldn't have misread it. She was still for Jack Thornton. She had to be. She'd laughed when she kicked him out after tea. That proved it.

"Jack!"

Heels clacked on paving stones in the darkness behind him. Emma hurried into the wet lamplight. She wore a long cloak, its monk-style hood covered her head.

"You walk extremely fast, Mr. Thornton." Her face was nearly invisible under the overhanging hood. "I started not twenty yards behind you," she panted, white puffs of moist breath shooting from the hood. "Did you not hear me call your name?"

"No, I heard nothing. Didn't even know it was raining until just now, I was still deaf and dumb after seeing you."

She edged the cloak back, her cheeks and nose reflected the dim light.

"What a lovely thing to say."

He drew a dirt-smeared envelope from inside his coat pocket. Rain pelted it, streaking the grime.

"My letter," she said breathlessly.

He nodded. "Your letter. My most precious possession."

"But it tells little, in truth. We mustn't act in haste. You know very little about me, about my past, about why my father has to drag young men home from the office. Why they only stay interested until someone tells them about . . . " The words cascaded out of control. She frightened herself to a halt. The rain gusted onto her face, wetting it.

"I saw you and Charlie in the hayfield," he said. "I guessed why you were in Newland with your uncle."

She shoved the hood back, hurt.

"And," he continued. "For some reason, Miss Wilson, I don't give a tinker's tiny fart about Charlie or anyone else who came before me."

Emma could have cried and he'd not have seen it in the rain. But she would not.

"We'll have to work on your manners and your language, Private Thornton," she said evenly.

"Corporal, if you please, miss. Got promoted, I did." He put the letter back into his coat.

"A week from tonight. You will call for me at eight PM, in at least a hack — four-wheeler if you can afford it." She gave the orders as crisply as d'Esterre. "Evening dress — dinner jacket will

249

do. We go to the Alhambra for their one-year anniversary of Arthur Sullivan's performance of *The Absent Minded Beggar*. Please ensure you have a guinea — two, if possible."

Then she was gone under the hood and into the night. Jack Thornton felt as though he could run all the way to Hampstead and still not sleep tonight.

• • •

"No, of course not." Edmund set his teacup on his desk, aggrieved at Jack's proposal. "A decent dinner jacket with low, crowned hat is miles better than rented evening dress! D' you want to look like a damned organ grinder's monkey in a leased tile and tails?"

Jack slurped his own tea and shrugged. "Who would know?"

"Good God! Every single person at the theatre will know!" Swinglehurst actually stamped his foot with frustration. "Even a backwoods Gloucester man must realize that."

"But she said evening dress was best, so . . . "

"But she quite sensibly said dinner jacket second, if you don't own evening dress. She didn't say go out and rent a clown suit."

Jack smiled.

"You own a dinner jacket, please God, say you do."

Jack fidgeted. "Yes, naturally, but it was made for me when I turned seventeen and it's bursting at the seams. I have my father's and it fits very well, but . . . " he trailed off, expecting another tongue-lashing.

"But it's old fashioned? Out of date?" Edmund coaxed.

"Well, yes. That's why I thought to rent, because I can't afford the money or time for a tailor to alter my own clothes."

"Why that's superb — your father's dinner dress. Does it show obvious signs of age — bit shiny on the elbows?"

"Yes, unfortunately . . . "

"Excellent — your father's duds will be perfect," Edmund sighed with relief, picking up his cup and sipping contentedly.

"Are you serious?" Jack was mystified by the contradiction. "Its lapels are narrow, and the cuffs are well worn."

"Even better! Heavens, Thornton, strapping on one's pater's togs for an evening out is first rate. Shows tradition, respect, and . . . well . . . don't you understand anything about fashion?"

"Apparently," Jack shrugged, "I understand nothing."

Swinglehurst laughed. "This Emma sounds rather formidable — ordering your affairs — but eminently perceptive. She's obviously seen your weaknesses."

Jack sighed.

"I trust she's horrible. This must be a duty call — paying respects is it?"

"Edmund," Jack fixed him with a serious eye. "They don't come horribler."

• • •

He compromised. The late November evening was cold and foggy but no rain. Train to town, walk to Chelsea to save money, then a four-wheeler the last few streets to the Wilson house. The fare to Leicester Square and return should leave him better than a guinea. "Imperious" answered the door again. He failed to recognize Jack's name and left him once again in the ferns to see if Miss Wilson was in. Jack foolishly sputtered after him, "Of course she's in, I'm taking her to the Alhambra."

The morning room was opened and he entered the place of his previous social debacle. Mr. Wilson was absent. Mrs. Wilson was surprisingly warm in her welcome.

"Well Jack, don't you look smart. Just right, too. Some people wear evening clothes anywhere — even the Alhambra — but then where's the standard? How can one wear the same clothes to the Alhambra and then to say, the Savoy, later? Surely we must make distinctions between theatre and music hall?"

"My sentiments exactly, Mrs. Wilson." There, that was better. He even inclined his head in a tiny bow.

"Would you be so good as to pour us a sherry, Jack? Emma will be a few minutes."

He accomplished the job smoothly, so much easier to behave normally without Emma lurking. Mrs. Wilson took her glass — her eyes flickered twice to his scars.

"I suppose you must miss the warm African sun on such dreary English days." She hadn't waited long to revisit Africa. He sensed her interest in the war, but did not know how far to speak on the subject.

"In truth, no, ma'am, I don't. The African sun creates an oven from which one cannot escape."

"Mmm," She looked directly at his cheeks. "Especially hot, if you are lying out under enemy fire, I expect?"

"Especially." He paused, considering that this might be an opportunity to mend fences. "About last week, Mrs. Wilson. I don't know what came over me. My war discussion was much too frank and it must have been distressing. I do beg your forgiveness for my behaviour."

She smiled, with a trace of Emma's sparkle. "I know what came over you."

He gulped his sherry audibly and vowed to keep his mouth shut unless asked a direct question.

"I do appreciate your downplaying the severity of your injuries," she eased the words out as though they were an afterthought. "To spare Emma's feelings, of course. But it must have been excruciatingly painful. And, my word, such a sanguinary wound. Did you faint?"

Well, if that wasn't a direct question, nothing was.

"No, but I nearly did when I spit my tooth out."

"Really," she exhaled heavily. "It wasn't shattered?"

"No, odd thing, isn't it? The bullet hit my face," he touched his left cheek, "uprooted the one tooth and popped out the other side clean as you like."

"And a face wound, particularly heavy haemorrhage I should think?" she asked hopefully. She held her glass out for a refill.

"Like a running stream," he smiled and topped up the glass.

"How awful," she smiled, eyes busy on his face.

The doors opened behind them and Emma swept in.

"I'm late, so very sorry, we must be off," she said pulling on a pair of gloves. "Mother, you haven't been interrogating poor Jack, have you?"

His mother merely sniffed, then knocked back her sherry like a sailor in a gin shop.

"I thought we had plenty of time," Jack remained calm, urbane, self-assured. But only because he was cautious enough not to look directly at Emma.

"Not since Mr. Sullivan died." She thrust a long wrap toward him. "Help me on with this."

Mrs. Wilson darted for the shawl but Jack was quicker. He held it open and despite his resolve to behave properly, nearly gasped with delight. Emma wore a rather plain, cream dress, only a fraction down the shoulder, but her white sweep of neck, the long nose, high forehead and, of course, deadly, green eyes, flailed him.

"Died? Who?" He managed to squeak as she pirouetted into the wrap and fastened the clasp.

"Gilbert and Sullivan, unknown in Gloucestershire?"

"Oh, that Sullivan. Died has he?"

"Terrible tragedy for the nation," Mrs. Wilson interposed. "Apparently died in great agony."

"Hearsay, Mother," Emma collected her bag. "The point is, we have reservations for *The Absent Minded Beggar* which is the last show Mr. Sullivan ever conducted. And *that* took place exactly one year ago at the Alhambra, so tonight's performance has suddenly assumed great significance, now that Mr. Sullivan has passed away."

"Mobs of people scrambling quite unashamedly for boxes," Mrs. Wilson said. "Your box . . . ?"

Jack shook his head.

"Your seats may be in peril," she finished smoothly.

Emma faced Jack. She curtsied. "Will I do, Corporal Thornton?"

"Emma!" Mrs. Wilson snapped, scandalized at the reference to his previous low station in life.

Emma's wrap fell open. Three tiny, silk, pink bows dotted the front of the dress, leading to a subtle floral stitching around the bodice. Three tiny, pink, silk, bows dotted the front of Maisie Downs' corset before she tore it off when she, they, pretended to be Emma and Charlie. Jack felt sick at the memory, kicking it away.

He took her hand and raised her up. He squeezed her fingertips and swallowed. "Miss Wilson. When the mob sees you." He had just enough sense to glance at Mrs. Wilson when he spoke. "They will forget who this Sullivan person ever was."

Emma blushed; Mrs. Wilson's face fell, her lips pursed anxiously.

• • •

He handed her into the cab. "Quick, Jack, the front window, is Mother there?"

He looked — the curtains twitched. "Yes."

"Excellent, you haven't wasted your money — she'll tell Daddy about the four-wheeler."

Jack would have been very content to throw the guinea at the driver and ride through the London fog until the money ran out. Emma chatted about Gilbert and Sullivan — a shame they never collaborated again after the 1890 quarrel — wished she had seen him conduct. Did he have the tickets? Were they in the amphitheatre?

"No, first circle," he said, "pit."

"That's six shillings each," she remonstrated, plainly delighted that he'd spent the extra money for good seats. He let her voice wash over him. The street lamps flashed through the door window revealing her, then plunging her back into the dark. Each flash like a different pose, a new picture of her. He let his besotted mind revel in these small pleasures, answering her questions, but asking none of his own.

Leicester Square was thronged. The garden in the center of the square looked as though it was the theatre, full of patrons, waiting for the curtain to raise. The driver forced his way along the pavement, but eventually mired down in the pack just short of the theatre itself.

"I'm sorry, sir, but this looks like it," the driver bellowed.

"Do you mind?" Jack asked, opening the door and peering up at the strange, moorish domes and keyhole-style windows on the theatre.

"Mind!" She laughed, excited. "It's wonderful."

She seized his arm with a grip that would have done Liz or Maude proud, and pulled him to her side. Shoulder to shoulder they drove a wedge into the crowd. The entrance door marked PIT was nearest them but it was screened by a rugby scrum of young swells, city men and their girls, hawkers, and a heavy sprinkling of prostitutes. The sharps in shiny, billycock hats and dirt-glazed waistcoats were offering twelve shillings a ticket for any seat in the pit. One accosted Jack but Emma smacked him smartly between the eyes with her reticule and he backed off, roaring with laughter.

"Well done, my lady! Watch her, sir — she's a tartar."

Jack and Emma laughed with him, revelling in the freedom of the very English mob.

"Thornton! You devil!"

There, in his face, Edmund Swinglehurst, eyes riveted on Emma. "I should be taking advice from you — not t'other way round!"

Edmund's introductions were severely curtailed by the shifting mass of people and by the fact that he appeared to have been drinking more than would be strictly customary before the theatre. His young lady, one Lotti of no last name, giggled and occasionally squeaked.

"He's a deep one, Miss Wilson." Edmund spoke loudly enough to be heard above the general rumble of the crowd. "First, he bags tickets to a show that scarce merited notice a week ago — then our Arthur Sullivan ups and pops off — making them the hottest seats in town."

Lotti squealed something about Edmund promising to find them seats and, so far, nothing doing. He deftly pinched her somewhere out of sight, calling her a daunting taskmistress. She shrieked, slapped his arm, then giggled.

"And then," Swinglehurst continued, fixing Jack with a stern eye, "he lies to his Uncle Edmund about you, Miss Wilson."

Emma joined in the game, demanding an explanation.

"He didn't half describe the true wonders of your beauty, Miss Wilson."

Lotti stopped giggling. She stamped a cross foot. The words "insensitive" and "cad" were clearly audible as she frog-marched the unfortunate Edmund toward the awning marked BOXES AND STALLS.

• • •

Although the performance had been retroactively refitted and sold
as a tribute to Mr. Sullivan, the audience was anything but sombre.
The spontaneity of the street seemed to carry inside where a glib
man in loud clothing introduced the show. He drew their attention
to Sullivan's music, Rudyard Kipling's words, and how they
combined in wondrous tribute to Mr. Sullivan and the English
heroes right now fighting on the veldt. The patriotic audience
interrupted him twice with clapping and cheers. This prompted a
call from the loud man for any soldiers of the Queen present to
stand up and be recognized. Two dozen men, all in evening dress,
rose to a round of applause. Emma practically dragged a reluctant
Jack to his feet. A spotlight danced about, highlighting each man
for a second of fame.

"Any of you brave Englishmen seen active service against the
Boer?" the loud man took his impromptu session to the next step.

All but Jack and two others sat down. Jack tried to, but Emma
thrust her arms across his chair to prevent it. The spotlight struck
him like a lightning bolt. He raised one hand to shade his eyes,
the other hand tugged ineffectually at Emma's arms.

"How was Capetown sir?" the man shouted, and the audience
fell silent waiting for Jack's reply. He squinted, disoriented and
tongue-tied, into the light. A huge voice — Edmund Swinglehurst's
huge voice — boomed from a box above.

"Capetown, nothing. He was wounded at Paardeberg!"

The crowd went wild.

Jack reeled, suddenly dizzy and upset. Kimberley's spotlight
blinded him, Palmer teased George about climbing up the light as
they huddled in the rain. Then the rain turned to Mauser hail and
Palmer's leg was a limp piece of half-butchered meat. He tried to
bow, smile at the Alhambra battalion. Soldiers in evening dress

257

goggled at the wounded hero who looked like he might be drunk, but what of it — if he'd been at Paardeberg. George and Billy and Bobbi number two and Wethered were still out on the filthy African veldt — Miles was underneath it. The Theatre Regiment couldn't cheer for them this evening.

"Jack!" Emma's face blazed in the light. She reached for him, pulled him down, took his hand. "I'm sorry, so sorry — what is wrong?"

He flopped down and the light sped away to interrogate the other veteran. She still held his hand. He squeezed, and she squeezed back.

"Nothing. Just a bit silly in the light."

She didn't believe him, but suddenly he was telling the truth because his African fears seemed to flow away through her hand. "Nothing at all, really."

• • •

The orchestra at the Alhambra was touted — by the Alhambra — as second best in London. This was pure bosh of course, Emma told him. But, it was certainly one of the best orchestras in London and they played above themselves this night. Jack clutched her hand most of the evening and was enchanted — the thrill of the music, the passion of the players, the glittering audience, Emma, and somewhere above in the dimly visible boxes a true, if misguided, friend. When the show ended they swarmed out into Leicester Square fog. Squads of theatre goers linked arms, marching down the street, singing the most popular verses and roaring out the punch line "*Pay, pay, pay!*" Emma expertly steered Jack east and south through the dense, white blanket. Gaslights hovered above them like large indistinct fireflies, but provided no clue as to street names or direction. She forced marched them, humming bits of the music, to a well-lit shop front. Pausing for him to get the door, they stepped into a small restaurant. She gave his name to the head waiter who ushered them to their reserved table.

"Well, you managed the theatre and the cab," she answered his puzzled look. "So I picked supper. I'm famished and couldn't really expect you to know where to find decent food." She picked up her menu. "Could I?"

Jack followed suit, gratefully noting that, although the place bespoke quality in its décor and service, it was not going to tax his skill with a wine list.

"Simple food, well cooked, that's the ticket," she piped up.

"That's Mrs. Toomey you're quoting," he replied. He took this as a hint and scanned the menu. The best fare in the house wouldn't come close to a guinea.

"What a marvel you are, Miss Wilson. Swinglehurst was right."

She kept her eyes demurely on the menu. "Café d'Esterre is perfect for discriminating and yet," she paused for a comedic beat, "nearly destitute Gloucestershire ploughman clientele."

She talked, he talked, of themselves and Gilbert and Sullivan and the fog and London. He hid his surprise at the name of the restaurant; thought briefly of the haughty young officer who issued orders like Emma; then forgot him. They finished the meal and a hackney cab was sent for. She reached across the table and touched one scar lightly. Her face was calm, serious.

"Last week, on Fulham Road. You showed me the letter, said you guessed, said it didn't matter."

He nodded, alarmed.

"It does matter. I'm still play-acting — sometimes. I've not reached the peace or even contentment that seems to come so naturally to you. But," she withdrew her hand, "I believe I know what love could be."

He nodded, vigorously, foolishly.

"We'll walk. Sundays, evenings, rain, snow or cold. Embankment, Hyde Park or St. James or Hampstead Heath. You will tell me everything, including the hayfield," she hesitated. "You will tell me the real war — the one that upset you tonight — and you will tell me the truth about . . . all that you are."

"Of course," he said, wondering how she knew that he wanted to tell her the truth about everything.

"And I shall tell you everything, including the hayfield." She stared unblinking at him. "Then we shall know — I will know what love is."

CHAPTER 15

Twice each week they met. They walked; they stopped in shops for tea; they sat on park benches when the sun made its infrequent appearances. Jack went to Offa's Rose for Christmas. He spent two hours in Charlie's company on Christmas day along with his mother, Vi, and a neighbour of Vi's. The name Emma was not spoken. His return to London in January signaled a resumption of their walks. Emma took to wearing woolen underwear she'd acquired in Newland because the first days of 1901 were bitter, damp, and obscure. The cold was harsh enough to form ice on puddles, but not cold enough to make cleansing snow. Emma wished they could be at Newland, free to walk miles up and down the Wye. He was shocked at such thoughts. He couldn't get enough of London. It had been so wonderfully good to him that he could stare happily at Apsley house or the Albert Memorial any number of times.

She told him, slowly at first, then with growing confidence, of her trouble — an infatuation with an older man who'd taught her how to take intimate pleasure. The man, married and a colleague of her father's, had been scarcely noticed when the affair surfaced. She, on the other hand, had been ruined at the age of seventeen. Used and hardened before she'd even properly dreamed of love, she had discovered — been taught — a taste for physical love. When the Wilson's society firmly closed its doors on her, she hovered between desperation and despair. She took a new man to fill the void. The second had been a young, city man eager to learn all she could teach him. That lasted not even three months before he fled. Her mother, just barely regaining a toehold on her social life, was devastated. her father became absent. Uncle Henry offered a bolt hole in Newland and she had taken it, to her parents' immense relief.

Jack and Emma walked arm in arm through St. James Park, the day dull but dry. Emma motioned to a bench and they sat. Her gloved hand slipped from his arm to his fingers, gripping them.

"Now for Charlie Cordey — now the worst," she said. "What you saw in the hayfield was the least of what I — we did," she began with a rush, like a swimmer running into the cold ocean to get the shock over with quickly. "Charlie was funny and friendly and so very much a man, unlike my London poodles. He was competent and strong and, you won't see this, but graceful in his work and his attentions to me."

"I saw it," Jack said, surprising himself. "I never imagined 'graceful' of course. But yes, I must admit I learned from him and, at times, couldn't help admiring him."

"Oh my, that's no help at all, Jack," her voice quivered. "You're supposed to hate him." She dabbed at tears.

"You loved him?" Jack's hand convulsed, crushing her fingers.

"I thought so at first — I may have done. We became physical lovers. The Forest was wild, lovely, free of London rules and so was Charlie, and when we made love . . . " she was crying now, flooding eyes bravely held to Jack's own eyes.

"When we made love," she recommenced, "it took my unhappy life clean away. I even sometimes thought that perhaps, in the Forest of Dean, Charlie might answer. But really, truly, no. I knew he could not and was not for me. He was the one who fell in love. He actually resisted my advances in the end — to prove his love."

"In the hayfield," Jack murmured, "I saw it."

"I was angry then. He no longer took my unhappiness away so I practically forced myself on . . . poor Charlie." She dissolved into tears now, face sunk in her hands. "I must disgust you," she blubbered, shoulders heaving.

An elderly couple approached the bench, looking from Emma to Jack with ill-disguised alarm. Jack slung his arm across her shoulders and pulled her to him.

"Not disgusted, Emma, not," was all his tight throat could manage. She cried quietly, so unlike the Emma he thought he knew, better than the Emma he thought he knew.

"Then you appeared," she hiccoughed and dabbed at red eyes. "Positively reeking of disgrace and your own unhappiness. But you took it, you worked in the muck and you sang at the harvest supper."

She smiled now and pecked him on the cheek. "As my letter said, I became your faithful observer. You are setting me free, Jack, I can feel it."

"Setting you free?"

She nodded, composed now. "Free of the girl who scandalized London and even the Forest of Dean. I think free."

"I'm not sure I understand exactly . . . "

"Me neither," she pushed closer to him. "But you know everything, I can tell you. Now you must talk to me."

No secrets now, Jack thought. That was freedom. He was free to love her without doubt or hesitation. He was for Emma, and she for him. His words came easily compared to hers. His petty pose of superiority on arrival at Newland. His resignation to serve his time as a labourer, the revelation at Tintern and his growing acceptance of his fall from grace. his father's lost money, his mother's debt to Vi, it all came out in the days that followed St. James Park.

Strangely, the episode with Mrs. Downs at her sporting house in Aldershot cost him no more than a blush. Emma actually seemed relieved to hear his one sexual confession. She was sympathetic when he explained the Cordey-Thornton debt and how it sent him to Africa. The Boer horrors were not suffered to gain status in her eyes and it eased her guilt. The war should have been a short, straightforward tale but first Miles, then Palmer's ordeal would not speak smoothly. They came forth with surprising rancor. The dying Canadian calling to his mother was another obstacle. An unexpected anger led him to rant the better part of one full afternoon on a Green Park bench about the enteric hospital. He shocked himself when he told her about the "rouge men" dying unmourned in their own filth. "Thrown on a cart and turned into the earth like so much night soil" was the phrase that came unbidden, and yet so truthfully. She bandaged these wounds with her presence and patience.

Then it was over. For nearly four weeks they had washed and scrubbed their hands clean. And they were happy — Emma even proclaiming herself in love — though she'd acted the part so frequently she wasn't absolutely convinced. They celebrated with another night at the theatre followed by dinner at Café d'Esterre. Mr. and Mrs. Wilson capitulated, accepting Jack, and a proper courtship began.

In the forenoon of a mid-February Sunday she came alone to Hampstead. He met her at the station and immediately sensed the tension. She forced loud laughter in response to the most trivial remark. Her hand lay on his arm like an iron claw. It was a mild day for February yet her face seemed cold, taut. He walked her slowly up the high street trying to fend off her nerves. He'd planned an early lunch at a small grill on Heath Street opposite the clock tower, then a walk in the country, returning in time for tea — but her manner left him uncertain. By the time they turned into Heath

Street they'd run out of conversation — the weather and Hampstead being exhausted in short volleys of words. Jack looked up the tall, square tower dominating them and checked his watch against it. He told her what he'd planned for the day, although it now sounded limp in the face of the stubborn silence that had descended.

She declared herself famished, but scarcely touched her lunch. He caught her watching him several times, almost as though she was spying. She would quickly look away or make an inane comment. His own appetite shrivelled.

"What is it, Emma? What's wrong?"

"Wrong? Nothing! Lovely day, hearty lunch, walk in the country — what could be wrong?" Her tone suggested "rainy day, rotten food, boring company."

"Is it because . . . ?" he momentarily lost his nerve. She gazed past him, out the window, as though she was lonely.

"Is it because we are so far from home with no chaperon? Are you afraid that we're imitating your past? What people will say?"

Her eyes searched him, wide and surprised.

"It is," he said. "But you insisted on coming. Why do so if it makes you uncomfortable?"

"Too late for chaperons — for me," she said quietly. "It's not what others say that counts anymore. It's me, what I have to say." She stopped cryptically short of explaining herself. "And I say," she brightened up, "I've never seen your digs — will you show me where they are — before we go on our walk?"

He obliged her, it was but a short detour to the red-brick, three-story cube that his widowed landlady operated.

"Plain, but solid and clean I should think," Emma said, standing on the pavement across the street. "Which floor?"

He pointed to the right side of the building. "Second floor, that is my sitting-room window right there. Bedroom behind it."

She stared quietly for a moment. "How strange to think of you here," she mused. "I often imagine you in that room you shared with Charlie over Mrs. Toomey's kitchen, but never visualize you here."

Wild images rushed him from all sides. She had visions of his bedroom — the hot, flushed bedroom on the night of the harvest dinner — Dilke and Fanny — Jack and Emma and Charlie. What did she imagine about his bedroom? Then, out of the muddle, a clear thought burst like a lyditte shell blowing all other notions aside. Emma was unchaperoned — "too late for me" — in a village where she was unknown. She was tense, hard, and lonely. She was "seeing" his bedroom. Jack turned his head slowly, as though in a dream. He looked deliberately at her. His wretched body rebelled against him and swarmed with lust. Was this where he would play the role of the old civil servant, or the young city man or worse, Charlie?

"Can you get me in," she asked, picking a mischievous voice. "Past your landlady? I'd love to see your rooms for myself."

He continued to stare at her, although she spoke without looking at him. It should not be a sneak in, sneak out, horrid memory, no.

"Yes, of course," his voice betrayed him. It sounded like a grunting pig to his ears.

She still did not look at him but her hand tightened its grip on his arm. They walked quickly down the next street, turned up an old mews and slipped through a gate in the garden wall. They went in the back door and up the servants' stairwell without a word. He stopped their rush outside his door, and half turned away from it. The door clicked open and his shaking hand put the key back in his pocket as she swept past him into the sitting room. She closed the door behind them. Chin down on her chest, she braced her back against it as though guarding against his escape, for all the world like Maisie Downs.

Her head came up and for the first time since the uneaten lunch she looked directly at him. Her eyes took him, unblinking and cold. She walked to his face; her nose not six inches from his chin. Her palms rose and cupped his face, pressing on his Mauser cheeks, pulling him forward, down to her. The kiss was fierce, almost a punch, mouths rubbed and locked like train cars coupling. He fought his hands back from their dash to her bottom and willed his jumping body not to press against her. Then she threw his head away and staggered back, but not to grapple with her clothes, not to clutch him better, not, thank God, and also regrettably, like Maisie.

The cold eyes turned green and her hard face melted. She transformed back to Emma as though an Alhambra magician had suddenly conjured her out of thin air. The frightening and hypnotically desirable woman was gone.

"I've done it, Jack." She smiled weakly. "We've done it. I'm free."

He managed to smile back. "One day our turn will come, but not today," he said as his lust-fuelled pulse subsided, disappointed.

She kissed him long and softly. They shucked their coats, threw coal on the fire and pitched camp in front of it. They scarce spoke a word, she settled against his shoulder, his cheek resting on her head. Later she inspected every detail of his home, noting pictures and furniture and books. She took the grubby, well-thumbed Hardy down from his small bookshelf and ran her fingertips down the spine, smiling. She made tea and toast which they ate on the carpet before the fire. She told him how she could now call him to her mind anytime — see him in his room at night reading Thomas Hardy — but, really, he should try Conan Doyle's mysteries. Childish maybe, but so much fun.

Jack thought of Tintern and Gloucester, of Redbrook, of his mother, his father, and Vi. Miles' mound of sandy dirt in the grove at Paardeberg and Palmer's angry face and empty trouser leg passed by. He was free now, as free as Emma.

• • •

"Edmund Swinglehurst," the young man presented himself before Jack's desk, "soon to become senior assistant to the Undersecretary for Trade." He held out his hand. "You may kneel and kiss the potentate's ring."

Jack took the hand, shaking it happily. "You cracked it. Well done. Must I call you Mister Swinglehurst now?"

"At the very least, I should think."

"Well, your new man will at least speak to you." Jack placed his index fingers lengthwise over his eyes. "Be a change from old eyebrows McKennitt."

"Yes, such a relief — a human being with which to converse." Edmund slumped into his chair. "Makes our old chap sound positively ape like! McKennitt is Irish you know. He should be a poet and a man who will sup his ale and make his juniors feel at home, but I never had a complete sentence from him during our entire history."

"McKennitt is an Irishman?" Jack was taken back. "Really?"

"Absolutely. You'd think the fellow was Scottish, or worse. Ever heard of such a thing?"

"No, my Irishman was anything but tongue-tied." Billy's lilting voice came to him. He'd sung "Ta-ra-ra Boom Dee-Ay" all the way back from Mrs. Downs' establishment to the barracks in Aldershot. Then there was the "Ballad of Colonel Aldworth" sung and edited and polished in the trenches on the Modder.

"Your Irishman? What's that? Bought one on market day, did we?"

"Nothing — a fellow in the army — doesn't matter. I say, when will you be moving to your new office?"

"Promotion takes effect June 30th, less than a month." Edmund suddenly leapt to his feet. "Less than a month to groom you for my chair, old son! What must you think of your Uncle Edmund? We shall set to work on your letter of application this very afternoon."

"Me? I've scarcely come through the door!" Jack's protest belied the hope swelling up inside. A promotion up to Edmund's old crib would give him the financial and social boost he needed. "They won't push me with only six months seniority."

"Of course they will. Even an old plough horse like yourself will eventually plod forward — provided I coach you."

Jack wanted badly to believe this was not just Swinglehurst teasing.

"What's wrong — don't you crave advancement like the rest of us mortals?"

"Well yes, naturally."

"Then stop making a face like a ruptured spaniel." Edmund slapped his shoulder. "This will be a cakewalk."

"Are you serious?" Jack sighed heavily. "I mean, this promotion could mean a lot to me, Edmund."

Edmund pulled Jack up from his desk and pushed him down into his own chair. "There, a perfect fit!"

Jack grinned, excited. It would happen if Swinglehurst set his mind to it.

"Why are you leering like the butler pinching the master's port? And what is 'it could mean a lot to me' supposed to mean?"

Jack sat up to the desk and rested his elbows on top of it as befit its new proprietor. "A perfect fit, indeed. This will be my future, Edmund — my perfect future. I owe you a great deal."

"Not offering you the Viceroy of India shop just yet, old boy. Let's not fatten our heads too much."

Jack, still unable to stop grinning, stood and took Swinglehurst's hand, pumping it heartily. "Better than being the Viceroy, Ed, miles better."

"Good Lord!" Edmund pulled his hand back as though he'd just touched a hot stove. "You're not thinking of the 'M' word? Surely not!"

Jack's silly grin widened of its own volition.

"You're much too young to clap yourself in irons! Oh I should have seen it coming," Ed pressed the back of his hand to his forehead. "Promotion, pay rise, future in the service, then respectable married man. It's a slippery slope — many have fallen foul of it. I'm safe naturally, much too intelligent, but I should have watched you more closely. Saw the symptoms, of course, but never thought you'd gone terminally ill."

Jack stepped forward, flush with maudlin emotion for his friend. "I'll marry her, if she'll have me."

Edmund pushed him away. "And stop trying to pump my fin!"

"You'll still help — show me the ropes?" Jack asked earnestly.

"Assist in your suicide?" He took Jack by the shoulders and shook him. "I suppose I must, now that I've set it in motion. But only because it's the divine Emma you've set your sights upon. Uncle Edmund fully approves of your intended harness-mate. A touch too sensible perhaps, but she is a beauty, Jack."

"You know, I don't think of her as particularly beautiful," Jack said. "She says her nose is a bit long and she has those freckles that she can't seem to hide. Also, she's nearly as tall as me with a slim figure, and her forehead, according to her mother, is much too . . . "

"I said beautiful," Edmund stopped him. He made an odd little smile. "*Not* pretty. Lotti is pretty, very pretty, indeed, but she's not beautiful. One wouldn't marry Lotti unless a substantial sum of money were involved. But Emma, yes, one would marry La Emma given half a chance."

"You approve, then." Jack was relieved, scarcely aware that he'd been asking for Edmund's approbation.

"Leave her unattended," Edmund's smile changed to a wolf's grimace, "and you'll see how much I approve."

"That's all right, then. Get me my promotion and we'll name our first son Edmund."

Swinglehurst cuffed him for that.

• • •

Edmund Swinglehurst was to civil service politics, what Lord Kitchener was to the Boer guerillas. His primary munitions were Jack's competence and excellent work record — no exaggeration; Jack's service record — somewhat exaggerated; and Jack's fine family pedigree and London connections — mostly fabrication. He fired these rounds with deadly aim at perfectly-selected targets, anyone carrying influence with Mr. McKennitt. The bombardment was subtle, yet devastating. Best of all, nothing was ever placed directly before McKennitt, except Jack's actual modest letter of application.

Senior men who'd never given Jack a second glance stopped to ask him about Paardeberg. Others commented on what a splendid home office man Wilson was, and fancy that Jack knew him so well. One memorable afternoon, Jack was tasked to hand deliver a confidential memorandum to McKennitt's superior, wait for that great man to append his opinion to the memo, then return it directly to McKennitt. The man actually recognized Jack, called him by his correct name, and declared that they needed more young men with knowledge of mining and agriculture in the ministry. Jack's respect for Edmund Swinglehurst turned to awe.

The last week of June, Jack and two other hopefuls sat outside McKennitt's office. The first competitor was younger than Jack but with a full year's experience, a very confident manner, and a lovely suit. He lasted nearly a half-hour with McKennitt and emerged quite calmly, departing without a glance for Jack or the other candidate. Jack knew the second fellow, Frederick Wheeler. He was at least ten years older than Jack and still a junior clerk. A plodder with no family, no style, and no connections. Edmund was angry that he should have been invited to an interview, not because the fellow was a threat, but because he was harmless and did not deserve to be set down publicly in front of younger chaps. Apparently, this was a favourite little cruelty McKennitt perpetrated for his own amusement.

Jack had been surprised at Edmund's sensitivity for Wheeler's situation but Wheeler seemed naively full of hope. He winked at Jack, straightened his tie and whispered "best of luck" before he entered the lion's den. Not five minutes later he lurched back through the door, face shining red, unable to meet Jack's eye as he hurried away. Jack's own fluttering nerves took full flight at the sight of Wheeler's disgrace. He rose weakly and dabbed his handkerchief on his forehead. His future happiness now depended upon a few minutes with a capricious villain who judged men by the width of their lapels. For a moment he froze, dithering outside the door. Then George Grigg's voice came clearly to him. The same words he'd spoken when the Cornwall Light Infantry charged Cronje. "The colonel said British soldiers. That's us. Let's go."

Jack put his heels together, squared his shoulders, and touched his thumbs to the seams of his trousers. His future happiness did not lie in Mr. McKennitt's hands — it lay with Emma, promotion or not. He strode into the office, stopped three paces before the desk, and stood easy. McKennitt's balding head was bent over a sheet of typed paper. He was writing in the margin of the paper. His hand moved slowly, deliberately ignoring Jack's presence. Jack noted the perfect silk cravat, impeccable suit, and snowy linen cuffs. The furniture in the spacious office was clearly McKennitt's personal property, delicate chairs clad in soft leather, a carved sideboard with silver tea service, and expensive drapes framing the window that over looked King Charles Street. At length his head raised, and his eyes appeared from beneath the hedgerow brows. They regarded Jack for a moment then dropped to his pen. He replaced the cap and turned it slowly, one revolution per second, until it screwed itself into place. He carefully laid the pen in a narrow mahogany tray above the blotter, and gazed at it for a moment. The hands placed themselves, palms down, on the desk top and he looked up again. Jack, irritated by the display but determined not to show any more emotion than McKennitt himself, met the eyes. A staring contest ensued, Jack willing himself not to blink. Finally the woolly eyebrows raised in question marks.

"Thornton, sir. Candidate for chief clerk position."

The enemy eyes swiveled away, searching Jack's clothing for lint, poorly tied cravat, weak crease or general lack of taste. Inspection passed, they returned to study his pen. A low mantel clock beside the tea service ticked loudly. The top half of a hackney cab driver with his bowler rammed low over his ears, moved past beneath the window. Surprisingly little traffic noise invaded the room.

"Much talk about young Thornton recently," he said to his pen. The eyebrows dove together, frowning. "Mostly good."

"Thank you, sir."

The brows and eyes shot up in reprimand at such unnecessary chatter. This time Jack looked away.

"The work of Swinglehurst, I think. Not appreciated."

Jack shuffled to attention.

"Father M.A.," he glanced down at the typed sheet. "Good. Doesn't say your school?"

"King's School, Gloucester, sir. Mostly day boys and mostly choristers for the Cathedral."

The eyebrows danced at this. "You? Chorister, Thornton?"

"Yes sir," Jack tried to keep the surprise out of his voice. "But only second rate and my voice broke early so . . . "

"Well, that is very good. Very good indeed. Why didn't you say so in your original application?"

Jack, overwhelmed by this barrage of conversation, stumbled in his reply. "Why, I never thought it, you know, was, ah, significant."

McKennitt referred to the page again. "Decent war. Good wound. Acquainted with Wilson, home office — promising. Swinglehurst teach you anything?"

"Why yes, sir. He was very kind to me."

The eyebrows levelled and the eyes locked onto the pen tray again for an interminable silence. Finally, "Carry on Thornton."

Jack left the office, walked back to his own desk in a daze, and sat heavily. What was he supposed to make of that? Edmund studiously ignored him. A narrow, cream-coloured envelope lay on Jack's desk. He idly opened it and unfolded the letter inside. It was a brief acknowledgement that he'd been promoted to chief clerk. It was signed by G.L. McKennitt.

"Came about five minutes after you left for the interview," Edmund said without looking up from his file. "Good news?"

"Yes," Jack said. "I suppose. I've been given the job. It also says that my assistant is to be Fred Wheeler."

• • •

Emma simply had to see 221B Baker Street, Sherlock Holmes' address, and she insisted on taking an omni bus. Saturday, July 1st, 1901, was a glorious, sun-filled day. They should have been in the country — but failing that, they would do something adventurous like ride the top of a bus in the afternoon sun. Daring greatly that Mr. McKennitt would not be travelling Baker Street, Jack agreed. Emma entertained him by examining their fellow passengers and based on the condition of their shoes, or the contents of their shopping baskets, deduced where they lived, how they earned their keep and what type of person they were.

"Baker's wife, two children, and generous of spirit. Lives over a bakeshop in Paddington," she whispered in his ear, nodding toward a heavy woman in a large, old-fashioned bonnet seated halfway down the other side of the omni bus.

"Why is she a baker's wife — because she's fat?" he whispered back, wishing mightily that he could just nibble the soft white earlobe that brushed his lips.

"Oh Watson," she scolded him. "You've learned nothing of my methods."

"Right," he said, suddenly reckless. "Let's see, shall we?"

He rose, and began to cross the jiggling top of the bus.

"Jack!" she hissed. "You wouldn't! Jack Thornton come back here this instant!"

He doffed his hat and bowed slightly to the woman. "Excuse the intrusion, ma'am. Would it be all right if I enquired as to how your husband's bakery is prospering?"

The woman's eyes widened in surprise. "Bakery?"

"Pardon, ma'am, am I mistaken? You're not a baker's wife?"

The woman beamed. "But how kind of you, sir, to ask. Of course we are bakers. My Arthur will be pleased to hear you spoke up. We've only been open in Paddington these past two months — fancy you noticing our little shop. Yes we're doing well enough and we were lucky to get the rooms above the bakery so I can help Arthur and keep touch with the bairns upstairs."

Jack's smile froze on his face. He tipped his hat and turned to leave.

"You've got such a wonderful young man, miss, if you don't mind my saying," she bellowed to Emma. "Wait 'til I tell Arthur and the children that a gent paid his respects to me on the omni today."

They kept their composure until the next stop at Portman Square then fled to the street, leaned against one another and let the laughter flow. Recovered, they walked arm in arm the short distance up Orchard Street and onto Baker, only to discover that Baker Street was but a quarter-mile long and numbered 44 to 85 only. 221B was a fabrication. Undaunted, Emma strolled them to and fro, studying the famous street, imagining her heroes at work. She eventually deduced that 221B must be a generously proportioned four-story on the west side between George and Blandford streets. Their detective work complete, they continued north at Jack's suggestion to Regents Park and found an unoccupied bench in the warm sun.

"Seriously, how did you know that woman was a baker's wife from Paddington?"

"Surely you noticed the residue of flour on the welts of her shoes? Then there is the old, over-sized bonnet to . . . "

"Emma! Really, you've got me stumped."

"Didn't you notice her get on the omni?"

Jack shook his head.

"Well, as we approached her stop, she was hurrying out of a print shop. When she passed us to take her seat I peeked into her bag. It was full of freshly printed handbills — advertising a newly opened bake shop with a Paddington address. Her age made her a baker's wife, not his daughter."

"Well, hardly deduction. Just snooping, really."

"One always loses the admiration of one's assistant," she sighed, "when the facts are laid bare."

"How did you know about two children and her nature?"

"Didn't." She gave him a wide-eyed stare. "They were total prevarications. Pure luck that she turned out to be a happy soul and I've no idea how many children she has."

"Prevarication is it?" He squinted at her. "What a wicked thing you are. Any other deductions you'd care to make?"

"Well," she removed her oversized, straw boater and fiddled with the ribbon on its crown. "I am fairly certain that your first day as chief clerk went well. You have the look of the cat who's swallowed the canary."

"Does it show that much? So obvious?"

"If you were any more smug it would be unbearable."

He tipped his hat condescendingly to her. "Thank you, miss, I am feeling very pleased with myself."

"I take it that Fred Wheeler didn't make himself awkward then?"

Jack shook his head. "Not a whiff of resentment. Started the morning by shaking my hand and congratulating me. Then worked like a Trojan and made pleasant conversation while we had tea. Has a wife and three children. They live somewhere east of where it is acceptable, but seem quite content."

"He could have used the extra money," she said seriously.

"Can't imagine wife and family solely on the junior wage." Jack let a pang of guilt interfere with his happy mood. "Even after the unspeakable way McKennitt treated him, he still spoke proudly of being at the Colonial Office. A Whitehall man through and through, he calls himself."

"Oh buck up, Watson." She jabbed him in the ribs with her hat brim. "Not your fault, you'll treat Fred well."

"Yes, I am anxious that we get on. I told him about my troubles — fall from grace . . . "

Emma's head shot around, eyebrows raised. "You didn't!"

"Well, yes. I told him so that he'd feel we were more equals, partners." Jack found himself shifting uncomfortably under her stare. "Don't want to lord it over him, rub his face in it."

"But he'll think the exact opposite — that you're patronizing him." Emma tapped her hat making the point. "Do you know him well enough in such a short time?"

"Oh, Fred's a brick." Jack said it too quickly. "He must hate McKennitt. My secret is safe with him, don't worry."

"He sounds too good to be true. Maybe McKennitt knows something we don't." She laughed. "Fred's dark secret!"

She lifted the boater and fitted it carefully back on her head. The brim cut a shadow diagonally across her face. "The sun is wonderful but I suppose it will freckle my enormous beak like — "

"Holmes," Jack interrupted. Her delight in Conan Doyle, her sympathy for Wheeler, the sun on her face, and her concern for him — all small trivial things — but suddenly the most important things in his world. He dug into his waistcoat and pulled out a tiny box, hiding it in his palm. "See if you can deduce what's in my hand."

She tapped his knuckles. "A sweet."

He uncurled his fingers. She took the box and opened it. She stared at the ring then removed it and slid it onto her left hand.

"Oh, Watson." She kissed him.

• • •

Neither wanted a large wedding, nor a long wait. They had few good friends or relatives and both were burning for the wedding night. Mr. Wilson put up a token resistance to the whole idea, hinting his fear of another scandal if it failed. Mrs. Wilson gave her blessing quickly; explaining to her husband that this would remove scandal. She agreed the wedding could be small but absolutely insisted that they could not marry so late in the summer. Early next spring was the best she would tolerate so March 12th, 1902 became the official day.

Every morning Jack regarded his face in the mirror and laughed at his own good fortune. Some of Mrs. Wilson's friends even took to inviting Emma along to tea, confident that dinner invitations were not far off. Every weekend of a golden autumn found Jack and Emma wrapped in each other's company. Picnics where they read Hardy to one another were in vogue at first. Then walking tours of Conan Doyle's adventures with a copy of *Strand Magazine* in hand were *de rigueur*. Even an afternoon tea at the Swinglehurst pile was enjoyed. His parents turned out to be quite near the right hand of God — living in Belgravia. Their season was over but they were late to leave for the country so, lacking true society, they allowed Edmund to bring Jack and Emma home for an afternoon. The Swinglehursts were proud of their son, working his way up the civil service, but were plainly ill at ease. One thing for a son to win his spurs at the front line — quite another to consort with actual front-line troops. Edmund was charming. Mrs. Wilson was thrilled to hear they'd breached such a lofty Belgravia bastion.

October began as golden as September. His delighted mother wrote him almost daily — demanding that he bring Emma to see her. Vicar Wilson wrote warmly and with evident pleasure that he knew they would make a good match and a happy marriage. Fred

Wheeler turned out to be the best of office partners. McKennitt occasionally broke into full sentences and Jack even got him to trust Fred with small independent tasks. But October 1901 was not gold for Six Company, Second Battalion, the Gloucestershire Regiment in South Africa. Detailed for outpost duty at Dewetsdorp near Sanna's Post, they were overrun and wiped out by a surprise Boer attack. The same day that Fred Wheeler made a surprise visit to Mr. McKennitt's office to launch an attack of his own.

CHAPTER 16

Jack presented himself early on that October morning to McKennitt's office. After only a brief wait, he was called in. A different aura was immediately sensible — at first Jack mistook it for a softening in the man's attitude — perhaps even a recognition of services performed and greater confidences to come. There was no preliminary waiting game. The eyes met him immediately and the voice followed.

"Ah, Thornton. Prompt as usual. Please sit."

Never having sat in McKennitt's presence, Jack hesitated before easing himself into a chair facing the desk.

"Now let us review the Thornton file," McKennitt actually smiled — or a least refrained from frowning. The eyebrows rode high and light on his forehead as he consulted an open folder with various sheets pinned inside.

"Mother from the Cordey family — prominent in mining," he glanced up and smiled. Jack was mystified by both the subject matter and the uncharacteristic good humour. "Prominent in that her family actually worked in the mines."

He wet his finger tip and flipped to a new page. "Ah, yes. Father M.A., Chapter of Gloucester Cathedral. Also responsible for unauthorized use of church funds, loss of said funds and subsequently disgraced — posthumously."

Jack might have fought back in different circumstances but McKennitt had recited only facts. The real truth, not his own omissions and half lies. Instead he crossed one leg over the other and leaned back in the chair He would take this like a soldier. Deep inside he'd known this day existed, he'd just convinced himself it would never come.

"Experience in agricultural management." The eyebrows positively leapt about here. "You worked as a common farm labourer!"

Full sentences, emotion, these things seemed so incongruous that for a moment Jack wondered if he was dreaming. McKennitt stared at him incredulously, as though he, too, wondered if it wasn't all a dream. "You," he pointed a finger, "actually worked as a hauler of muck and herder of sheep!"

Jack nodded, strangely serene. There could be no denial or excuse now. He was on a sinking ship and damn all to be done about it. He felt sorry for McKennitt, almost. The man was facing perhaps the worst trauma of his life.

"You don't deny it! It is true?"

Jack nodded. "True, sir."

"And, and the worst . . . the absolute worst, possible abomination." McKennitt now flipped clumsily through the folder. "Officer with the Gloucestershire Regiment, wounded at the great victory of Paardeberg. You, in fact, served as a private soldier! Can this be true?"

Jack shook his head. "Only in part, sir. Strictly speaking I was promoted to the rank of corporal after my sergeant was killed at Paardeberg."

A delicate palm slammed itself down on the desktop. "*Corporal!* Oh, fine, that's so much better. Let's just carry on then, shall we? I'll be the sergeant, shall I?"

McKennitt gasped audibly for air, as though he'd been gutshot. All pretense of dignity vanished. He goggled at Jack like men at the circus stared at the bearded lady or the Siamese twins. Jack returned the stare as steadily as he could manage. McKennitt sat back and broke eye contact, breathing heavily. Eventually he rose, walked to the window and stood looking out, hands clasped behind his back. His voice was angry but, once again, under control.

"Then how did you pass the examination? Where did you learn to speak like a gentleman? Farm labouring soldiers do not obtain employment with Sir Harold Brakspear — nor do they become engaged to a senior civil servant's daughter. My God, sir! This is nothing short of an . . . an apostasy!"

Jack had no explanation that would make sense. One either understood that working men were corporeal humans who occasionally sneaked into the officers' whorehouses — or one didn't. Jack contended himself with a simply reply.

"Miss Wilson and I are, in fact, in love, sir. That is how we came to be engaged."

"In love, he says." McKennitt spun around on his heel, eyebrows high with outrage. "But you were once a chorister. What manner of spurious cad are you! Were you really a chorister?"

It was Jack's turn to stare in confusion.

"Yes sir. And I did attend King's School where I was well educated. I did perform a proper clerical apprenticeship. I was wounded at . . . "

"Enough," McKennitt said quietly. He knew that a bridge would never be built. He strode back to his chair, seated himself and carefully closed the file folder.

"Bad business, all round. Bad for me and the service. Especially young Swinglehurst."

Jack felt his first true shock. Edmund's support for the hiring and promotion could certainly do heavy damage to his career. The eyebrows knit and the eyes wandered away as McKennitt lost himself in thought.

"Short staffed. Premature dismissal only make situation worse. Keep a lid on it. You," he allowed his eyes to rest on Jack, "will continue to serve as senior clerk until I arrange for your quiet replacement. Department will not lose face. Best if you stay. No reference if you go."

Jack stood. It was the most he could hope for. They would cover over the sore, bandage it, and let it go quietly away. He would descend to junior clerk, for eternity. No official reprimand. No messy sacking of employees. Perhaps no damage would come Edmund's way. He wondered how the truth had come to McKennitt's attention. But a moment later the curiosity died. A dozen possibilities existed, all of them irrelevant now, because McKennitt was in possession of the truth. He would not struggle against it. The eyebrows flicked toward the door. Jack let himself out.

• • •

The morning room in Chelsea was grey with cloudy, afternoon light. Jack was conscious of Emma standing close by his side. Nearly a year ago he'd first visited her here, swooning and stumbling and swearing. He'd lived a whole life in the twelve months since. The Wilsons were flanking the mantelpiece, trying to sound angry but making a poor show of it. In fact, they were defeated, in retreat from their daughter who would not leave them in peace. They wanted rid of her and now it appeared Jack, their one shaky hope for deliverance, had failed them miserably.

"Wedding's off," Mrs. Wilson said in despair.

"Never!" Emma fired back.

"You can't seriously consider living on a junior clerk's salary for the rest of your days," Mr. Wilson said it without conviction — hoping somehow they might just manage it.

"Won't have to, Father," Emma spoke firmly, well in control. "Jack has savings from Newland — Uncle Henry's bonus — and his army back pay. That plus my dowry will set us up modestly but comfortably in Paddington. Then . . . "

"Oh dear, Paddington!" Mrs. Wilson wilted under the blow.

"Yes Paddington! It's hardly Spitalfields, Mother."

"If I may," Jack placed a restraining hand on Emma's arm. "My plan is to look for a different position in the city in the new year. Mr. McKennitt has promised a neutral reference if no further scandal breaks out before then."

He looked to Emma's father, trying to sound in control, reasonable. "Assuming I find a position that attaches less importance to status — say import-export . . . "

"You will," Emma shrilled. "He will, of course, find a position. He's one of their best people at the Colonial Office — Eddie Swinglehurst said so — several times."

Jack blushed. He squeezed her arm and she relented. "Assuming I find employment with a decent future, then we see no reason for the wedding to be delayed."

"If not?" Mr. Wilson asked.

"Then we'll wait until I do." Jack shot Emma a restraining glance. She bridled herself. She had only with great reluctance agreed to this caveat. She was determined to show her bravery and loyalty — "marry if you're the crossing sweeper" had been her bold statement.

"So there is a chance this won't leak out?" Mrs. Wilson perked up slightly.

"No, ma'am, it's out." Jack was firm — no more half truths or pretense. "But there is a good chance it will be ignored so long as I keep my station quietly."

"Well," she fluttered like a nervous bird. "That will have to do then, won't it?"

• • •

The Boer War had brought prosperity to many — Charlie and Vicar Wilson among them — in 1899 and 1900. But by 1901 the costs were mounting and it was the colonies who took the prosperity. Jack saw it in the reports he filed and copied. It was Indian and Australian and Canadian horses that carried the British army. It was Argentine and Australian and American beef that fed the army. It was colony wheat and oats that fueled it. One report in early 1902 detailed how a bushel of wheat grown in Manitoba, Canada, could be shipped all the way to a flour mill in Essex and still sold at a profit for the Manitoba farmer. While the Essex farmer's taxes, wages, and property costs alone exceeded the sale price of the bushel. And now the volunteers were coming home and demanding their jobs back. City stock firms shrivelled, traders closed shop. Manufacturers fared well, but the rest of the British economy tightened its belt and dug in.

Jack Thornton, sharing a cell with Fred Wheeler at the Colonial Office, watched helplessly as March, then April, then May 1902 slipped past him. London winter had been wet, cold, and eternally foggy — spring, not much better. His savings lay waiting, dusty and intact for his wedding day. That day seemed to vanish along with the golden London of their courtship. Emma's strenuous efforts to carry through with the wedding had slacked off. She still protested her determination, but the hope was dimming. She knew it as well as Jack, though neither admitted it openly. She went to Newland for July, to visit her uncle and Jennie Mitchell. Jack, terrified at her absence and the lurking proximity of Charlie Cordey, suffered nightmares of outrageous scenes involving Emma, Charlie, Sir Charles Dilke, and Maude, the miner's wife. She returned in August, weeping to see him, and he nearly wept with relief. She was still for Jack and Jack was still for her. But how long could they survive? Engaged over a year was almost a fresh scandal in itself.

Jack grew desperate. He answered any advertisement for any position that promised the remotest possibility of a future. But he was fast turning into Fred Wheeler. 'Twenty-three years old — still a junior — odd that. What's wrong with the chap?' He was slotted into his place and there would be no escape. His days were well and truly numbered into the future. In late June a report crossed his desk. It included a reference to a letter in the *London Times*. The letter was written by one Reverend George E. Lloyd on the prospects of land ownership and farming in Canada. Western Canada. The words leapt at Jack. Sergeant Kerslake, Bobbi, Captain Arnold, a starry night on the march to Paardeberg where he dreamed of Rocky Mountains and red Indians. These images and thoughts swamped him. They sent a tingle down his spine. Canada. A bushel of wheat from Manitoba could make a man wealthy. He bought the *Times* back issue and took it home. He poured over the letter, devouring every word. The letter might as well have been addressed to him personally.

"The Canadian Wheat Belt," it began. "Finest agricultural land in the world — millions of acres — 160 acres free to new farmers — thousands of Americans rushing to take up farms — where are the English? — why not form British groups to settle the new land? — why not a large party for next March?"

Jack slept a couple of restless hours and was in to the office early the next day. He retrieved the report and discovered that it was based on a campaign being mounted by the Department of Immigration for the Dominion of Canada to attract the right kind of farmers for the west. They wanted the help of the Colonial Office in recruiting English and Scottish farmers. These were to offset the influence of European, American, and worse, Slavic Catholics who were already farming successfully in western

Canada. "Englishmen of good muscle who are willing to hustle," said the report.

Jack laughed at the crude poetry in a government document. Billy would have transposed it into a song in no time. He looked at his own hands. Once brown, thick-wristed and hard, now white and soft but still strong, still of good muscle. The report said that Reverend George Exton Lloyd was an Anglican priest who had lived in Canada — he would be the pastor to the British flock. A Church of England man, Reverend Isaac Barr, would lead and administer the colony. He had been licensed by the Archbishop of Canterbury, no less, to act as deputy of the Colonial and Continental Church Society in this matter. Reverend Barr had served and travelled extensively in Canada although at present he was stationed at St. Savior's in Tollinginton, London. A pamphlet was available. Jack wrote for it.

CANADA FOR THE BRITISH

Prospectus

Now that the British people are at last waking up to the vast importance and splendid possibilities of Canada along the lines of cereal and stock production . . .

The pamphlet — actually a small book — covered everything from homesteads to hay rakes. It explained how a little England would be organized, established and farmed. There would be instruction for the untrained, cooperative living for the bachelors, instant one hundred sixty-acre land grants with another one hundred sixty available to married men or proven farmers. Some of the 'colony' ideas made Jack squirm — rules of conduct — supreme court — expulsion criteria. But mostly it held him in thrall. The exact costs of travel, living, livestock, implements, even seed had been tallied. It was far less than the total in his savings account.

England would hold him as a junior clerk because he'd been a farm labourer. But Canada would make him the lord of three hundred twenty acres for the same sin. And it was not a fraud nor a cheat. The man had been anointed by the Canadian government and the Archbishop of Canterbury. He wrote Isaac Barr. Isaac Barr wrote back. Jack Thornton was exactly the type of man they wanted.

• • •

Jack blundered with Emma. He descended on her with his pamphlet and letters like an evangelical bible thumper demanding that she convert to his new religion. It resulted in their first true squabble and ended with him off to Hampstead in a huff. But even in his snit, he possessed enough sense to leave the pamphlet and Barr's letter with her. When he called, full of apology and babbling remorse the next Saturday, she forgave him on the spot. Moreover, she had caught the emigration fever. Her youthful disgrace and banishment combined with Jack's present working exile were like prison clothes upon her. Barr and Lloyd had suddenly given her a future bright with opportunity. It was their chance to escape clean, and start anew. Besides, unlike Jack, she had enjoyed rural life with Uncle Henry. It thrilled her to think of what they could do with a hundred and sixty acres. Actually, three hundred and twenty, Jack corrected her, if they were diligent.

How to break this to her mother and father?

• • •

The Wilson's Chelsea morning room, Jack mused, scene of all the great events of his London existence. He and Emma sat waiting for her parents on the same settee where he'd first rediscovered her eighteen months ago. She held his hand expectantly, nervous and very prettily flushed. She'd broached the idea of emigration with her father by giving him Lloyd's newspaper article and Barr's pamphlet. His job was to see the sense of it, which she was certain he would; then convince her mother, which was very uncertain. She prayed for their blessing but was quite willing to argue for it and even go without it, if necessary. The door opened and she sprang up like a terrier. Jack read the faces; Mr. Wilson harassed, Mrs. Wilson ascendant.

"We have some questions, my dear," Emma's father started, ignoring Jack's presence. "Is this a notion to emigrate or — "

"You can't be serious, truly," Mrs. Wilson finished his sentence with an instinctive boxer's step forward. "You mustn't give up England just because of a delay in your plans."

"Yes, Mother," Emma ignored her father's presence. "Actually we are very serious. It is an opportunity that won't come again and we want to seize it."

The two women stared hard and long. Both men found carpet patterns that seemed to demand their fullest attention.

"You're running away."

"We're going forward. This is progress, not retreat."

"It's beneath your station."

"Our station? And where would that be? Junior clerk for the next thirty years?"

This hard truth took her mother full aback. It was not to be easily countered because she was a staunch supporter of the code that had exiled Jack.

"I'm afraid Emma is right," Mr. Wilson stepped into the lull with a gesture towards Jack. "He has little prospect for advancement."

Emma's mother stood her ground tight lipped.

"And this All-British colony in Canada will have good, solid English values." He put his hand on her arm, searching her face "The organization is impeccable. Reputations will be made there. The owner of hundreds of acres cannot be ignored — once they are successful in Canada."

Mrs. Wilson's back sagged down a degree and her squared shoulders softened. She looked to her husband.

"How much land does Henry have?"

"He has title to twenty acres and lease to another sixty," her husband's voice brimmed with hope. His demeanor was plain — he'd have been thrilled for Jack and Emma to emigrate to the Antarctic if it could be done gracefully. "And the church — the Archbishop of Canterbury — has blessed the enterprise. It is in the finest tradition of the empire."

"It could be said," Mrs. Wilson clasped her hands as though in prayer, "that this is almost the duty of our best young people . . . to go forth as it were."

Her father beamed at her. Emma rushed to embrace her mother, who fought back tears.

"Jack will go out first to establish accommodation, secure land title, engage staff, and such," Emma's father fanned the flames, enthusiastically burning Jack's bridges. "Then in a month or so Emma can join him. We will remit her dowry when she actually goes out."

Up to this point Jack had been happy to be treated as though he was already gone to the wild west, this was Emma's show. But now, he found himself speaking as was his habit in the Chelsea morning room, without thinking first.

"Actually sir, Reverend Barr has specifically declared that he will not be accepting remittance men in the colony."

Mrs. Wilson dabbed her eyes and seemed to recognize his presence for the first time. "What on earth is a remittance man?"

"Incompetent, inconvenient, useless men whose families send them abroad and keep them abroad with remittance payments from home," Jack said flatly.

Mrs. Wilson gasped, hugging Emma tightly. Emma shot Jack an arching expression of exasperation. They were home and dry! What in God's name was he thinking?

"Sir! Are you accusing me of paying my daughter to leave my house?" Mr. Wilson neatly cut his wife off. He posed outrage but his eyes pleaded with Jack to rejoin the pantomime.

"Not exactly, no. I simply mean to say . . . " Emma's green-lit eyes focussed on him and his icy prickle of pride melted clean away. He spoke his heart, which was all he could do when she connected herself to him like this.

"There is a new country waiting to be built and I mean to do my part — be one of the first. I hope to do it right, to make it a good and prosperous place. But I have no expectation of success whatsoever unless Emma is with me. I am for her and she is for me. With her, I have no expectation of failure or need of remittance from home."

Mr. Wilson coughed with embarrassment at such an artless display of private feelings. Emma laughed the same way she'd laughed when she had evicted him from the morning room the first time. Mrs. Wilson grew thoughtful and said, "if my sums are correct, I calculate Emma and Jack could have four times as much land as Henry. Extraordinary."

• • •

March 12th, 1903, exactly one year late, Jack and Emma were wed. It was also exactly thirteen days before Jack and his fellow members of the British Colony for the Saskatchewan Valley were due to set sail for Canada. In keeping with her promise, Mrs. Wilson arranged a small wedding at Chelsea Old Church. Reverend Henry Wilson travelled from the Cathedral of the Forest, Newland, to preside. And, although the wedding was scheduled early at 10:00 AM, Edmund Swinglehurst arrived under the obvious influence of brandy. But it was just enough to make him jolly, not disruptive. He practically wrestled a reluctant Fred Wheeler into the church with him. They mopped the rain from their faces and waved to Jack. Strictly speaking, neither man was invited. Mrs. Wilson omitted Edmund from the invitation list because she was afraid he'd snub them. She omitted Fred because she felt obliged to snub somebody. Jack, however, issued verbal invitations to both men and felt a deep sense of gratitude at the two kinds of courage his friends displayed this morning. He strode to them and shook hands.

"Look at you!" Edmund pumped his fist a tad too long. "Slippery as a Bermondsey eel. One minute down and busted; next minute off to your castle and barony in the new world with the delightful Princess Emma by your side." He winked at Fred.

"Yes. Congratulations on your escape," Fred echoed Edmund rather stiffly.

"Edmund, Fred," Jack said emotionally, "all you've done, the way you two have stood by me, it's very decent. I mean to say . . . "

Fred blushed waves of crimson up to the roots of his hair and looked quickly aside.

"Huff and puff, be quiet before you make Fred blubber." Edmund deflected him. "Here now, speaking of tears, where are your future in-laws?"

Jack pointed out Mrs. Wilson in the second from front pew. Swinglehurst blanched.

"Not too late, old son." Edmund adopted a secretive manner. "My man," he slapped a still-blushing Fred Wheeler on the shoulder, "has a swift pair of steeds without. Say the word and we'll make good our escape. How far can the old dragon breathe flames anyway?"

They chatted and laughed away Jack's pre-wedding jitters. Edmund surreptitiously produced a silver flask and insisted they drink a toast. They filed into the Chapel on the South and huddled in the corner behind the down-sloping archway.

"Jack and Emma," Edmund whispered and they each took a sip in turn. It was extremely smooth brandy and sat very warm in Jack's belly.

"Thank you, Edmund."

"Wait! Wait!" Edmund hissed, unscrewing the flask again. "Where is your courtesy — sense of history? We are in Sir Thomas More's chapel — can't just nip in and out without paying our respects can we?" He raised the flask, "to Sir Thomas More!"

They each took another tipple then Fred pocketed the flask and hustled Edmund to the rear of the nave. Edmund stopped to protest that surely Lord Dacre and his fine memorial deserved a moment's homage, but Fred was having none of it and got them both seated at the back. Aunt Vi was perched like a large, black spider alongside his mother on the side of the church opposite Mrs. Wilson. Vi caught Jack's eye and grinned broadly. His mother pretended not to have seen the episode in More's chapel and Mrs. Wilson did the same, with a shudder. Then Vicar Wilson appeared, took Jack by the elbow and steered him, robes flowing, rapidly across the chancel and into the sacristy.

"What is it, Vicar? Something gone wrong?"

"No, my boy — everything is going as it should." He beamed at Jack and pointed to a long, narrow wood box. "I just wanted you to myself for a moment, to give you this silly gift."

Jack knelt and flipped the lid open. A scythe blade, edge gleaming silver bright, lay beside its ash handle nestled in the box. He looked up.

"I knew you had it in you from that first hay crop we took in together."

But I didn't — I mean, I hated the idea of farming."

The Vicar positively twinkled. "You thought you did, but you are a man born to make your living from the land — Bobbi felt it when she chose you to handle her. Even when you left us for that African war, we knew the sword would be beaten into a ploughshare one day."

Jack rose. Was it faith? Was it even true? He might be home, broken in a year. Then he thought of his fine speech to the Wilsons and finally saw the Vicar for the wise man he was.

"Thank you, sir. This means a great deal to me."

"Twenty, no, even fifteen years younger and I'd be going with you, Jack. How I envy you."

"Surely not!" Jack was mildly shocked.

The Vicar pointed through a small window that overlooked the Thames flowing beneath them. Grey sheets of rain swept from Battersea, across the equally grey river and threw themselves against Chelsea Old Church, painting it dull and dark.

"Humanity in its tens of thousands living in ancient sin upon the ruins of nearly two thousand years of their predecessors. Probably been a church here, on this spot, since the first Christians arrived. It is old and worn and magnificent. But it's yesterday we see here."

Jack looked at him sharply. The Vicar's face was calm, even happy.

"The Northwest Territories Jack! It's new and green and hardly been touched. *You* will be the first. *Your* foundations will be built upon by the thousands who follow you."

He took Jack's hand in both his. "Be proud of what you're doing. Don't worry about us — we're old. Go forward, be new."

• • •

The music, the Vicar's words, and even the drumming rain faded away to nothing when Emma began to walk up the aisle. She must have been on her father's arm but Jack didn't notice. It was nearly as bad as that first tea in the Chelsea morning room. Her tall figure — white, slim, gliding to his side — mesmerized him. When the veil lifted and she smiled at him, he reeled mentally and for all he knew, physically. It took an act of focussed concentration to get through the ceremony. Vicar Wilson, beaming like a latter-day Pickwick, would have married them twice, just for the fun of it.

Jack regained his senses sufficiently to make a proper exit under a roof of dripping umbrellas. He shook hands, kissed hands, uttered happy nothings and, by the time their carriage made the short trip to the hall for their breakfast, he was behaving rationally again. Emma, absolutely radiant, manoeuvered him safely through a platoon of her mother's friends. Mrs. Wilson's theme seemed centred on three hundred and twenty acres — she poured it out with the sherry to each guest, as often as she could. The food was excellent and Jack found himself hungry. Fred Wheeler stayed in the background and ate whatever was on offer — in whatever quantity offered. Jack thought for a moment he saw Fred in Canada. Emma dismissed the idea as ridiculous. Fred was a Whitehall Man, period.

Speeches and toasts and a flood of conviviality surrounded the newlyweds. They floated in it, as happy as any man and woman in the great city. During her father's rather long and tedious speech, Emma dropped her napkin. Jack leaned over to retrieve it but instead of taking if from him, she slipped her hand under the cloth and clutched the top of his thigh, giving it a powerful squeeze. Jack nearly shot out of his chair and had to feign a coughing spell to cover the disruption. A minute later he turned to look at Emma. She turned to him. He fancied for a wild second that he could see green flames in her eyes. Suddenly he wanted to be out of the reception, desperately. God alone knew what his own face showed because Emma coloured fiercely and turned away. At least nobody had noticed their exchange. Except Vi, of course. Looking out over the guests he saw her beady eyes twinkling at him as she waved her napkin.

The wedding breakfast progressed well into the afternoon, fueled by a half-case of champagne — E. Swinglehurst's gift. Jack's mother clung to him twittering non-stop about how proud she was of him, of Emma, and of their bold move to the frontier. Although half prattle, as was her habit, she did pause to talk seriously of his father. She paid him genuine homage and, despite the "debt" and the scandal, she declared her steadfast love for him. Jack was not to doubt that, whatever else he thought. He'd never heard her make such a statement and wondered whether either of his parents had ever actually said the words to each other. But that didn't matter — she was passing their heartfelt blessing to their son and his bride. It echoed his Tintern dream, updating it and making it better.

Vi bluntly pulled him away from her sister and tapped his chest with her rolled fan.

"You saved my bairn from the war, Jack."

"Bairn? Oh, yes," he gave her his full attention, "Charlie."

"Thee dusn't remove the death of three babes by saving one," she snapped.

"I think I finally reckoned that up myself," Jack replied softly. "I'm sorry for what happened between us, Auntie Vi."

"But ahm that grateful for it all the same," she smiled at him. "Your Mam and I, we've found a peace together. She doesn't owe me anything — not now."

She turned before Jack could speak, locked arms with Gladys and walked them away.

Then the feast began to break up. The champagne gift, save one bottle stowed safely in the newlywed carriage, was dwindling. Edmund had disposed of a fair portion of his own present and was now quite the worse for wear. Emma and Jack waved one last farewell then fled hand in hand through the unending downpour to their carriage. They were pursued by several brave souls flinging soggy flower petals and Mr. Swinglehurst who was tooting the "Tally Ho" on a small brass hunting horn.

• • •

Two nights in the Grosvenor Hotel — not the best room — but still the Grosvenor, had been his mother's and Vi's gift. Jack alighted under the curved awning that funneled gushing rain water away from the grand entrance. He handed Emma down and they were ushered into the elegant lobby by a doorman who looked to be an old soldier. Just inside the door stood the Wilson's butler, "Imperious" as Jack had come to think of him. He approached them, half bowing, with his hands clasped behind his back.

"I hope you don't mind, miss . . . ," a quick cough, "pardon me, I should have said ma'am. But I wanted to provide a personal service for you today. I have installed your bags in your rooms, ensured the fires are proper lit, and obtained your keys."

Emma, clearly touched by the gesture, thanked him profusely. Then they both coloured at the unexpected intimacy.

"With your permission, Mrs. Thornton," he continued formally, "I'll take one minute of Mr. Thornton's time to deliver the keys and make final arrangements."

Emma took the cue and seated herself on a large, circular couch near the lifts. Imperious drew near Jack and passed him the keys.

"The Grosvenor staff is well briefed as to your new-married status, sir, I've run a professional eye over them and they should provide satisfaction. The manager will require vacant possession of the room no later than one PM on the 14th."

Jack, still nonplussed that the bully had kowtowed, could only mutter his thanks.

"One more item, sir, of a confidential nature." Imperious shuddered with a tremendous quiver of self-consciousness.

"Yes, well, what is it?" Jack's patience was thinning rapidly.

"You'll be off to the Saskatchewan territory soon, sir?"

"That's right."

"One hundred and sixty acres to any man possessed of the ability to farm it? A homestead claim I believe it's called?"

"Correct."

"Do you think . . . ah, would it be possible . . . " he choked on his own temerity in broaching the subject. But the light finally dawned and Jack could not suppress a short, laughing bark.

"You want to go out — homestead?"

The red face bobbed up and down vigorously.

"You would give up your position in a fine house to go be a dirt farmer?"

More nodding and blushing.

"Who would you bully? Who would you look down your nose at? Your livestock?"

Imperious stiffened, hurt and humiliated — a little man who could serve up insults but not take them.

"Sorry. Joke. Not in good taste," Jack stammered, once again the loser in their encounter. "You're too late for the March sailing but Mr. Barr has indicated that only half the colony land will go to our lot. A second wave is to follow. You may certainly begin the application . . . "

"I know that, sir. I've read all the pamphlets. What I need to know is . . . could I do it? Do I have what it takes?"

Jack examined the man, for the first time really. Mid thirties in age and with an almost cat-like grace, Imperious also had broad shoulders and power in his frame. He was sharp-eyed and watched Jack with intelligent calculation. A man, after all, not a machine.

"Do you know? I think you might do it — given the capital and some instruction."

"I agree, sir. I think I might." He smiled, impulsively grabbed Jack's hand and shook it. Then horrified at his own behaviour, fled into the rain.

They ordered tea and drank it slowly and quietly before their small, fourth-floor window. They watched each other and they watched the rain pelt into Buckingham Palace gardens. It turned the grass bright green, in contrast to the black and grey of the rest of the city. All the hustle and noise and voices of the day fell away. They savoured the solitude of an afternoon's empty hotel and the absolute privacy it afforded. Emma rose first, trailing her hand across the small parlour table. He took it and let her draw him to his feet. She led them to the bedroom, dimly lit by a streak of cloudy light coming through the streaming window. She started with his collar, then his waistcoat, then his cufflinks — carefully unfolding his starched cuffs. He turned her and slowly unhooked her back — no vision of Mrs. Downs now, only Emma. She stepped from the dress, dropping it to the floor. He untied petticoats and peeled them down one by one, staring at the true shape of her body as it emerged from its layers of silk and cotton.

Then she regained the initiative, faster now, her freckles showing, cheeks reddening. Shirt, trousers, hose, deliberately but firmly removed. Her fingers ran over his shoulders and down his chest, more contact than necessary to remove the clothes. He responded to the mounting tension, removing and discarding her corset, then, with a gasp, her chemise and bloomers. Emma stood, her face turned gently aside, naked before him except for her stockings. He let his eyes trace down her neck, shoulders, breasts to the sweeping curve of belly and thigh — white in the afternoon dimness.

The moment broke and she closed with him, one hand entwined in the hair at the back of his head, pulling him to her. The kiss was as fierce as it had been in Hampstead but this one was real, human, and urgent. The urgency smashed through the years of patience and swamped them. They touched and kissed each other how and where they could, racing to explore, to give pleasure and take it. Jack heard himself grunting and tried to check it, but failed. He found himself on the carpet lying on his stomach while she lay full length on top of him, biting his neck and shoulders. The next minute they were on the bed and he was kissing first her earlobes then her ankles. Then, like an unpredicted volcano, they coupled facing each other, eyes open and staring, one of Emma's legs slung over his hip. They finished noisy, unrestrained and delighted with one another.

● ● ●

"Goodness," Emma ran one hand lazily over the nearest pillow. "We never even drew the counterpane or removed the pillow slips."

Jack, sleepy and ruined, popped one eye open. "Next time then, eh?"

They dressed for dinner intending to linger over it, but found themselves gobbling their food. They rushed back upstairs to re-consummate their wedding on the settee in the small sitting room by the light of only one lamp — haphazardly lit. Finally, in the bedroom under clean sheets, and fuelled by the Swinglehurst champagne, they spent themselves one last time and slept.

CHAPTER 17

They lived happily ever after, for a fortnight. Jack's landlady bent her "sober bachelors — only" rule because Emma charmed her shamelessly. They wallowed in each other's company the first few days, then set forth to pay respects and have tea with the unavoidable social commitments her mother had made. These were mercifully few and brief. They spent two of their precious days towing his mother and Vi about the city and were immensely grateful to Vicar Wilson — Uncle Henry now — for his attendance on these journeys. Emma shocked Jack when she opined that Henry was interested in his mother. She mortified him by suggesting that she could help things along with a bit of subtle matchmaking.

The Vicar and the two Cordey sisters departed for Gloucestershire three days prior to Jack's emigration date. Their leaving marked the end of the honeymoon and the beginning nibbles of the great loneliness Jack knew would come. Thankfully the days were jammed with work. The first job was money. They mailed a cheque to Mr. Barr for boat and train transport to the colony lands. They pored over Mr. Barr's lists of the purchases necessary in the new world and totalled what they thought was a reasonable figure for the first year. "Jack the clerk" then added fifty percent for safety. It accounted for half his savings and that one thought gave him a great relief. Without a penny of Emma's dowry nor a farthing of farm income he would be able to keep them for two years at worst. They speculated with mounting excitement what their estate would be in two years time. A hundred acres of cash crop, a fine home, livestock, perhaps even a start on the next hundred and sixty acres. It glittered and it defeated, temporarily, the fears of separation and loneliness.

Mrs. Wilson gave Jack a beautifully-tooled, soft leather belt with a wide, double-stitched recess in the back for his money. Surprised at its obvious utility and her now firm confidence in his ability to succeed, he'd nearly embraced her. They completed banking arrangements, purchased sensible clothing for travel and farm life, retrieved train and boat tickets, made reservations and shopped for the hundreds of items they deemed necessary to their adventure. Jack would travel light, taking only items of practical value. Emma would ship the furniture, carpets, china and other necessities in June. She would follow in July. The last night before the boat train they spent locked not in physical love but conversation. Emigration dreams had become their antidote to fear of the unknown. They clung to Mr. Barr and the British Colony for the Saskatchewan Valley vision and felt themselves carried by it toward a very bright future.

"See here, nothing extravagant now, Watson." Emma was reading the estimates for housing costs — again. "I shall be heartily disappointed if I'm not allowed to endure some hardship in the new land."

"No, not extravagant, but certainly comfortable." Jack enthusiastically followed her lead. Their new home, full title untaxed and independent, was one of their favourite topics. "See, I'll have a local builder put up a basic bungalow — rectangular, simple, but well-sited near woods and water. Then in a year or two when we've got all our equipment and livestock in place we can use the farm profits to add to the house."

"Yes, the building site will be most important," Emma touched his arm excitedly. "I do like the sound of that. I should think a hilltop, woods on the slope, and a pond or stream nearby."

"Look here, I've been thinking something like this," Jack sketched a rectangle on the back of Barr's pamphlet. Then he added two longer wings at right angles to make an H. "The original house can be renovated into an entry hall and morning room. Then the wings can be used for kitchen, scullery, storage on one end and our private bedrooms and dining room on the other."

She took the pencil and made some alterations. "I agree, but better to have the dining room here, closer to the kitchen. You've made the scullery and storage much too large."

Jack watched her eager face in the lamplight. Eyes shining, strong fingers drawing rapidly to fashion their new life on Barr's paper. By God, they would be a force in the Saskatchewan Valley. This felt so true and so powerful that he found himself wishing he was on his way already. Sooner gone, sooner there, sooner Emma and he in their future rather than only dreaming it.

"Jack?" A frown over the green eyes.

"Oh, sorry, what was it, Holmes?"

"Will there be competent builders? I mean to say, if the original bungalow is poorly constructed then our future house will be based on a weak link."

"I'm certain. You've seen Barr's preparations. The man has thought of every possible contingency. Of course there will be hardship and upset from the unexpected but at bottom it's a sound venture. I'll be tenting for a couple of months but, compared to Africa, that's a cakewalk. And rest assured, I'll supervise construction closely. When you arrive in July we shall be meekly but comfortably settled."

"Settled on Newland Estate," she pulled him close for a soft kiss.

Jack laughed. "I loathed Newland but it brought us together and taught me to farm. I could never have foreseen this future — never. Yet looking back I can't help but see that it was all part of some kind of plan — destiny. "Newland Estate" indeed."

He returned her kiss and that ended their conversation of farm dreams. As young lovers, they were bound to spend their last night fulfilling romantic ones.

• • •

Euston Station was approaching pandemonium. The conductors still pretended to be in control. They threaded the massive crowd that threatened to overflow the platform and swamp the boat train. Blue-coated, brass-buttoned symbols of English imperial efficiency, they refused to admit defeat but, really, there was no hope of ensuring the right passenger in the correct coach at the proper time. For the Saskatchewan Territory Colony circus had come to Euston this March evening of 1903. Two colonists played squeezebox tunes; a violinist in shabby clothes with his hat on the platform for money played sad Irish songs of departure; a group of young men — boy colonists really — sang "Goodbye Dolly Grey" to great cheers. Quick, destitute girls darted past the harassed baggage guards to sell flowers illicitly on the departure platform. They were joined by hawkers of baked potatoes and matches.

Families swirled like miniature cyclones. Those actually emigrating formed the "eye", while grandparents, uncles, aunts and envious little cousins swirled around them laughing, chatting advice, determined not to be downhearted. The odd single man, perched on his baggage, eyed the spectacle with quiet amusement. It was to one of these calm eddies in the torrent that Jack and Emma gravitated. A solid man, about a dozen years Jack's senior, sat crossed-legged and bowler-hatted on two trunks and a duffle bag. Jack dragged his own trunk — not a handcart or porter in sight — up to the man and parked beside him. Emma, both hands straining on Jack's large valise, arrived a moment later puffing from the exertion. The man nodded, tipping his hat to Emma; they smiled in reply.

"There, you've made a friend already," Emma whispered.

"Oh yes, Em," he laughed. "I'm certain we'll become inseparable comrades."

"I'm just worried about you being alone in that huge land." She bit her lips and eyed the man critically from under her broad hat brim. She'd dressed as though for church, as had most of the women present. A fitting send off she'd said. "He looks strong and practical — be his friend."

Jack clutched her arm. "I'd propose marriage to the fellow if I could — he looks just my type!"

She slapped his shoulder. Then, without warning, she seized him and kissed him, clinging tight as though she would fall if he let her go. Jack's bowler hat friend smiled, envy plain on his face, then discreetly looked away.

"Four months is nothing — no time at all, Watson," she quavered into his ear. "July will come before you know it, if you're brave enough not — "

Her tears came, finally, and in great rolling streams. Jack's throat constricted. He tried to reassure her but he only croaked as far as "Holmes, it will be fine." Then he had to be quiet for fear of crying himself.

They sat huddled on his trunk until they recovered. "I'm glad I wept now," she said, dabbing up the last tears with a sodden hanky. "I want to laugh and cheer when you leave, not blub like a coward."

"I say, look here." Jack led her to a nearby schedule board. A cluster of bills were posted on the reverse side. One poster stood out, garish and bright. WESTERN CANADA — THE NEW ELDORADO. The letters were printed in yellow on a background of green wheat sheaves. Circled pictures dotted the poster. One showed lush fields of grain neatly tucked between thick forests on gently rolling hills. Another portrayed a large two-story Georgian home with barn, trees, corrals and outbuildings. A third depicted a man, pipe in mouth, atop a wagon dwarfed by its load of grain. Four magnificent shires pranced at the end of his reins. THIS IS YOUR OPPORTUNITY. WHY *NOT* EMBRACE IT? HOMES FOR EVERYONE — EASY TO REACH — NOTHING TO FEAR! FREE 160 ACRES — WESTWARD THE STAR OF EMPIRE TAKES IT'S *WAY*.

"That's us, Emma. It's really going to happen to us."

She flung one arm about his waist and drew him to her, smiling now, radiant and excited. "Oh how I wish I could come with you. To see Canada for myself. I feel like a great adventure is slipping past me."

She reached up, tore the poster free of its tacks, folded it and stuffed it into her bag.

"There, our first souvenir of our life's adventure," she said firmly. They returned to the trunk. The billycock hat had been joined by a younger man — perhaps eighteen — in a large, flat, cloth cap. They were talking.

"No go, Alf," flat cap said. "Baggage bloke is all at sixes and sevens."

"What d'ye mean, no-go," bowler hat snapped. "We're never leavin' for Canada wivout our kit."

"'Ee sez if you wants to be sure yer bags go wiv you — best load 'em yourself. I sez, Mr. Barr promised baggage and transport for us."

Flat cap spat on the platform defiantly. "'Ee sez, then let Mr. bleedin' Barr load your bags coz there's no enough porters ner bag men to make sense o' this mess."

Bowler hat glared. "An you sez?"

"I sez, get my trunk loaded sharpish now or my brother will batter you."

Bowler hat laughed. "So, is he coming?"

"Naw, told me to go to blazes."

Bowler hat stooped, hoisted the end of one trunk and laughed again. "Let's get 'em loaded Davie."

Flat cap spat again. "Aw Alf, don't give in to the sonofabitch."

"Pick up your trunk," bowler hat ordered. "An don't be spittin' ner cussing in the lady's presence."

Emma coloured sweetly, then quickly snatched up Jack's valise to follow the billycock and flat cap brothers. Jack tailed behind lugging his trunk, delighted at her practical, quick action.

• • •

Alf and Davie Buxton, introduced and hands shook at the baggage wagon, stood quietly nearby, smoking their pipes. Emma drew two, narrow, boxed packages from her bag. "I brought you something for the nights on the trail and around the campfire."

For one horrified moment he thought she'd got him a harmonica. She opened the first box to reveal a pipe. White matt stem, silver band, and dark gnarled briar bowl. He didn't smoke, but instantly knew that it was perfect. He'd envied the men in Africa their satisfaction at a pipe and mug of tea but somehow felt foolish — like a child aping grown men — when he'd tried it himself. But no longer. He was a man. The realization startled him. Hard manual labour, government service, war veteran, and now married farmer and landowner. No more indecision or doubt. No aping or acting a part. He was going forth to succeed or fail by his own merit. A man needed his pipe. He looked at Emma as she showed him the tobacco pouch — mild blend to start. The bowl was well-blackened and the first trace of a light stain blemished the stem. She saw his look of puzzlement.

"I burnt it in for you," she whispered in his ear. "So it would draw well the first time you used it. And so you would think of me."

"You?" He was astonished. "Sat in your room puffing this pipe, burning it in?"

"No silly — I sneaked into the garden," she giggled. "Mother would have had conniptions if she'd smelled tobacco smoke coming from my room. Nearly made me ill, the beastly thing. But once I got the hang of it . . . well, I found it to be quite pleasant."

• • •

They boarded at midnight. The entire crowd sang "Auld Lang Syne" as the coaches filled. "The Old Folks at Home" followed, sung from carriage windows to the teary-eyed relatives left behind. Jack hung out one of the windows as the train lurched in a false start. Emma, hat now in her hand, stood calm and clear-eyed in the crowd — twenty paces from the train. He waved but she did not. Then the train lurched again and began to roll. She raised her hat like a cowboy and waved it in the air. Her voice broke strong and powerful through the maudlin singing.

"Three cheers for the Barr Colonists!"

The crowd stopped singing. A lull fell over the entire platform.

"Hip, hip!" Emma shouted.

"Hooray!" The throng erupted.

"Hip, hip." She punched the air with her hat, laughing.

"Hooray."

"Hip, hip." She blew him a kiss and began to cry.

"Hooray."

Jack slammed the window up and blinked rapidly, averting his face from Alf and Davie.

"Alfie! That was Mrs. Thornton leadin' the cheers," Davie said.

"Aye," Alf replied. "Her husband's a lucky barstid an' all."

• • •

The Buxton boys were taciturn but not rude. By two AM it became clear there would be no sleep, so they smoked — Jack a half bowl — played cards, and spoke of Canada until a bright dawn saw them deposited in Liverpool. Mr. Barr's string of omni buses whisked them to the Beaver House Hotel on St. George Square for a full breakfast, then down to the docks. The Buxtons were brother butchers in their father's Stepney shop — a shop that barely supported father. They bucked up greatly after demolishing a full tray of sausages between them and confessed to Jack that they knew nothing of horses, farms, or live cattle but were certain they would grow rich raising cows and pigs.

"We know what a good cow or porker should end up like — so we're going to grow 'em ourselves an' cut out the middleman."

When they learned Jack had spent two years farming, they decided to adopt him. For better or worse, Emma's wish had been granted.

• • •

Jack scratched his cheek scars. Three years since the Glosters had formed so orderly and quiet on the floating dock. It might have been three minutes. He found the stock gangway he'd led Bobbi down and almost fancied he could hear Miles' curses when she'd balked at the bottom. Then a swarm of squealing children, yapping

311

dogs and cranky parents swept onto the dock and transformed it back to the present.

"Mr. Thornton!" Davie Buxton yodeled, waving. "Here, our gate, over here."

Jack joined them at the "single men" embarkation gate where Alf was checking his watch again. Nearly ten o'clock and the great bulk of SS *Lake Manitoba* still sat like a rock out in the Mersey. No steam up that Jack could see but Alf refused to accept that their boarding time, already an hour late, could be delayed much longer.

"Where is Mr. Barr or the sailors? Why don't somebody tell us what's going on."

"Should I go find out, Alf?" Davie was the scout. Alf held the fort. It was their habit.

"No!" Alf rammed his bowler down so far it curled his ears out. "You'll bugger off and they'll call us to board."

Jack glanced significantly at the black and white ship shining in the morning light. "Still getting steam up, I expect. No tugs in sight. I think we're looking at a good delay."

Alf checked his watch, squinted at the sun, then nodded, releasing Davie like a greyhound from a gate. The gay family groups so prominent at Euston Station presented a sad spectacle ten sleepless hours later.

"You were smart, to leave your missus behind." Alf volunteered. "Could be a long journey. Mr. Barr says some hardship to start with. Best to leave wives and kiddies 'til we're established, proper like."

Logic bade Jack agree but the thought wrenched him. They'd only had each other for a few days, how could he believe they'd done the right thing when others were sailing with babies, puppies and parakeets? A rank of dark clouds swept up the Mersey and it began to drizzle. A young matron nearby struggled through a welter of hand luggage to find Macintosh coats for her two children. They whined almost without cease, the littlest crying when the first drops hit. Then they fought her as she dressed them. Her husband stood aloof from the fray. He seemed comfortable in a tweed hunting cape and matching deerstalker hat, but frowned when he had to shield his cheroot from the rain. About forty-five years old, he sported a close-cropped greyish beard and fine moustache. He wore a regimental tie — Jack thought the colours were Essex Regiment — and nipped from a silver flask. The wife, twenty years younger and very pretty, finally shrugged her own cloak on over her wet dress. She looked up and Jack caught her eye.

She wasn't angry, or tired, or frustrated. She was afraid. Fear sat on her face like a mask. He looked away, frightened and uneasy for her.

• • •

Jack and most of the passengers braved the cold afternoon mist to line the deck and watch Liverpool slip away. At least a third of the women were crying openly. The rest were on the verge. Most of their men were grim faced, failing in their efforts to look cheerful. The deerstalker man had a fresh cheroot lit and was regaling a small crowd with the story of his regiment's departure for Africa. A knot of ex-soldiers stood nearby, smirking. One nudged Jack.

"You were out to see the elephant I'll wager."

Jack, surprised, admitted it was true.

"Always tell a Boer veteran." The lean hard face winked. "No fuss over a bit of a rain or a few hours delay." He pointed to Jack's face. "Shrapnel?"

"Mauser, Paardeberg," Jack said.

The soldier put out his hand. "Freddy White — London Fusiliers. Ate some dirt at Paardeberg myself."

Jack introduced the Buxton boys. Davie, clearly awed by the older man's loud tale and regal bearing piped up, "He was an officer, a major he says."

Freddy White whistled a little tune through his teeth and smiled knowingly. "Major Nuisance you mean? One o' the lads here served with him. Sailed with the Essex Regiment all right, then found a staff job in Capetown. Went home after four months on account of sick headaches from the heat."

"Oh," Davie retracted his awe.

"Remittance man, I'd guess," Freddy said. "Wife's a corker, though. Pretty thing looks like she'd fling herself overboard if it wasn't for the little 'uns."

Mrs. Major Nuisance was crying. She sobbed, "Oh England, my God, England." Then she pressed a hanky to her lips to stifle the weeping. Her children, for once quiet, stood holding her skirts as Liverpool and England faded into the mist. The well wishers on the dock began to sing a hymn. The colonists did not reciprocate.

• • •

The single men slept in three-tiered bunk beds made of hard planks and jammed eight deep in a large forward dormitory. The midships deck was steadier, had small cubicles for privacy, and was allocated to the families. The single men thought this eminently fair. The single men ate in shifts at a long table with benches running the length of their deck. They served themselves because there were only enough stewards to serve the families' deck. The single men accepted this as fitting. The families were given eggs, meat, and bread. The single men took the excess cabbage and biscuit. The single men didn't like this, but who would take an egg or meat from a kiddie? There were grumblings that Mr. Barr had cheated them. Their passage should at least include the same food for all. But they were at sea, so they put up with it. Besides, most were too seasick in the first thirty-six hours to eat. The meals consumed so far had been thrown up — usually into one of several buckets made available — sometimes onto the sawdust-covered deck. The nauseous wretch was then required to shovel it away.

On the third day, a heavy set, unshaven steward appeared with buckets of breakfast oatmeal, some bread, and praise be, a large tin of jam. He flung these at the heaving table and the jam can missed, spilling itself on the greasy deck. Freddy was the nearest passenger and he raised a howl of disappointment. The steward scraped half the jam off the floor back in the tin and slapped it on the table with a surly scowl.

"We're not eating that!" Fred grabbed the steward's collar. "Bring us a fresh tin."

The steward wrenched free. "No more. Eat that or go without."

"We'll have a new tin and right now," Fred's anger sparkled. A crowd began to gather.

"There's your fresh jam." The steward flicked a lump of jam with the toe of his boot. "Good enough for bloody emmigrants." He turned to leave.

This, the single men would not tolerate. A roaring Freddy White seized the man, spinning him around. The steward was a veteran of more shipboard brawls then Fred had square meals. He came about easily, punching left to Fred's gut and a jarring right uppercut that snapped White's jaw shut with a bang.

"*Fight.*" The steward roared.

Before Fred regained his feet, four steward reinforcements arrived, wading forward to get a lick in at the colonist. Jack vaulted over the table, knocking the jam to the floor a second time. He levelled a lucky punch square on the temple of a tall, lanky steward who was aiming his boot at Freddie's face. The man dropped. In his mind's eye, Jack had leapt the table to pull Fred clear but his fist had seen the easy target and punched of its own accord. Appalled, he collared Fred and pulled him back into the crowd. One of Fred's soldier pals traded a brief flurry of blows with the original steward, then both sides broke contact. The stewards backed to the exit, hurling insults and daring any man to fight. Jack's victim lay limp on the deck in no-man's land. The soldiers and single men formed a human wall opposite the stewards.

Stalemate.

Alf Buxton went forward and stooped to help the steward to his feet. "Enough!" he bellowed, steadying the man. "Behave yourselves!"

The "jam tin" steward darted up as though to hit Alf, but stopped short and delivered a volley of curses instead. Alf pushed the punch-drunk man toward his friends and shouted for order but he was shouted down. Davie pushed to Alf's side. Jack joined them.

"Davie, quick now," Alf said. "Get up to the boat deck and fetch Mr. Barr down here or there'll be a riot."

"Won't let me on the boat deck — no steerage allowed." Davie had scouted the ship thoroughly. Alf eyed Jack's tie, collar and suit. "Take Mr. Thornton — show him the way — let him do the talking."

Davie moved like a beagle in bracken, zipping through a small bulkhead door, down two corridors, then up a series of steel ladders. Jack tailed him. They emerged on the main deck and made their way up a flight of stairs to the upper deck. An immaculate steward materialized and drove Davie down a step with a single glare. Jack pulled Edmund Swinglehurst to mind and looked brightly at the steward.

"I say, excellent timing. See here, I must speak to Mr. Barr immediately on urgent business."

The steward nodded and without a murmur led them around to a small, teak, sunlit deck. Davie nudged Jack and smiled. Two men sat in deck chairs, a third stood by the deck railing. Isaac Barr was leaned back in his chair, face to the sun, eyes half closed. He wore a white naval officer's hat, cleric collar and thick moustaches. Otherwise, his dress was plain. Beside him lounged a study in elegance. Tall, thin, high soft boots and immaculate tweed suit, the secretary for the colony, George Flamanck, watched Jack and Davie approach.

"Sorry to disturb, sir, but there is trouble in the single men's deck." Jack nearly stood to attention as he reported but remembered the Swinglehurst slouch just in time.

"Trouble! What now?" Flamanck rose. "And you are?"

"Thornton, John Thornton. A fight with the stewards over food — could turn ugly. If Mr. Barr could come, I'm sure his presence would . . ."

Barr sighed heavily and made to rise up but Flamanck touched him with a restraining hand.

"Mr. Barr does not break up brawls in steerage."

Barr seemed to accept this and eased back into his chair. "The men shouldn't be fighting," he said to Flamanck. "This is an English Christian colony."

Both men looked past Jack, as though this solved the problem.

"Jolly right," Jack forced himself to stay with Swinglehurst. "But they are fighting and bad luck for us — I fear it will take a gentleman of Mr. Barr's status to bring order."

"I believe there are many gentlemen who couldn't obtain cabins on the boat deck." Flamanck looked directly at Jack for the first time. "Many gentlemen were obliged to travel third class — can't one of them clear this up?" He paused, smiling wickedly. "I believe Major Jordan is in the married quarters. Fetch him. Or perhaps yourself, sir. You could take the situation in hand."

"Oh no," Davie's voice shot out from behind Jack. "It was Mr. Thornton here what cold cocked the big steward. They won't listen to him, I don't think."

That effectively ended the interview. Both Barr and Flamanck twisted away, but the third man standing at the rail burst out laughing. Very tall, cadaverously thin even in his priest's cloak and broad-brimmed cleric hat, his eyes were bright and lively. "That true, Mr. Thornton?"

The Swinglehurst bravado evaporated. Jack nodded and removed his hat.

"Well, Christian Englishmen or not, we can't have a riot in the middle of the north Atlantic. He threw off his cloak revealing dog collar and dark clergyman's suit. He strode past them. "Let's go preach some "Goodwill toward Man" shall we?"

$$\bullet\ \bullet\ \bullet$$

The belligerent forces had closed to near arm's length. Their shouting filled the room, pushing the oxygen out. Freddy White, bloody-lipped and wild-eyed, was within an ace of charging the steward lines. The Reverend tugged his hat down, smoothed his beard and pushed through the doorway past the surprised stewards who wheeled about expecting a sneak attack from the rear.

"Quiet! Quiet please, gentlemen!" The minister's voice was strong. Its command was obeyed. "I'm Reverend George Lloyd — chaplain for the Saskatchewan Valley Colony."

He let that sink in and stepped between the battle lines turning slowly so all could see him.

"You have the look of a soldier," Lloyd said genially to White.

"I am, sir," Freddy snapped back. "Two years in Africa."

"Fighting over spilled jam?" Lloyd asked. "I can't believe a British soldier, veteran of severe hardship and mortal dangers would do such a thing. Surely not."

Freddy White wilted. The blow hit much harder than the steward's fist.

"But you are entitled to decent food, I grant you," Lloyd smiled sympathetically, restoring Fred's dignity. He turned to the steward, plucked the breakfast chit from the man's tunic breast pocket, and scribbled a note on it.

"There now. Take that to the quartermaster and draw two large tins from the boat deck stores."

The steward nodded meekly.

"But let us not forget," Lloyd raised his voice to sermon tenor. "We *are* British men, bound to make a better life for ourselves and to bring civilization to a wilderness. We must behave as civilized Britons."

He took Fred's hand and the steward's hand, joining them. Fred grinned and shook. The steward, embarrassed beyond resistance, shook back.

● ● ●

The fifth day at sea, halfway from England to Canada, the Saskatchewan colony got its sea legs. Reverend Lloyd crammed the main dormitories for lively church services in the morning. Roast beef, pudding, potatoes actually cooked right through, and ladles of hot gravy appeared before every passenger. The sun shone brightly on a deck thronged with colonists taking in the cool, salt air and light sea. Three good-natured boxing matches declared a colony boxing champ complete with small trophy. Mr. Barr even gave a lecture on land titles and set up an office where men could go to pick their one hundred sixty acres from a map pinned to the wall — speed up the homestead claims once they arrived in Canada.

Fred White and the other Boer veterans had gone to queue up at the land office but on Jack's advice the Buxton boys had decided to wait until they reached Canada to make a claim. They sat on the deck, backs propped against a white bulkhead, soaking in the reflected sunlight. Jack read from his African edition of Hardy. He mused on how much Thomas Hardy's stories had changed. In Africa, they had represented his hope for Emma. Now they reflected his memory of her. A north breeze carrying iceberg-cooled air played over them. Two small girls raced past them, shrieking, then laughing, then shrieking again.

A moment later one of the girls peeked around an air funnel protruding from the deck. She was about seven years old with blonde wispy hair rapidly coming adrift from its plaited tail. Jack idly glanced her way and she squealed, jumping back to hide from view. Gales of laughter pealed from the funnel. Jack kept his eye on the hiding place and was rewarded a minute later by the smaller girl's eyes peering out from cover. He winked with great exaggeration. The little girl, perhaps two years younger than her sister, was also blonde and clutched a soft, cloth doll. Her mouth popped open in surprise, she dropped her doll, and fell backwards producing more shrieks.

"Got a way with women, that's for certain," Alf pushed his hat up from where it had shaded his eyes. "Look here now, the game's afoot."

Two skinny arms reached out, picked up the doll, and made it dance a little jig. When it stopped, Jack, Davie, and Alf applauded. The arms made the doll bow, then whipped it out of sight. A little voice shrilled, "Ready, Steady, *go!*"

Two blonde rockets shot from behind the funnel and raced squealing past the men.

"Hello, Mr. Dimples!"

Alf looked at Jack. "Mr. Dimples?"

Jack shrugged, vaguely guilty again. Somebody was taking those two little porcelain children into the Saskatchewan wilderness; he should have let Emma come. The expedition certainly looked to succeed easily.

"Uh, oh, here they come again," Davie warned.

A flurry of flying feet and flailing arms bore down on them.

"Hello, Mr. Dimples!"

The older girl made the safety of the funnel but the little one, victim of an untied boot lace, crashed headlong into the deck, doll rebounding from the bulkhead. A second of calm descended before a storm of crying erupted. Alf was up and giving aid before Jack could get to his feet. He retrieved the doll and brought it to the scene of the accident. Alf pressed a clean handkerchief to the well-skinned knee while the little girl perched on his lap crying her eyes out. His beefy hand gently brushed the hair back from her face and he rocked her to and fro.

"Well, well, what a tumble we've had then, miss. Never fear now, it's going to be fine. Oh, oh, poor little girl . . . "

The quiet prattle represented more sustained conversation than Jack had heard from Alf over all the last five days. Jack knelt and held the doll out awkwardly.

"Look who's come to see you!" Alf took the doll and tucked it into her arms. "Is your doll's name Mr. Dimples, then?" The girl's sobbing decreased as she hugged the doll and endeavoured to reply. "*No*, she's a girl, see?"

She thrust the doll into Alf's smiling face, displaying its frock, bonnet and long ringlets. Alf examined it.

"How silly of me. How could such a pretty doll be named Mister Dimples."

She snuffled a smile at this.

"Is this your sister?"

The older girl was edging carefully toward them.

"Yes. That's Mary."

Alf beckoned to Mary. "Come up now, your little sister's fine."

Mary darted to the casualty and stared at the red blotch on the handkerchief.

"That looks awful, Kitty, does it hurt?"

Kitty nodded tearfully at these drastic words, but Alf neatly headed off a relapse.

"But she's being very brave, aren't you, Kitty?"

Kitty's little jaw clenched.

"Besides, she has to take care of Mr. Dimples, he had a terrible fall too!"

"*Nooo!*" Kitty protested, shaking her doll in Alf's face again. "My doll is a *girl*, remember?"

"Well now, I've done it again!" Alf laughed and the girls laughed, too.

"Catherine! Mary! What on earth are you doing?"

Their mother, in full flight of worry, indignation and embarrassment swept down on them. Jack recognized her, Mrs. Major Nuisance — Mrs. Jordan, apparently. The men rose, doffing their caps. Alf cradled Kitty in his arm.

"Kitty fell, Mama, and this man is a doctor," Mary improvised quickly. "He's bandaged her."

The mother was blonde like her daughters and as beautiful at close range as Fred White had speculated from long range.

"Doctor?" The pretty face frowned in obvious disbelief. "Is my daughter injured?"

"No, ma'am," Jack stepped forward to save a now silent Alf. "The girls were playing around us, hide and seek, I think, when Kitty — Catherine, fell. Mr. Buxton's not a doctor but he has worked a miracle on that scraped knee."

"Oh girls! I told you to play quietly and here you've run off to bother these gentlemen!" She reached for Kitty and shot Mary a cross look.

"But Mother, Mrs. Dimples wanted to see Mr. Dimples," Mary explained quickly.

The mother blushed fiercely. Alf took the doll's arm. "So this is Missus Dimples!"

Kitty and Mary laughed.

"Who, pray tell, is Mr. Dimples?"

The girls suddenly fell shy, darting glances at their mother, who looked as though she wished the deck would open and swallow her.

"Oh, this is frightful." She looked at Jack and smiled apologetically. "I'm afraid this is partly my fault. You see, Kitty's doll has large dimples sewn into her cheeks."

Kitty held the doll up again for inspection. Alf peered closely, jabbing the indentations and giggling in a woman's voice, much to the girls' renewed delight.

"Before we go farther, I should introduce myself. I'm Alice Jordan. My husband is Major Jordan."

Jack introduced himself and the Buxtons, shaking hands on their behalf. She clung to his hand and made her explanation.

"I'm afraid the girls were asking about Mrs. Dimples' . . . ah, well, dimples . . . yesterday when you walked past us on the deck and . . . I'm so sorry, no harm was intended you see . . . "

The light dawned and Jack hurried to put her out of her misery. He poked his index fingers into his scars.

"*I'm* Mr. Dimples!"

Alf and Davie roared with laughter. "O' course you are! What a lot of dense men we are, Kitty!"

Mrs. Jordan smiled with relief. "How very understanding — you're so kind, Mr. Thornton."

Her eyes couldn't help staring briefly at Jack's face.

"South Africa, ma'am, Paardeberg. Boer rifleman gave me my dimples."

Her eyes widened with sympathy. "I didn't mean to pry . . . "

"Not at all, ma'am," Alf now came to her rescue. "'E dines out regularly on them dimples. What's more important is Miss Kitty's knee repairs — there's a real injury."

They made their way back to Mrs. Jordan's base camp: a deck chair, a book, and a scatter of bags containing children clothing, biscuits, and toys. She rummaged until she produced a small, tin medical box. Alf took charge. His large fingers deftly cleaned the scrape, dabbed iodine, shushed Kitty's squeals of pain, applied a small gauze bandage, and sealed the deal with peppermints from a bag in his vest pocket. Mrs. Jordan wisely stood clear, at Jack's side.

"He has a way with children, marvelous really," she said frankly admiring his first-aid skills. "His children are fortunate."

"Alf's a bachelor, Mrs. Jordan," Jack corrected her. "Confirmed bachelor, I'd say. I've only known him a few days but he's one of the best men in the forward dormitory. He'll make a go of the new world."

She arched her eyebrows quizzically. "Because he's good with children?"

"No," Jack bristled slightly. "Because he's punctual, hard-working, has a sense of humour, and has a solid plan.

"Mr. Thornton," she said, studying Alf anew. "I find that very easy to believe about Mr. Buxton."

"And," Jack continued, mollified, "he was the only one on our deck to stop a fight that could have turned very ugly. He's a natural leader"

"Thornton! The fight! Of course." She turned on him. "You're something of a celebrity. Major Jordan told me — you're the one who laid out the steward!"

Jack cringed and muttered something about a momentary lapse.

"Major Jordan has gone to file a claim. Not you?"

"Our plan," he said. "The Buxtons and I, that is. Our plan is to tour the colony before we settle a claim. I've farmed some poor soil in Gloucestershire and I want to see what we're getting. The Buxton brothers and I plan to file on adjacent quarters, pool our labour and . . . "

Jack recited the plan for the "Newland Cooperative", as he'd come to call it. The fear that he'd seen on her face in Liverpool returned. He stopped his lecture, afraid he'd given offence.

"I wish to heaven we had a plan," she murmured.

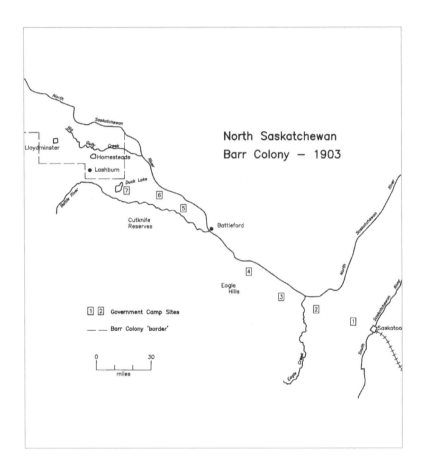

North Saskatchewan
Barr Colony — 1903

Lloydminster

Homesteads
Lashburn

North

Saskatchewan

Gully Creek

Duck Lake

7

6

5

Battleford

4

3

2

1

Saskatoon

Cutknife
Reserves

Eagle
Hills

Eagle Creek

North

Saskatchewan River

South Saskatchewan River

Battle River

1 2 Government Camp Sites

——— Barr Colony 'border'

0   30
miles

Ploughshares

CHAPTER 18

Canada, 1903

Jack was reconciled to the claustrophobic troop ship arrangements on the SS *Lake Manitoba*, until he emerged on deck at dawn of the eleventh day out from Liverpool. Before him lay Saint John, New Brunswick. Then, suddenly, he'd had more than his fill of the crowded, stinking ship with its petty intrigues and squabbles. He was desperate to be away for the Saskatchewan territory. A heavy, cold mist sifted in from the Bay of Fundy, but it had a smell of land that Jack found exhilarating. He consulted a pamphlet Isaac Barr had issued yesterday. "At Saint John the party shall step from the steamer onto the train and shall not be compelled to seek shelter in an immigration shed or in hotels. If the train is not quite ready when the steamer arrives, we shall remain on her until it is. There will, however, be no delay".

Jack laughed. Barr had a certain style. Absolutely no touch with the reality of the expedition — but plenty of style — and nerve. Two days earlier, Barr had ordered the ship's cooks to bake all the colonist reserve flour into bread for the train ride west. Then he declared the bread would be sold at ten cents a loaf to cover "expenses". Lloyd was publicly furious and an ad hoc committee of concerned colonists had stormed Barr's office demanding an explanation. The man was proposing to sell them their own bread! Major Jordan was prominent on the committee.

Over the last five days Major Jordan had been in the forefront of several colonist versus Isaac Barr confrontations: poor accommodation; poor food; and the land claim office fiasco. Jordan discovered that his "prime" quarter section had been given out again twice over. He'd learned Barr was not keeping a proper record of claims filed and, indeed, had no authority to issue land. Alice Jordan had told him of Jack's Newland Cooperative plan and he quickly joined it — without asking permission. On learning Jack had been a corporal and the Buxtons were east-end butchers, the major un-joined, nose in the air. Jack had been relieved but the pragmatic Alf saw the major as a source of influence and money, assets that outweighed his arrogance. Alf had a word with Mrs. Jordan who, in turn, convinced her husband that the working men needed him. Jordan saved face by declaring he'd gladly take command of the Newland Cooperative after all. He referred to Jack as Jack and Alf as Buxton. He did not refer to Davie at all.

Jack drew a lung-full of the moist Canadian air and blew it out, trying to picture the Saskatchewan country — the new world. Alf accepted money and influence as necessary evils but they tainted Jack's own dream. Alf had slipped into the role of helper, servant, butler, and nursemaid to the Jordan family. Mary and Kitty adored Alf. Their own father, when not on committee business, spent most of his time smoking and tippling. It was a complication that Jack had grown to resent. It would be paramount that the cooperative make good progress on land claims, breaking the soil, seeding the first crops, arranging shelter . . . a million things to be done. He was sympathetic to Alice Jordan and her children but would they jeopardize his and Emma's future?

Jack peered through the mist at the grey shoreline and said aloud what he imagined Emma might say. "Ah, well, money and influence can't hurt, Watson. Even remittance men have their uses."

• • •

The colonist trains were ten hours late, with luggage in chaos, and they departed only because of the herculean efforts of Reverend Lloyd. The first train carried single men who needed jobs to Winnipeg. The second train carried single men with money to Saskatoon. The third train conveyed families, and the fourth, all the luggage. Moments before the second train's departure, Alf the punctual, Alf the fastidious disappeared. Jack and Davie flew up the Saint John platform in opposite directions to find him. Jack spotted Alf shifting a stack of Jordan family trunks toward the baggage cars under Alice's directions.

"Thornton! Jack, my boy!" Major Jordan's rasping voice called him from up the tracks. "Seen my wife have you?"

The major strode toward Jack, a daughter trailing from each hand. "I've got a committee report to prepare — damned train arrangements are a disaster — and she's lumbered me with the children."

"He's managing your baggage for her, yonder. Alf!" Jack shouted. "Our train is leaving — this minute, hurry now."

Alf ran up, bobbed his red face at the major and started to explain the arrangements. A moment later Alice arrived to repeat the story. Jack took Alf's arm, "Enough now! We are in danger of missing . . . "

Alf pulled free. "Wait a tick — got to say goodbye to my girls."

"No time!" He shoved Alf and broke into a run. "Come on, for God's sake!"

"'Til Saskatoon lads — wait for us in Saskatoon."

"Right you are, Major — safe journey."

• • •

"If you take Barr's guarantees and cut them in half, then you will only be badly disappointed," Fred White declared. This started another round of complaints among the men queued up to cook their billies of porridge on the single, tiny stove. Jack Thornton did not join the chorus. He was already fighting a mounting sense of dread that was eating at his confidence, like an angry sea eats at a weak shoreline, caving it in inch by inch, relentlessly. His fears came partly from the obvious truth in Freddie's declaration. Barr, however well meaning, was in over his head. Simple arrangements such as trains, baggage, and meals had been bungled. The CPR, Canadian Immigration men and Reverend Lloyd had salvaged each situation, barely. If Barr couldn't even get them properly from ship to train — what would happen when they reached Saskatoon?

He fingered his money belt. What if the promise of wagons, implements and livestock had been bungled? What if there was no free land? What if — as Freddie and Major Jordan often said — what if Barr was a crook? Would he go home to Emma as a duped failure? But these were early morning fears — daylight and logic calmed them. The CPR and Canadian Government were not Barr's henchmen. The colony might muddle through, regardless of Barr's incompetence. His real fear, the gnawing dread, came from Canada itself. False dawn illuminated the country outside his train window and it did not banish his Canada fears. The place was staggering. It overwhelmed, as even South Africa had not. Two days on a train had conquered the Karoo, but it seemed that here, two days on a train meant nothing.

The train seemed to move on a perpetual treadmill through a long, narrow tunnel carved from a primeval dark forest. Occasional patches of open sky appeared where villages and a scatter of farms had been hacked from the boreal evergreen jungle of spruce and fir. The celebrated and much anticipated Montreal was bypassed as a horizon light one night. Ottawa, and its attendant river valley,

DAVID RICHARDS

provided a few hours of civilized, inhabited country, before they plunged back into the trees to go north of Lake Superior. When he first glimpsed the vast, ice-packed, inland ocean, Jack raced to the platform at the end of the carriage. Sky above and miles of lake below gave soul and mind a chance to breathe before the frigid air drove him back inside. Then the rock and trees returned to snuff the openness like the last candle extinguished in a dark room. The Forest of Dean was no forest at all. It scarcely existed.

This fourth morning, waiting in line for hot water for his tea, added to the sense of dread. Trees again. No animals, no birds, no humans. Rock, trees, water, and trees. Impenetrable forest sped past the window in the gathering light. The conductor said Winnipeg and the prairies would appear today but Jack found no solace in this. The train, speeding faster than an English train, would take more than two days to cross the prairies to Saskatoon — "The Promised Land" — Mr. Barr's pamphlet said. And Saskatoon was in the middle of the vast prairie. My God, it would never end. How would two London butchers, a clerk, Emma, and a remittance man with a desperate wife penetrate this empti-ness . . . this vacuum. "Newland Estate" he and Emma had enthused. This country would eat Newland Estate and leave not a trace of their passing. If only Emma were with him. If only they could be together on the married train with the Lloyds; he could face it. But his strength oozed from him on this crowded, noisy train full of inexperienced young men hurtling toward oblivion.

• • •

Jack hoped, wildly and illogically he knew, that Sergeant Kerslake would appear at the Winnipeg train station. He did not, of course. Winnipeg looked grand with its expansive main street, brick and stone buildings. Newspapers declared two thousand wealthy, upper

332

middle-class Englishmen were accompanying a Mr. Barr through the city. Every person Jack met on the brief stopover asked him two questions: "Are you one of Barr's Colonists?"; then, "Would you like to buy a watch, or hat, or shovel, or horse, or dog?"

Jack, depressed and irresponsible, said yes to the dog, astonishing himself. Re-boarding the train he dug a haversack from his valise and deposited the quiet little tricoloured hound into it. Weaned three and a half months, the man had guaranteed. What on earth was he to do with a dog? Davie fell head over heels in love, producing bread, water and even a little sausage for it. The cooperative needed a dog, he said. Every other colonist had brought a dog from home and Mr. Thornton had done well in his choice because a beagle would find rabbits and grouse for them. Beagles were English hounds, Davie said, and you couldn't do better than that.

A flaming sun went down on the ocean-flat horizon as they sped westward. It filled Jack with a longing for the green hills of England, a longing that was more terrible than any he'd experienced for Gloucester in Newland or for Newland in Africa. Swinglehurst and Wheeler would wake, soon, to go to work. Emma would breakfast in the morning room of a Chelsea sunrise. The Vicar — Uncle Henry — and Charlie would be harrowing or seeding with thoughts of a pint in the Ostrich later. What in hell was he doing on this endless, treeless ocean of frozen, dead grass? Jack cradled the sleeping pup in his arms.

"What will you name him?" Davie asked, unable to resist stroking the little hound's long silken ears.

"Ostrich," Jack said without thinking.

"Are you serious?"

"Yes."

• • •

The station in Saskatoon could not accommodate one-tenth of the trunks and cases and crates that Barr's lambs had brought to the "promised land". In the end, the baggage cars simply opened their doors and dumped their contents. If you were lucky, they landed on the prairie grass; if unlucky, in the muddy ditch beside the tracks. The prairie stretched to three naked horizons. Only the west side of the tracks showed signs of habitation. A tall slope-shouldered grain elevator stood like a proud giant near the tracks. Farther on, the two-story, wood-frame, immigration hall towered over a swarm of army surplus, bell tents. The tents were aligned in streets and rows reminiscent of the plague hospital at Bloemfontien, except these tents bore traces of sleet and snow and they marked the end of track. Beyond them, a brief scraggle of houses and shops bravely delineated the western limit of civilization. Saskatoon. So long awaited, so often dreamed of, so heart breaking in reality.

Claustrophobic, exasperated colonists rushed for baggage, then for a wet, cold tent. Fights, both verbal and with fists, erupted because the baggage was jumbled and the tents were too few. Freddie White, Jack, and the other Boer War veterans dug into a mountain of canvas and rope and pitched two dozen more tents near the immigration hall. Reverend Lloyd ensured everyone was at least under cover. Neither wood nor water was to be had and not a hint of food, but at least shelter from the freezing wind and sleet. Barr holed up in the immigration building, all others were denied access.

Freddie pointed out one advantage gained in spending the remains of the day setting up tents. The rest of the colonists had already retrieved their luggage from the CPR mess. The attendant fist fights and furor were over. Thus, the last few trunks and bags lying lonely in the ditch at nightfall were the property of the tent builders and, by default, were easily identified and claimed.

Jack skidded his trunk into the tent he shared with the Buxton boys. Davie had wrapped himself in three layers of clothes, then rolled up in his blankets, Ostrich had wisely taken refuge with Davie. Alf's blankets were neatly laid out but Alf was absent. Jack swore quietly. Ostrich yipped at the sound of his voice.

"Has he gone to see Mrs. Jordan?" Jack asked.

Davie hedged. "Maybe — couldn't say for sure."

"Davie?"

"Yes, I guess he did." He sat up, blankets and dog spilling down. "But don't be wexed, he had to go. The major is at a committee meeting at the hotel. They're getting a claim to dun the CPR for the baggage mess and . . . "

Jack was already gone, striding along the tent lines. Hungry, cold, and anxious, he gave a spark of anger its head, nurturing it into a fury by the time he arrived at Major Jordan's tent. Night had settled and it highlighted his prey. Lantern lit, stovepipe puffing nicely, the smell of frying bacon floated around it. Most of the other tents were dark, their occupants huddled like Davie against the cold.

"Alf!" Jack shouted.

No answer.

"Alf Buxton!" Somebody opened the tent flap inward and Jack stepped through without further invitation. The lantern fluttered brightly. Mary and Kitty perched on stools near the glowing camp stove eating bacon sandwiches. Alice sat on a cot, nicely made up for the night with blankets and quilt, likewise eating, a mug of tea at her feet.

"I say, you've done well, Alf, very well indeed." Jack's sarcasm was either missed or ignored. Coatless, with sleeves rolled up, Alf was heating a basin of water. He proudly explained how he'd already been to town to procure the stove and bacon, then unpacked some of the Jordan furniture and created a snug camp for their first night in the promised land.

"Davie is lying hungry in the dark on a muddy patch of grass. Did you think to offer him a bit of bacon? We spent the whole day getting people under shelter. We've had nothing to eat or drink. What about my snug camp? Is this a cooperative or are we indentured, bloody servants?"

Alice sipped her tea, staring into the mug.

"I'm never indentured — whatever it means." Alf straightened up. He met Jack's eyes and his voice turned hostile. "Davie's a man, you're a man, these is women and children. I'm not leaving them . . ."

"She's got a man, for God's sake!" They would soon have to attack that endless horizon and he was afraid. He wanted Emma and he wanted England and he wanted a bacon sandwich. Most of all he wanted Alf strong and at his side. "Major Jordan is her man! Not you. You are only "Buxton" their performing ape!"

Alf took two great steps, slammed one thick, flat palm onto Jack's chest and Jack flew back through the tent flap tearing it half away. He landed on his back. The stars of Cassiopeia played above him in the black sky. The tent flap secured itself shut. Jack returned to his tent, picked up Ostrich, and rolled into his blankets.

"Is he coming home . . . or staying with them?" Davie's voice was plaintive in the dark tent.

"Home? Funny word for a leaky tent on the cold prairie, Davie."

Davie didn't defend himself.

"He'll be home soon," Jack said, disgusted that his own voice sounded as plaintive as Davie's. "I pray to God that Alf will decide to come home."

Ostrich burrowed under his arm in a way that suggested he missed his mother and littermates. Jack lay sleeplessly reviewing the cooperative's status. One posturing, remittance man, fond of drink. Remittance's young wife and babies, unable to survive without servants. One over-age bachelor wearing blinkers, and servile. One grass-green boy. One homesick, lovesick colonist already fighting with his tent mate. And one beagle puppy. They were beginning to founder and they were only one hundred paces from the train tracks. Soon they would have to penetrate over one hundred miles of the wilderness. "God, please grant me the courage and strength for the trials before me."

"Amen to that," Davie said.

• • •

Even Jack, a minister's son, did not expect God to grant wishes. But the next day, a bright, warm, sunny Sunday, went a fair way toward restoring his courage and strength. Reverend Lloyd led the service in a huge government marquee tent with wooden floors and warm stoves. The major stayed with his family, and Alf pretended to forget the previous night's squabble. Jack and Davie happily followed his lead. In fact, Alf had procured a second camp stove. They spent the remainder of the morning rigging its pipe through the awkward belltent, putting a thick layer of straw on the ground, setting up cots and laying a table of sorts on Jack's trunk. Then they cooked and ate a huge breakfast of oatmeal porridge, bacon, and sweet tea. They lounged in front of their tent, contentedly smoking pipes, comfortable on the prairie grass which dried quickly in the sun.

Visitors came by. Fred White and some veterans stopped for a smoke. Young men who had befriended Davie on the boat sought him out. All poor London boys, they travelled on the largesse of a well-to-do philanthropist named Miss Sisley. She was paying their way, equipment and all, to make a fresh start in the promised land.

337

"Jack Barr, your leader's brother and here to provide you with the best animals at the best prices."

The farm instructor made to introduce himself but was blithely elbowed to one side as Jack Barr conducted them to a large pair of chestnut-coloured horses. He and the major immediately fell to discussing fetlocks and shoulders and spavins — stroking the animals, checking their teeth. Jack sat on the top rail of the corral as Barr walked the pair around demonstrating their gentility and training. They were impressive horses, not of Bobbi's build, but they must be western-bred and, therefore, hardy and reliable. Yet something didn't seem right about them. The major was wary of Barr, instinctively distrusting every word he said, but eventually had to admit the animals looked good.

"Your brother has let us down badly," he began his bargaining. "But these chestnuts will suit me. How much?"

"Five hundred dollars," Barr said coolly.

"What! That's, why that's . . . " the major's beet face flushed with outrage.

"That's near one hundred pound." Davie made the calculation.

"Your brother said a good team would be sixty pounds, that's a fifty percent soaking," Alf snapped, jamming his bowler down tight against his ears.

"Well said, Buxton." the major smoothed his moustaches. "Three hundred dollars, harness included."

Jack Barr laughed harshly. "They'll sell for five hundred, easy; I could get six from a green horn."

"Never!" The major became very regimental. "You will sell these horses for three hundred dollars or not at all."

Barr smiled and tipped his hat. "Good day to you then, sir. And good luck pulling your wagon without horses."

He turned to welcome a colonist who was hurrying up to the corral.

Although deadly religious, she had inspired them with a pioneering spirit that soared high and infectious today. The Jordans in Sunday best dropped in for a civilized cup of tea. Alice had found a cow, bought some milk, and brought it as a treat. The major, Jack, and Alf held a long, but exciting, planning session. Using Mr. Barr's pamphlet as their shopping list and Jack's farming experience as a guide they discussed their equipment and livestock purchases for the next day. The major was adamant about horses — a gentleman's animal — while Alf was plumping for oxen. Alf was going on the advice of a local man he'd met in town and Jack, although hearing the practical logic of Alf's argument, couldn't see himself calling an ox "Bobbi". He was for horses, as well.

They would each have their own wagon, harness, team, plough, tent, cookstove and basic tools. They would share costs on harrows, mower, and binder. This equipment would be used communally for the first year or so. They would buy their crop and garden seed in bulk to get the best price, then divide it three ways. Alf asked why Barr's list showed both harrows and disk harrows. Jack assured him that, once ploughed, a good set of smoothing harrows with round teeth would prepare the seed bed. Disk harrows might be useful in heavy land or in newly-cleared land but there seemed to be little danger of tree or hedge roots on this prairie. They were just ploughing grass, never-ending grass. How difficult could that be?

It was exciting; it was warm in the golden, spring sunlight; it was civilized and methodical — three like-minded men finally making real plans to tackle the Saskatchewan Valley wilderness. They smoked and sipped from the major's flask. Alf spoke as an equal, eschewing his role of "Buxton", much to Jack's relief. For a moment he could believe it would be the grand adventure he and Emma had planned. The major held a match for Alf's pipe and Mr. Barr's Colony was good again on this bright Sunday of optimistic dreams. Davie and Alice and the little girls laughed and played with Ostrich. The beagle adopted Kitty and Mary as his littermates and even he howled with baby-hound delight.

• • •

Jack got up, started the fire, made tea and porridge, and then sprinted for the immigration hall before Alf or Davie showed a leg the next morning. He was first in line when the post office opened and was rewarded with two letters from Emma. He ran back to the tent, dished up breakfast then sat outside facing the rising sun, eating and reading. Neither letter said anything new or important but each word was devoured slowly and carefully. He touched Emma's signature: 'With all my love, your Emma.' He looked up at the semicircle of sun breaking the eastern horizon. That sun was already looking back on a London afternoon. In three months Emma would follow it out to him and this barren place. Yesterday's courage fought his bedrock of doubt and won, barely.

Alf repeated his concern over the disk harrows as they walked toward the Jordan tent and Jack allowed that they could certainly afford a set at only six pounds — split three ways. They decided to let it be a low priority. If they acquired all their other kit and had time then they would get a disker, but Alf and Davie would have to transport it. Major Jordan, beet-faced and hungover, stood sipping a cup of tea waiting for them. The two little girls were whining for their breakfast as a flustered Alice struggled with an overheated pot of porridge that was flinging boiling lumps of oatmeal onto the stove where they immediately burnt. Alf pointed like a bird dog but the major reined him in with a gruff, "Leave her to it, Buxton. She has to learn some time and we've got a big day ahead of us."

The four men set off, eagerly discussing horses versus oxen and the best wagon styles. They agreed that transportation had the highest priority and that the good wagons and animals might sell out quickly. They hurried down First Avenue toward the wagon yard where two surprises awaited them.

First, only one style and size of cart was available. The slab-sided, high-box, unsprung Bain wagon, painted bright green with red wheels was the only thing to be had. It would be the only thing for at least two months. The second surprise was price. Barr's pamphlet specified fifteen pounds per wagon. These were twenty, not including seat, hoops, or canvas cover. Major Jordan nearly left to inform his committee of the swindle but Jack persuaded him to stay. The Bain wagons were new, sturdy, general purpose vehicles that met their needs. Only fifty were available at the moment although the CPR promised delivery of more "soon". These wagons would be sold before noon, and their buyers would be first on the trail and first to choose land. They bought three Bains. Alf and Davie blanched at the unexpected cost but, when the agent tacked a SOLD receipt to their rig, they beamed with pride. They proceeded directly to the horse sellers, excited now that they'd made their first deal.

A Dominion Government Farm Instructor was engaged in an animated discussion with the proprietor of a corral full of horses. The proprietor, a vaguely familiar man, immediately broke off his conversation upon sight of his first customers of the day.

"Welcome, gentlemen, welcome." He glad-handed them all in turn and patted Ostrich. "Wise men, I can tell by looking at you. The smart colonist will spend his time and cash on the best horses he can find. Your team will make or break you in this country. Early bird gets the worm."

"My sentiments exactly, Mr. . . . ," the major said.

"Damned Barrs!" The major's eyes popped at the impudence.

"Bound to be better deals around, Major." Jack hopped down. "Remember the bread on the boat? There must be local prices available."

The man with the "Farm Instructor" armband sidestepped over to them. "I'm afraid not. A decent team will be four to five hundred dollars, sadly."

"But the pamphlet says . . . " Alf produced his underlined and well-worn copy of the Saskatchewan Valley Colony document.

"That is not, I repeat *not*, a realistic guide." The instructor smiled sympathetically. "Listen gentlemen, I'm not meant to interfere on prices. I'm here as a civil servant to help you find land and farm it. But I feel compelled to speak."

"Then speak," Major Jordan ordered.

"Bluntly, those horses look fine, but they are blind."

"Good God!" The major reached for his flask. Jack felt as though he'd been punched. All his courage evaporated. Prices one-third or more higher than anticipated he could manage, but they simply could not venture forth with bad animals. Alf and Davie were on a much tighter budget than he — they could conceivably leave Saskatoon broke, or not leave at all under such ruinous costs.

"Look here," the instructor drew them into a confidential circle and lowered his voice. "My bosses don't want you dealing with Canadians or Europeans, the All-British Colony, right?"

"A sound policy, too," the major breathed whiskey fumes at them. "You're not suggesting we consort with Slavics — peasants?"

The inspector's eyes hardened. "Northeast of town, trail leaves from the other end of First Avenue. Six miles out you will find two outfits selling livestock. Same prices as here but it's good stock. And, if I was you, I'd leave the horses. Oxen are the ticket. Horses need barns, hay and oats. An ox will live on this." He kicked the thick, woolly grass. "And a good pair costs one hundred twenty dollars. Pass the word to your friends."

Then, guilty at his betrayal of the Colony Policy, he slipped away.

Jack looked at Alf. "Well, I'm sold. Ox and ox for me."

Alf exhaled heavily. "One hundred twenty, we can manage. Thank God for that man."

"Six miles out and back, let's be off. Barr was right about one thing, the early bird gets the worm." Jack spoke loudly to drown the inner voice that was shrieking doubt.

"I'll not collude with a European and that's flat," the major warned them.

"No need to collude, Major Jordan," Davie said, clearly shocked. "Just buy their oxes is all we're after doin'; leave their women alone, I sez."

The major looked through Davie. "Canadian seller of Canadian horses is fine by me and confusion to the Barrs. But not Europeans!"

• • •

Six days later, on April 24th, 1903, the first wagons struck the westbound trail from Saskatoon, bound for the All-British Saskatchewan Valley Colony. A crowd assembled to cheer them on their way. Jack watched somberly, annoyed at Ostrich's happy barking. Freddie White and six veterans in two fast, light buckboards had already departed yesterday. Their plan was to make a quick trip, claim the best land, then return to buy equipment at their leisure. They had precipitated a "land fever" and added to Jack's terrors. Stories flew through the tents daily — some of the colony was good land — most was rocky and thin. The first hundred colonists would fare well, the rest? All the good land near

Saskatoon and Battleford was claimed — the reliable man who sold them their animals had confirmed that story. Their only hope was to push on rapidly up the river valley to untouched territory.

Yet here they sat, waiting another day for the major to get oats for his prize team. Hay and grass weren't good enough for the black matched pair that he drove around Saskatoon so proudly. Alice and the children could have been in a royal landau rather than a green and red Bain wagon, judging by the excitement on their faces. Even Alf and Davie seemed content to play with their wagon and oxen, taking drives out onto the prairie to practise handling the big animals. Jack had suggested an initial drive to test the harness and wagons. After a few minor adjustments he had found the ox team quite simple to handle compared with horses and he'd been able to teach Alf and Davie to drive, easily.

But he had created a monster. They drove now every morning as a recreation. They fussed over water and feed and cleaning the wagon in the afternoons. Then they retired to the tent for supper, pipes and visits, content to play at pioneer. The cooperative had its equipment, priced from twenty to fifty percent higher than expected. In the end, they couldn't afford both a mower and binder so they bought the binder as it was needed to bring in the all-important first crop. It was to be freighted out to them in late July. There were no further preparations required in Saskatoon and they were ready to go, but they didn't. They would not take the situation seriously. Jack's credibility had taken several bad lumps. The worst was plough buying. He'd described the plough he had used with Charlie. It cut an eight-inch furrow with an iron moldboard. Two different salesmen and finally the farm instructor laughed outright at his specifications. The instructor at least laughed kindly. This was undisturbed sod — one hundred sixty acres of it. A real man's plough cut fourteen-inch furrows on a steel blade with exaggerated suction and a swooping, wide moldboard to flop the sod over. Otherwise, the farm instructor said, eyes twinkling, you end up cutting a thousand pretty, little lines in the grass.

Jack shook free of the embarrassing moment. His old fear of leaving the railhead to strike into the unknown now butted head on with a new fear that their only hope — good productive land — would disappear if they didn't strike out onto the trail, and soon. He walked back through the tent lines battling his conflicting tensions and nearly crashed into Alice Jordan.

"Ah, Jack, I was looking for Buxton."

"Gone to practise driving the wagon," he replied tersely. They entered the tent and he tethered Ostrich to the centre pole.

"Yes, it seems to have become a habit," she said, folding her arms. "A bad habit, I fear."

Jack's head snapped up. Here was an unexpected ally. "Bad habit?"

She nodded. "Driving and committees and visiting keep us stuck here. We must go now, either home," she walked to the tent flap and gazed eastward down the rail tracks, "or on to the colony. But we must take action. This camp is false, it's unnatural."

Jack's spirits began to rise. There was anger just below Mrs. Jordan's surface, good anger. He needed to bring it up — use it.

"Unnatural, strange choice of words?"

"I shall speak plainly, then, Jack." She sat on their trunk table, he knelt beside her.

"You know the major's style. He enjoys the company of other men. He likes to drink and plan and enact committee agendas. He's at a meeting in the big marquee right now, attacking Mr. Barr's profiteering. But we, his family, will suffer if this continues. He must seem to you to be a frivolous man. But I believe that all he needs is real work, a real challenge. If he doesn't get it, then the committees and conviviality will ruin him. If we could get on with the trek and our farm, then there is hope."

"And Alf Buxton?" Jack said quietly. "Can you manage a trek without him as your handservant?"

Her eyes widened, eyebrows raised. "You speak bluntly, Mr. Thornton."

"New country — we are laying the foundation for future generations — a wise and good friend told me that. I feel it presumes plain, blunt speaking when important issues are discussed."

She studied his face, her eyes sticking briefly on his scars.

"We are speaking of an issue that is critical to my future, Mrs. Jordan." He returned her stare. "I'm in deadly earnest here. I soon won't be able to afford to go home. I believe Alf and Davie are very near the point of no return right now."

"Bluntly?" She sighed. "If I could hire Buxton, I would, on the spot. I am afraid I might not manage by myself but I'm more afraid of staying here in limbo. It will surely bring disaster for all of us."

"Well, Mrs. Jordan, I have a deal to offer you." He stood and untied Ostrich. "I will find a bag of oats, deliver it to your husband, and push him to agree to leave within twenty-four hours. You talk to Alf. Between us we will break the inertia."

She rose, smiling. "Deal, Mr. Thornton." Her voice was strong and she shook his hand firmly.

CHAPTER 19

Isaac Barr, his staff, and a few loyal colonists mounted in a squadron of buggies and light wagons set forth from Saskatoon the next morning. Many said he was fleeing his critics and good riddance. Others were outraged that he had failed to organize guides and wagon trains, another lost promise. But he drew a large convoy in his wake. He seemed to break the jam and colonists flowed after him. Major Jordan led the Newland Cooperative. Although Alf said the major was more in hot pursuit of his enemy, Barr, than leading pioneers on a grand adventure. The trail was wide, deep, and relatively smooth having cut below the surface grass to a hard-packed earthen highway. The Jordan wagon, crammed to the top of its canvas hooped cover, set a spanking pace. Jack and Alf, much more modestly loaded, plodded behind him. Unable to form a bond with the huge swaying beasts before him, Jack simply called them Ox One and Ox Two. They seemed happy with this arrangement. The sun was up and a fresh, east breeze blew them on their way. The major reined in when the Saskatoon grain elevator was just about to slip below the horizon. He leaped down from his wagon and, as Jack's outfit caught him up, he raised his hat.

"Come on slow coach!" Jordan was dressed in riding breeches, high boots and a bright yellow waistcoat for the momentous day. "*Westward the Star of Empire Takes its Way!*" he cried.

"Westward!" Davie echoed from behind. Jack laughed and waved, standing up in the box. He saw Emma pinching the poster in Euston Station. "Westward the Star of Empire" it read. He thought of her pluck, leading the crowd in three cheers. And he saw her tears.

"Ostrich," he said, sitting down on the bouncing seat. "Wait 'til you meet Emma. She is going to make this all worthwhile."

The hound cocked his head quizzically, sad, brown eyes almost seeming to understand.

• • •

The Jordan wagon disappeared over the western horizon just before noon when the east wind turned cold and strong, and blew heavy, dirty clouds over the two ox-powered wagons. There were other wagons far behind them in the east and a surprising clump of trees on the distant, southern horizon. Otherwise the dead, grass plains stretched away on all sides to melt into the dull sky. Jack called a halt. They unhooked and walked the oxen a half-mile to a pool of snowmelt water where the animals drank very little. Then Jack gave them a bit of hay which they ate indifferently. The humans made a small fire, boiled tea, and chewed bread and cheese. Ostrich was the only one with anything to say, racing back and forth between the burrows of squeaking ground squirrels — gophers, the farm instructor had called them. His baying, galloping approach allowed the gophers easy escapes and he lacked the instinct to dig after them. His horizon was the few yards of grass beyond his nose. Jack, Alf and Davie couldn't help staring at their huge, grey world. Its vast emptiness deadened their conversation.

They hooked up, pointed out the pond to a group of newcomers, and resumed their journey. An hour later, the Jordan wagon reappeared as a motionless white-capped dot in the distance. Jack whipped up his team from a plod to a walk and stood up on the seat to see what had happened. A shallow lake, shores rimmed alkaline white, held the Jordans in its grip. The trail led arrow-straight into the slough and reappeared on the far side. A secondary trail skirted the slough on a half-mile detour. Two wagons were just completing the detour and were rejoining the main trail beyond the slough, ignoring the tiny cries for help from the Jordan vehicle. Jack pulled his team to a stop, Alf reined in beside him.

"Trail must have thawed under all that water," Alf pronounced. "Everyone's going round on dry ground."

"Not everyone," Jack replied.

"What now, Mr. Thornton?" Davie still called him mister. Alf had dropped the formality.

"I don't know, Davie." Jack let some of his fear edge into his voice. "Why couldn't the bugger just go around like everyone else, instead of charging forward?"

"What did you do in Africa when a wagon or a gun got stuck?" Alf asked.

"Unloaded it, hitched extra teams, and pulled it clear," Jack said, Klip Drift suddenly clear in his mind's eye.

"Let's do the same," Alf said simply. "Show us what to do, Jack."

The two ox teams drew their wagons in slow procession around the slough. Major Jordan's bellows for help turned to cries of relief when he realized who they were. Alice fluttered a white hanky at them like a lady at Ascot waving to her favourite. At the main trail junction they unloaded both wagons leaving two tidy piles on the prairie. Jack wiped the cold perspiration from his brow and swallowed mightily as he climbed back into his wagon.

"Ever driven through water like this in Africa?" Alf's voice called in a falsetto behind him. Jack shook his head

"What if we all get stuck? It's getting cold and late," Davie observed, drawing dirty looks from both Alf and Jack.

"Get up." Jack snapped his lines, fully expecting the oxen to refuse, but they didn't. The easygoing brutes simply sloshed forward, drawing the empty wagon easily with them. Mud from the soft bottom spun up off the wheel spokes spattering Jack and his new wagon but he scarce noticed.

"Well done, One, well done, Two. Good lads, good boys," he crooned to them, noting with relief that the water was no more than a foot deep. He heard Alf and Davie's animals splash into the slough behind him but stayed focussed on his own pair. One and Two gave an aura of calm competence that began to relax him.

The Jordan family rejoiced to see the stalwart steers plunging to their rescue. Jack stopped well short of the mired wagon; his approach seemed to upset the exhausted horses. Caked in mud, trembling and belly-deep in cold water, the horses were near panic. They would be of no further use, Jordan had pushed them too hard. The major stood, whip in hand, at the front of the wagon, completely dry. Blast the man. If he'd led them by hand, the horses might have won clear.

"Welcome, boys! Welcome, heroes!" Alice called gaily, the children repeating her calls. Ostrich barked a happy reply.

"Major! Unhook that team and lead them up onto dry ground," Jack ordered.

"Better idea, old chap," the major took a cheroot from his mouth, grimacing at Jack's tone of authority. "You hook your bullocks up in tandem to my girls and we'll walk out."

"Your mares are knackered and frightened," Jack barked. "One more pull and they will tip you over."

"I think I know my own horses best," Jordan answered coolly. "Buxton, hook up your cattle, there's a good man. Sharpish now, the day is waning."

"*Get those goddamned horses out of here!*"

Seven miles west of Saskatoon, in the middle of an unnamed salt slough that would be dry in two months time, Jack Thornton lost his temper and won unchallenged command of the Newland Cooperative. The major waded waist-deep in the muck hole churned by his horses, unhooked them, flipped their filthy traces up over their backs and walked them out of the slough. He tethered them to the Buxton stores, lit a fresh cheroot and opened his flask.

The hoop and canvas covered wagon was a nuisance because they could only unload over the tailgate. It took an hour to shift the two half loads and the Jordan family onto the rescue wagons and plod to dry land. Alf and Jack then unhooked their beasts and led them, sloshing through the ice water, back to the Jordan wagon. Connected to the wagon by two lengths of chain, four stout sets of shoulders strained, and suddenly the empty Bain popped free of the muck. All three wagons were finally reloaded on dry ground just as the sun lit a crack in the clouds before sliding out of sight.

The men cut dry grass, wiped down their animals and shivered in wet clothes as snow began to fall. The miserable group huddled on the freezing prairie looked silently to Jack. He felt like screaming at them. He felt like slapping their defeated faces. What right did city-bred Englishmen have flinging themselves out onto this wilderness, then look to him for salvation? Two years on the Vicar's farm did not qualify him for their trust. He stifled these thoughts and tried to say what George Grigg would have said.

"We're a good four miles from the first government rest stop, and it's getting dark. We will camp here."

Nobody argued. He plunged on.

"Davie, you feed and water the animals. Major, get your family's beds sorted inside your wagon. Alf, use some grass to start a fire on the mud bank. There's a mountain of old, dry buffalo dung back on the detour. The major and I will fetch it for the fire. We can dry our clothes over the cooking fire. Mrs. Jordan, if you please, dig out some oatmeal. We will need a load of hot porridge in our bellies for this night."

They turned, like children, to do as they were told. The actual children stood shivering in the blowing snow, staring at him.

351

"What should we do?" Mary asked in a voice that angered Jack all over again. The two little girls should be tucked up in their beds at home, not stranded on a freezing prairie he thought.

"You, Mary, and you, Kitty," he said very seriously, "have an important job. You must play with Ostrich, tire him out so he sleeps quietly tonight."

Jack rooted a spade and buckets out of his wagon. They should shovel up the buffalo manure before the snow dampened it. The major joined him to tramp back down the detour.

"Cheer up, Major Jordan. It's only dry buffalo shit, could be worse."

Jordan turned a red-streaked, baleful eye on him. "Worse, how?"

"Well, sir," Jack said *à la* Billy Webster, "it could be night soil."

• • •

Alice made them hot tea, boiled over the last of the buffalo dung, before dawn. None of them had slept well in the freezing dark and nobody complained of the early start. The clouds were gone and the prairie was dusted white. The slough sported a thin crust of dark ice. The major led but never opened so much as a fifty pace gap between himself and the ox teams. One and Two blew thick white jets of condensed air from their noses. Alice, Mary, and Kitty walked with Ostrich to warm themselves.

"Puff White — Nothing — Puff White — Nothing," the girls chanted a little song in time with Two's breathing. "The cold has turned the ox into a steam engine," Mary observed.

"Daffodils will be blooming at home. All bright yellow," Alice said quietly. "How will you grow wheat, Mr. Thornton, in the snow?"

Jack shared her exasperation for a country that froze and snowed on April 26th. "That is a good question," he played up, trying to sound cheery. "I'll ask Mr. Barr and get back to you."

They struck the first government camp an hour and a half later — a large marquee surrounded by a half-dozen filthy bell tents. A stovepipe from the marquee belched smoke, and a welcome cord of wood lay stacked outside. Two dozen Bain wagons were parked at the camp but only a few people stirred. They pulled in at the edge of the camp. Alf and Davie waited like soldiers for Jack's orders; Major Jordan lounged against a wagon wheel in a great show of independence but, nonetheless, waited quietly for Jack to speak. Jack felt a small surge of last night's anger but suppressed it as pointless.

"Next rest stop is nineteen miles according to our directions, which so far seem surprisingly accurate. We came up short on the first day's trek, but only by four miles, so I think the animals can do the nineteen today. That will put us in Camp Two on schedule."

All nodded in assent. Dismal Camp One was not the place to spend a day of rest.

"Let's dry our clothes properly in the marquee and cook a good meal of bacon and bread. We won't have to outspan the animals so we can save unpacking time. Then we'll march through the day. We'll eat a full supper at Camp Two."

• • •

Sunshine and warm air melted the prairie. Grass-bottomed sloughs of brown water and rivulets of grey water cut the trail every mile. Most were driven through successfully — even with some element of disdain once they gained experience. But then a huge, alkaline flat stretched north-south to the horizon and two miles wide across the trail. No detour possible, they hitched all the animals to each

353

wagon and pulled them through the floury muck one by one, walking the teams back each time for the next wagon. The crossing was completed before mid afternoon, but the men were so tired from slogging miles through the sucking mud that they simply camped, washed, ate and slept. The next day was also sunny, warm, and very slow going on the spongy trail. The second government rest camp was indeed only nineteen miles, but they just managed to reach it at sunset on the second day out from Camp One. They gave up the notion of trekking twenty miles a day, and the idea of a "schedule" was dismissed. They marched until darkness or exhaustion forced a stop; that was the new "schedule". Today it was simple luck that they made Camp Two at quitting time. But Jack was pathetically grateful for a heated, wood-floored tent this night. A whiskered leathery old man built like a string of gristle had command of the stove when they entered.

"Ladies and gentlemen, welcome to Jimmy's cooking class," he cackled. "Gather here, now, and I'll show you how to fry a loaf of bread quick as a wink and easily done over a campfire."

The smell from Jimmy's frying pan drew them into his presence. Jimmy leered openly at Mrs. Jordan and motioned her forward.

"You can help me."

A month ago Alice would have cut him dead. This evening she darted forward, anxious and hungry. The little ferret of a man had a pan full of fried bacon which he emptied into a large tin. Taking flour, baking powder, and two spoonfuls of the bacon grease, he mixed all together with some brownish slough water. The resulting dough he kneaded quickly and lightly for only a minute, then flattened it out into a round cake. Too thick and the centre would be gluey; too thin and it would burn. Alice followed his example, carefully constructing her own flap of dough. The cakes were then fried in the pan, flipped once and suddenly bread appeared or, as the old timer called it, "bannock". He tested Alice's loaf and swore, "Son of a bitch, missus!" He chewed a bit more, thoughtfully. She blushed at the oath. "Mr. Barr is paying me to teach you people something in my camp here, but damned if you don't need Jimmy's help. This is near as good bannock as I make and, by God, I'm one-quarter Cree warrior — bannock is in my blood!"

Jimmy gave them some of the bacon. Alice beamed as though royalty had complimented her on her table. They took Alice's triumph and the bacon and sat unceremoniously on the wood floor to eat. Every few minutes a new party, cold and mud-spattered, entered the tent and presently Jimmy fried up more bannock for the newcomers.

Jack finished his last crumb, licking his fingers, when a man, woman and two children literally staggered into the tent and flopped onto the boards nearby. Jack recognized the man's eyes. They were red-rimmed, wide and staring. He'd last seem those eyes on two DCLI soldiers huddled on the Paardeberg plain, shocked at the Mauser death they had narrowly escaped.

"You look knackered, chum," Davie said. "Go get some bannock, it's lovely."

The man gazed vacantly at Davie. He was unshaven and filthy. A freshly clotted cut ran the length of his jawbone. His shirt collar was stained with dried blood.

"Are you all right?" Alf asked. "Nasty cut, there. Have you cleaned it?"

The man shook his head, stunned by the questions, seemingly unable to cope with conversation.

"Let me have a look, eh?" Alf stood. "Can't march on westward ho tomorrow in that condition."

The man waved him off. "Not westward tomorrow, eastward. Quitting, going home."

"Surely not already," the major said as kindly as he could manage. "Come on, man, buck up now. Bound to be a setback or two. Mustn't be quitters."

"Setback is it?" The man's voice steadied and his eyes cleared, focussing brightly on the major. "Quitters are we?"

He laughed bitterly and nudged his wife. "Quitters, Lucy, that's us."

Jack exchanged embarrassed glances with Jordan.

"We got to this tent two days ago, *chum*," the quitter hissed. "Jimmy showed us how to make bannock and we were jolly well proud of ourselves. Come through quicker than most. One of Jimmy's first customers. Then yesterday we hit Eagle Creek, five or six miles west o' here."

The Newland Cooperative leaned forward, like children listening to a ghost story.

"Trail drops down this hellish steep ravine to the creek at bottom. The creek's full and fast, cutting across the trail to join the Saskatchewan a half-mile north."

"The North Saskatchewan River?" the major asked.

The quitter nodded.

"Excellent! Finally in the Saskatchewan Valley, wot!"

"Excellent, oh yes," the man said sarcastically. "First hillside is good, trail switches back across it, but then it turns and with no warning drops like a sinner to hell, straight down fifty feet or more to the water. Brake was useless, we were smashing into the horses' breeching, whipple tree skinned the tendons off the rear legs of my best animal. They took off — I gave 'em their head — had no choice. Hit the creek, bottom is soft, horses went over, wagon went over, hoop ripped me this."

He ran a finger along the cut jaw.

"My daughter was thrown and trapped underwater by the wagon, drowning in front of me. Horses screamin' and kickin'.

Can't see Lucy. My son and I tore our heavy gear out of the box and she floated an inch in the current, got the girl free at last."

They stared, round-eyed, at the child, still coated in dried mud, already asleep on the bare boards.

"Lost all our food, wagon damaged, one horse lame. Half my tools lost in the creek, took the rest of that day and all today to limp back here. Only got twenty pounds left. At least one hundred pounds damage. We're finished. If we get to Saskatoon with no further loss," he paused as though calculating their odds. "then we can sell the wagon, horses, harness, tent and all. Should be enough to get us home. At least we haven't passed the point of no return. The "great adventure" is over, *chum*."

He turned on his side and joined his family in their deathlike sleep.

"Well I blame Barr," the major whispered. "He encouraged these poor people who are clearly unsuitable and underfunded. Promised cooperatives and guides and instructors. Completely unrealistic and irresponsible. Imagine, only twenty pounds left to their name."

Davie looked wildly to Alf and Alf shook his head slightly. Davie stayed quiet.

• • •

"Doukhobors? Russian serfs! Certainly not!" The major flared insubordinately at Jack's suggestion that they venture into the village for eggs and milk. They were stopped at the top of a low ridge overlooking a shallow valley running at right angles to the trail. The valley gradually sank northward into the steep bluffs and streak of water that was the North Saskatchewan River. A small cluster of tidy, whitewashed huts perched near a creek that wound through the valley floor.

"Fresh eggs and milk," Davie murmured dreamily.

"Absolutely *not!*" The major rounded on him. "This is the All-British Colony — Canada for the British is our motto and you seriously expect me to trade with . . . Russian peasants?"

"Could eat the eggs to celebrate our entry into the Saskatchewan Valley," Davie persevered.

"They use their women to pull their ploughs!"

This piece of doubtful logic seemed to sway the decision. Jack had made the suggestion only because he felt obliged to for the children's sake. His own stomach was in a fine state of tension. The western horizon was no longer barren prairie. A line of hills, purple and dark-wooded, ranged beautiful and menacing before them. Prior to the hills they would cross Eagle Creek. Further discussion with Jimmy Bannock last night had fixed the creek just past the Doukhobor commune. Jimmy also confirmed Eagle Creek as the worst obstacle between Saskatoon and the colony site. Jack had thrashed wakeful all night. Alf looked even worse, perhaps no sleep at all. He and Davie were approaching their epiphany.

"Let's get on," Alf snapped. "Go see the elephant and get it over with."

"Elephant? That creek? Come, come, Buxton. Don't get the wind up." The major, alone unconcerned, laughed. "A dawdle, I'll wager. That quitter didn't do a proper reconnaissance and obviously has no talent handling a team."

"Get up, One. Get up, Two" Jack thwarted the simmering squabble. Alf was right, get it over with one way or the other.

A half-hour later they stood atop a high, round hill looking down at the rapidly flowing waters of Eagle Creek, one hundred feet below them. Jack chewed his cheek scars nervously and the major reached for his flask. He took two long pulls before the colour returned to his cheeks. He turned to Jack.

"Let's walk it, first."

Jack nodded and they set off down the trail. The first fifty feet switchbacked steep, but reasonable, just as the quitter had reported. Then came a sharp turn and a sickening drop as the trail narrowed through a stand of poplar and hit the ford. The ford itself was badly chewed — evidence that the task had been done by others, but not easily.

"Run the switchback, then install the chain brake and skid to the crossing?" The major tugged at his moustaches, eyeing the ground.

"Agreed." Jack surveyed the tall, thin poplars on the steep bank. "But we'll cut poles and stick them through the rear-wheel spokes as an added precaution. We'll walk each team down, individually, and brace them up the other side the same way."

"Right. I should go first. I owe it," the major said quietly but firmly. "Made a hash of that first slough — time to ante up now."

The high load nearly tipped on the first corner. Jack sang, crooned, and begged the mares to stay calm. He walked beside one, holding her bridle strap, Alf walked beside the other. Davie very bravely walked directly in front of the team, giving it a reason to move slowly. Two wheels creaked and lifted an inch into suspended nothing before banging back down onto the hard earth. The major swore violently, Jack nearly bit through his scars.

They inched down to the turn and stopped. Davie fastened the chain brake and slipped the newly-skinned poplar pole into place. They walked the horses forward until chain and pole clapped up tight to the tail end of the wagon box. The rear wheels locked solid and began to gouge ruts in the trail.

"Westward the Star of Empire takes its Way," the major muttered and touched up his horses. It might have taken them a half-hour to descend the fifty foot drop — or it may have been a half-dozen minutes. The words *now, now, now* called in Jack's head, waiting for disaster just as he had waited for his bullet at Paardeberg.

The back wheels scraped loudly in his ears. *Now, now.* He smelled the rotting, wet leaves carpeting the ground beside the trail but he fixed his eyes on the horse, willing it to stay calm. Then his feet were wet, and icy water filled his boots. Davie whooped, Jack swallowed rapidly, giddy with relief. The horses sensed the human emotion and nickered with tense energy. Jack removed the chain and pole. He slapped their rumps and with a cry of delight the major deftly drove them up the long, gradual ascent to the prairie above. The others scampered behind, ready to block the wheels should they lose momentum.

"Hooray, Papa! Well done, Major!" Mary and Alice's triumphant cries came from the hillside above them. Ostrich barked his approbation.

Jack grinned broadly at Alf. "Point of no return, Mr. Buxton?"

"Piece of cake, Mr. Thornton." Alf grinned back. "With the oxen and low loads — well, hardly a challenge to experienced carters."

And so it was. Men who had two months earlier toiled as Stepney butchers — who had never held reins in their hands — drove a wagon carrying all their possessions across Eagle Creek in the wilds of the Saskatchewan Territory. And they drove it with high confidence. The morning clouds disappeared to let the sun shine brightly on the now-conquered and therefore lovely Eagle Creek Valley. Alice Jordan stood atop the bank, gazing back up the creek to where the mighty, ice-choked Saskatchewan gobbled it up.

"Let's *quit!*" she shouted, laughing, turning her face toward the sun.

"Quit?" Alf asked, smiling at her.

"Quit for today. Let us camp here on the clean grass. We have real water, real wood, and sunlight. Let's stop here and celebrate. The major and Ostrich can hunt. I'll make bannock and roast grouse. Let's, please, take some pleasure, just for today."

"Grouse, my dear," said the major indulgently, "are English. Perhaps a rabbit may be found but . . . "

"Then what is *he* hunting?" Alice retorted, pointing into the valley.

They rushed to her vantage point on the rim of the coulee. A lean, grey dog weaved slowly and stealthily through a scatter of willow bushes on a benchland below them. Several hen-like heads moved jerkily through tall grass beyond the willow. The coyote flattened, patiently attending the birds' approach. Suddenly a dozen rapid paces carried him low-slung from the willows through the grass. The covey burst upward flapping for altitude, their high *gup gup gup* calls of alarm preceding their heavy-bodied climb to safety.

"Watch where they land!" the major shouted excitedly.

But Jack could not remove his eyes from the bold, quick coyote who trotted proudly beneath them, limp bird in its mouth. It sat, dropped the bird, and howled up to Jack a high clear message of victory. Then he picked up his kill and disappeared. Wildlife. Predator — prey. All his time in the African desert among thousands of noisy men he'd never seen anything more wild than the jackals licking Miles' blood from the gun carriage. He had assumed this empty wilderness was . . . empty. But he'd been wrong, thank God. Happily, wonderfully wrong. Others lived here — it was alive and it would turn green and grow. A piece of Jack's dread broke off like a calving iceberg and drifted away.

"Yes. Why not? Let us do quit," he said.

The major raced for his twelve-bore. Davie collected Ostrich and tied him to a long piece of rope.

"I want to be able to reel him in if the coyotes decide they'd like beagle for dessert," he explained. Then he and Jordan were off like little boys, stalking toward the aspen at the edge of the ravine where the grouse had landed. Ostrich quartered instinctively but with puppy incompetence at the end of his tether, sniffing eagerly, feeding off of Davie's excitement.

"Like us, I suppose," Alice said. "Puppies searching, but not really certain why or for what."

"After today, more certain than ever," Alf said. "This will be our home one day. I feel it."

Alice clasped her hands behind her back and walked slowly toward the wagons without replying.

Alf and Jack pitched a bell tent then went for wood, of which there was an abundance. They would have a big fire, all night. The major's shotgun boomed twice and seconds later twice again. Ostrich barked in the distance and Davie's voice echoed him.

Cooking game came naturally to a butcher, so Alf declared and proved. The three fat grouse, plucked, cleaned, and roasted with bacon strips were unbelievably delicious. Alice watched Alf do the first two, then tried the third herself. Jack was startled by the thought that Emma would be at least as helpless as Mrs. Jordan. He resolved to advise her to learn to cook — his very next letter, tonight. But he must be tactful.

Two more wagons as well as the "Royal Mail" crossed late in the day. The mailman was a sinewy, older fellow the colour of tree bark, riding a western pony and leading a packhorse laden with red canvas bags that had RM and a crown stenciled on them. The Newland Cooperative shared its fire and tea. Alice proudly gave the last of her bannock and half a grouse to the appreciative newcomers. The mailman ate quickly, then pushed on into the dark. The rest sat around the fire until late, smoking, sipping tea, and sharing their dreams. Later, rolled in his blankets with Ostrich, Jack felt peace. Near midnight a coyote yowled from Eagle Creek. Another, then another, answered. They sang their songs for the better part of an hour. They were singing of grouse and gophers and perhaps even deer. Jack slept and dreamt of Emma. No nightmare of dread disturbed him.

• • •

The grass prairies of Saskatoon and south seemed like another world now. For two days the trail wove them around the Eagle Hills, sometimes in sight of the river, sometimes in thick poplar, aspen, and willow. It seemed that half their day was spent straining uphill, the other half braking down. Then this morning flat land again, but not the wasted, bald prairie. It was undulating savannah, dotted with clumps of thick-growing poplar and trembling aspen, farms, telegraph poles, and traffic. "Old Timers" were the settlers who had been here ten or fifteen years. They waved from substantial log homes with proper corrals and barns. This landscape, in turn, evolved into a solid, conifer forest. Even the oxen sensed the excitement of Battleford and practically raced north toward the river. They made their greatest distance this day, nearly twenty miles, and they made it in good fettle. Jack's wagon led through a belt of spruce and pine. The fresh, evergreen scent was a tonic after the prairie sloughs and alkaline bogs. The sun touched the western horizon when he broke free of the trees and halted the wagon with a cry of surprise.

He was perched on a height of land. A gradual, open slope fell down to the river valley. The Battle River's shiny, narrow line wriggled southeastward, parallel to the great North Saskatchewan as though resisting its pull. But it lost the struggle just at the bottom of the slope and fed itself into the big river. A sturdy bridge — a real post-and-beam wood bridge — took the trail, transformed it into a road, and carried it over the Battle into a village. Houses. Shops. Stables. All illuminated by the setting sun. Jack led the excited Newland Cooperative to a billiard table-flat piece of ground short of the bridge, and they camped. Their mail would come here, Battleford, North West Territories, now. Saskatoon was irrelevant flotsam in their wake.

Voices woke Jack the following morning. He and Alf rose quickly and emerged from the tent. Davie waved frantically, pointing to a group of people near the riverbank.

"Indians! Hostile, maybe!" Davie whispered in a voice that was easily heard at fifty paces. The girls gawked without shame, deliciously frightening themselves with thoughts of a "war party". The flat land was campground to at least two dozen colonist wagons. Each tent was issuing English men, hurrying to see the "red men".

The Indians were moving along a deep-cut trail near the river. Their range of appearance was startling. In the lead were two men, tall, lean, and muscular. They wore bright, cotton shirts, fringed and beaded deerskin leggings, and soft moccasins that tied off at mid-calf. Each rode a shaggy horse with a long back and a large head. Jack nearly cried "Bobbi" out loud at the sight of these tough ponies. The men cradled rifles whose stocks were studded with large, brass nailheads. They rode with slick familiarity, as though horse, man, and gun was one multi-limbed animal. Like mounted Boer commandos, Jack thought. A group of women followed the men. They walked, leading horses that drew squealing, two-wheeled carts whose cargo was covered by buffalo hides. A cluster of children and dogs walked with them. At the tail of the column straggled men and women who would have fit easily into the slums of Whitechapel or Spitalfields back home. Incredibly filthy, either drunk or deeply hungover, they wore rags of both European and Indian clothing.

A dozen of the latter broke from the trail and went for the settlers. They made universally recognizable begging gestures, and muttered guttural threatening demands. The Barr colonists contracted into a tight knot at the sight. Alf stepped protectively in front of Alice and the girls, his fist balled.

"I think they are harmless," Jack said, touching Alf's sleeve.

"Harmless?" Alf turned, belligerence on his face. "How would you know?"

"They're defeated. Look at them. I saw the Boers in their laager after the surrender at Paardeberg — these are the same."

Alf relaxed his stance a trifle. "What about those two?" He motioned toward the mounted men who were turning their ponies onto a course cutting between the beggars and the colonists.

"They are different, I'll grant you," Jack replied. "But they are still defeated, I can feel it in them. We need someone who can talk with them."

As if on cue, Reverend Lloyd's tall figure strode from the near end of the Battleford bridge. His right arm was upstretched toward the Indians.

"*N'Sjayasis* — Brothers!"

The Indians stopped but did not appear surprised to hear their language spoken by a man in clergy dress. The colonists were, however, amazed. Lloyd intercepted the mounted warriors and spoke slowly, with animated gestures. He produced a packet of tobacco and gave it to one, then called to the English for a quarter-pound of tea. A colonist fetched it from his tent; Lloyd gave it to the other mounted man. The Indians, looking down at Lloyd, made no move to dismount nor any gesture of thanks. They simply turned their ponies, called sharply to the beggars and returned to the women to resume their march.

"Arrogant devils," Alf said.

"Proud ones, I'd say," Alice replied. "At least proud once upon a time."

Lloyd walked to the colonists and they surrounded him, eager for an explanation of this "red Indian" phenomenon.

"Nothing to fear," he said, smiling. "Some of the Poundmaker Cree people in town to trade and drink. They are going home now."

"What did you say to them, Reverend?" Davie asked.

"Told them who we were and what our intentions are. I told them we would be travelling near their reserve in a few days but that we would be making our homes to the northwest." He spoke slowly in the same cadence as he had spoken to the Cree. "I don't believe they will even bother to make contact with us. They think," he said laughing, "that we are a poor lot — dirt farmers — who drive cows instead of horses."

"Us a poor lot!" A murmur of nervous, lighthearted outrage rippled through the English crowd. "Say, Billy! Go get your tea back and give 'em a piece of your mind, instead."

"They were nothing more than tramps!"

Lloyd's eyes sparkled at this and he raised his voice. "Do not be mistaken!" He pointed to a heap of charred timbers and rubbish piled at the end of the flat campground. "That was the town of Battleford eighteen years ago."

They fell quiet, not understanding.

"Poundmaker's Cree caught Colonel Otter's column of four hundred infantry, police, and artillery at Cut Knife Hill up yonder, in 1885." He pointed along the trail Barr's two thousand would soon take.

"Those tramps," he paused for a wicked smile, "defeated Colonel Otter, killed and wounded twenty-five of his men, and sent the rest back here in retreat. Then they sacked the town which used to be situated here, on Telegraph Flats."

Jack started at the mention of Colonel Otter.

"They are harmless," Lloyd continued. "But do not make the mistake of insulting or antagonizing them."

"How came you to speak their lingo and know so much about them, Mr. Lloyd?" Davie asked, bright-eyed at the tale of Indian warfare.

"I was one of the twenty-five casualties," Lloyd said, casually. "Shot through the lung and only survived by God's good grace."

This blunt statement, shorn of drama and emotion, struck them dumb. Jack's mind revolved at the fantastic coincidences piling one upon the other. Reverend Lloyd, Cut Knife — Colonel Otter, Cut Knife. Then Otter, Paardeberg — Jack, Paardeberg. Lloyd shot through the lung, Lindsell shot through the lung, French Canadian soldier shot through the lung. Indian ponies with Bobbi-big heads. Not coincidences, rather connectors. Somehow these events and people were harnessed together. He was meant to be here. Vicar Wilson had felt it — Jack Thornton was meant to come here, to farm this land. Another piece of his new-world fear broke and fell away. He was buoyed up, reborn.

He thought of the Cree deerskin leggings and moccasins. He looked at Alf's billycock and Davie's flat, tweed cap. The plains "red men", proud warriors and hunters once, had passed their time. The London butchers and clerks had passed their time. Jack stared up the tall banks of the North Saskatchewan River. They pointed northwest. He felt a powerful urge to limber up One and Two and follow that river, right now. The wild west was no more; London, Gloucester, England were irrelevant. The pioneers would step into the vacuum and fashion the new country, and it would fashion them. He was anxious, not with dread but with anticipation, to see what this Saskatchewan Territory would make of him.

• • •

There was a letter from Emma at the Battleford post office. Oddly, it was the fifth letter she had written. She referred to subjects raised

367

in four previous letters, of which he had only the first two. It didn't matter. Her hand had written, her voice was in the words, the actual message was secondary. He posted his own accumulated letter — eight pages long — which included a description of the Cree and his growing confidence.

The major received his first remittance cheque from home. He and a number of other colonists questioned the wisdom of travelling further. This discussion was fueled by the contents of his refilled flask. Why press on into "Indian Land" when Battleford was such a splendid little place with plenty of strangely unclaimed homesteads south and east of town. The railway was coming soon, land prices would rise, here was the "promised land", surely.

Jack couldn't argue these points, but the narrow triangle of land wedged between the Battle and North Saskatchewan resonated the Wye and Severn. At home the land was limestone with a thin blanket of soil. Here, the open land to the south was similarly pushed high and aside by the rivers. The spruce and pine cover looked false. He voiced these concerns uncertainly, so the major proposed an experiment. He took his shovel and led a survey to three of the potential homesteads. In each case, he randomly dug a hole one foot deep. The top inch or two was dark earth, then nothing but sand and grey, thin gravel. Even Alice, newly enamoured of Battleford's shops, houses, and especially the immigration hall, blanched at the sight of the scrawny soil. They topped up flour, oatmeal, sugar, salt, and tea stocks, gave the animals a good feed and rest, then pushed on without a backward glance.

• • •

The land did not improve. It turned into thick, scrubby woods, bogs, and if they were lucky, firm-bottomed sloughs. At least one wagon each day became stuck. This necessitated a wet, mud-spattered orgy of balking horses and stubborn oxen lurching to pull the victim free. May 4th, Jack's feet and hands turned numb pushing the Jordan wagon out of a slippery hole in a snowstorm. May 5th, he had to take off his coat to push his own wagon through alkaline mush in the hot sun. May 6th, they won free of the jungle and camped on the dry grass savannah.

"According to that rancher bloke back at Paynton we should be through the worst of it," Jack said, hanging wet socks on a willow stick near the fire. "The open, grass meadows and small patches of aspen — parkland he says — should be our lot from now on."

"Amen to that," Davie said, scraping great blobs of half-dried muck from his boots.

"Six or seven miles to the last camp, just inside the colony boundary." Jack pulled out his pipe, thought of Emma as she had hoped he would, and thumbed tobacco into it. "Then thirty miles on good trail to Mr. Barr's headquarters camp in the "promised land". We will establish a base there and search out the three best homesteads to be had."

He lit his pipe and drew contentedly on it. "If the wet and snow are finally finished — and I believe they are — we may even enjoy the last two days on the trail. Why, it's so warm, I may sleep under the stars tonight."

The evening campfire had become a ritual, in fine weather anyway. It drew other colonists camped nearby to swap stories of the day's hardships and triumphs. Tea, pipes, and a bit of Alice's bannock around the fire became their much-cherished balm, smoothing over the day's troubles. The major never failed to add to his teacup from his flask, but he pulled his weight on the trail now and that was all that counted. Jack lounged full-length near the flames, propped up on one elbow, thinking of the homestead — his one hundred and sixty acres. It didn't seem possible that they were finally on hand. He wondered again about a house, water well, barn. The old-time settlers along the trail doled out all kinds of dire warnings and good advice about building homes. Barr's colonists looked forward to picking up their lumber at Headquarters, most planned to build for themselves and save the cost of a carpenter. Jack remembered his plans with Emma. A small but well-built bungalow. Costs might be fifty percent more than they had envisaged but even so, it would be worth it to go for proper construction. The major and his committee — few of whose members had pushed past Battleford — were convinced there would be neither wood nor carpenter nor even land guides at Headquarters. Such little faith had they in Barr that they doubted the colony land itself, now.

Jack was sympathetic. Barr had failed on many promises, but at bottom the colony was succeeding. They were equipped, near the end of the trek, with better land in sight. He glanced at the familiar faces around the fire. Browned, bearded, lean and tired they were, but also tougher, unafraid of hardship, competent with their animals and wagons. Even Alice, the English posy, was now a wild, prairie rose. They could camp, find water and feed themselves efficiently. Perhaps the miseries of the march had been a blessing, an acclimatization.

"There it is again, on the western horizon, watch for it." Alice was standing clear of the fire, pointing. Jack stepped away from the light and stared into the heavy darkness.

"I see it now," Alf said, slipping close to Alice's side. A bubble of red light rose, defining the west rim of the earth, then seemed to burst and die away. Moments later the phenomenon of red light repeated itself.

"Perhaps a flare, from the sunset," Alice suggested.

"Prairie fire more likely," the major said. "Settler near Battleford warned me about them. Flame wall, twenty feet high, galloping at the speed of the wind and devouring — "

"Not so soon, surely," Alf cut him off in response to Alice's anxious face. "We've only had a few dry days, ground is barely thawed."

"Didn't say I believed the blighter," the major rebutted. "Give a fellow a chance to finish, Buxton. I was going to say that the chap was doubtless exaggerating — you know what these people are like."

"Besides," Jack hastened to add, "wind is from the southeast so it will push a fire away from us."

"Even if it is a fire," the major said, jutting his chin forward, "We'll simply use shovels and buckets to put it out. Only a grass fire, after all. Had plenty of those things to contend with in Africa — jolly well fun — bit of fire fighting, eh?"

• • •

Next morning the wind shifted, strong and warm from the northwest. It brought a thin haze that smelled sweet, unlike wood or coal smoke. Jack reckoned them to be less than a mile from the next camp which was purported to be on the shore of a large slough full of ducks and geese. The major could shoot them a fine lot of birds for supper tonight. They might even push past the rest camp and make inroads on tomorrow's trek to the finish line. The trail was firm and dry — they were almost certain to complete the journey tomorrow. The Buxton wagon led the Newland Cooperative, followed by Jordan, then Jack. A dozen wagons preceded them up a low ridge running at right angles across the trail. Jack walked, lines from the oxen draped over his shoulder. It was better than the jolting wagon seat. He climbed up onto the box rim and vaulted into the wagon, then stood on the seat, straining to see over the ridge. He could not.

"Davie!" he bellowed. "Can you see Duck Lake — the camp, yet?"

Davie likewise stood up and waved in reply.

"Yes, just over the hill."

Better time than he'd hoped. Jack jumped back down. Two twitched and pulled One sideways. One snorted and jerked Two back.

"Now, boys, settle down," he clucked, flicking the tip of a rein on Two's rump. But he jerked again and began to increase his pace. A heavy plume of smoke engulfed them for an instant then fled on a wind gust. Jack looked to his left, startled, but the smoke seemed to have materialized from the empty prairie. A wave of hot air struck his face and it sucked another dense puff of smoke around the left end of the hill. The smoke whipped low and snakelike over the ground, hit him, frightened Two, then was gone.

"Must be a grass fire — no need to worry, Two," he said calmly yet flicked them forward all the same. The lake would be best.

A tiny line of smoking flames crested the left end of the hill where it flattened into prairie a half-mile away. They crept almost imperceptibly down the spur, nibbling the grass. The flames were scarcely higher than the grass they ate. Jack sighed, relieved to actually see the menace. "Walls of fire" indeed. Still, might as well get over the hill and into camp, the oxen wouldn't stand for any amount of smoke or flame. The Jordan wagon stopped. The major dismounted and began digging in the box. He emerged with a shovel and empty burlap sack as Jack drew near.

"Woot, One, Woot, Two." The oxen obediently pulled right to pass around the Jordan vehicle. The major dipped the sack in their water barrel and waved it at Jack.

"Come on, Thornton, let's put the blessed thing out."

"Oxen are nervous, Major. Reckon I'll get them to the lake first. Then I'll come back and help."

"Well, fetch the Buxtons with you. We'll show these locals a bit of English pluck, eh? Little thing is hardly worthy of the name fire, yet they let it eat miles of grassland."

"Best perhaps if your wagon stayed with us?" Jack asked, unwilling to interfere with the family, yet uneasy at the thought of Alice and the children alone.

"I can drive to the lake," Alice said matter of factly. She boosted the children up onto the seat and untied the reins.

"You? Drive?" Jack and the major spoke simultaneously, surprised.

"Buxton showed me," she replied, avoiding their stares.

"Alf taught you to drive?" Jack repeated as Alice climbed into the seat. For answer, she snapped the reins and the horses moved off. The major laughed, tweaking his moustaches.

"Jolly well done, old girl! See, Thornton! There's English pluck for you, right there."

Alice whipped up the team and Jack fell in behind her. He walked, looking back over his shoulder. The major strode toward the twinkling light of the little fire carrying his shovel like a rifle at the "shoulder arms" position. Smoke spiraled straight up as though the fire was about to lie down and die of its own accord. The wagons ahead of Davie had nearly disappeared over the ridge. The last two were whipping their teams, charging the crest, foolishly wasting horseflesh. Then, suddenly, Davie was shouting to his oxen and slapping them with his cane. A moment later the Jordan team lurched into a trot. One and Two tried to follow suit with an oxenly lumber.

"Whoa, easy, whoa, boys," Jack pulled back, annoyed at the amateurish race for the lake. One and Two ignored him. He began to jog to keep up. A roar of what seemed to be a heavy waterfall struck Jack's ears. Flames shot up over the crest of the hill less than quarter-mile to his left — high, leaping, yellow flames. One and Two actually began to gallop and Jack ran with them, lacing them with his willow switch, urging them on to the top. The hillcrest revealed the full horror of the prairie fire. Thick billows of grey smoke shot low over the ground. A wall of bright flame bent before the wind that drove it forward. The flames charged in a long-angled line, the nearest end about to follow the small spot fire around the hill, the farthest end of the line still a mile from the lake. A marquee and cluster of bell tents below were a hive of activity. A dozen teams were ploughing parallel fireguard furrows between the camp and the flames. A mob of figures with buckets and sacks dashed to the lake.

One and Two pointed their noses at the big slough and actually increased their speed. The wagons streamed down the reverse side of the slope. They would make the safety of the water easily. Jack's eyes prickled from the advance guard of smoke. He turned back to look for the major, prepared to laugh at the older man pounding up the slope, perhaps shovel flung away in panic. He was not pounding up the hill. He was flapping his wet burlap on the little spot fire, unable to yet see to the danger.

"Major! *Run, man! Fire!*" Jack shrieked over his shoulder as One and Two tugged him onto the hillcrest. The major couldn't hear him. He wouldn't see the real fire until it flowed around the end of the ridge. Then it would be too late; the wall of flames would cut the trail before he'd got halfway up. Alf had heard Jack, so had Alice. It was her voice that came over the noise of wind and fire.

"No, Alf! Please, *no*, Alf. You can't save him!"

Then Davie's plaintive wail. "AAAALfred!"

Alf, bowler rammed down over his ears, bulldog eyes glaring fiercely above a hanky tied across nose and mouth, ran back up the trail. Whether it was logic or emotion that had prompted Alice's cry — she was right. Jack measured the distances with his eye and knew it would be too close. Alf pelted toward Jack without so much as a sideways glance. His eyes were riveted on Jordan.

"Buxton, don't be an ass!" He plucked at Alf's shirtsleeve without success. "You're not his servant."

Alf never broke stride. Jack ran on behind One and Two over the hilltop. Something from Africa ate into him as he ran. It was Palmer's crawl for safety; George Grigg's warm hands on his wounded head; the Gloster Machine Gun Section going into the Paardeberg night.

He took a running leap onto the wagon box and wrapped the lines tightly around the seat springs then jumped clear. One and Two knew exactly what they were doing; they had no need of a driver. Racing back to the hillcrest, Jack saw that he was already too late. Major Jordan was running away from the fire that now chased him. He tried to turn uphill and disappeared into the smoke that led the flames, now threatening to cut the trail. A moment later he emerged staggering and retching. He was either in retreat or disoriented because he began to run before the wind again. Alf, seeing the mistake, cut a long detour to intercept the major. He entered the smoke and reemerged just in front of him. A brief struggle ensued then both men turned back up the trail, Alf holding Jordan's hand.

But it really was too late. The trail was completely obscured by smoke. The actual fire was less than one hundred yards behind the smoke. The men plunged into the grey mass. Jack coughed and wept at the top. The flames were clawing up the ridgeline, from both sides now. The fire seemed to have taken on a personality, as though transformed into a living creature. It came for him like a slinking predator. He'd have to run, and soon. The prairie fire now took full notice of Jack and turned to trap him. Jack stared back down the smoking hill, a calm corner of his brain telling him to fix the spot where the men's bodies could be recovered later. Then he turned to go.

"Thornton!"

Jack swiveled at his name. Dr. Fiset, ant-like, humped Captain Arnold's limp body out of the smoke toward him. Except it was Alf, and the rim of this bowler was glowing. Jordan's bulk lay draped across his shoulders. Then Jack was beside them, taking Jordan's legs and chasing Alf who clutched the major's armpits.

"Your hat is on fire, Alf," Jack said, laughing and choking.

"Damn," Alf wheezed.

• • •

The rain was only heavy once, for about half an hour in the morning. Then it settled into a soaking drizzle for the entire day. One and Two looked as though a naughty boy had played them a prank, painting their legs gloss black. Jack's boots and trousers were soaked with soot the consistency of glue. His hands and, he suspected, his face made him a parody of a black man. The trail past Duck Lake turned north and drew them up a steep slope to a plateau overlooking the government camp and the lake. They paused to rest the animals at the top.

"This country's the very devil." The major's voice cracked, finishing the sentence with a small cough. His eyes stared red from a soot-blacked face. The tips of his moustaches were craggy, burnt stubs. Davie laughed. He tried to restrain himself, but his laughter burst forth as a large guffaw. The major, stunned by such insubordination from the lowest strata of their little society, turned a fierce glare on Davie. The result was exactly the opposite of what he intended. Davie dissolved into shuddering giggles.

"Sorry, Major," he hooted. "But your poor face . . . it's the very devil's face."

Alice turned rapidly aside, stifling a snort. Alf, Jack, then the children were instantly infected. Even Ostrich, resembling a miniature, black Labrador retriever, began his puppy-hound howl. The major stamped to the wagon seat, retrieved Alice's bag and fished out her small mirror. One glance was enough. He took a long swallow from his flask and, to everyone's delight, he joined them, laughing until he coughed up a lump of black sputum. Drawn by the same thought they faced back down the trail. Low, grey clouds clung to the horizon. Duck Lake's kidney shape shone metallic silver beneath the spitting clouds. At the far end of the water a tiny cluster of white tents huddled on the patch of brown grass saved from the fire. Clumps of leafless poplar and aspen, their circumferences singed, dotted the plain. Otherwise, every square foot of country was black. Prairie fire had indeed devoured everything that dared show itself above ground. The plateau was, likewise, soot to the north and west horizons. Drizzle pattered on Alf's bowler, its tiny drumming the only sound. Prairie fire had bitten off one corner of the hat brim and left a watery blister on Alf's forehead. Rainwater trickled through the gap and down his face.

"Well, we are now officially on Colony land," Jack broke the silence. "For better or worse, welcome to Barr's promised land."

The others turned unenthusiastic eyes on him as he pulled his spade out of the wagon and stamped it hilt-deep into the soil. "Might as well know the worst," he muttered. "Let's try the major's experiment, shall we?"

He heaved on the handle and turned over six inches of sod. The soil was almost indistinguishable from the burnt grass it lay upon. The others gathered around him.

"Fire would burn down that deep, would it?" Alf asked.

Jack plunged his shovel in again, and then again. Just over a foot down he reached a trace of grey-brown till. The major knelt and picked up a handful of the dug dirt, squeezing it in his fist.

377

"It's cool and moist. Look, the grass roots are white." He put a piece between his teeth. "Roots are fresh, sweet." He spat. "This is better than a foot of heavy loam, lady, gentlemen, and children. And we're at the edge of a plateau. If it's a foot deep here, then it will be up to two feet deep northwest of here, where we are bound."

Alf and Jack's faces lit up like pirates opening a treasure chest.

"Is that good? Is loam good?" Davie asked.

"Davie," Jack laughed, taking the mudball from the major. "If my Uncle Henry had land like this in Gloucestershire, it would be worth five hundred pounds an acre."

"An' we got one hundred and sixty acres, for ten dollars," Davie breathed.

"Each of us." Jack knelt to put his hand into the hole. "If we can plough it and stick to it for three years."

The major jumped to his feet. "Not a single, ruddy duck on the whole thing," he said, "but who cares, eh?" He scooped Mary up in his arms and faced her to the lake. "Good riddance, Duck Lake!" he shouted.

"Goodbye, Duck Lake," Mary squeaked.

"Begone, Camp Desolation," Jack hollered.

"*Adieu*, Camp Starvation," Alice's sweet voice sang.

Alf smiled at the Jordan family. Jack sobered quickly. Was it only twenty-four hours ago that Alf had risked his life, and the cooperative future to save the major? It did not seem possible but the memory was clear — as clear as the vignette of Miles and Palmer and Arnold when the Mausers took them. Did Alf think it would one day make him their social equal?

CHAPTER 20

"Too flat, not enough trees, less chance of good water," Jack repeated emphatically.

"But it's close to the new townsite — closer to the railroad when it comes. Land value will skyrocket *if* we stay close to town." The major had long since given up issuing orders but he was persuasive, nonetheless.

"You talked to Mr. Rendall yourself," Jack replied. "Two wells over twenty feet deep and each one dry as a springtime fart."

The major looked down his nose at such vulgarity and Jack regretted his lapse into a Charlie Cordey expression.

"There are seepage wells for now," Jordan said to Alf. "And if the Rendalls choose to be near town then that's where we should be."

They stood in early-morning debate beside the government land office, a large tent stained from the priaire fire ash. Jack kicked at the blackened, woolly grass at this feet. Fresh green shoots were rising like magic from the ash. In a week, the old timers prophesied, the land would be a riot of bright-green grass and wild flowers. Prairie fire was dangerous and benevolent.

"No lumber for a house. Only a handful of land guides, no well diggers or carpenters." The major pressed his points on the Buxtons, ignoring Jack. "Just as I foretold. We have to stay close to the townsite, first to maintain committee vigilance over these Barr blunders and, second, so that we will be close at hand when proper supplies and services arrive."

"But the land here is nearly all gone," Jack pitched to Alf. "We'll be split up all over these townships. How will we farm cooperatively? And we can't waste time chasing Barr or doing committee work. We need good land with good water."

His Boer War enteric nightmare had never left Jack. Some of the first people into the colony were already suffering from dysentery, and it frightened him. His instinct was for the river valley, north or east. Not the flat, alkaline sloughs here. They must stay together. Splintered across a thirty-six-square-mile township, their chances dwindled.

"Davie and me are for open land and stick together," Alf declared. The major fumed but stopped short of mutiny, much to Alice's relief.

A creek flowing northeast of the Headquarters Camp cut a wide ravine that ran for several miles to join the North Saskatchewan River. The chief land guide oriented them to the large map pinned up on an easel in the Land Office. Appropriately named Big Gully, the creek was wooded and sandy, but south of it the land was excellent for about twenty miles east of the Headquarters. He advised them to follow the Big Gully east, then strike south. If they could use a compass and "reset the declination from English variance", then they could find their own homesteads. Otherwise, it would be a two-day wait for a land guide.

The major produced a compass. All previous arguments healed, they set off in his empty wagon as fast as his horses could go. Already land claims were being jumped, swapped and fought over. They must not only find their land, but race back to register it at the Land Office before someone else took it. The horses seemed to fly. After fifteen days behind One and Two, Jack felt as though he was riding in a steeplechase. Major Jordan, for all his reservations, seemed to have been bitten hardest by the land bug. They drove due east, covering ten miles in less than two hours, to strike Big

Gully. The land dropped as steeply and deeply as Eagle Creek, and the flat bottom was nearly a mile wide in places. They pressed on, following a trail that cut the prairie on the southern edge of the ravine for perhaps six more miles.

They rested, fed, and watered the sweating horses, while Jack pored over the map. Facing them was essentially flat grassland dotted by a maze of aspen groves. No trail nor marker nor even cowpath seemed to point the way. The land bordering Big Gully for two miles might prove thin and sandy, they would have to go well south of it.

"Well, General?" Jordan asked. "Ready to launch the campaign? Orders?"

"Drive three miles south to hit good soil." Jack tapped the map. "Then when we see something promising, we'll find the township marker and . . . ah, go from there."

"That's it?" Alf asked, scratching his burn boil and wincing. "Could take days wandering around like that to find one iron marker stake."

"Buxton's got a point," the major said. "Rather vague, old boy, isn't it?"

"Look here, then." Jack showed them the map. "Each township is six miles by six miles, thirty-six square sections. The north edge of our township line runs along the edge of the gully, right where we're standing. If we find land three, four, five, or six miles south of here, then we know we're in township twelve, and roughly where in that township."

"Why didn't you say so — piece of cake." The major stood, lighting a cheroot. "Let's be off before somebody beats us to it."

"The land agent has marked the only four quarter-sections that have been claimed, all unseen. None of these people have arrived in Headquarters camp yet, so we've got lots of time and leeway," Jack said, restraining his own eagerness. They must do this right, be accurate. But the major's fever had infected Davie. He hopped into the wagon. "But the land agent's one of Barr's boys! He might be swivven us — might be dozens o' his chums out here already."

Davie's words seemed justified a half-hour later when, two miles south of the gully, they rounded a bluff of trees and drove past a bell tent. Two men — brothers they looked — were trying to hitch their team to a plough not one hundred yards from the tent.

"Hallo! Hallo, there!" A woman, bent over a cookstove sited near the trees, waved to them.

"Good God," Jack yelped, surprise followed immediately by apprehension. "What the devil are *they* doing here? The land agent — "

"Was Barr's man, and he was wrong, by heavens." The major drove toward the men. "Who knows how many others have preceded us?"

The older man extended his hand. "Good day. I'm Bob Hill, this is Oliver. Southbound, are you?"

Jack quickly unfolded his map. The major and Alf made small talk, probing the Hill brothers for news of others in the area.

"Just us, for now," Bob said. "We each have a quarter but only one plough, so we'll take turns if we can get the thing to work." He smiled.

Jack showed him the map. "This is your land here, then?"

Bob looked. Oliver looked. Both shrugged and smiled. "Land guide put us in here two days ago. Don't know about your map but we're the southeast — here, and southwest — there," he pointed, "quarters of section twenty-eight."

Jack marked the map with their names. "But the land agent told us you weren't on the ground yet."

Bob and Oliver just shrugged and smiled. Their mother approached from the stove. "Land guide brought us here with three other families. We were the only ones with our claim already settled, on the boat, over a month ago."

"Three other families, Mrs. Hill?" Alf doffed his hat.

"Oh, yes, them," Oliver laughed. "Forgot about them. But they didn't have land claimed yet so I didn't think you would care . . . "

"Which way did they go?" Jack snapped, his worst imaginings now back in full flight. "Sounds like the place is crawling with colonists."

"Eastward," Mrs. Hill answered tartly. "Last we saw them."

Jack eyed the east horizon as though looking for enemy horsemen.

"You haven't claimed yet?" she ventured, eyebrows raised.

"No, thought better to see the land first," Alf replied with a worried glance in Jack's direction.

"Aye, well," Mrs. Hill indicated the stove. "I have tea and bread, but I'll imagine you want to press on — good land like ours will be going fast. We claimed on the boat, you know."

The Jordan wagon fled south, all its passengers now entertaining visions of a lost land race. At least, Jack thought, concentrating on the map and compass, we know pretty much where we are, if only we knew where those families had wandered to. The major whipped up the team, racing forward to . . . what? This was insane panic.

"Slow up, Major," Jack forced himself to be calm. "Go easy, so we can have a good look and stay on the compass."

"There!" The major hauled in the horses excitedly. "Looks promising."

A large slough, green, not alkaline white, lay in the distance just east of their course. A long fringe of trees ran along the north shore.

"It's all water!" Alf protested.

"Good water for seepage, lots of ducks and some grouse, I'd wager," the major replied. "Perfect for me. I want to shoot and I want woods."

"Can't farm woods as easily as prairie."

"Let's have a look," Jack interrupted, "the ground appears to rise south of the slough so it will be well drained. You and Davie might go that way, Alf."

The major was already trotting the team toward the water, eyes shining at his "estate" as he had come to refer to the homestead. The slough revealed itself to be about forty acres, with a thick belt of trees on the north and east shores. A knoll rose at the east end and the trees climbed its north face. The south side of the knoll swept smoothly and gently down, then up in a gradual undulation to flat, open ground for the next mile south. The major wanted the lake and trees. The Buxtons wanted the south upland. Jack wanted the knoll. "I should think a hilltop, woods on the slope, and a pond or stream nearby." Emma's voice came to him. It was what they had envisioned — yet it was nothing like England, and nothing like what he had seen in his mind's eye in Hampstead. But it was all he wanted, now.

They pored over the map, estimating distances from the Hill homestead. Jack was certain he and the major were somewhere in section fourteen. The section due south, number eleven, was not free. It was a school section. But immediately east of the school land, section number twelve was free. They drove to it, dug in it, and Alf pronounced it perfect. There was an extra quarter bordering each of their claims so they could preempt another one hundred and sixty acres. Even though it was mid afternoon and the horses were wet and tired, the men had no thought of rest. They needed to verify their claims, exactly, in order to register correctly. They drove slowly south of the "Buxton land" as they already called it. Jack, Alf, and Davie walked fanned out at hundred-yard intervals, wide of the wagon. Alf spotted the tall, iron stake first. They converged on it in a triumph that was short-lived. The iron rod marked the southeast corner of their township. They need only measure one mile straight north to verify the Buxton claim on section twelve. But the charred grass around the stake was well trampled and wagon-wheel tracks departed in all directions. Even as they stood in the slanting rays of the late afternoon sun, a usurper could be claiming their land. There was no way of telling, the only course was to press forward.

They tied Alf's red bandana around a spoke at a rear-wheel rim, rolled the wagon forward one full revolution of the wheel, and measured the distance covered. Davie divided it into five thousand two hundred and eighty and calculated the number of revolutions for a mile. Then with Major Jordan driving exactly behind him, Jack walked north, compass in outstretched hand before him. Davie and Alf counted the bandana revolutions, tying a knot in a piece of string every hundred. The mile worked near-perfect to the southeast corner of the "Buxton land". Another mile west and north confirmed Jack and the major's homestead claims as residing in section fourteen. Satisfied as to the accuracy of their claims, they camped near "Lake Jordan". All were nervous, snapping over trifles, minds' eyes wandering to headquarters camp and the land agent's tent. The long day and miles marched scarcely touched them with fatigue.

What if the good land was all gone? What if they had to trek south off the colony to try their luck? These thoughts rose inside Jack, then were shouted down by logic. My God, there were hundreds of miles of nothing behind and before them. Surely they would find land. They crowded into the Jordan wagon to sleep.

• • •

385

Jack awoke. He crawled to the open end of the wagon. His watch by moonlight read one AM He would sleep no more, that was certain.

"You awake, Alf?" Davie said, from the dark.

"Never went to sleep, boy."

"Right, same for me." The major kicked off his blankets. "Let's go now, we'll be first in the agent's tent at dawn."

"In the dark?"

"Moon's up — three-quarters is bright enough to read the compass," Jack said, rolling up his blankets. "Colony Headquarters should be a bit north and west of us. We can march southwest 'til we hit the main trail and follow it in. Should cut five miles off our journey of yesterday."

The others were already shaking out the harness and running down the horses. The fear of possible loss gave the land a luster that none would have recognized a week earlier. Indeed, the slough, trees, knoll, and rising upland were much the same as hundreds of sloughs, trees, and knolls already passed on the trek. But these seemed like the pot of gold at the end of a long rainbow. They drove as fast as they dared, oblivious of the beauty that the moon gave their new homeland. At four fifteen AM, Major Jordan stopped the wagon behind the land agent tent and tethered the horses. They walked to the front of the tent and were astounded to find five men wrapped in blankets, sleeping like so many sausage rolls in a line before the door. Now, thoroughly alarmed, Jack sat down on the damp, sooty ground, right beside the fifth man. The major, Alf, and Davie followed suit, the major hitting his flask, the rest puffing pipes that glowed in the rising dawn.

The moon set, as sunlight brought the eastern horizon into focus. Three men trudged toward them out of the sunrise. Haggard and limping, the newcomers' shoulders drooped even farther at the sight of the queue. They sat in behind Davie. There was no conversation. Each man mulled his own furtive thoughts and worries as the camp came to life. The land agent showed no surprise when he arrived to open for business. In fact, he made a speech about behaving like Englishmen, and declared that if he had to break up just one more fight or arbitrate one more altercation between men claiming the same land, then he would close the office. An argument immediately broke out between the first two men in line over land in township twelve. The Newland Cooperative was township twelve. The agent lost his temper but forgot his threat to decamp and, instead, made both men go to the end of the line where they began shoving and cursing each other. The remainder of the queue moved forward, ignoring the squabblers' misfortune.

Inside the tent, Jack quickly traced Big Gully on the large map. He found twelve and his eye shot fearfully to the southeast. Nothing was written in the little paper squares. The sections were empty. He leaned forward, squinting. Section fourteen and twelve, absolutely devoid of human occupation. He popped his head outside the tent and grinned broadly. Soggy, filthy from soot, and red-eyed, the Newland Cooperative whooped with delight.

• • •

Jack turned One and Two loose. He climbed to the top of the knoll, and slowly turned three hundred and sixty degrees. The Jordan tent was mushrooming nearly three-quarters of a mile west — at the far end of the lake. Alice would not let them call it a slough. The Buxton wagon crawled like a sooty, green and red beetle across the sweep of grassland toward the edge of the Buxton land, nearly a mile southeast. A chickadee sang its dee-dee-dee in the trees on the north side of Jack's hill. Ostrich found a patch of grass that had already outgrown its burned bed. He rolled in it. The chickadee fluttered past Jack's head. He let his eye measure half-mile sides to an imaginary boundary around him. One hundred and sixty acres. It was huge. He breathed in deeply. Morning air that had never carried anything on it but nature. He expanded his lungs with it. He drew more until they hurt, then he exhaled with a tremendous bellow —inarticulate, joyous, and victorious. He threw his cap in the air and roared like a lion, then howled like a coyote, staggering and gasping. Ostrich cocked his head, half wondering if he should have gone with Davie. Jack picked the dog up and planted a sloppy kiss on its head; it licked him in return.

"It is here we stay, Ostrich. This is our place. May I borrow your grass?"

He sat in the newly-grown greenery, its remnant of dew penetrated his trousers. He pulled a square of paper and a pencil from his waistcoat pocket — much as he'd pulled his mother's note out on a spring morning four years ago.

My Dearest Emma,
I am writing from Newland Estate. Not much yet, but there
is a hill with trees and a pond below. There are one hundred
and fifty acres of prime farmland besides. I cannot do it justice
with this pencil, but here is my best attempt . . .

• • •

The promise of fresh grass and wild flowers was kept. Jack's acres blossomed vigorously. He scarcely noticed that he was without human contact for the next three days. He and Ostrich crisscrossed their land. They carefully paced out its boundaries and marked the corner of the section. They found a small, natural depression at the edge of the trees at the bottom of the north side of the knoll. He hammered three skinned saplings into a tripod over the depression to mark his future water well. He dug a hole near the slough and each evening dipped out the buckets of water that had seeped through, strained, at least, of bugs and larvae. He religiously boiled this and topped up his water barrel. He dug a deep latrine in dry land beyond the south side of his hill, near where he paced out and staked the dimensions of his barn. He marked the corral for One and Two, although they seemed content to wander from slough to grass patches, drinking and eating to replenish themselves after the long trek. A corral might be low priority. He also staked a five-acre parcel beyond the corral. This he did carefully, almost reverently. It would be ploughed for oats. His first crop.

He and Ostrich lived in the tent on a ledge just below the crest of the hill on the bare, south-facing side. Sunrise woke and warmed them each morning. A dozen building sites for the house were carefully examined for convenience, proximity to water well and barn, and vistas of the surrounding country. Jack finally decided that the top of the knoll would be best suited. The fourth morning he woke to the sound of wind, but the tent sides were not flapping. Curious, he and Ostrich climbed the short distance to the top of the hill and were struck by a cold, north gust. Clouds scudded rapidly toward him from the north horizon, riding the arctic air that smelled like snow. Ostrich turned his backside to it and crouched close to the ground. A harsh blast shoved Jack. He turned, imitating Ostrich, and knelt to offer a smaller target. Twenty paces below them the tent quietly soaked up the morning light. Jack grinned and slapped a palm against his forehead.

"I think that wind is telling us something rather obvious, Ostrich."

The beagle gave up the cold and trotted down to the tent.

"Got it in one." Jack followed him. "Emma will be impressed with you, little hound. Let's discuss house design over breakfast, shall we?"

They cooked and ate a full breakfast including the last of Alice's bannock, hoarded for a special day. Jack found himself chatting to the dog, twice calling it Emma by mistake. House, well, barn located and plans for ploughing ready, today they would visit the cooperative and compare notes. He could spare a day's labour, indeed he ought to go visiting. Talking to your dog was bad enough, but confusing it with your wife — three thousand miles away — that was serious.

Jack found, somewhat to his dismay, that the Buxtons were much farther advanced than he was. Of course, twice the labour counted for much. Still, it was a surprise to see that they had not needed his guidance in establishing their farm. They had made several trips to a wooded bluff just south of their land. A substantial stack of firewood lay neatly cut and piled by their tent. A sturdy web of aspen poles formed the box frame for their house. Davie, as it turned out, had a natural talent for carpentry. The house was sixteen feet by twelve with a sloping roof. They would use sod for walls and poles, and sod for the roof. They could not even consider the cost of lumber yet. Similarly, a wider, higher frame for the barn was under construction. The real surprise was the well, good water at ten feet down. For this, at least, Jack was given full credit; he had picked good land with good water.

Jack's ego was then further bolstered by the sight of their plough. They hadn't been able to assemble it correctly and were anxious to start ploughing. The instructors and land guides had repeated the absolute necessity of ploughing a good fireguard and getting a few acres of crop in to feed their animals over the winter. The fireguard sod could be used to build the house and barn. Jack convinced them to accompany him on a visit to the Jordans. They would arrange a ploughing class with the major, and trade some flour for Alice's bannock. They stopped on the way past Jack's knoll where he was proudly showing them his plans for house, barn, well, and field, when he realized they were only wood stakes. His actual accomplishments were two holes: the seepage well and the latrine. They continued on into the wind. Clouds had covered the sky now and a flurry of white snow whipped past them as they rounded the west end of the slough and hurried toward the Jordan tent.

"Hallo! We've come visiting!" Jack called, suddenly conscious of the fact that nobody was about. The tent flap opened and the major stepped out. He was clean-shaven and natty in gaiters, corduroy trousers, and wool cardigan. He puffed a cheroot, waving to them. A scraggly heap of twigs and deadfall logs was piled outside the tent. An axe lay in the grass. Nearby, a bow-saw with broken blade had been similarly abandoned. The wagon, still partly loaded with chairs and a china crate, was parked, but no horses were in sight.

"Tea, my dear, we have company," the major announced as the three men ducked under the canvas. Mary sat quietly with Mrs. Dimples near the far wall. Alice, hair roughly tied in a bun, face pasty white, wore the dress and apron she had worn on the trek, still stained with soot.

"Lovely. How pleasant," she said, but her eyes were afraid, the same fear as on the Liverpool dock. "Please come in, gentlemen, the grass is thick and soft." She forced a laugh at her own joke.

They laughed much too loudly with her and sat cross-legged by the centre pole. She dipped water from a bucket and strained it through a piece of cheesecloth into a kettle on the campstove. Jack shot Alf a quick glance, and Alf frowned. Drinking slough water, not even a seepage well. There had been no toilet facility visible, either. The major sat on an empty cot and began talking about the shooting. He had procured duck or grouse for dinner every night.

Alf interrupted the major, "Where's little Kitty got to, Mrs. Jordan?"

Alice nodded at the cot behind her. It was piled high with blankets and a tiny voice squeaked from beneath them.

"I'm here, Alf. You can't see me."

Alf didn't humour the girl's invitation at hide and seek. The little voice was sick.

"She sounds terrible, Mrs. Jordan. Is she ill?"

Alice gulped, blinking rapidly by way of reply.

"A touch of flu, some fever. I think she's rallying now," the major's words were casual, but even his voice cracked, worried.

"May I see?" Alf moved to the cot and pulled back the covers. A red-blotched face emerged. Kitty's blonde hair had been sweat-plastered to her forehead, but was crisp and dry now. Her eyes were glazed. Jack reeled. Not enteric, please, God.

"Well, aren't you a pretty picture." Alf touched his lips to her forehead then turned. "Why don't you let Davie show you how much Ostrich has grown while Mommy and Daddy and I visit."

Jack followed them outside, sick at heart. Alf dispensed with any notion of propriety.

"It's scarlet fever — seen it a hundred times back home. She needs a doctor. What in the devil are you doing? Why haven't you gone for Doctor Amos at Headquarters Camp?"

Alice barely controlled the tears. "I know, I'm so terribly worried . . . Buxton. But we can't go for a doctor."

Alf looked to the major, angry. Jack began to make placatory sounds, but the major spoke up.

"Horses ran off two days ago. Can't find the brutes anywhere."

Jack and Alf waited for him to finish, but he fell into an awkward silence. He examined the wagon and puffed his cheroot.

"Well, what are you planning to do, now?" Alf asked patiently, giving the major a chance to say the right thing.

"Do? Nothing to be done! No horses means no doctor. If we had claimed land near the townsite my daughter would be well cared for."

He blew an indignant cloud of smoke at Jack, but the snow-squalling wind whipped it away. While he'd been mooning over Emma and playing at farming, poor Kitty had been lying seriously ill. Jack swallowed audibly, but Alf refused the pathetic excuse.

"Why not come see us? Take the oxen," he demanded. "You let Kitty suffer because you're sulking over lost horses and your precious town?"

"Now, see here, Buxton." The cheroot was spat out and ground into the earth.

"Stop it!" Alice stamped her foot. "It's serious. Kitty needs help, so just stop. I won't listen to it." She looked to Jack, pleading eyes brimming with tears.

"Right. You're right, of course, Mrs. Jordan. I did bring us out here so I'll get Kitty to the doctor." He let the words out in a rush and they steadied him, a plan formed itself inside his head. "Mrs. Jordan, wrap Kitty up as warm as you can. Make a sling out of a blanket — like a cradle for her to ride in. It's just under sixteen miles to Headquarters Camp. The major, myself, and Alf will walk it, take turns carrying Kitty. We'll go hard — make it in five hours."

"Walk? But why not take the oxen — fetch the doctor here," she said.

"Oxen are too slow, take them all day. And Doctor Amos may be out on a call. This way, at least Kitty will be in the hospital tent with nurses and proper medicine. If we three go now and trade Kitty off when we're tired, we'll be in camp by early afternoon."

"Agreed," the major said. "But take Davie with us, he's the youngest and strongest."

393

Alf started to protest, but the major cut him off. "And despite his tone a moment ago, Buxton senior is the man to look after my wife and Mary. Davie is just a boy."

"Bring your compass," Jack said. "We can't take a chance on losing our way."

Alice gave a little sob of relief and wiped her eyes on her cuff. She rushed into the tent with her husband. Jack and Alf waited outside.

"Davie and I won't be back until late tomorrow. The major will be gone for at least four or five days . . . " Jack faltered.

"I'm not going to attack the woman the second her husband is gone." Alf poked him and grinned. "Give me some credit."

"Sorry. Just for appearances sake . . . ah, not suggesting you, or she, would be . . . "

"Improper?"

Jack laughed. "Listen to me. Appearances I'm worried about, and not another human within ten miles."

"I'll tell you what, Jack Thornton." Alf looked him in the eye. "I wish to God I'd let the shiftless bugger die in the fire." Then he laughed too.

• • •

Davie went like a thoroughbred. He carried Kitty eight miles, up and down ravines, crashing through small woods, running around large ones. Jack scrambled to keep them on compass course — the major barely kept the pace. Jack did two miles with Kitty; then the major one, gasping and wheezing and cursing the cheroots. Davie took her back with a fine, long look down his nose at the two of them. He raced them along and they intersected the main trail just short of Headquarters Camp. Moments later, a swift moving democrat rattled up the trail behind them.

"Here! Slow down! We need a ride." The major's rasping breaths puffed white in the cold air. "Sick child."

"I say. That you, Jordan?" The buggy drew up. One of the committee men from the boat was driving. Reverend Lloyd was the sole passenger. "Well climb aboard, men, we'll have the little chit into the hospital lickety split. Dear me, she doesn't look well at all."

"Scarlet fever, I fear, but I think we've got her here in time." The major mopped his steaming face and smiled gallantly. "Sixteen miles in just over three hours. Horses gone off, had to do a forced march."

The Reverend said nothing, but the committee man whistled through his teeth. "Jolly well done, Major Jordan, good going."

"Couldn't have done it without these fellows," the major said generously, in a tone that suggested he'd carried all of them.

Reverend Lloyd gave him a hard look, but continued silent.

"All's well that ends well," the committee man said cheerfully. "You will be the first in camp to hear the big news — Barr is gone."

"Never! Scampered with our cash?" Jordan's eyes lit up. He reached inside his coat for his flask, then froze and slid it back. Reverend Lloyd was severely opposed to the "liquorite element" of the colony.

"Not likely," the man replied. "We voted him out — meeting in Battleford two days ago. Reverend Lloyd and a committee of twelve will administer the colony now. Couple of hotheads were up for shooting Barr, or lynching him, but the gentlemen took things in hand. There will be no further irregularities, I can assure you."

"Who is to be on the committee?" The major fairly salivated at this news.

"Three so far. Myself, Nate Jones, and Robert Blackburn were elected from the colonists still stuck in Battleford. We'll have nine more elected from those of you already on the front lines. You must let your name stand, Major Jordan."

The major, puppy-like, looked to Lloyd.

"Anyone and everyone who is sober," Lloyd paused significantly, "and competent, may stand for committee election. It's not just for the gentlemen. You would, of course, be welcome to join us should you be elected."

Jordan mistook this verbal slap and chuckled. "Thank you, sir. I think I know my duty and I shan't let you down."

Reverend Lloyd shifted his gaze to Kitty, still in Davie's arms. "Mmmm, yes, quite. Duty is the thing, Major. Tricky sometimes, finding exactly where our duty lies."

He smiled at Kitty and praised her for a brave girl, and a fortunate girl to have such stout friends.

• • •

White and yellow and blue, the wildflowers burst in the warm sun four days later. It had taken them a day to find the horses — grazing happily at the bottom of Big Gully. Then they had dug a seepage well and a latrine on the Jordan homestead. Davie had enclosed the toilet inside an aspen-built outhouse. Jack and Alf sawed up a large stack of firewood. Alice fed them bannock, porridge, bacon, and the last duck. The men slept on their own land each night.

Then it was time to plough. The major and Kitty remained at Headquarters Camp — Doctor Amos' orders were that she not be moved again until fully recovered. Jack went through the plough assembly with the Buxtons, naming all the parts and fitting them together. Alice and Mary watched intently, blonde heads shining in the morning sun — hats and parasols hadn't survived past Duck Lake. Alice's metamorphosis from English beauty to sunburned frontierswoman was striking. She repeated the words along with Alf and Davie.

"Share point and heel actually cut the ground. Moldboard turns the furrow. Frog, the frame for all the other bits. Beam, the keel. Clevis, the hitch to attach the horses. A two-horse — or ox — walking plough to cut a fourteen-inch furrow."

Jack twisted the graceful, gooseneck handles and the ploughshare lay poised on the thick grass. He slid the heavy leather collars over the heads of One and Two. The backbands — meant for horses — barely straddled the broad, ox bodies. He clipped the chain traces onto the collars and ran them back to their individual draught bars. Jack was struck with a sudden sense of performance now, as though on stage for an historic scene. He slid the S hooks of each draught bar through the rings on the ends of the iron whipple tree which had one ring in its middle. That would concentrate all the ox power from straining neck collar, along the taut traces, through the draught bars onto this one point. He walked One and Two to the plough, lined up the clevis and whipple tree, and dropped the final pin into place, connecting animal to implement.

A peaceful satisfaction flooded him. Wind hissed in his ears as he knotted the leather reins. He dropped the looped lines over his neck and took the handles. Sunlight flashed from the ploughshare blade. Grass rippled as a green sea, waving, giving substance to the prairie breeze that hummed through it. The flowers scented it lightly for his nose. It cooled his face. He looked at his "class" standing expectantly to one side. Jack heaved on the handles and set the blade tip into the earth. He sighted down the beam between One and Two. His marker stake awaited him a quarter-mile distant.

"Up, One. Up, Two. Woot, One. Woot, Two." The Gloucestershire ploughman commands sounded in his ears over the wind. The plough bit sank, and slid under the turf. A long, slow wave of black earth curved up and along the moldboard. It turned over, smooth as a sounding whale, and formed a dark ribbon on the earth's surface. Wind swirled out of the uprooted grass and curled up his trouser leg.

Welcome home, Jack

He shook his head. The sound of tearing linen drowned the breeze. It was the prairie ripping. Ten thousand years of untouched roots and humus. Grass, upon buffalo dung, upon grass, ten thousand times over. It split and surrendered to Jack Thornton. His last shred of doubt evaporated. He sucked the magic wind into his lungs. This wasn't what he had expected. He was not the conqueror of this soil. He was joining it.

Welcome home, Jack.

Alf, Davie, Alice, and Mary walked beside him, grinning like children on Christmas morning.

"Westward the Star of Empire takes its way," Jack said.

CHAPTER 21

Jack was pleased with his potatoes. No doubt of it, the potatoes were doing well. A little less than a half-acre, ploughed, and quickly chopped by the disker — good enough for potatoes. They would be welcome this winter. But the oats were his delight, his pride, and on July mornings like this, his wonder. Only two acres, true, but then the prairie soil, like everything else in this country, had fooled him. The plough had done its job, yet the long ribbons of overturned sod could not be seeded. They, in turn, needed to be broken up into a finer bed for the oats. He'd run the little disker back and forth three times before the stubborn land had relented. By then the Buxtons were literally standing at the edge of his field, anxiously waiting for the disker to till up their furrows. He'd done the harrowing relatively quickly, all the time cursing himself for buying too much harrow and too little disker. Thank God, Alf, through instinct and blind obedience to Barr's pamphlet, had insisted on at least one set. The purchase of binder over mower had been foolishly optimistic, as well. He could scythe the few acres of oats easily — the binder was envisioned for vast acres of crop, which had not been possible this first year. Whereas the mower would have made haying so much easier and, God, what a fool he'd been . . .

Still, he had got his oats seeded the first week of June, and two rains and plenty of sun since then had caused a volcano of green to erupt. They were already high, thick, and rippling in the first breeze of the morning. Bright sunlight seemed to draw them up from the earth. Jack talked freely to the wind when it rustled his oats. He had abandoned his early embarrassments. The first day that he'd answered the hissing wind, he'd stopped mid-sentence, looking around sharply for someone to mock him. One and Two seemed not to care; the only humans were over a mile away. He'd laughed, and finished his sentence. Now he chatted quietly to all of them: the wind, Ostrich, One, and Two. He'd also cursed, loudly and with venom, when the mosquitoes had come. Into his eyes, ears, mouth, biting his wrists and neck to a bloody mess. They had coated One and Two, chasing them neck-deep into Lake Jordan on several occasions. But most of the mosquitoes were in July remission, and the prairie wind chased the few remaining pests back into the grass.

Emma would love this land. She had to love the oat field, if nothing else. Nineteen nights, then she'd be here. She would see his oats and marvel at the barn built of sod taken from the fireguard that ringed their field and home. Home was still a tent and that pricked him. A bungalow was out of the question. Major Jordan's three hundred-square-foot hut had cost him two full months' remittance. Jack shrank from that cost. He broke land instead, hoping Emma would agree to a sod house for now, but not having the confidence to actually start construction without her approval. Nine more days. He would plough for six, then get the blade sharpened. That would break nine more acres. He'd buy a new disker in Saskatoon. Next year, then, he'd have a real crop. He made his way toward the barn, already performing his favourite mental arithmetic. Nine more acres, eight miles up and down the fourteen-inch furrows for each acre broken. Seventy-two miles. Well, he was nothing, if not lean and fit.

A solitary rider approached along the trail from the Jordan property to break his thoughts. The rider wore scarlet and rode a powerful horse. North West Mounted Police. The three-man detachment at Headquarters Camp, now christened Lloydminster, patrolled the entire colony, but this was their first visit to the Newland Cooperative. Tall, well-built, English, ginger hair and moustache, Constable Roberts could have modelled for a recruiting poster. For all that, he was friendly and genuinely interested in Jack's farm. Jack found himself eagerly showing off his barn, well, potatoes, eighteen broken acres and, of course, his beloved two acres of oats. He even showed Roberts a picture of Emma.

"I say, Mr. Thornton, you're a lucky fellow." He squinted closely at Emma.

"Jack."

"Pardon me?"

"Call me Jack. Everyone does."

"Well, Jack," Roberts handed the picture back after one last glance, "your wife is lovely. When is she coming out?"

"Train into Saskatoon in nineteen days. I'm taking the oxen in nine days — leaving myself ten days on the trail — just to be certain I'm not late."

"Don't blame you. This section must attract pretty women. Just met Mrs. Jordan. By heavens, there's a beauty . . . " he broke off, embarrassed.

"It's all right, Constable," Jack laughed. "You'd not be human if you failed to notice Alice Jordan. Blessed few women to be seen at all out here — pretty or otherwise."

"Which brings me to the point of my visit, Mr. Thornton."

"Jack."

"I understand you are friends with a colonist by the name of Frederick White — Boer War veteran?"

"Yes, we were acquainted on board the ship," Jack answered cautiously, wondering if a head-punched steward was making trouble.

"Sad news, I'm afraid," Roberts continued. "Seems Mr. White has gone a bit doolali — woman trouble."

"Woman trouble? He came out alone, like me."

"That's the trouble. His fiancée back in London wrote to break off the engagement. She's refusing to come out."

Jack's sympathy for Freddie White was tinged with apprehension. Then he saw Emma, punching the air with her hat at Euston, leading the cheers. Emma wouldn't balk.

"Sorry to hear it; he seemed like a steady chap to me."

"I've seen it before," the constable spoke briskly, as though discussing a late, spring frost. "Even a few weeks alone out here — especially the ones from London — the empty land, the wind. It gets to them. Found one fellow south of Saskatoon last winter feeding whole trees into his stove. Door of his shack open — tree sticking out — snow drifting in. Wouldn't use his axe for fear of hurting the tree. Barking mad, he was. Singing, talking to himself. Claimed there were voices in the wind."

Jack laughed, nervously. The policeman shot him a hard look.

"Not funny when you see it happen. Could hit anybody. There's insanity in the wind, and loneliness — just like there's bugs in the water. It's real."

"Anything I can do for Freddie?"

"Actually," Roberts shook his head, smiling, "it's what he can do for you. He's bent on going home to see his fiancée, but he's nearly flat broke. Wants to sell his horses to raise the fare but, when another colonist offered to buy them, White punched the man silly. That's how I became involved."

"Freddie's in jail?"

"No. Because he is a bit crazy, no charges were offered by the victim."

"I don't understand how this affects me." Jack ran his hand down the police horse flank, admiring the strong, clean lines.

"White's horses came by rail all the way from Illinois to Edmonton, matched pair of Clydesdales. He must have paid over a thousand dollars for them. He wants you to buy them."

"Me?" Jack laughed "I can't come up with . . . "

"He wants to sell 'em to you for three hundred dollars because, he says, you fought for him on the ship. Says if you won't buy them he will shoot 'em and walk home. Doolali, like I said."

• • •

Freddie's homestead was immaculate. He had a small, wood-and-sod house, a neat, sod barn, good water, and a two-pole corral with a bit of hay already cut and stacked. He welcomed Jack like an old friend. He prepared tea and bannock for them then sat relaxed, puffing his pipe while they ate and drank. Jack looked for a crazy man, but saw nothing.

"Not much ploughing done, Fred," he observed, during a lull in the conversation. Constable Roberts stiffened, alert and tense.

"None." Fred smiled, slowly. "What's the point to ploughing when your future wife — betrothed and promised — refuses to let you plough?"

"Eh? How's that?" Jack asked, missing Roberts' signal to be quiet.

"Blast and Damnation, man!" Freddie jumped to his feet and kicked the water bucket. It flew and clanged off the stove, water hissed on the hotbox.

"My Clydes are cart horses! Don't you know? I was a carter before the war — Clydes and shires for Worthington's Brewery. Can't put cart horses in a plough unless the wife says so. And she says *No! No go!* Won't budge on it, Jack."

Freddie was full-flown crazy, now. Fists clenched, eyes starting from his head.

"I have to go get her, bring her here, and then I can plough. You must see that."

"Certainly, of course, Fred," Jack spoke in the same voice he used to coax another furrow out of One and Two at the end of the day. "My mistake. I see your point."

Fred calmed instantly. "Right, then, here's the deal. You take my Clydes, three hundred dollars, take care of them. Don't work them, unless you feed them grain, mind. Hay for light duties, but if they work they gets oats. I'll be back next spring and buy them off you for four hundred dollars. You'll not be out of pocket. Otherwise, I shoot them right now. Deal?"

He stuck his hand out. Jack shook. "What do you call them?"

Freddie looked at him quizzically, eyebrows raised. "Blast and Damnation, Jack, haven't you been listening to me?"

• • •

Jack rode Blast and led Damnation the fifteen miles back to his own homestead. He gave Constable Roberts a draft for the three hundred to return to Freddie, then kicked One and Two out of the barn to make way for the Clydes. He'd have to build a pole corral, cut hay, and talk the major into financing some cooperative grain for the horses. He'd get no more ploughing done before he left for Emma. And there was definitely no money for a wood house now. But, by heavens, he'd drive to Saskatoon in style, and in half the time. The Clydes were magnificent. Freddie White would return to his senses in England, Roberts had assured him, but Freddie White would never return to the Saskatchewan Territory.

• • •

He was up at four AM, having hardly slept, excited as a flea. Emma was coming. He drove One and Two over to the Buxtons. The oxen pulled a wood sled across the grass, Jack's plough lay on the sled. Alf and Davie would double their breaking and disking while he was gone. It struck Jack that if the Buxtons were able to take a crop off next year on all their broken acres, they would no longer be the poor members of the cooperative. He was anxious to be away, but he hadn't seen the brothers in nearly a week so he was obliged to stop for a cup of tea and a pipe. The Buxtons stayed on their land and worked every daylight hour that came their way. The cooperative idea had worked very well; tools, equipment and labour shifted efficiently between the Thornton and Buxton members, at least. But little time was spent in frivolous visiting. They were already counting the weeks left before winter, setting priorities — "before snow tasks" — Alf called them.

The major had two acres broken, too late for a garden or crop, because he'd spent most of his time "visiting". This had resulted in his election to the governing committee, and he often spent up to three or four days away at Lloydminster on committee business. At least it kept him sober and active, for which Alice was thankful. She had cribbed their water well during one of his absences. She also became expert with the axe and bucksaw. She and the girls coped very well on their own. Better, in fact, than when he was at home demanding attention. Once a week, she walked with the girls to deliver fresh bread to Jack, then the Buxtons. She had a proper stove in her house now, and had mastered Canadian yeast cakes to make wonderful, light loaves. Nothing was said overtly but everyone, even the major, recognized that the bread was her way of thanking them for getting the Jordan family safely established on their homestead. Kitty was absolutely devoted to Davie. Her only memory of the scarlet fever was Davie's face and the snowy sky above her when they made the run for the hospital.

The Buxtons were excited about Emma's arrival. Their few hours in Euston Station with her had somehow transformed from a casual meeting to a firm friendship. They often told the story of Emma leading the cheers as the train pulled out, and never failed to remind Jack that he was extraordinarily lucky to have her. They did so this morning and, once One and Two were safely ensconced in the Buxton corral, they sent him on his way with wishes of godspeed. He hurried back to his own property. The battered Bain wagon was already loaded for the trip. He had borrowed the Jordan hoops and canvas so that he and Emma could sleep in the wagon. He had washed his mattress tick and stuffed it with fresh-mown grass — Vicar Wilson's scythe's first cuts in the new world. It was neatly made up with clean blankets on the wagon bed. He'd even installed a special bracket on the box wall to hold a lantern. He thought of Emma by firelight in the Grosvenor Hotel, and his hands trembled as they fitted the lantern into the holder.

Pulling a nearly empty wagon did not qualify as work for Clydesdales but Jack fed them a tin of oats each, anyway. They sensed his excitement and returned it by fidgeting when he threw the harness on them. A nervous two-thousand-pound horse is a dangerous thing. Jack forced himself to talk calmly to them and they responded in kind. He walked them quietly from the corral to the wagon, fitted the tongue, pinned the whipple tree and climbed aboard. He whistled for Ostrich who was sniffing the manure pile, then gently snapped the lines. He spared one backward glance at his oat field. On the hillside the sun lit the white canvas of the tent, collapsed and bundled against any storm that might come in his absence. He swallowed an unexpected lump in his throat. In eight weeks this little square of grass and trees had become his home in a way that London, Newland, and even Gloucester never had. A late-hunting coyote yelped from the trees bordering Lake Jordan. Jack stood and called Blast and Damnation into a brisk pace. They flicked their huge hooves up proudly as only purebreds can do. Jack threw back his head and howled at the coyote. Ostrich bravely echoed him.

● ● ●

Emma Thornton had married with absolute contentment. She'd faced her wedding night, not with trepidation like many of her peers, but with enthusiasm, appetite even. But today she felt as nervous as a teenaged bride in an arranged marriage. How to account for it? It was more than an absence of three months. It was more than the physical separation of ocean and continent. It was this awful country — raw, different from anything she held as remotely familiar. Jack had hinted at it in his letters, but he'd failed to convey the overwhelming scale of the place and, consequently, of their new life. If Jack had spent three months in Wales she'd not have had these thoughts. Even his time in Africa couldn't compare because there he'd been surrounded by the British Army and he'd eventually come home. But was this home now? What had this coarse, gargantuan land done to Jack? Would her old Watson wait at the station or would she meet a stranger?

The tracks curved into a long, slow bend that ended at a small jumble of wood-frame buildings with the peculiar oversized square fronts, pretending to hide the small, gabled shop behind. What pretentious silliness, as though even a child would be fooled into thinking the store was a two-story establishment. She had been hoping the much anticipated Saskatoon, Saskatchewan, would be a grand prairie city like Winnipeg. She pressed close to the greasy window to confirm her disappointment. Saskatoon — so exotic and alluring on the map in Hampstead four months ago — now rather ridiculous. The prairie rolled deadly flat and monotonous to the small town and it deadened her, as the endless trees and rock had done two days ago. She checked her bag again, everything packed for hours. She must not let depression in. It was just the effect of seven days in the smelly, cramped, colonist sleeper. Sleeper . . . she'd hardly slept, and had virtually nothing substantial to eat. Jack would set it all to rights. They could stop over in a hotel, bathe, get a decent meal, then she would be ready for the adventure to begin. But, my, what a dismal, end-of-the-world moor Saskatoon was. So much for Mr. Barr's promised land.

• • •

Two young men with Scandinavian accents pushed past her and jumped to the platform. Emma waited on the stairs for a porter to put a stool down. Next, she was shoved by a large American woman herding her brood off the train. A crowd milled on the wooden planks below. Somewhere nearby a hound bayed, then was silenced. A man pressed up behind her, breath reeking of whiskey. She swung her bag out and let it fall, then leapt the gap. She stumbled, straw hat tipping forward over her eyes. A beagle darted through her peripheral vision and, in an instant, had his leg cocked above her valise.

"Ostrich! *No!* Bad dog!" A hoarse male voice bellowed.

Emma aimed a slap at the dog and he danced clear, then sat and howled at her. Ostrich. The Newland pub — this little brute was Jack's dog. Her dog, now. She straightened up, pushing her hat back. Jack stepped around the American buffalo-woman. They faced each other, separated by an armslength. His face was tanned brown as mud but his cheeks were oddly pale. The red bullet scars were prominent. A startling hatline cut his forehead, above white, below dark. He needed a haircut, badly. He wore the identical suit she'd last seen him wearing at Euston. One large fist clutched a bunch of flowers, yellowish daisies mostly, and some purple thistles. He stared at her, wide-eyed and nervous. Her old Watson, on the surface anyway, not much different from the first day in the Chelsea morning room.

"For me?" She pointed to the flowers.

He thrust them forward. "Yes. Wildflowers, picked this morning. Summer has killed off most of the spring flowers."

She took them. The crowd swirled around them. She was disoriented, suddenly fearful. Only this tiny station perched on the prairie with a tall granary nearby. No porters, no gateways, no fences, no order to the place. Jack and the beagle stared at her. Four round, brown eyes on her as though she was a painting in a gallery. Why didn't she do something? She had never felt so awkward in all her life. In that instant she knew that she'd made a mistake, somehow she wasn't meant to be here.

"It is rather warm . . . hot," she said, weakly, fanning her face.

"Yes. Been hot for three or four days now," Jack's voice was wrong, cracked and hoarse. "Drove here in the rain, though, caught a cold."

"Are you very ill? Your cheeks seem pale."

"Oh," he touched his face self-consciously. "I shaved my beard off yesterday."

"Beard? You?"

"Shaving takes time, needs water. Never bothered when I was on my own, at home." He stopped. The word "home" sounded so strange here. "But I shaved for you, for today."

He spoke in stunted clips, like a Crusoe just rescued from a desert isle. Completely flustered now, she reached down to pick up her bag. She had to move, end this tension. Ostrich darted in and got one handle in his teeth, growling. Two hands slipped quickly under her elbows and pulled her back up. Arms encircled her and pulled her tight. Jack's face filled her vision.

"My goodness, Emma. Forgive me. I think I had forgotten how much I love you," and he clung to her.

"Watson," she whispered into his ear, hugging him with all her strength. "You scared me half to death just now."

They walked down the main street of Saskatoon to the hotel. Her baggage car had been left in Regina, no reason given, and would come up with the next train this evening. The furniture she had shipped two months earlier from England had not yet arrived, and all Jack could get from the CPR man was "check again in August." Jack was neither surprised nor upset at this news. The hotel looked horrible but Jack assured her that it was much better than the boarding houses, so they went in. The price for one room, one night, was scandalous. And a room is precisely what they got. Rough planks on floor, walls, and ceiling. A small, dirty window, one bed frame with hay-filled mattress, one chair, one wash basin. The bath was extra and expensive — especially when she asked for hot water. Jack hauled the buckets up from the heater — a porter cost extra.

Never mind, she was desperate to scrape off the grime of her long journey. She undressed down to chemise, then suddenly and, again, inexplicably, she became shy. Jack dumped the last bucket into the tub and fled the room. The bath, though expensive and crude, revived her. She dressed in a simple blouse and light, cotton skirt, then descended to join her husband for an early supper. The waiter gave her an odd look when she asked for a menu, yet he never glanced at Ostrich, sleeping at Jack's feet. A dog in the dining room was *de rigueur* but a menu was frowned upon.

"Pork or beef. Potatoes. Pie and coffee, ma'am."

"Beef fresh, is it?" Jack asked.

"Was fresh, once, I would imagine," the waiter replied deadpan.

"*Pork!*" Emma fairly shouted. Jack laughed with the waiter and she flushed, disoriented, childlike, resenting Jack's camaraderie with the loutish waiter.

The meal was served in less than five minutes. It was salt pork, half fat, and nearly inedible. The potatoes were fried as was an unexpected egg flopped on top of the meat. She managed the egg and potato. Jack ate like a miner, all of his, plus her leftovers. The rhubarb pie was good and the coffee a welcome finale. The bill was ruinous and when Jack laid ten pence down as tip, she snatched it back up instinctively.

"The tablecloth, if that's what this rag is, wasn't even clean, Jack. You can't offer a gratuity!"

"The food was abominable. The service rude and," he laughed, taking her hand in his rough paw, "the decor execrable."

She sighed, tremendously relieved to see that she hadn't somehow been transported to a different dimension, as in one of HG Wells' stories. He did see the same reality as she.

"Then why would you let us eat in such a place? And a tip, for heaven's sake!"

He grew serious, searching her face for she knew not what, as though he had terrible news to impart and wondered if she could stand it.

"What is it, Jack? Tell me!"

"Emma, we ate here and I tipped because this is far and away the best restaurant in a one hundred fifty mile radius."

"Disappointing, I suppose," she squeezed his hand. "But scarcely a shocking hardship. I shan't be expecting restaurants when I'm on a pioneering adventure."

"No, you don't understand. Everything about this country is like this hotel, this restaurant. Lumber, feed, tools, supplies, clothing — everything — if you can obtain it. Expensive and one size fits all."

She shook her head.

"It's a wonderful place, Emma. I have come to love it. Rich soil, freedom, opportunity, it's all we hoped for. We have a hill, with trees and a lake. We have good water, hay, and a field heavy with grain. But we have neither wood nor carpenter for our house. No fresh meat unless we hunt it ourselves. We live by sunlight and candles because paraffin is as dear as gold. And precious few candles at that. The railway is not coming to us for at least two years. Until then, we fend for ourselves. There are hardships we never imagined, Emma. And winter in a couple of months will make all this so far seem like a picnic, they say."

It came like a rushing wind, a confession of things he'd not told her in his letters. He gripped her hand fiercely, as though afraid she would run away. She suddenly realized that he was afraid she would desert. His lack of faith sent a shot of anger through her. She dug her fingernails into the back of his hand. He flinched.

"You think I'm a coward?"

"No!"

"This Jordan woman you write so much of, she is brave and strong, but you assume I'll run home weeping."

"No, not at all. But Alice never had a chance to . . . "

"Alice, is it! Not Mrs. Jordan, but Alice?" Her anger sputtered and died at the hurt look on his face.

"It's the hardships I didn't have the courage to tell you of." He looked like Ostrich's brother, ears back and shoulders drooping. "I know you are strong. I was wrong, I suppose, to doubt your commitment, but his country is so damned . . . I don't know . . . "

"Frightening." She finished his thought, smoothing the scratches on the back of his hand, fully aware of her own doubts just hours ago on the train. His anxiety had not been so far out of place. "But if this Alice can manage with the man she's got — you weren't fibbing about him, too, were you?"

He smiled, shaking his head. "No. He is hopeless, most of the time."

"Well then," she continued. "If this hot-house rose Alice person can cope with her man, just imagine how well I shall do with you."

He lunged across the table and kissed her. She returned it fully. Not the done thing at the Savoy, or even Café d'Esterre, but then this was the new world and doubtless there would be new "done things".

· · ·

Both of them were timid. The bedroom was like a dog kennel. Travelling salesmen, in rooms on either side, snored clearly through the walls and Ostrich made several determined assaults on the bed. Jack finally admitted that he had been sleeping with the beagle on his blankets these last months. They did nothing more than sleep in each others' arms that night, with a small hound flopped across their feet.

Sunrise came at five AM and it was delightful. Emma looked back at the eastern horizon to see it silhouette the disappearing Saskatoon skyline. They were the only wagon on the trail. The air was calm and so fresh, rising from thousands of square miles of green, bedewed grass, that she fancied she was drinking it rather than breathing it. The Clydesdales' broad, powerful bodies seemed not to even notice the wagon that rattled and banged over the ruts behind them. Jack had to check their pace twice for fear of damage to the wheels. She held on to the spring seat and shouted aloud with excitement when they plummeted down a ravine, B and D pushing back into their breeching. She couldn't bring herself to call them Blast and Damnation. Was she a prude? Hardly what her mother's friends would have labelled her, but in this country . . . who would name their horses curse words? An

Englishman driven partly insane by loneliness and empty skies. Jack claimed he couldn't retrain the horses to new names, it would confuse them. But she felt certain he loved bellowing the words, especially when they had stepped down the middle of Saskatoon's high street this morning.

She shifted close to him and slipped her arm through his. He smiled and kissed her cheek. His suit was packed. He wore long, wool underwear, flannel shirt, heavy, cotton coveralls with a bib and shoulder straps, and a weathered, sweat-stained hat that looked as though it may have been a Mounted Police stetson at one time. Canada had changed him. She would be foolish to expect otherwise. It was already changing her. She was now in the habit of tying her hair into the practical hardknot that Mrs. Toomey favoured. She wore a broad, straw hat from Uncle Henry, and her blouse had not a single brooch, pin, nor cufflink attached. Her shoes of best leather had unfashionably low heels and laced up well above her ankles. She was being practical; Jack, she couldn't help thinking, was being careless.

"Tell me again about Newland estate," she said, trying to imagine how this grass tabletop would transform itself once they reached the river.

"From Lloydminster, from the north or west, is the prettiest approach," his voice became soft, almost dreamy. "We travel past the Jordan homestead along the north shore of a lake that covers nearly fifty acres of their land. This shore is ringed with aspen and poplar trees, pretty, but not suitable for building material. The east end of the lake curves away from a hill, and the east tip of the lake laps on Newland Estate."

She squeezed his arm and he stared at her, his eyes bright and lovely.

"Trees cloak the north and west slopes of the hill. Our trail winds through the woods, past the water well, and up to the summit, which is clear. From the peak a vast, broad upland spreads to the south and east horizons. The Buxton place, a mile away, sits like toy buildings beneath us. Our house — building site, rather — is nestled on a ledge halfway down the southern slope, taking advantage of the sun's course. Below are barn, corral, vegetable garden, and two acres of oats ripening into feed for Blast and . . . for the horses this winter. A full eighteen acres adjacent to the oats lies broken, black and rich, waiting for our first cash crop next year."

"You sound like Uncle Henry preaching," she said. "As though this place is a religion."

He shrugged, mildly embarrassed. "Not religion, but something spiritual, I would say."

"Now that I am here," she changed the subject because the image of a mad Englishman began to replace Jack. "Uncle Henry expects you to write to him. He interrogated me mercilessly in June when I visited to learn cooking from Mrs. Toomey."

"Did you let him read my letters? If so, I hope you censored the personal bits."

"Jack Thornton!" She cuffed him. "As if I'd let anyone read your love letters."

• • •

Late that afternoon they reached a huge marsh, stretching nearly to the horizon north and south. The shores were dried white and sent heatwaves wobbling up to the hot July sun that now struck them full in the face. Wind gusted, whipping a white dust onto Emma's perspiring face. Salt, when she licked her lips. A stench of brackish water and rot filled the air.

"Right." Jack leaned forward, shading his eyes and staring intently at the point where the trail crossed the salt flat and entered the slough. "That's where the firm bottom goes."

"How can you tell?" Emma, just now realizing their intention was to plunge into the smelly mess, tried to sound confident.

"Well, the Jordan wagon got stuck on the way out, just near a bit of a mud bar which deceived them into thinking the water was shallow. In fact, it was deep with a soft bottom. But that was in the spring and there was more water then."

He pointed to the left. "That's it there, I believe. So if we stay well to the right of it, we should be fine. Keep your eye on that mud bar for me. We must not lose sight of it."

Not daring to imagine what would happen if they mired down in this disgusting bog, Emma glued her eyes to the brown, weedy strip of mud that surfaced halfway across the slough. Blast and Damnation strode fearlessly into the water and the wagon lurched alarmingly. Water and mud flew up off the front wheels.

"Coom, yeh, Blast. Coom, yeh!" Jack snarled.

The Clyde heaved herself against the wagon shaft. Damnation staggered, hooves changed tempo churning the slough into a stinking cauldron that splashed wads of muck against Emma's skirt. She scraped it off with one hand, clutching the bucking wagon seat with the other. Then the horses calmed, the wagon straightened, and they steamed smoothly through the water, only a foot deep now. Jack praised the horses, soothing them.

"Where is that bar? I lost sight of it getting the horses out of that hole," Jack asked, urgency in his voice.

"Oh dear, Jack." She searched the water frantically. At water level, the weedy bar blended with the shoreline and other peninsulas. She'd been so distracted by the flying mud and the wagon which seemed like it had been about to tip . . .

"You lost it?" There was no sympathy in his demanding tone.

416

There! A hump of ground just left of their course, she had it. "Go right, Jack. You're aiming almost directly for it."

"Woot, girls. Woot, now." Jack eased the reins over and the horses gradually veered right. Emma ignored the sludge still clinging to her clothes. She riveted her attention on the hummock. She had nearly failed him in her first, simple task on the trail. She would not waver until they were safely past the danger. The horses sloshed heavily now, their pace slowed as they neared the centre of the slough. Jack's head tracked the mud bar.

"You did well, Em, to keep your eyes open," he said. "A lot of people would have panicked a bit when we hit that hole back there."

She accepted the rebuke and vowed to be braver.

"It is a little thing. But out here, little mistakes can mean . . . Oh, what's wrong now? Hup, girls, come there, Blast, git up, Damnation."

The wagon seemed to be on a gradually-sinking elevator, the horses suddenly up to their knees in water. But the mud bar was well to their left. Blast and Damnation slowed. Unable to lift their hooves clear of the mud in unison, they lost their cadence. Jack stood up, urging them on, slapping the reins across their rumps, but in a matter of seconds they stalled, water just below their great bellies. The hot wind sent waves lapping against the bottom of the wagon box.

"Fancy that. There are two markers out here," Jack said. "We must have lined up on the wrong one."

Not twenty yards ahead lay a small, weed-covered bump of ground. Emma knew that it was the bar Jack had originally pointed out to her. She had picked the wrong hummock.

"Jack, I am so sorry." Her words were pathetic, futile, and hung in the hot air, worse than no words at all. A hawk circled high above them. Emma felt like stranded carrion. Jack smiled, thin lipped and squinting.

"Not your fault. I must have got you lined up on the wrong marker. Anyway, finding blame is just a waste of time."

"But what will we do?" She did not attempt to sound confident, that was gone now.

"Two possibilities. I think the horses just lost their momentum. The wagon is light; they are strong and not upset yet. I can lead them by hand and they'll probably just walk out."

"Do you really think so? What if they can't — what is the second option?"

"We unhitch, walk to shore, wait for another team to come down the trail and get some help." He said this as a matter of fact, handing her the reins. "But I really don't want to have to rely on that. Now, you'll have to hold the lines while I lead them. If we get going and they start a good pace, I'll jump clear. You whip 'em up and keep them going until you're out of the slough."

"Me? Whip up? On my own?" Her stomach shrivelled into a hard, tiny ball. She'd driven a pony and trap under Charlie's supervision before. Two tons of horse and wagon through a bog was beyond her.

"Well," Jack climbed down, gasping as the water rose up his thighs, "the only other one here is Ostrich, and I hesitate to give him the lines."

The beagle, hearing his name, leapt from their bed where he'd been sleeping, up onto the seat beside her. Even the dog expected her to fail; is that what Jack wanted? To see her weakness? She felt sick. Jack stroked each of the horses, wading around them, talking quietly to them. Then he pulled gently on the bridles and began walking backward. They followed him with tentative, sliding steps. Jack was soon up to his waist, water began to run into the box around Emma's feet. They sank deeper, the horses slowed, Jack's murmuring voice never changed pitch. Emma bit her tongue, resisting the urge to ask for reassurance. Ostrich barked fiercely at a muskrat flushed from the weeds on the mud bar, now beside them. She snapped at him to be quiet. The horses slowed to a bare plod, but did not stop. Water receded from the box and Jack's belt, waist, then legs reappeared above the water. The horses sensed victory and began to step in a uniform cadence again. Jack stumbled, tried to turn around, but caught in the mud, he fell. He pitched himself sideways and called out to her.

"Don't stop, Emma. Keep 'em rolling!" Then he went under water. Emma found herself standing up in the swaying wagon, terrified the wheels would crush Jack, trying to decide if she should attempt to turn the team, knowing she couldn't, then slapping them hard with the lines and yelling.

"Hup, Blast! Hup, Damnation. Go on, girls. Hup!"

The horses' feet broke surface hurling great clods of slimy mud back into her face. "Blast and Damnation," she cried, spitting the muck out. "Go on! Go on!"

The water was shallow now and the horses pranced forward, pacing like racers. Ostrich began howling, baying in her ear. Jack's voice chased her. "Well done, Holmes! Bloody well done!"

Emma found herself calling wildly and she slapped the horses again. They hit the white-salt shoreline, shot across it, up the low bank and suddenly she was alone on the prairie. Ostrich abandoned ship with a daredevil leap over the tailgate, and she was flying across the green sward. Her hat was gone, sun and hot wind whipped her face, the glistening brown bodies at the end of her reins pounded up dust with thumping hooves. The wagon jolted and rattled in protest, she rode it lightly on the balls of her feet and laughed triumphantly.

• • •

"How did you stop them?" Jack stood beside the trembling horses, dripping slime and brown water.

"Why, hauled on the reins and shrieked at them," she said breathlessly, conscious of perspiration running freely from her hairline down her face. Jack climbed up, took the reins, and hugged her — mud, sweat, water, and all. They kissed hard, her tongue and his releasing four months of passion, his hand hard on her bottom, pulling her into his belly, she squirming against it, urgent. Then she broke clear.

"Where do we camp?" she demanded, stroking his muddy hair.

"Nice bit of trees off the trail two miles up. I marked it on the way in." His voice was hoarse, but not from the head cold.

"Well, then, let us drive on and be quick about it."

Of course, there was nothing quick about it. They found the little freshwater pond with its fringe of willow bushes — not real trees. Then the horses had to be completely washed down, brushed, and fed. Jack waded into the pond, scrubbed himself and his filthy clothes, then set them out to dry in the evening sun. Emma had washed herself relatively clean and sponged the worst of the muck from her clothes. Jack, clad only in a woolen one-piece suit of underwear and wet boots, collected enough wood to start a fire, just as the sun began to set. They had not eaten in nearly nine hours. Despite the hot day and nervous exhaustion from crossing the slough, Emma found herself desperately hungry. She made no effort to interfere with Jack's meal preparations, which bore little resemblance to Mrs. Toomey's teachings. He fried bacon in a pan, mixed a blob of doughy substance in a fire-blackened tin, then deftly scooped up the dough, poured the bacon into the tin, and flattened the dough into the greasy frying pan. Emma put the teakettle on the fire and tried not to look too closely at the mugs waiting on a nearby rock.

"Where are the plates and cutlery? Shall I lay our places in the wagon?"

Jack looked up from his frying pan. "Lay places, my word. Haven't heard that phrase for months." He laughed, but stopped abruptly when he caught her expression. "Sorry, Em, I know it's nothing like home and I hope you'll be able to make our place a true home, but for now . . . "

"Well, do we eat with our hands?" she asked, trying to block the now-familiar sensation of childish disorientation.

"Hands! No! No, of course not." He jumped up, ran to the wagon and brought back a grubby towel. He unrolled it to reveal two knives and two forks which he stood in their mugs. "Table is set, ma'am, dinner served in . . . well, right now, actually."

Was he mocking her or just trying to humour her? Either way it hurt. She turned half away from him, but a marvelous smell wafted past her. Hurt feelings and introspective relationship problems were surprisingly easily dismissed. Her hunger took charge. She turned back, the smell emanated from the fried dough he'd just torn in half. He scooped half the bacon back into the pan, dropped half the bread into the tin, and handed the tin to her. What should have been revolting and inedible actually caused her to salivate. Jack sat cross-legged on the ground, knife and fork poised over the pan. She sat beside him and they devoured the food like dogs, pausing only to make and slurp tea. The thought that she was surrendering to the coarse new world much too quickly crossed her mind. Then she dabbed the last of the bacon grease up with her delicious bread and ate it. The word "sublime" occurred to her, incongruous though it was.

"Lovely bread — or what would you call it? I suppose even bread isn't bread in this topsy-turvy world. Bacon bread?"

He shook his head, smiling.

"Grease gobs?"

He shook again.

"Rumplestiltskin loaf?"

"Bannock."

"Of course, bannock, my very next guess."

"Mine is good, but Alice . . . Mrs. Jordan's is absolutely wonderful." He grinned sympathetically at her. "Seem to be getting it all wrong, don't I, Holmes? It's just there is so much hard work to be done to make a bit of forward progress in the Saskatchewan colony. I've let anything non-essential slip. I haven't even touched Hardy or Conan Doyle in a month. Then I make you feel badly for noticing my slovenly ways."

Emma snapped up this tidbit of contrition, even though instinct told her that it wasn't enough. She wanted so badly to reunite with Jack, but this man with rough manners and monstrous horses was only occasionally her Jack. Still, she could not resist it.

"Here's something I can do," she darted to the wagon and dug a book from her bag. "Lie down beside me. Close your eyes now, drink your tea."

He obeyed. She began reading to him and he smiled, squeezing his eyes tight shut.

"From, *The Case of Identity*," she began. "My dear fellow, said Sherlock Holmes, as we sat on either side of the fire in his lodgings at Baker Street. Life is infinitely stranger than anything which the mind of man could invent."

Ostrich, still licking a bit of bacon grease from his muzzle, crawled into her lap.

"Remember the afternoon we ran up Baker Street on the omnibus?" Jack murmured.

"Like it was yesterday." She reached out to stroke his face. "And now we sit beside a fire in the North West Territories."

"Have I dragged us into a desperate folly, Emma?"

She recommended without answering his question. "We dare not conceive the things which are really mere common place of existence." Her voice settled over them and apart from occasionally feeding the fire, Jack lay at her side, silent. The story and characters and places of London flowed, unbroken, for nearly an hour. Then a siren wailed out of the falling darkness.

Emma leapt, grabbing for Jack's arm. A wolf — on the other side of the pond — only a few yards away. Its howl brought the hair up on the back of her neck. A half-dozen others joined it in an unholy choir, like demented sopranos singing for the devil. Ostrich began to shake and whine, burrowing into her lap. The sun had gone, making the willows opaque, black shapes against the fading light.

"Jack, get your gun, wolves."

"Coyotes, not wolves." Jack picked up Ostrich and stood, peering into the bushes. "And I don't have a gun — the major hunts for all of us. It's one of his few skills."

Emma leapt to his side, pulling him near the fire. "No gun! How do we defend ourselves? Will the flames hold them at bay?"

"They don't attack humans," he said in a schoolteacher tone. "But they would like to have Ostrich for supper, if they could."

"Jack! Don't be horrible."

"*Stop that noise!* " Jack suddenly roared. The howling ceased. Two black dogs trotted past, not twenty paces from the fire, and disappeared into the dark.

"That's it?" Emma felt somehow let down. A thrill of wilderness adventure had been rising involuntarily inside her. But these fierce, wolfish predators were, in fact, nothing more than whining beggars.

"That's it." Jack drew her to him. "Not very dramatic, I'm afraid."

"Well, it was rather, ah, exciting. For a moment."

Jack threw his head back and howled. Ostrich, careful not to leave Jack's arms, followed with a feral bay of his own. A coyote answered with a brief yap.

"You try it, Em."

"Oh no, I couldn't"

He nudged her. "Nobody will hear you. We are truly alone. Forget London."

Astonished at herself, Emma laid her head back and stared up at the first stars overhead. She began singing in the highest key she could manage.

> *With cat-like tread*
> *Upon our prey we steal,*
> *In silence dread*
> *Our cautious way we feel,*
> *No sound at all,*
> *We never speak a word,*
> *A fly's foot-fall*
> *Would be distinctly heard*

The coyotes answered immediately. From the pond willows, from the prairie, from far off beyond the trail — a pack of yearning, wild dogs called to her.

"Excellent! *The Pirates of Penzance.*" Jack beamed at her, his face glowing in the firelight. "At least a dozen replies and I'm willing to bet they were all males."

He cupped the nape of her neck, gently pulling her head back. "Again Emma, again."

She sang, wild, and flooding with aroused passion. The coyotes sang back. Then she took his hand and dragged him to the wagon. They did not even get the lantern lit. Ostrich sat quietly like a very wide-eyed observer at the end of the mattress. He whined when Jack and Emma howled together, coyote-like, a few minutes later.

• • •

Two days later Emma sang Gilbert and Sullivan again but, this time, it was to relieve fear, not kindle passion. Jack took the Clydes and wagon on an apparent attempt at suicide, plummeting down the bank of a steep ravine toward a narrow creek. She hurried behind the wagon, steadying the poplar pole shoved through the rear wheels' spokes to brake them.

> *He is an Englishman! "* She gasped.
> *For he has said it, and it's greatly to his credit*
> *That he is an Englishman!*

Her heart leaped into her throat and pumped in rhythm with the song as the descent sharpened and the Clydes whinnied in alarm.

> *For in spite of all temptations,*
> *To belong to other nations,*
> *He remains an Englishman!*

Then the Clydes' hooves shot great fans of spray from the creek, the wagon stalled motionless for a second, and Jack was shouting, "Now, Holmes! Now!"

She heaved on the pole with all her strength. It shot clear and she sat heavily in the creek, ice water rushing up her dress. The wagon lunged forward and up the opposite bank. She scrambled after it, pole at the ready, barely conscious of her soaking clothes.

CHAPTER 22

From a distance, the lake, with its north shore forest, was beautiful. As they drew near, the faint odour of warm, stagnant water drifted from it. Nothing like the alkaline sloughs on the bald prairie, hardly an English lake, either. From a distance, the Jordan homestead, tucked into the trees, looked tidy and comfortable. Up close, the house was unpainted, the yard was littered with debris from the woodpile, and the barn looked as though it was built out of dirt. A clothesline stretched from a tree to a pole near the house. They rounded the back of the house, Jack announcing their arrival with a shout.

"Good heavens!" Emma had steeled herself to be diplomatic, kind even, toward Mrs. Jordan, although intuition dictated that Mrs. Jordan would disappoint. But this was unspeakable, well beyond diplomatic niceties. "That is disgraceful!"

Jack, crestfallen at her reaction, helped her down. "What now?"

She pointed to the clothesline. He looked and shrugged. "She's washed out her dusters and hung them to dry. Come now, Emma, no scullery maids here to clean up after us."

"Jack!" she said hotly, still caught by surprise. "Those are *not* cleaning rags!"

He stared at her, as though she was a recent and highly eccentric acquaintance. "Then what are they?"

She flushed. Of course Jack wouldn't know, neither would the major, nor even the Buxtons. Why would Mrs. Jordan, completely devoid of female companionship, bother to be discreet?

"Poor woman, alone out here," she murmured. "I'm sorry, Jack, I was mistaken. She must have been cleaning especially hard for our arrival."

"Alone? She's got all of us and her children," Jack said, still puzzled, but relieved. "The woman is never alone. In fact she gets too much attention from the likes of Alf and the police. They've "patrolled" here twice in the last two weeks, just to meet her, if you ask me."

"Don't be such a gossip," Emma said, staring at the fluttering row of wynciette cloths. "She is as alone as a woman can be, in a way you'll not understand."

Mrs. Jordan emerged from the house, two little blonde girls with short, bobbed hair and brown faces clung to her skirts. She advanced, hand outstretched, grinning broadly.

"Oh welcome, Mrs. Thornton, welcome to the Newland Cooperative."

She shook Emma's hand with a hard palm nearly as callused as Jack's. She was — or certainly had been — very beautiful. The sun had bleached the fringe of her blonde hair and browned her face.

"You can't imagine how much I've looked forward to the arrival of a female ally."

Emma pulled her hand free of the embrace and smiled. This woman was ready to cling, suffocate.

"You will be my friend?" Alice tried to say this lightly, politely, as befitted a Belgravia tea room, but it reeked of earnest desperation.

Emma's eyes flickered to the clothesline, she couldn't stop them. Alice Jordan winced. "Oh my, please forgive me," she said, mortified. And Emma saw herself turned away from an old friend's front door, her mother crying with humiliation, cut dead by their own society. She laid a hand on Alice's arm.

"Whatever for, Mrs. Jordan?" She winked. "Every competent housekeeper must surely wash her "dusting rags" at least once a month."

Alice brightened. "Exactly, Mrs. Thornton."

"And I should imagine the men appreciate your efforts at housekeeping." Emma found herself enjoying the conspiracy.

"Ah yes, the men. Well, they don't really understand the rhythms of homemaking." Alice laughed and was no longer a desperate, possessive menace.

"I shall look to you for advice in coping with such matters, here in the wilderness."

Alice beamed. "I have tea — in china cups, mind you — ready to pour. Would you care to . . . ?"

"Mrs. Jordan, I would love tea from a china cup."

• • •

The trail skirting the trees was pretty enough, especially when it entered the woods and began to wind up a gentle slope. They stopped beside a tripod set above a water well, no pump. A pulley and rope hanging from the tripod spoke of much labour hauling water up, a bucket at a time. Jack insisted on dipping a pail-full up for her. It tasted slightly of iron, but was very cold and very fresh. She nodded her approval. The well was cribbed with wood poles and rocks. The original earth walls were just visible and a pretty, crenellated pattern was worked into them.

"What is the purpose of that decoration, Jack?" she asked idly, kneeling and slipping her hand down one of the smooth, vertical grooves.

"Actually, those are the spade marks from where Davie and I dug the hole." He knelt beside her indicating the perfectly repeated, heart-shaped impressions. "This was hard going, had to carve out each shovelful."

She stared at his hand, large, scarred, and heavily creased. Powerful as a vice grip, it was still gentle when it wanted to be. She thought of the wagon last night.

"Why not use an auger, like Uncle Henry did for his sheep pond at home?"

"No auger between here and Saskatoon so Davie and I went at it like navvies — two solid days. Eleven feet down we struck a gusher; she rose up five full feet, six when it rains. Alf thinks we hit a spring."

"Eleven feet of these?" She touched his hand that still rested on the groove.

"No such luck," he laughed. "When we hit clay at the four-foot mark we could only hammer the shovels in halfway. Had to expand the opening then get the pick into it for the last seven feet."

Emma rose, staring at the simple well that represented so much labour. "Non-essentials" Jack had said. How little she had understood. They drove through the trees and emerged onto an open, grassy knoll where they climbed down from the wagon. Prairie, dotted with clumps of short trees, stretched to the horizon. A dirt building lay a little farther on, adjacent to a manure pile and a corral fenced with weirdly-contorted poplar poles. Beyond this was a small field of grain. To her right and down the sloping ground stood a dirty, white tent. The tip of Jordan slough — Lake — extended just past the knoll. Jack beamed at her expectantly, like the proud father of a newly-born son. Hill, woods, water and south-facing view, technically true. But all Emma could see, try as she might, was a low ridge with scrubby brush on one side and a slough of dead water below. It took a conscious effort to smile.

"Newland," she said simply, a catch in her throat. Jack mistook her emotion for joy and his arms enclosed her, hugging the breath out of her as he swung her about in a circle.

"Our future, Em! Our Estate! One hundred and sixty acres — double that in three years. I knew you'd love it!"

She let the tears trickle down her face. She let him think they were happy. She wouldn't show her disappointment. Two men burst from the tent.

"Surprise!" One wore a flat, wool cap, the other a bowler with part of the brim missing. "We set your tent up, got it cleaned, and built you a bedstead!" Davie shouted. "Alf said there was no chance he'd see Mrs. Thornton sleeping on the ground — so I made the frame myself from straight spruce hauled all the way from Big Gully."

Ostrich ran barking to Davie for a hug. Alf whipped his hat off.

"Welcome, Mrs. Thornton. Me and Davie are at your service. Ah, pardon, ma'am, are you all right?"

Jack released her from his bear hug and walked rapidly toward the Buxtons.

"Never fear, Alfred. Tears of happiness, my man. Tears of pure happiness."

Emma lost her composure and wept. The boys were thrilled.

• • •

After the middle of July, the cooperative looked to its hay. The days of hot sun had baked the prairie hard, and breaking it was impossible now. The major returned from Lloydminster the night of Emma's arrival so the entire cooperative met at his house to make plans for the next day. Major Jordan was an untainted Englishman and, despite her predisposition, Emma immediately warmed to him. Neat, cotton suit, trimmed moustache, clean shirt and collar, he took her hand with a murmured gracious welcome and held one of the two chairs for her. He took the other one while Alice, like a parlour maid, scurried about with tea, bread, and jam for everyone. Jack and the Buxtons in their coveralls and collarless shirts sat on boxes.

The major held forth, articulate and well-informed. The committee was managing the colony with calm assurance. Great strides had been made in Lloydminster itself — hunt club, choral and drama societies established, and plans for a proper church drawn up. They would start cutting logs this autumn for spring construction. Emma could not resist it. This was the original dream coming true. Sixteen miles from the Newland homesteads a new England was being created. Hardships were being overcome in both places, but the town victory seemed more faithful to home. The major's priority had been land and house, then community. It seemed natural and at least as productive as two acres of oats. Tea and bread consumed, the meeting changed pace and it was Jack who took control without so much as a squeak from the others. Major Jordan fidgeted momentarily, as his clay feet were so clearly exposed to the newcomer, then he lapsed into a subservience that Emma found disturbing.

"My blunder, but no time to wallow in self-pity," Jack said. "We have a binder arriving in Saskatoon next month, but really no crop to cut and bind. We have no mower, yet we have a need for tons of hay."

He nodded toward Jordan. "The major's generous purchase of feed grain for the four horses will greatly increase the efficiency with which we can employ the animals, but we still require a mountain of hay for the winter. Suggestions?"

"You're the dab hand with a scythe, Jack," Alf said. Emma wondered how a Stepney butcher had supplanted a British

431

gentleman so completely. "You cut, Davie and me will rake and load. The major drives better than anyone; he can use two wagons and two teams of horses to transport. He will haul one load while we fill the other and so on."

"Agreed," Jordan spoke emphatically, glancing at Emma." We shall start with the hay on the south side of the lake."

"No. It's slough grass. Mr. White said to cut up on higher land — dries quicker and better quality. We'll go to slough grass as a final cut if needed."

"White doesn't know everything," the major opined quietly. "Mustn't let the colonial chaps take command."

"He's farmed here for ten years. He's a government instructor. The fact that he's Canadian doesn't make him wrong or hurt my feelings," Jack said, with an unnecessary harshness, Emma thought. She tried to catch his eye but failed.

"Then the best grass is up on the railway quarter, north of Davie's claim. We'll cut there first. A few tons of hay are the least the CPR can give us after those colonist cars."

"Cut the railway land without permission?" Emma asked. It didn't seem right, couldn't be right. "I mean to say, is it legal? What if the police catch us?"

Davie laughed loudly — Alf elbowed him. Jack studied the ceiling, bullet wounds glowing red. Even the major harrumphed and stroked his moustache.

"Excellent point, Mrs. Thornton, but I assure you there is no need for such concerns." Alice rescued her. "The CPR and its branch lines are not very popular, even with the police. Those few acres of grass will very likely burn in the autumn wildfires so there is no loss to the railway."

"Thank you, Mrs. Jordan." Emma found herself repeating the formalities. She sounded like one of the ladies at her mother's charity meetings. She was stiff, pretentious, and awfully like the very things she detested about society. Yet she couldn't seem to control it. "I know I'm . . . green, I believe is the expression. Just explain these things to me and I'm certain I shall learn."

Alice refilled Emma's cup. She rested her hand on Emma's shoulder and gave it a small squeeze.

"Oh, you're not so green. I understand that you drove the team out of the big mud hole west of Saskatoon, and you've come through Eagle Creek as well."

"She handled the brake pole down Eagle hill and right smartly, too," Jack said eagerly. "Calm as you like — singing opera all the way."

"I was not calm; I was terrified," Emma smiled at him. "Jack got us through that awful place."

"Jack?" Alf winked at her. "Why he had to go clean out his pants after his first look at the creek."

"Buxton! That is enough, if you please." Alice swatted Alf lightly.

Emma recalled her thoughts of parlour maid and was pinched with regret. "I will learn," she thought. "And I will stop judging poor Alice Jordan."

" . . . hay is put up by the middle of August, we should have a clear month to haul wood. Even if White is exaggerating," Jack was speaking again and paused to smile at the major. "The winter will be much more severe than most we have experienced back home. The stove may require wood up to twelve or fifteen hours a day on the worst days from what I've heard. Since we have three wagons, I propose we set up a temporary camp in the west region of Big Gully and cut wood until all the wagons are filled. Then Major Jordan and Alf can begin driving and unloading while Davie and I stay on cutting. Emma can cook for us in the camp — Alice for the drivers at this end. That way, we should be able to establish an effective shuttle and stockpile plenty of wood by early September."

"And we can cut some good, straight spruce to frame and roof your soddie, Mrs. Thornton." This was Davie, anxious to make amends for his earlier gaffe.

"Soddie?" Emma was still digesting the news of her role as lumbercamp cook. "I'm afraid another explanation . . . "

"Your new house, Mrs. Thornton! Alf and me and . . . " he looked toward the major.

"Sorry, old chap, but I'll simply have to attend to committee business once the firewood campaign is concluded. Much regrets, but there it is."

"Anyways, Alf and me and Jack are going to build you a grand house — it's all arranged. I'm the best carpenter, so I'll be in charge of framing and bucking the doors and floorboards and such."

"Why, Davie, what a wonderful surprise." Emma lifted her teacup and held it up in a toast to Davie before taking a sip. "I am confident that I can face a few more weeks in that beastly tent if I know what awaits me at the end of the rainbow. And Jack never mentioned a word." Emma searched her husband's face, but he could not meet her eye. She had complained rather loudly this morning about the tattered, old tent and the fact that her cooking stove — a beautiful new Aga — stood open to the skies. A log home sounded rather wonderful and, judging by the scant thickness of even the Jordan bungalow walls, a log home might be the best alternative.

"Jack, why didn't you say? This soddie sounds just the thing."

Jack grinned stiffly. "Surprise, my dear. Didn't want to tell all my secrets at once."

"Why is it called soddie — rhymes with loggie? Is that your cockney, Davie Buxton?"

Davie was so happy to be in her good graces that he fairly burst with humour. "No, Mrs. Thornton, but I wish I did have a Stepney song for you — I'll get right to work on it, so I will."

"Soddie," Major Jordan smiled malevolently at Emma. "Pertaining to the root word sod, ma'am. Sod being the top four inches of dirt and grass turned by the breaking plough. Hence soddie, a house constructed primarily of bits of sod. A dirt home to be exact. Shouldn't wonder but that the Doukhobors invented the word to describe their earthen hovels."

Emma smiled, then realized with a shock that Jordan was not joking. And he was no longer the gentleman she had warmed to. He had delivered the definition with clear intent to cut her, and thus Jack — a petty revenge. But a mud hut for her marital home?

"Then, Davie, in spite of your very welcome and good intentions, I shall decline the soddie. I will not live in a cave, nor a ditch, nor a dirt home. I thought it hard that the animals must live in such conditions — I will not."

"But, Mrs. Thornton! It's not like the barn at all! We've got tarpaper for a double roof, and two proper windows, and I'll build you the best split-log floor."

Emma found herself outside the house, striding through the trees to the edge of the lake. Anger, dismay, disappointment all gave way to a sense of betrayal. How could he? How could the Jack she married have spent their house money on a disk machine and a pair of horses? She turned to watch for his apologetic approach, to spurn all possible explanations and repay him for . . . But Jack was not approaching. The house remained shut. Doubtless they were conducting cooperative business, still, and that business was of greater importance than she. Ostrich trotted up and sat by her for a moment, sniffing the hem of her skirt. Then he, too, grew bored of her silent mood and ambled off, snuffling for better scents.

• • •

She prepared supper silently, not out of anger, but dignity. A dirt house. There had to be some sort of limit to the "essentials only" policy. Perhaps the major was blind to the true necessities of making a homestead but at least he housed his family in a proper shelter.

"The truth, which I've never hidden from you," Jack stirred the boiling rice, "is that we simply do not have enough money for lumber."

"What about," something stung her wrist and she slapped at it. "What about a log house? All those pine and spruce trees at the Big Gully Davie keeps talking about?"

Jack slapped his forearm and began rolling down his sleeves. "Hauling timber for just the frame will take more trips than we should really ask of the cooperative. An entire log house would be out of . . . "

He wiped a hand across his cheek and smeared a thin streak of blood from his scar.

"What is wrong with your wound?"

"Not my bullet holes — mosquitoes are back."

Suddenly she had simultaneous feather touches on her neck, hands, and face. The touches turned to tiny stings. She swept the pests away, disgusted. The bites began to itch. Following Jack's lead, she quickly pulled her sleeves down and buttoned up. He fetched her hat and pulled it down tight on her head. The mosquitoes descended on her face and neck like a small cloud. Jack started a fire in the small campstove inside the tent, then threw green grass on it and left the stove door open. Smoke puffed out filling the tent.

Emma wore a thin, cotton blouse and the bugs were now biting through it on her shoulders and elbows. She ran to the tent while Jack finished boiling the rice. They shut the tent flap tight — eating between wheezing coughs. Gradually the smoke thinned, leaving them to finish the meal in peace.

"Mosquitoes are the devil's torture." Jack tried to sound light-hearted, but it was an obvious effort. "Walls on a sod house are twenty-eight inches thick, no mosquitoes, cool in the summer, warm in the winter."

"No," she said, too tired to argue, too disheartened by the onslaught of biting insects.

"Then the only other course is your dowry."

Jack's face was genuinely surprised, as though he hadn't spoken the words. He blushed and hung his head.

"Sorry, Emma, I don't know what came over me, I should never, will never again, ask for a remittance from home. Never. I'll find a way for a house. I'll think of something."

The mention of the dowry was treason to Jack. Not in her mind — she felt he was too hard on his remittance principles — but the mere fact it had escaped his lips was significant. What had this miserable country done to her Jack? She moved to sit beside him and put her arm around his shoulders, wondering at her own resilience.

"I know you will — we will," she said, stopping short of actually offering the dowry. It looked to be a close shave, this Canadian adventure. Should they founder, her dowry would be their only salvation — their lifeboat. She would be strong. She would not cast their lifeboat adrift.

• • •

The lovely, gold hayrick certainly was a reward for previous disappointments. Of course, in Canada, it wasn't a rick but a "stack". The Buxton and Thornton winter supplies of hay were cut, raked, and stacked in huge piles near the barns. Another few hot, August days would see the Jordans likewise prepared. Jack had risen to an unassailable stature in the cooperative by his stellar scything performance. Between the smudge fires at night and the twelve-hour days cutting in the broiling sun, he had also risen to a reeking prominence. Emma had finally tackled him one evening, stripped him, and bathed him. The tension over the house and dowry had cracked and they had made love on the wobbly, spruce bed. It had been the first time since the last night on the trail, but now it was their ritual, their "love bath" Jack called it, every Sunday. Oftentimes, Jack lay nearly unconscious from his long day's labour and she had to manage the event. These were the times she loved best. When he was hers again and, for a leisurely hour, they would be clean and happy and free of Canada.

Tonight was bath night. A steady wind blew from the west grounding all but the most determined mosquitoes. Emma made a show of bringing the tub into the tent after breakfast. They exchanged raised eyebrows of scandalized shock, then laughed together. Jack declared that he was too filthy to work and needed his bath now. But that would ruin the anticipation and, besides, she liked him tired and slow and malleable. She told him this and he declared he would be distracted all day and she was wicked. Then, he'd harnessed Blast and Damnation, hitched them to the wagon, and set off into the sunrise when the major arrived with his outfit. Mary and Kitty rode with Jordan today — they loved to ride home high atop the swaying piles of hay. The two wagons trundled toward the Buxton claim, calling, "Thank God for fine weather! Let us make hay!"

"Let us make hay" — the Forest of Dean hayfields with Charlie — Jack watching unknown. That hot day, pressing into Charlie's hard body, deliciously dangerous in the open field, formed an indelible memory. The thought that Jack had watched them, feverish from his place in the hedgerow, caused her to shiver. She replayed the scene, allowing Jack to replace Charlie in the memory. She would visit the memory many times today. Perhaps she'd walk the mile and a half to the hayfield and spy on Jack.

She washed breakfast dishes — no more eating from the frying pan — then descended to the barn. Today was her day to muck out the stalls. She told her plans to One and Two as she turned them out, careful to check that the fence around the haystack was intact. The lazy fellows would raid the cut hay. They were not in the least shocked by her frank words. She no longer worried about the fact that she talked to oxen, they were excellent listeners. The days were long and her work hard. The simple task of making dough in a tent, then raising and baking it on a stove outdoors required a major effort. Everything else was likewise complicated. Why not pour out her heart to One and Two? She climbed back up to the tent and let her gaze run over the battered, zinc tub. Her most alluring piece of furniture.

"Welcome to my boudoir, young sir. Is it not the most exciting, nay, intoxicating place of amour? Pray enter and take your ease."

"Why, thank you."

Emma leaped. Alice Jordan stood in the open tent flap.

"But I believe I'll settle for a cup of tea, if that's all the same to you."

Not yet true friends — Emma wasn't certain what a true girlfriend might be — they were free and content, now, in each other's company. She laughed and blew the breakfast embers back into life for the kettle.

"I've come for Mrs. Beeton again, if I may, " Alice said.

"Of course," Emma retrieved the cookbook from her trunk and passed it to her. "But I say, let's have our tea in the breeze, at the top of the knoll. It is such a fine, windy, mosquito-free day."

They carried their cups, pre-sugared, and teapot to the hilltop where they sat unceremoniously on the grass.

"Boudoir, is it?" Alice asked.

"I must be slowly going mad, in a very gentle descent, mind you," Emma said.

"What a lovely way to go; you're so lucky in your marriage."

This was dangerously frank for their relationship.

"Well, really, we're still newly wed. Count the days actually spent in each other's company and we are very fresh to the game. And we do have our troubles. This beastly sod house business has formed a wall that we, neither of us, seem able to scale."

"You and Jack will surmount it. I can see that plain as day." Alice smiled wistfully. "That time you quarreled at our house — over the soddie? I envied you that quarrel. It had feeling, passion even. You're closer in your fights than the major and I . . . "

"Don't take on so, Alice," Emma held her hand. "We all have our ups and downs."

"If only we had ups and downs," Alice withdrew her hand. "If only our marriage wasn't as flat as the prairie."

This was more than Emma could console. She sipped her tea and gazed over the uplands. The Buxton house and barn were tiny, but prominent on the empty landscape. Alice wanted to talk, not take advice — there was no solution to her situation. Emma became like One and Two, a good listener. A half-hour later Alice left, bright and cheerful. Emma returned to her tent and ran a hand along the tub. Perhaps this lonely country, full of hardship, was driving them all a bit off course. Perhaps no one could see it because no one was normal any longer. One had to snap like Fred White, go barking mad, as Jack called it. Otherwise, one's little antics simply went unremarked.

Mrs. Beeton's book lay on the trunk.

Emma snatched it up and ran to the top of the hill, hoping to call Alice, but she wasn't going home. Alice was following the narrow path that cut from Thornton to Buxton. What was she up to? Surely the men were out haying. Emma ran after her.

Alice disappeared inside the humped-back sod house. Emma hurried forward. The door stood ajar; she peered inside. Alice was humming a hymn. She picked up a bowl from the rough table, examined it, and replaced it. She ran her finger along the edge of a shelf made from a packing crate. Neither Alf nor Davie was home. She went to the bed — same design and construction as Emma's — and smoothed out the grey blanket with the palm of her hand. She hummed louder, stroking one of Alf's shirts hanging on a peg. Was she mad? An obsession with a man of lower class who was denied her? Then it all came at Emma, hitting her like hailstones. The hayfield with Charlie — obsessed with a lower class? Her own life trapped outside society — cut dead and drifting toward Charlie's excitement. Until the harvest dinner when Jack sang. When she saw life, and she knew Jack would make her alive, and she was not going to stay dead forever.

That must be what Alice saw in Alf. Her life. Except she couldn't have it. She could watch it and talk to it. She could let it help raise her children. But she could not have it. Jack claimed that Alice wept for Alf, not her husband, when they were thought dead in the prairie fire. Emma had put it down to melodramatic gossip.

"Alice."

Alice continued humming and turned slowly.

"Does Alf know you visit him — his things — when he's away?"

"I've never told him, but he knows. He must sense that I've been here."

Emma scanned the one-room house; it was her first time actually inside. The wood floor was constructed of uneven, split logs, but it was clean. The Buxtons had somehow wallpapered the interior walls with the pages from a *London Telegraph* newspaper. It was a snug and tidy house. And it was cool.

"It's lovely in here, out of the sun," she said.

"Soddies are cool in the summer and warm in the winter," Alice repeated Jack's testimonial on sod homes. "If they are properly constructed. Alf and Davie made a proper job of this one."

"You can't have Alf," Emma said.

"I know."

"What will you do? It must be terribly, what? Distracting, I suppose, is the word."

"Do?" Alice smiled. "I'll do nothing for as long as I can stand it. Then I don't know what I shall do."

"You said I was lucky in my marriage," Emma said.

"And you didn't believe me."

"Oh yes, I believed — or rather, I knew and had forgotten." Emma walked across the floor. How pleasant to be off the dirt and grass of the tent.

"The boys will build you a better soddie than this." Alice tapped the newspapered walls. "Then you and Jack can be perfect again."

"Shall we walk to the hayfield with a lunch?"

Emma held out her hand and Alice took it. They started back hand in hand, to Newland Estate.

"You will ask Jack and Alf to build you a soddie now, Emma."

"Yes," said Emma. "Of course."

• • •

It was the best time to be in the tent. The knoll deflected the sunset up over the canvas, yet a half light glowed inside. Emma struggled with the bucket of boiling water. Her gloved hands slipped on the handle but she didn't slop any of the precious hot water. Jack held the tent flap for her. She sidestepped through and poured it into the tub. Steam billowed up the centre pole and hovered in the peak of the tent. The wind had stayed; the mosquitos were grounded; and the low-walled tub was perfectly hot. Jack stripped and sank into it with a groan of satisfaction. He reached for the hard, yellow bar of soap, but it was not in the towel. Then he felt it scrape across his back. Emma knelt behind the tub and ran the bar methodically across his shoulders and neck, lather gradually building. His head sagged forward, chin resting on his chest.

"I don't think I can withstand more than an hour or two of that, Em."

She used one hand to rub the soap in low, slow strokes down the small of his back. With her other hand she undressed herself. When she wore nothing but boots, she dropped the yellow bar and quickly unlaced them.

"Are you tired?" he asked without looking up.

"No, just give us a minute."

She fished the soap out of the tub and stepped into the water, her feet on either side of him, drawing his head up and back against her belly. She poured a cupped handful of water over his hair, then slid the soap back and forth, massaging the lather into his scalp, making him moan and push his head into her. She thrust forward against his taut neck, nearly losing her footing, and guided his head down, underwater, rinsing his hair. He surfaced and drew her forward. She knelt, hands braced on the edge of the tub, for him to scrub her back and thighs. She rested her chin on her knuckles and pushed back, slithering her cheeks against his stomach, all pretense at bathing ended now. They began slowly, but the tempo of their lovemaking soon accelerated. She revelled in the long body contact, in the splashing water, in the glowing air around them, in attaining their ecstasies, her, then him, howling like coyotes.

Afterward, they towelled and went to bed naked, praying mosquitoes would not invade.

"Davie works miracles with those green trees," she said drowsily. "This bed is really quite wonderful."

"Mmmm, best bath night ever."

"I understand he's an absolute wizard at constructing sod barns and houses and such," she tapped his chest.

"Whatever would we do if we had neighbours close to hand," his eyes popped open, alarmed, "no noisy bath night activities then."

"Jack?"

"Yes?"

"I'll have a sod house, please," she said, brushing his eyes shut with her fingertips.

"So we can have privacy for continued bathing?"

"Precisely," she said. Why not enjoy her marriage? Why taint her one pure joy over the construction materials used in their house? And she could keep that dowry intact, as a bonus.

CHAPTER 23

Blast and Damnation would not work at the near-stationary pace of oxen, and they were not stubborn enough to break the hard September sod. Jack borrowed the Buxtons' oxen and now he ploughed with all four of the huge animals. They were slow, maddeningly stubborn, but they did break the earth. He was cutting four long furrows about twenty yards inside the fireguard he'd ploughed in May. The fresh-cut sod was then sliced into twenty-eight inch lengths, each fourteen inches wide and four inches thick. Alf sliced. He and Alice loaded them on the wagon. Blast and Damnation pulled the wagon uphill to the housesite. Emma proudly drove the sod wagon, and basked in Mary and Kitty's admiration for the way she handled the big Clydes. At the housesite she helped Davie unload, but he would not let her set a single sod in place. This was to be his architectural triumph and he was like a jealous prima donna — setting and squaring each piece exactly. Sturdy spruce logs formed a solid frame box eighteen feet long, twelve feet wide and just over six feet high. This sat square on a level bench cut into the side of the hill where the tent had stood. Davie built the walls by laying the sods alternately cross-wise and lengthwise, grass-side down. He employed a plumb line and fastidiously trimmed any dirt or grass that did not conform to his specifications.

For the entire first fortnight of September the assembly line continued, Jack joining the cutters and haulers once his furrows were finished. On September twentieth the walls were complete.

Davie was congratulated and each labourer placed a small memento in the northwest angle of the walls — the cornerstone, Davie somewhat grandly declared. The men then began skidding and hoisting logs up onto the top of the walls, laying them side by side, with a small second layer forming a ridge down the centre

The house construction coincided with yet another change in climate. Canada relented in September and showed its true potential for beauty. Two cold nights — cold enough to drive Emma to bed in all her undergarments, plus two nightgowns, plus wool cap — finally stifled the mosquitoes. The trees on the lake and ridge turned golden yellow. The grass dried to a sweet, hay-like quality, springy underfoot. A warm sun in the endless blue sky merely offset the cool, north breeze. Meadowlarks, redwing blackbirds, flickers, and flaming-red robins that dwarfed their English cousins gathered in multi-coloured flocks prior to their departure south. Geese filled the skies with honking Vs winging down from the arctic north. The long stretch of warm September days pulled them to earth where they filled Jordan Lake and most other sloughs in the township. The major grew jaded, the hunting was too easy, but the succulent goose flesh was irresistible, and they all feasted from his shoots.

Emma's house grew in this almost magical time of calm and plenty the old timers called "Indian Summer". Then a prairie fire appeared on October first, just as the last, main roof logs were being laid. It burned a red menace on the south and west horizon, each of the next two nights. Smoke skimmed above the Newland farms each day but the fire stayed close to the Battle River. The major hurried home from Lloydminster. He, Jack, and the Buxtons immediately burned their guards. This entailed the tricky job of setting fire to the dry grass between the two belts of furrows surrounding the homesteads. Emma, Alice, and the girls were armed with wet, burlap sacks with which they swatted any burning pieces of grass that flew into the enclosure.

Jack shrieked like an hysterical woman when a bit of flaming debris fluttered over the guard and into his precious oat field. The oats had been cut and the sheaves stooked. Emma extinguished the offender before it scorched six inches of stubble. There was no cause for alarm, but Jack shifted all his sheaves into the woods near the slough and flagellated himself for the risk he had taken. They returned to the roof, laying thin poles between the logs to close off the ceiling completely. Then the wind shifted, hot and whirling from the southwest — the fire set course for the Newland Cooperative. Roof work ceased again and everyone returned to their homestead. Jack and Emma filled buckets with water and sacking; damp clay from the wellsite was dumped at strategic locations along the fireguard. The Buxtons were completely prepared and even the major had a credible, defensive position. His proximity to water and trees made his home the easiest to protect. Jack volunteered to drive south to scout the fire. Emma climbed into the wagon while he was harnessing the horses.

"I don't think you should come," he said when he wheeled the horses up and backed them into place.

"Whyever not?"

"Might be a bit dangerous."

"Jack, don't be ridiculous," she laughed. "If it is dangerous then you should stay at home. How would I cope on my own if you were caught down south in the fire?"

"Well it's not dangerous, but . . . "

She waited, quietly amused at his struggle between the traditional Englishman that still lurked inside and the plain, new-world truth of the situation.

"But it's not the place — the thing — scouting, that is, for a woman."

"Woman, me, that is, in the North West Territories may live in a tent, cook outdoors, cut sod, drive the team, lime the latrine, and stook oats. But scouting is beyond the pale?"

"You've certainly been busy the last two months, I'll grant you that." He laughed. "I hadn't really thought of all the new talents you've acquired."

"All!" She leaned over and took the reins from him. "That is scarcely the tip of the iceberg. Let's see, I feed the oxen, water the potatoes, mend the fence around the oats and hay, shovel manure . . . "

She snapped the lines and gave a small "hup." The Clydes hit their collars, and the wagon was rolling. Jack caught the tailboard and swung into the box.

"You've only mucked out the barn twice," he protested.

"Operated a logging camp cook tent, raked hay, stacked hay," she paused, glancing thoughtfully at him. "Oh yes, and I prepare a bath for the lord of the manor once a week."

• • •

The smoke was still high, but it scented the warm air blowing directly in their faces. The horses followed the tracks cut into the grass — they knew the trail to Lloydminster. Emma held the lines slack. She found herself thinking more and more like a Nor' Wester. More and more insane? Or just less and less English? She couldn't say. But she did instinctively count the miles, look for landmarks, and wonder when a village might be established closer to township twelve.

"Trail's in good shape," she said.

"Amazing," Jack answered. "The mark of man on the land. When Davie and I ran Kitty to the doctor, what — only four months gone — we had to use a compass to find our way. Now, there is a clear trail. Next year half this land will be claimed."

"I know." She smiled at him. "I'd never have thought this place could be anything but empty. Yet Mrs. Hill claims that in two or three years prairie fires will be extinct. All the land ploughed, no grass to burn."

"Amen to that." Jack squinted at the smoky horizon. "Still, years from now, it will count for something. Being first, I mean. Being the ones who broke the sod and fought the fires and blazed the trails."

"Blazed the trails?" She handed him the lines and kissed his cheek wound. "What a romantic silly you are."

"Silly, is it? Well then, Mrs. Thornton, just exactly why did you insist on joining the scouting party?"Emma sat up, surprised at his perspicuity.

"To see the fire. Curiosity, I suppose."

"*Ha!* Liar!" He stamped his feet like a nasty little boy. "Let's have the truth."

"You brute. All right, the truth is I wanted to be part of it, be the one to see it first. I may have been jealous, a little tiny bit jealous, of the rest of the cooperative having braved the spring fires. I wanted to prove myself."

He slung his free arm around her shoulders and squeezed her. "Knew it." A prairie fire suddenly appeared in the west. Leaping, yellow flames like tiny devils dancing all across their view. Jack pulled the team up.

"That's probably the head, right there. I'd say six or seven miles. North and south flanks, twice as far behind."

Emma was frightened as she had been frightened of that first trip to Hampstead to visit Jack. Anticipating the test, yet fearful lest she should fail. Jack was calculating direction and speed but she scarcely heard him, the flames were entrancing. Imagine, a whole country on fire. It was the essence of this free, open land. Nobody controlled it, they just coped with it.

"Well?"

"Well, what?"

"How far have we come from Buxton's place, do you reckon?'

"That's easy," she said proudly. "Eight miles to the big white rock on township twelve line, then a half-hour on is another three miles to make eleven all told to here, so seventeen or eighteen miles from the head of yonder fire to home."

"My thoughts exactly." Jack sniffed the smoky wind. "She's coming slowly now. Almost evening, wind's slowing, so she will lay down and sleep in another two hours."

"That means, if the wind picks up after dawn, the fire will still be six miles off," Emma paused to calculate. "It should hit us about an hour or two after sunrise."

"Well done, scout. Let's go home." Jack clucked "woot" and the team started to turn. She laid a hand across his arm.

"Can we watch it for a minute longer?"

"Why you romantic old silly, of course we can."

• • •

Three hours after the sun cracked the eastern sky, the prairie fire rode a suddenly fierce southwest wind into the Newland Cooperative. The flames whipped up high one moment, then bent forward in a rushing assault the next. The worst part of the fire, the head, came straight up the Lloydminster trail and engulfed the Buxton homestead. Emma watched from the top of her hill. Alf and Davie darted like frenzied, black ants along the guard, flailing wet sacks. Then a wave of smoke obliterated her view and the flames seemed to wash right over them. A white-tail deer and her nearly-grown fawn burst from a bluff near the Buxtons and raced,

white flags waving high, not ten yards past Emma to the safety of
the trees surrounding Lake Jordan. A red fox followed them. The
wily coyotes probably departed last night, she thought. It was her
last coherent thought; everything began to happen at once in the
fiery chaos.

*The fire races across the flats then charges undaunted up the slope
toward her. She runs to her station by the haystack. Jack goes to
the corner of the guard nearest the fire. A rushing, crackling, hellish
wind fills her ears. Smoke. In her eyes, mouth, nose, lungs, snatching
oxygen from her. Jack pelting left, smacking at a flame inside the
guard. Ostrich barks at his heels. Jack gone in a billow of smoke.
Two flaming straws riding the wind strike the haystack. Her turn,
now, in the firing line. She almost welcomes the hits — easier to
thump the wet sacking than to watch the wall of fire coming for
her. Ostrich runs past her like the fox, heedless of her calls. Pray
the little dog has enough sense to run into the slough. She kills both
sparks quickly. A shriek of wind tears a strand of hair loose and
flings her hat away. Hot, roaring flames call from behind her and
throw a half-dozen sparks onto the stack, high up. She gets them,
barely, with her wet bag, on tiptoes. Then a clump of burning grass
hits near the top of the hay mountain, well beyond her reach.
Miniscule flames ignited. Blast, Damnation, One, and Two would
either starve or eat now. It is up to her.
She shoots up the haywall like a squirrel up a tree, clawing and
kicking. Her own voice sounds above the wind, swearing, like Alf
and Jack when a whipple tree breaks, coarse oaths she'd rarely
thought and never said. The fire is going into the stack, her wet
burlap is useless. Emma digs her hands under the burning patch.
She dives deep to her shoulders and catapults the burning hay high
— the wind whips it up and over the barn. It lands on ploughed
land and withers. Something scorches her cheek. The loose hair*

glows, tips burning like slow matches. She crushes it in the wet sack, smearing soot on her face, then slides down the stack and resumes her battle. Jack is gone, alive, burned, unconscious from smoke, she knows not. She may have taken her eyes off the hummock in the slough, but she will die before she'll let her hay burn.

"Thirty minutes?"

"That's about it," Jack replied after he finished retching.

"Seemed longer."

He straightened up, white eyes in a soot-blacked face stared at her. "Your hair! Are you burned?"

"No. Well, just my ear, a little." She touched the tender blister on her earlobe. A ragged, foul-smelling strand of burnt hair stuck to her fingers. She pointed to the small hole at the top of the haystack and explained what had happened. Jack dipped his handkerchief in the water bucket and gently dabbed her burn.

"I really didn't think there was any chance the fire would leap the guard, much less hit the hay, but that wind . . . " he placed the palm of one hand on her neck to steady her while he cleaned the blister, "that wind was straight from hell."

Emma closed her eyes, basking in his gentle attentions, hearing the concern in his voice. She hadn't thought of personal danger but, now, the image of herself atop a torching haystack brought a shiver of horror, reminding her of Charlie's India stories of suttee.

"You saved us from tremendous loss, Em," Jack said quietly into her burned ear. "Maybe even ruin. No hay and not enough money to replace it. I'd have lost the Clydes this winter."

"You exaggerate," she said modestly.

"I do not." He kissed her ear lightly. "This will scar but I'll tell you now, Emma Thornton, you should be as proud of your wound as everyone seems to be of my Paardeberg trophies."

She kissed his cheek in return. He was her Jack, the Englishman she loved. "I'm for Emma and she is for me". His Chelsea morning room words came to her. But were they the same, or had she fallen in love again, with an entirely new man? Two people singed, filthy, and half overcome with smoke, clinging to each other on a patch of grass surrounded by black desolation.

"Aye, well, we made it, then. We'll take the rest of the day off, clean up. Get back to work on the house tomorrow," Jack said.

A mournful hound bayed from the top of the hill. Ostrich emerged from the soddie doorway and threw his head back to bay again.

"He thinks you were lost in the fire," Emma said. "Otherwise, he'd have never deserted you."

"Nonsense." Jack whistled loudly, waving. "The first whiff of smoke and he was off and devil take the hindmost."

The beagle trotted toward them, tail up and wagging furiously.

"Not very loyal but deuced intelligent — hiding in the house."

• • •

This prairie fire did have two benefits. There would be no dry grass for spring fires, everyone agreed with relief. But it also demonstrated the glazing quality of Saskatchewan River Valley clay. Emma was helping Jack spread the damp clay on a few hot spots outside the guard. One of the clay piles had been fired into a crude, hard lump of china. The next day when the men were tacking a double, crisscross layer of tarpaper over the roof poles, she took the wheelbarrow to the well. She loaded it half-full of the clay spoil from the digging. She fetched up two pails of water and emptied them into the barrow. By the time she returned to the house, the clay was sloppy. She wheeled it into the house unnoticed. Ten minutes mixing with the hoe and she had a smooth slurry of molasses consistency in the barrow.

The first handful was cold and slimy, but it stuck to the sod wall. She smeared it with her palm and it spread smoothly. Excited, she applied a second coat and the porous sod disappeared under the smooth plaster. A third application failed. Perhaps it needed the bits of grass and earth from the sod to form an adhesion. She scraped the slipping layer off without harming the initial coats. Two veneers it was, then. She worked out from the original patch, ignoring the mud splattering her clothes and face. She rapidly honed her technique. The barrow was empty and a smooth, brown rectangle three feet long by two feet wide graced the back wall of her new home.

She knew it would dry and likely fall off chunk by chunk, but if it didn't . . . well, it would be wonderfully clean and perhaps it could even be whitewashed. She tried not to raise false hopes. If the men saw it they would doubtless laugh or find some "Canadian" reason why it could not work. She busied herself making lunch. They ate, then the men began hauling the last of the cut sod up onto the roof, laying it over the tarpaper. Emma slipped into the house. The back wall had not crumbled. In fact, it was drying into a pale-brown smoothness, and aside from some tiny, hairline, surface cracks, it seemed solid. She tapped lightly. Her fingernails clicked against the hard clay. She struck at it with her knuckles, then rapped sharply on it. Not so much as a flake came free. Emma ran for the wheelbarrow and, with Ostrich as her only confidante, she returned to the clay pile.

Three hours later the men laid the last of the roof sod. The October sun was waning and the air was falling chill. They entered the house to dig the cellar hole in the floor for potato storage and were greeted by Emma, virtually coated with clay.

"Cor, Mrs. T." Alf actually dropped his shovel in surprise. "You're the mud woman."

Emma stepped aside, her confidence suddenly evaporating. What the hell? Mud on walls? Waste of bloody time — won't last. Where'd you get such a notion? All the comments she feared were plain on the men's faces. She should have asked; she had wasted her time; God she felt like a child again, a stupid —

"Did you mix straw in with the clay?" Alf asked, but not with ridicule.

"No, I found that the dry earth and bits of grass in the sod wall seemed to bond with the wet clay, hold it on."

"O' course Alf! That's where we went wrong." Davie cut her off excitedly. He crossed the room and examined the driest section of wall. "Hard as a nun's heart, beautiful."

He whirled around, eyes glowing. "See, Mrs. Thornton, me and Alf tried the same trick, but we mixed straw with the wet clay to give it some body."

"Poor man's brick, Cockney bricks back home." Alf joined Davie and tapped the wall. "But it dried quick and fell off, so we gave up. Pasted newspaper to sticks and propped 'em up."

"Wonderful work, Emma." Jack slipped his arm around her waist. "It really is fine, and it will help keep the cold out."

"It may crack when the house settles," Davie said critically, the master builder taking a second opinion. "But I laid these sods exact and we dug into the hill to level her, so she won't shift much."

"I thought to keep a pile of clay warm inside the house, then when cracks appeared I could do running repairs this winter." Emma tried to sound clinical but a thrill of acceptance, accomplishment, bubbled behind her voice.

"Right, Mrs. T," Davie turned to her. "We lay your floor and cut your stovepipe roof hole tomorrow. But the very next day you'll take us on as your apprentice plasterers, like. We'll finish here, then you'll have to come help Alf and me do our shop."

Emma felt the half-dried blobs of clay on her face crack from the huge grin she could no longer suppress.

• • •

"The best thing. The absolutely best, most marvelous thing is that we don't have to creep around bent over in that miserable tent. And now that we have our furniture," Jack tottered through the low door with the bed rails. "Well, at least some of our furniture. We can finally live like human beings again."

Only a kitchen table, three wood chairs, one armchair, one carpet, and the bed had, in fact, arrived. The packing-crate shelves, trunk for a wardrobe, and flour-bag curtains would have to continue in service. The CPR had no idea when, or if, the rest of her furniture would appear. In truth, there was no room for the missing dining-room set, stuffed chair, settee, or cabinets and wardrobes. Emma didn't mind much.

"No, Jack," she said, gazing over the snug, little, earth house, cradled like a baby on the bosom of the hill. "The very best thing is that we built it ourselves. This truly makes it our land. Think of all the places in England — on the whole earth — that are leased or "held" or occupied on sufferance. Now look at us. This is our land, our place. We can build ten houses and dig a hundred-foot well if we want."

Jack appeared in the doorway, a sleepy smile on his face.

"Did you say better than England?"

"*No!* I said different. I don't know if I shall ever submit wholly to this country." She saw his face fall. "But it's something. To be first. To be the ones who blazed the trail."

His smile returned. She thought of her dowry — their life boat — and smiled back.

"And look! November fifteenth. A touch of frost, to be sure, but none of the vaunted snow blizzards. We've got it made, Em. Hardly worse than a Lancashire or Scottish winter I shouldn't think. We've seen the worst this country can dish out."

• • •

The major bought runners and shifted his wagon box onto them to make a fine sleigh. Jack and Davie managed to carve runners out of two-inch planks bought from an Edmonton river scow. These were attached in place of wheels to the wagon frame. They were awkward and not articulated properly, so turning was a long, arcing process. But they worked and were a huge improvement over the snow-bound wheels. The snow lay ankle-deep, hard, and crisp, perfect for winter travel. The major decreed they should go to Lloydminster for Christmas. Since the Mounties had forbade travel in the late afternoon fearing colonists lost in dark, winter nights, the major arranged for them to stay overnight at a committee-member's townhouse. Emma found herself in a social fluster — tried to deny it — then became even more flustered. She had two decent dresses, but there was the Christmas Eve carol service, the Christmas morning church service, and the ball. Could she wear the same dress twice and get away with it? Jack stared at her as though she was barmy when she broached the subject.

"Emma, half the people in the colony are lucky to be dressed, fed, and sheltered at all." He began ticking the points off on his fingers. "Major says nearly two hundred families are destitute in government shack tents in town. Over twice that number are barely hanging on to their homesteads. Nearly forty percent of the colony livestock is already dead. By those standards, we're royalty! Nobody will notice!"

She knew the sad statistics of the "summer grasshoppers", as Alf called them. The people who hadn't built proper homes or barns, or even grown vegetables. But she also knew many ladies from successful homesteads would be pulling out all the fashion stops, and she didn't want to show up badly. It was her first social affair in seven months and the chance of some dancing, music, and gaiety was like water to a parched throat. The winter, not nearly as severe as expected, had still been cold enough to halt all activity, save tending the animals, cutting wood and hauling water. The short days and long nights spent cloistered on the homestead were beginning to stifle. So she fussed and enjoyed the novelty of it.

The Christmas celebrations were a delight — crude, raw, and rough — but a delight. The Hall & Scott General Store seemed palatial after the homestead soddie. Tall, wooden walls, brightly lit, decorated, full of people. At first Emma found herself stunned by the crowd and even uncomfortable in it. Like a hermit emerging from a cave, she winced at the noisy voices. As a cure, she joined the choir for the carol service, against mild resistance from some of the town members, who had been practising for a month. Reverend Lloyd's service was so English and wonderful that she was certain Jack — the Vicar's son — had to fight back tears. The banquet was filling and palatable. Constable Roberts lead the Mounted Police into the hall triumphantly bearing a huge plum pudding, which was excellent. He then danced frequently with Alice Jordan, much to Alf's annoyance and the major's obliviousness. The major spent most of the evening secretly boozing and ranting over townsite problems with other concerned citizens.

Jack and Emma danced until four AM and fell in love again. English clothes, voices, manners, and music took them home to England in spirit and soul. "Home Sweet Home" was sung to general weeping at four thirty, then "God Save the King". They drove home in bright moonlight and light frost. Ostrich barked at the coyotes who whined at the moon. Blast and Damnation stepped smartly through the snow throwing up a fine, sparkling, white cloud that floated around them like the snow in a Christmas glass ball. Emma snuggled beside Jack on the cold, high seat. Alf, Davie, and the Jordan ladies were warmly cocooned in straw in the box. The major snored alcohol fumes in a corner by himself. Sunrise hit them an hour from home. The snow blazed with reflected light. They laughed to see it. Emma found herself looking forward to the homestead. She still couldn't call it home, especially after this very English Christmas, but it was where she wanted to be just now.

$$\bullet \; \bullet \; \bullet$$

The last day of January, Emma hosted a dance in her sod house for the residents of township twelve. Furniture was shifted to the barn, the floor spread with sawdust, and two frozen geese were thawed and cooked, their heat and smell filling the house before guests arrived. The Jordans, Buxtons, Hills, and an older couple with two teenage daughters attended. The latter, the Bowens, homesteaded on the lip of Big Gully. They, and the Hills, had travelled the farthest and would stay overnight. Counting the young Bowen girls, as Davie eagerly did, there were plenty of partners for dancing. The dreamy Oliver Hill accompanied them on the violin with a great range and skill. They waltzed, two-stepped, and polkaed in shrieking whirls. The Bowen girls demonstrated a schottische — then everyone tried it. Even the major did his duty. At one o'clock in the morning, Emma and Alice fed them soup, fried potatoes, goose, bread, jam, and dried apples in syrup. The soddie was warm and snug. It brimmed with conviviality — the major taking this in a literal, liquid sense — and camaraderie. Then the fiddle began sawing again and they danced until past three. By then Kitty and Mary were sound asleep with Ostrich in the bed, and the major, mostly unconscious, slept in a corner using Emma's clay pile for a pillow. Rather than disturb them, Emma put Alice to bed with the girls. The Hills and Bowens shifted their bedrolls to make room for Jack and Emma on the floor.

Alf and Davie donned boots, coats, and mitts and said their goodbyes. Up until that moment, the house had been filled to the roof-poles with music and voices, but now they fell silent and a high, keening sound came. Davie opened the door and winter, the old-timers' winter, rushed in. A floursack of snow burst on Davie, coating him instantly white. The wind was a north, howling fury that the ridge blocked, but the turbulent undercurl whipped snow down onto the Thornton house. Davie laughed in surprise and slammed the door. Emma pressed her face to the largest window which revealed an extraordinary volume of snow rushing past on the wind.

"Now that's a snowfall!" Davie wiped his face and eyes. "Better tie ourselves down, Alf."

They pulled earflaps down from their caps and knotted the strings under their chins.

"Maybe it would be best to wait until daylight," Emma said uneasily. "So you don't lose your way."

"It's a mile and a sniff!" Alf laughed at her fears. "We've made a path a foot deep between your place and ours, we could walk it blindfolded. We'll be home in fifteen minutes."

"I know every tree, shrub, and bump," Davie said joining Alf at the door. They braced themselves.

"Right-O, we're off." Alf whipped the door open, plunged out, and slammed it behind them. Emma's stomach lurched. She looked to Jack.

"Come, Em." He tossed her a blanket. "You can't get lost between here and Alf's place."

"Hardly a polar expedition," Mr. Bowen said, settling himself on the floor.

Emma topped up one lamp and set it in the deep sill behind the large window. "I'd feel better if we let that burn until daylight."

"Waste of precious paraffin," Mrs. Bowen muttered, already half asleep.

Emma caught Jack's eye and his protest died. The floor was colder than the air higher in the room. Emma pulled on a cardigan then burrowed into the blankets beside Jack. She watched the lamplight in the window and listened to the stove crackling. There was something unrestrained, wild, about the wind battering the soddie. Like a prairie fire, it did not acknowledge their presence as anything significant. She closed her eyes and the long, day's exertions brought sleep. A dream came, but it did not fool her. She knew she was dreaming, even as she slept. She and Jack wandered an African battlefield looking for Bobbi who had bolted and left them on foot. Long-bearded, Boer men gave them advice on finding a horse lost on the veldt. She tried to follow their directions but all Jack could say was "lost, lost." She opened her eyes, tired of the vaguely disturbing dream. The stove was down to coals, she could see her breath in the lamplight. The other sleepers sent tiny streams of condensed air puffing up like so many train engines on sidings.

Lost.

She sat up, cold air rushed into her warm blanket. The wind spoke to her.

Lost.

461

Good God. It was not the wind. She leapt from the floor and rushed to the window. It was a human voice.

Lost —ost.

Two voices, echoing each other. Alf and Davie dying out there; she could hear it in the high-pitched cry of their voices.

"*Jack!* Major, Bowen, Oliver, get up!" she screamed, as a shrivelling horror filled her. She threw on her coat and boots, searched frantically for mitts.

Lost. The voices were fading, they were walking away — they hadn't seen the light. She found her mitts and pulled them on. Jack stood beside her, shivering in his underwear and socks.

"What is it, Emma?"

"Alf, Davie! They're still out there, lost. They're going to die."

She reached for the door latch. Jack's strong hands gripped her arms. He shook her, violently.

"*No*, Em. You're imagining it."

She struggled. "I heard them calling, Jack. We have to go get them."

"It's the wind, Emma," Jack shouted directly into her face. "It speaks crazy things to you, tries to trick you. It wants you to go out there. Listen, it's a full blizzard, the Buxtons went home two hours ago. It can't be them. It's the wind calling you"

It checked her. She stopped struggling and looked into his eyes, aware of the others sitting up in the dim light, staring at her. Jack's eyes were bright, flitting back and forth. He really believed the wind could speak to him, her? Is this what Fred White's face had looked like to Jack? Was she seeing the same inroads of madness in Jack now? Then his actual words sank into her conscious thoughts. He was right. The Buxtons left two hours ago. They couldn't be outside; it was impossible. Jack saw the madness in her — that she had been drawn close to the edge of a flimsy reality. She fancied she could hear the others breathing above the shrieking storm; could feel their eyes upon her. It was not the dream carrying over into wakefulness. Rather, it was her own mind readily embracing the impossible notion that a force of nature could speak English.

Loooost.

She twitched as though slapped. Even now the word, faint to the point of nonexistence, came to her on the blizzard's breath.

"I heard it," Mary stood up in the bed then jumped down beside the stove. "Just now, Mommy. Somebody said 'lost', but like they were crying."

"Hush now, Mary. It's not the time for games." Alice reached for Mary, embarrassed.

"Me, too! From the stove," Kitty tried to crawl over Alice. Ostrich raised his sleepy head and yipped.

"Quiet!" Oliver Hill commanded. He leaned on his elbow, head cocked to one side.

Loooost. Emma held her breath. Both Mary and Kitty's faces lit up.

"Somebody *is* out there," Hill said quietly. "The wind is somehow carrying the sound down or across the top of the stove pipe. It must be acting as a kind of collector."

The room erupted into chaos. Jack dove through bodies for his clothes. Mr. Bowen was swearing, looking for his boots. Children, women, dog, men's voices burst into a cacophony of order and counter order. Emma seized the door and pulled it open. Surprisingly, little wind met her. She stepped into the darkness and stumbled against a snow wall three feet deep. She plunged forward and after five high-stepping strides was standing, panting, in thick, dry snow up to her waist.

"Alf! Davie! Here!" She yelled, but her voice was pitched nearly the same tone as the wind, and her words disappeared at the edge of her lips. She floundered ahead and the snow shallowed out to knee deep. She was off the house ledge and going down toward the barn. She increased her pace and fell, conscious already of her head and arms stinging from the cold, despite the heavy coat, but her lower body was relatively warm under the deep snow. She struggled to her feet and tried to bellow, deep-voiced.

"Here, boys! Here!"

She hurried down the slope to the bottom. She stopped to listen, cupping one mittened hand over her ear to deflect the wind.

Lost— lost — lost.

She was closer; they were closer; they must have heard her. She leaped forward, bounding through the drifts, gasping, "here, boys, here."

Lost — Lost.

She changed direction and plodded through the wind toward the voice. Now beyond the ridge's protection, the wind came through her clothes as though she was naked. It froze the hair in her nose solid; tiny icicles prickled her. She put a mitt over her face to thaw them. One of her ears was no longer hurting — it must have frozen. She tripped over a stone, a furrow perhaps, buried in the snow, and fell.

"For the love of God, help us, please."

She could not see him. She crawled, hand outstretched, and touched him.

"Alf?"

"Mrs. Thornton," Alf said formally.

She could just make him out, sitting cross-legged in the snow, holding Davie's body curled like a baby on his lap.

"Can you walk? Is Davie . . . " She spoke into his ear.

"Yes, we can, for a bit, but we're near done."

"You're just by our corral," Emma said calmly. "I'll lead you back. We'll follow the lamp in the window."

"What lamp?"

Emma whirled about, face into the flying snow. It couldn't be more than fifty yards, but the lamp was gone. She fought back a sudden jolt of panic. The fingers of her right hand were numb — they rattled like frozen sausages in her mitt.

"Then we shall simply follow my tracks."

"Right you are, Mrs. T," Davie's weak voice came to her.

They rose and leaned into the north wind. Snow packed into their eyes. It melted for an instant, then froze their eyelashes shut. Emma put her dead hand up as a visor, took Davie's hand and pressed on. A minute later, she realized she was breaking new trail. She had lost her tracks. She stopped, disoriented, back to the wind.

"Can we lie down again? It's warmer in the drifts," Davie asked

"*No!*" Alf shouted. "We're going home, Davie. Stay up. Go on, Mrs. Thornton! Go on, now."

Emma turned. They must charge the wind, go north until the ground started to rise. She couldn't miss the hill, surely. She struck off, pulling Davie.

"*Emma!*"

Jack's voice — behind her. How could that be?

"Jack!" she tried, but her own throat was cold, hoarse. A smudge of light flickered to the right. She threw herself at it. It extinguished.

"*Emma!*" Jack again, but to her left. She changed course. The light reappeared, and a figure beside it. Jack holding a lantern, shielding it from the wind.

"Jack," she wheezed. He came to her and lifted her bodily into his arms. Oliver Hill took the lantern. Mr. Bowen picked Davie up and Bob Hill grappled Alf. They lumbered uphill. A second later the major tottered toward them from the soddie.

• • •

Jack had to feel his way to the woodpile — only ten yards from the house. The mostly-sober major clung to Jack's coat. The two men brought in large armfuls of wood to feed the stove. Emma sat on the floor, feet outstretched to the heat. Alf crouched beside her, massaging useless hands near the hotbox. Mrs. Hill rubbed snow on Davie's face, partly for the frostbite, partly to revive his senses. Kitty held Davie's limp fingers in her warm, chubby hands. Alice fed the fire and prepared a kettle of tea. The Bowens had gone back to bed, the Hill boys hovered quietly in the background waiting any orders their mother might issue. Alf looked to Jack, then Emma. His hair stood nearly on end and his face was waxed marble. In the vague lamplight he was an upright corpse, except for his glittering eyes darting to Emma then away, like a feeding hummingbird.

"Your wife," he spoke slowly, thickly, as though his mouth was full of bread. "Thaved . . . tha . . . saved me and our Davie."

His jaw moved but his lips and cheeks would not flex properly. It was macabre, verging on hideous. His breath stank, Emma smelled it. Alf had taken on the life of one of Mary Shelley's nightmare characters — a waking, dead man.

"I believe she did," Jack replied.

"The Buxton boyth," he paused to breath heavily. "We are in your debt, ma'am."

He took her good hand in his cold collection of stick fingers. Emma looked aside to mask her revulsion.

"Forever, Mithuth — Missus Thornton." He peered into her face. "Forever in your debt."

He shifted slowly onto his side, curled into a fetal position by the stove, and fell asleep. Mrs. Hill let Davie do the same. Emma felt a tingling, hot sensation under the scar on her left ear — blood returning to the frozen veins. Jack sat beside her, his strong arm around her, pulling her tight to him.

"Remember my debt, Em?"

"I do." She lay her head on his shoulder. "Except it wasn't your debt. And you went to Africa and nearly got killed because of it."

"Funny, though," he smiled. "Went to Africa because of the debt; met Canadian Bobbi in Africa; Bobbi took me to the Canadian soldiers; they took me to Paardeberg; Paardeberg water sent me home; and at home the Canadian letter caught my eye and here we are, freezing to death in Canada. Like a big circle, really."

"Don't be ridiculous. Life doesn't work like that — like a game of dominoes."

"Maybe it does. Maybe it is exactly like a game of dominoes, each piece leading directly to the other."

"You don't believe that," she said earnestly. "We'd be married regardless of that silly debt. We fell in love, but not because of a predetermined fate."

He did not argue.

"I hearby cancel the Buxton debt," she said lightly, her frozen fingers tingling now.

"Oh no, Em." Jack stared at her. "You can't. Like it or not the Buxtons are sworn to you. It's for them to decide."

"Stop that!" She returned his stare, uneasy now. "You're scaring me. This is like a gothic novel full of . . . "

"No. It's not a novel. It is real. It's like George Grigg and Billy Webster and Palmer and Miles and Wethered. I'm bound to them, regardless of where they are. Bound forever."

"But Miles was killed," she said, then regretted it. She wanted no more of this eerie conversation. The single lamp and a flickering glow from the stove threw Jack's profile into an ill-defined shadow on the clay-plaster walls.

"Dead or alive, it does not matter." Jack's gaze had not wavered; his eyes had not blinked. "You're bound to the Buxtons. You gave 'em their lives. You offered your own for theirs. You would have died with them, for them."

"That's not true! I didn't know I was taking a chance until I lost sight of the lamp. That doesn't count. I didn't make a deliberate — "

"Doesn't matter, and you know it. You brought them from death to life. Alf is right."

A shocking, hot pain struck her ear. Then it leapt to her frozen hand, darting like fire from one finger tip to another. Now the toes of one foot caught fire. She jerked back from the stove. Had she somehow come too close to it? The pain began streaking up and down her feet and hand. She shook them involuntarily.

"Jack, oh, Jack!"

He took her hand, alarmed "What is it?"

"I'm not sure. It's burning, oh heavens, it won't go away." She began twitching, her body trying to expel the pain. It stopped pulsing and settled into a deep, thick needle penetrating up her fingers and toes, glancing off her bones. She could scarcely concentrate her thoughts.

"She's thawing out," Mrs. Hill said matter of factly. "Major, fetch me some snow, if you please."

"*No!*" Alice's voice cut hard across the room. Emma heard the disgust and anger in Alice's tone. "The major can have another drink. He has no reason to lift a finger to help these people."

Jordan lurched to his feet.

"Steady, girl. By heavens, that's a bit raw. Chap can't be held — "

"Sit down." Alice fired the words like pistol shots. "Bob Hill, would you bring the snow?"

Hill jumped to the door, cracked it, and scooped up the snow. He brought it to his mother who began to rub it on Emma's hand. She felt the cool sensation on her skin, but the pain was inside her and it was intensifying. She began to cry. She cried like a little girl with a skinned knee. A moment later, Alf woke up with an oath. His face was bright red. His fingers were swelling enormously.

"I'm on fire," he said.

"More snow, Bob, please," said Alice.

• • •

It was thirty hours before the guests finally departed in bitter, bright sunlight, calm air, and harsh cold. The thirty hours it took the blizzard to exhaust itself had been the scene of harrowing trips to the barn to feed and water the animals. The major's flask was empty; he was sober, but he remained aloof and apart, tacitly refusing to volunteer with barn or house chores. He pretended his wife was an old-country servant — invisible. She gave him his food and maintained a servant's silence, setting his bowl in front of him, then turning her back to eat. All were embarrassed by the major's lack of action in the Buxton rescue and anxious to put it behind them. Alice would not let it heal.

She tended to Alf and Davie, nursing their swollen faces, cooking for them, and reading to them. Her eyes frequently met and held Alf's, even when they weren't speaking — she refused to see the major. She casually laid her hand on Alf's arm or felt his forehead for fever, yet she stepped with great exaggeration around her husband to avoid contact with him. When the children reached the end of their behaviour tether in the cramped soddie, Alice involved them with Alf or Davie, never their father.

The Jordans departed as a family for their frozen home. Jack and Emma, her head wrapped in a woolen scarf, saw them off. She tugged Alice's coat and spoke quietly through the scarf while Jack and the major checked the horses.

"It will be better when you get home, on your own, Alice. He can mend his fences in private."

Alice lifted Kitty into the wagon. "Nothing left to mend," she whispered.

"You can't mean that. There must be . . . "

Alice turned and placed her hands on Emma's shoulders, pulling her close. Her breath steamed Emma's face. "I've crossed my Rubicon, Mrs. Thornton. He's betrayed me and I can't forgive him. I can't leave him physically, of course." She waved one arm at the surrounding snow wilderness. "But I've done with him all the same."

"You can't have Alf."

"You told me that once before," Alice said, no longer whispering. "Yet it was you who saved Alf's life. Now you can let me have him."

She climbed onto the seat beside her husband and called, "Farewell, Jack, lovely party!" The sleigh carved blue ruts into the snow as it curved off toward the treeline.

"Take more than a woodstove to warm the Jordan house," Jack observed, wading toward her.

"I fear the worst, Jack. She'll leave him in the spring."

"Then he'll go home, too, and no great loss to the cooperative," Jack replied lightly. "Pretty minor scandal way out here."

"What about Alf — when he goes after her? What about Davie and us left here? Where's your cooperative, then?" she said crossly. "I don't give a fig about divorce scandal. But suddenly, Jack Thornton, I do give a fig about our lovely Newland farm."

Jack smiled. "Spoken like the heroine of Newland." He put an arm around her and kissed her through the soggy scarf.

"Eh?"

"Newland heroine," he laughed. "That's what Ollie Hill calls you."

CHAPTER 24

The seventh, and last, blizzard of the winter hit mid-March 1904. It struck one week before spring, raged for three days, and nearly broke the spirit of every English man and woman surviving snowbound on the prairie. It crushed morale as surely as it filled the trails with trackless, dry snow. For five days before the blizzard the thermometer over the soddie door never climbed higher than thirty-three degrees below zero. One memorable morning it was forty-six degrees. The cold froze all moisture into ice fog — then froze that until it fell on the snow. The air crackled with electricity at the slightest friction. Only the moon and coyotes liked the cold. At night, in the wickedly-clear atmosphere, the moon shone a harsh, blue light, sparkling the snow and driving the coyotes into a wild paroxysm of song. Emma and Jack stayed up nights bucksawing wood to feed the stove and stave off the cold. But the soddie held, the horses survived, the oxen seemed not to notice, and Ostrich took to yowling with the coyotes. "Barking Mad Beagle" Jack called him. Then three days of white horror that ended early one morning. It was only twenty degrees below zero when the sun rose. There was a softness that Emma hadn't sensed for weeks. The brittle, dry air was gone. The sky was blue, not washed white with ice crystals. This day might see nearly zero, Emma thought, perhaps better.

"Feels like spring," Jack said. He had taken to reading her mind over the last two months spent trapped in the soddie. He stood beside her, shovel in hand, looking much like a bear. Knee-high moccasins stuffed with felt and wool socks. Long underwear, trousers and baggy cords over all. Heavy, felt coat buttoned to the chin, collar up, and scarf tied around it and his chin. Wool cap surmounted by fur hat with earflaps tied down under the scarf, only his nose and eyes showed. Foggy breath streamed out from his face.

"Can you smell it, Em? I'll wager we hit zero today."

She had taken to reading his mind in retaliation, but he liked it. He was going to mention the lack of sun dogs, so she pulled her scarf down a notch and spoke.

"No sun dogs, then, Jack. That's a good sign."

He laughed and shovelled snow away from the entrance to the soddie. Emma began her plod to the woodpile, pushing thigh deep through the hard-caked blizzard drifts. She collected an armload and stamped back to the house, dumped her load inside and repeated the trip twice more, recreating the path to the wood. Jack had the entry clear so they trudged, single file, down to the barn, following the long piece of twine tied from the house as a safety measure. They merely trampled the snow down. Jack had given up shovelling weeks ago. He cleared the drifts from the barn door and they entered. He immediately went to fuss over Blast and Damnation while she fed One and Two, then led them outside. Jack followed her with the harness.

"Let's break trail to the Buxtons first, see if they want to come to Lloydminster with us," she said, knowing he was about to suggest it. They would go, turn and turn about, as lead sleigh breaking the snow to the main trail — much quicker if the Buxtons came along, and much easier on One and Two, she thought, scratching the reliable old One behind his ear.

"Agreed. Two teams breaking trail in turns works so much better than one."

She smiled. Cabin fever, the old timers called it. She and Jack
accepted it as just another of the little insanities one developed in
the Saskatchewan Territories. They had even turned it into a game
in the evenings when they grew tired of Hardy or Conan-Doyle
or Dickens. They played games, read silently, read to one another,
acted out scenes from the stories, and read each others' minds to
keep despair away from their soddie in the long, wasted nights.
Once a week they bathed, taking hours to melt snow and heat the
water. Then they made love in blankets sparkling with static
electricity. But only once a week, to keep it as a special treat.

"Then we'll go along to see what the Jordans need from town."
They finished this in perfect unison and laughed. "Major will want
to catch a ride with us." They repeated the trick and laughed again.
One looked at Two, arching a big, frost-rimed eyebrow. Two blew
jets of frustrated, moist air from his nostrils. Jack and Emma,
chastened, harnessed them and set off for the Buxton homestead.

Alf and Davie were faring less well than Jack and Emma,
psychologically. One night, Davie had shown up at their door,
sullen and morose. He'd eaten supper, complained about the skilly
Alf always fed him, ignored Ostrich, and made minimal conversation, except to say that he and Alf had quarreled. Emma, worried
something awful might have happened, went to see Alf only to
discover that there had been no quarrel whatsoever. Davie had
spilled some sugar and left the house silently, Alf said. But today
in the blue-sky, white-snow landscape the boys were ebullient.
They were already breaking a path toward the Thornton home
when Jack and Emma pulled out. The Buxtons waved, calling to
them. Davie jumped down and pushed on ahead of the oxen,
arriving breathless and giddy. He wore a bandit's mask — a cloth
strip with eye slits cut — tied around his head.

"Notice anything new?" he giggled.

"Well, if it ain't Dick Turpin," Emma said.

"No! It's me, Davie," his voice was disappointed. "I'm wearing goggles — see? It's to prevent snow blindness."

"Excellent idea, Davie," said Jack. "Do they work?"

"Oh yes, tried them last week before the blizzard." He adjusted his goggles. "Are you going to Lloydminster?"

"Yes, we need coal oil, flour, meat, tea, tobacco, sugar . . . " Emma replied. "Just about everything. Though we can ill afford it."

This brought an uneasy silence. The costs of equipment and travel had far exceeded Jack's estimates based on the Barr pamphlet. Then, the prices of the necessities of life had doubled, doubled, and doubled again over the winter. Jack had announced his decision to find work with the railroad once the crop was seeded this spring. Emma knew the only way he could afford to stay at home was to spend her dowry. She'd never offered — he'd never asked. She put the thought of their separation from her mind.

"Ah well, best not dwell on costs and budgets today, eh, Em?" His eyes wrinkled and she knew he was forcing a smile under the wrap.

"Already forgotten," she said.

Alf swung past, and Jack urged One and Two into his wake.

"Ostrich coming?" Davie asked, walking ahead of One and Two to help the oxen along.

"No, he sulks inside until all the trails are broken," Emma answered. "His only joy is sniffing the manure pile. Everything else is frozen dead."

Davie ran on to break trail for his own oxen. The Buxton team laboured around the treebelt on the slough. One and Two moved more easily in the fresh-ploughed grooves. They rounded onto the Jordan house, nearly half buried in snow. No tracks disturbed the white carpet.

"Odd," Jack said. "Usually Alice has been to the barn by now to see to the horses."

Emma thought again of the night of the dance when Alice had cut the last thread to the major. They still cohabited, but she ran the homestead, occasionally goading him into sawing wood or clearing muck from the barn. Emma strained her eyes against the glittering snow.

"Line's down to the barn. Probably didn't want to risk the trip last night," she said.

"Last night, yes," Jack shook his head. "But she should have been out first thing this morning. Muck will freeze and then she'll be sorry."

"My thoughts, exactly." Neither of them laughed. "Perhaps she's ill."

They drove on silently.

"Hallo inside!" Alf called cheerfully. "Come on out — the water's fine."

No faces appeared at the frosted window. Somebody must be awake, smoke came from the stovepipe. Emma tried to settle her anxiety on the reassuring sight of the chimney. They jumped into the snow and followed the Buxtons to the door. It opened and, to Emma's great relief, Alice's smiling face urged them inside. Kitty and Mary first asked after Ostrich, then dragged Davie off to see the playhouse they had made for Mrs. Dimples.

"Take off your coats — I'll reheat the kettle. Tea or coffee?" Alice bustled about the stove, pouring water into a large, black kettle. "Looks a simply lovely day — so beautiful after the storm — thought it would never end. Nearly drove us crazy."

She paused, glanced up, and laughed. "I mean crazier than we were already."

Emma laughed in reply.

"So is it to be tea or coffee?"

"Ta, Mrs. Jordan, but we were going to make trail to Lloydminster today and it could be a long slog, so we'd best skip the hospitality and be off," Alf explained.

"Why, Alf, Lloydminster is the other direction. " Alice looked steadily at him.

"Thought we might pick up some supplies for you," Emma said. "And offer the major a ride — so he could catch up on committee work."

"You mean so he could spend half our money on liquor and get drunk, don't you, Emma?"

Alice delivered this line with such cool, offhand frankness that Emma couldn't be certain she'd heard correctly. She looked to Jack. He'd stripped off scarf and hat and his face was bright red, but not from the cold. Alice was no longer playing the game, and Emma had nothing more to say than her embarrassed husband. Alf saved the moment. He strode to the curtain that divided off the bedroom and drew it back. "Let's ask the man himself. Major, are you up for a trip to town?"

The bed was neatly made. The tiny room was empty. Alf turned, puzzled. "Where is he?"

"Gone," Alice replied simply.

"Not to town on his own, surely!" Jack found his voice. "Not in the blizzard."

"No, not even he would attempt anything so foolish." Alice smiled.

"Then he left before the blizzard?" Alf prompted.

"Couldn't have," Jack interrupted. "His horses are knackered. He'd never have tried for town with them, even before the storm."

"I've not said he went to town," Alice snapped. "Really. It's quite simple. He's gone."

The men fell silent, baffled. Emma pulled off her hat and mitts, crossed the room, and sat Alice in a chair. She sat opposite her, held her hands across the tabletop, and looked into her unblinking eyes.

"Gone outside, Alice?"

"Yes, as I said, quite simple."

"But there are no tracks outside," Jack started but Emma stifled him with a quick look.

"When did he go out, Alice?"

"Last night, about seven or eight o'clock."

"In the storm?"

"Yes."

"Whyever for?" Emma squeezed Alice's trembling hands. Alice's voice quavered, now, but her eyes were dry and steady.

"Well, I fed and mucked out the horses yesterday morning. Then I melted snow for cooking and drinking because the well cover is frozen over. Then I got all the meals and, after supper, I went outside and bucked wood 'til dark. The girls helped me bring it in — played a game, didn't we?"

"Yes, Mama. We built a house for Mrs. Dimples out of the wood," Mary piped up. She knelt beside Davie but his attention was riveted to Alice. They were all held rapt to her narrative.

"Anyway, I was exhausted and cold from cutting wood in the blizzard. Major Jordan had spent the morning reading and the afternoon drinking the last of his brandy. I asked him to go check the horses. He ignored me at first and I'm afraid I lost my temper — storm and all — I suppose frays one's nerves." She smiled apologetically to have revealed such domestic intimacies before guests.

"We had rather a fierce row that ended with him going to the barn. Like I said, gone about eight o'clock, I should think."

"Father must have spent the night in the barn," Mary explained. "Mamma took the lamp out of the window after he went to see the horses."

Emma was weeping quietly, gripping Alice's hands. The men studied their boots, as though in silent prayer. For several, long minutes the little house was silent — even the girls sat quietly beside Davie.

"Best go find him, leave Lloydminster for another day," Jack said hoarsely. Emma intended to stay with Alice, but she began dressing in her heavy clothes.

"I'll come with you," Alice said. "Mary, Kitty, you stay here, girls."

Emma dried her eyes and followed them outside. Jack formed them into a line, each spaced an armslength apart, and they began a shuffling walk along the edge of the treeline toward the barn, a hundred yards distant. Emma's feet nearly disobeyed her, so fearful were they of treading on the major, but they made the barn without incident. They fed the horses, then shifted around and made a new line parallel to the first five snow furrows.

"We can assume he missed the barn since the safety cord was cut . . . " Jack's voice cracked in the cold air. "I mean broken. Sorry, safety twine was broken."

They stared at him, Emma tried not to think what Jack was thinking. "He likely hit the trees then realized he'd gone too far and turned around to try a back bearing to the house, but that wind was such a bitch . . . sorry. Strong wind, no light, likely lost his back trail and went out onto the open prairie. If he had a lot to drink, he won't have gone far."

He stopped talking and adjusted their aim to the open, white field that glittered beyond the house. They set off. Cold air burned Emma's nose but warmed in her dry throat. She breathed out heavily, fogging her face. Perspiration prickled under her arms and at her forehead, though her nose ached with cold. Each footstep punched through the snow released the smell of ice — odourless in England but tangible in the Saskatchewan winter. Perhaps the major could just stay out here. That might be best. Clean and icey and safe now.

Fifty paces left of, and two hundred beyond the house, Davie stumbled and went down.

"Got him," he said brusquely.

"He was damned close when he passed the house. Pity, no light in the window, " Alf muttered, plunging through the snow. "Here now, Davie, lad, come away. Mr. Thornton and I will see to Major Jordan."

Davie stood, snow caked. "I'm all right, Alf."

"I know you are, son. You get the women back to the house and fetch us a blanket, eh?"

"Lord, Alf. I'm sorry, so sorry." Alice's resolve broke. "Forgive me, Alf. Please, dear Alfred, forgive me."

She fell against Emma. Tears flowed and froze on her cheeks. Emma and Davie helped her to the house. Emma, unwisely, looked back. Jack and Alf had pried the body up, one arm frozen where it had been flung out at a right angle to the torso. The major's hat was gone. His face was clear as glass. His long, tipped moustaches, caked with ice, were perfectly lined up with the corners of his mouth — groomed just as he liked them. The men were struggling to break the outstretched arm so they could carry him without snagging it on anything.

• • •

The last patch of snow on the north side of the barn melted. The entire country ran with water, sloughs flooded, and the mud was knee-deep on the trails. Jack drove Alice to Lloydminster to bury the major. They had all travelled to town three weeks earlier for the major's funeral. The Mounted Police had done a perfunctory investigation and pronounced "death by accident or misadventure."

One of Miss Sissley's boys was missing and presumed dead in a blizzard, another young bachelor had tried to walk into town in February and, although found alive, hadn't survived. The major's accidental death was never questioned. Reverend Lloyd conducted the well-attended funeral service in Hall & Scott's store. Nobody, except Emma, wept — Alice was rather put off by the tears. The coroner had placed the body in a locked shed until the ground thawed. Alice wanted to inter her husband quietly, so Jack and Blast and Damnation were her only companions this spring day.

Emma and Ostrich and the Jordan sisters walked the higher ground, marveling at the anemones already pushing up through the wet earth, flowering impossibly-vivid colours on the cold prairie. Mary was occasionally thoughtful; Kitty's grief had been intense, but short-lived. She asked frightfully embarrassing questions about Uncle Alf or Uncle Davie, and why didn't they come to stay now? Emma had always been fond of the girls but, now, in the freshening spring, she found herself fascinated by them. For a day or two she wondered if she was broody, then she wondered if she was pregnant. She'd learned the mechanics of avoiding pregnancy in her teens, from her first illicit lover. She and Jack had, by mutual unspoken agreement, dispensed with them in the last month of bitter cold — a subconscious urge to create life in the dead, winter land. But instinct or urge were irrelevant for now. Her flags fluttered from the clothesline. Would she have a Canadian baby if the flags failed or would she insist on going home? Jack was still determined to go with Davie to work on the railroad this summer. He could earn good money with the Clydes, grading trackbeds. They would have enough acres of oats for the next full year's feed and even ten acres extra to sell to other colonists. Then next summer he'd stay home and farm full-time. They would seed the dreamed-of wheat crop and, if the railway came, they would be rich.

She could keep him this summer if she called for the dowry. But spring and little girls and new crocuses spoke strongly to her of babies. She would keep the dowry in case a baby came. It would build a proper house and give some comfort. It could even take them back to England, if that seemed right. A meadowlark bubbled its sweet call and a fresh breeze ruffled Kitty's blonde hair. Her baby, if it ever came, would be Canadian. That seemed right, today.

• • • *

"Ostrich! OOOOstrich!" Mary's voice carried over the ridge and the beagle, sniffing the fresh-turned earth behind Jack's ploughing, immediately pricked up his ears.

"Ostrich!"

He put his head down, galloped up the hill past Emma, and shot over the top, baying his welcome. A moment later the two little girls chased him back and Alice appeared, waving, smiling. She pointed to the line of flags Emma had just finished hanging. Emma shrugged.

"No baby for the month of May, then," Alice said as she drew near.

Emma led them into the house and gave each of the children a biscuit and a cup of milk. The milk came from a jug kept in a homemade ice box. She poured it nonchalantly.

"Milk and sugar with your tea, Mrs. Jordan?"

"You've got a cow!"

Emma grinned, putting the kettle on the stove. "Yes, and she's a beauty. Half-Holstein, half-Guernsey, sweet tempered and just freshening when we got her. I love her."

Then she blushed deeply — excited over a cow. "I couldn't say whether my Uncle Henry at home kept one cow, five cows, or no cow. It was a matter of total indifference to me and, now, well, I seem to be in love with one."

"I'm green with envy," Alice said. "Have you named her yet?"

"Promise not to laugh?"

"Promise."

"Buttercup."

Alice rocked with laughter. "Oh, Emma, such bold originality."

"Alice Jordan, you promised!"

They both laughed then, free and lightly, as they hadn't done in the weeks since the major's burial.

"Well, I suppose," Alice dabbed at a wet eye, "if your dog is Ostrich, your horses are Blast and Dee, and your oxen One and Two, then I suppose you need to offset the bizarre with the mundane."

"My thoughts exactly." Emma turned to get teapot and cups. "It's good to see you happy."

"Didn't feel it for a long time. Thought I'd never laugh again. Then I was afraid to; that others — Alf — might think me irretrievably callous."

"I can imagine, it must have been awful," Emma said mechanically, the words one always says.

"I doubt you can." The girls finished their treats, said thank you, and Alice shooed them outside. "If it hadn't been for those two I'd have walked into the snow instead of sending the major into it. But that's not what you meant, is it?"

Emma felt her eyes widen in surprise. Sending. Alice Jordan, murderess and tea guest. It jarred badly.

"Afterwards, in the days it took the snow to melt, in the cabin with the girls . . . it was awful, Emma. One of those nights I heard him calling — just like the Buxtons."

"Lost?" Emma felt the hairs rise on the back of her neck.

"Yes. Loud and dry like a hoarse, old man calling for his nurse. It was the major's voice — I thought — but really it was the wind."

"Jack says the wind here can speak," Emma admitted, then felt foolish, superstitious.

"I know. When Jack took me to Lloydminster for the burial in April, I thought . . . " Alice stopped, suddenly cautious.

"What? What did he say?"

Alice shook her head. "Never mind."

"Did he say something hurtful? Did he speak of the major?"

"You mean, did he ask me if I cut the safety rope and hid the lamp?" Alice smiled softly.

Emma recoiled at the frank exhumation of the truth, but nodded, nonetheless.

"He didn't. I half hoped he would, clear the air. In fact, he never spoke to me, above necessities, for the whole trip. Didn't he tell you?"

Emma shook her head. Jack, the Buxtons, and even she had quickly plastered over the incident, clinging to the police verdict of accidental death. They would have done a Belgravia society room proud; the rapidity and watertight strength of their denial had been impressive. Now, though, Alice seemed determined to wrench the major back above ground. And Emma, despite a macabre sense of impropriety, helped her.

"Jack didn't say anything, except that the major was properly interred." She hesitated, then heard herself say, "Did you? Cut the twine, hide the lamp after he left the house?"

Until the mosquitoes came, Emma liked to have the door open on fine days — she couldn't get enough of the sweet, wild air. Mary and Kitty's voices came easily into the sod house, as did Ostrich's barking. Even Jack's faint shouts to the horses were audible.

"Woot, Blast. Woot, Damnation."

Normal, real life wafted through the door on the May wind, but Emma could not accept it. She stared, hypnotized, into Alice Jordan's unblinking gaze. Alice nodded once, then rapidly looked away, breaking eye contact. She moved to the stove and poured the tea.

"Milk and sugar, how lovely. I can't tell you how much I've missed this simple pleasure."

Emma was nearly panting. She gulped down a breath and tried to back away from the brink of her next question. But she couldn't.

"Has Alf said anything — about the major or the circumstances of his death?"

Alice set the teapot on the table and resumed her eye contact with Emma.

"Alf has not spoken a single word to me beyond the strict demands of courtesy." She poured the tea. "There, I'll be mother, shall I? Just like England, home."

Emma sipped, savouring the taste, regaining her composure. "I suppose you'll be packing, soon, to go home. When do you leave?"

"Do you know it's a year today that we filed on the Newland Cooperative?" Alice asked.

"Why, no, I hadn't realized."

"Two more years and the Homestead Act regulations are met. I'll have one hundred and sixty acres," Alice continued, a spark of enthusiasm in her demeanor. "I have decided to stay, Emma. The property devolves to me as . . . widow . . . and the major's family has agreed to two more years remittances, if I stay."

"On your own? With two children? Farm this land yourself?" Emma found this almost as fantastic as their previous flirt with the major's death. "Who will break the remaining acres? The Homestead Act says you have to break and crop thirty acres."

484

"I'll learn. I was hoping Jack would teach me to plough. The Jordan family expect me to remarry or obtain title to the land within two years. After that, I'm on my own. I know I shan't likely remarry . . . "

She twisted her engagement band, tugging it half-off, then sliding it back into place, studying the diamond.

"Plenty of willing men." Emma said, "but few of your class."

"My class," Alice tapped her stubby, broken fingernails on her teacup. "My class became irrelevant a year ago when I bucked my first half-cord of wood while the major slept off his brandy."

"I suppose that's true — we've changed . . . "

"My class is irrelevant, but the damned working class seems to have kept its sense of duty," Alice continued, as though Emma hadn't spoken. "The working class saves worthless lives . . . "

She stopped, her breath came in short sniffs.

"Alf has not spoken to you," Emma paused — Alice nodded. "But you have spoken to him?"

Alice nodded again. "I know he is repelled by the lamp and the safety twine. He may never come past them. But I mean to stay and give him the chance."

They finished their tea in silence, then went outside. Below them Jack wheeled the Clydes expertly and began a new furrow. The oat field and the acres broken last year had been ploughed, disked, and harrowed, as had the garden. He would seed them next week and leave for the railway. In the meantime, he broke new ground at a frantic rate. He used One and Two from predawn until noon, then Emma fed and watered them while he took the horses out and broke sod all afternoon. She mucked the barn, milked Buttercup, and performed all the other chores to leave him free for breaking. In the evenings, they mended harness, hammered out ploughshare blades, and fussed over the animals until, staggering with exhaustion, they fell into bed.

Emma's stomach usually tightened at the thought of Jack leaving. And the knowledge that her dowry could keep him only made it worse. But not this day. She glanced at Alice's strong, brown face, and blonde hair pulled tightly back. This woman had fought one fierce battle and survived. She was going to face two years of the Saskatchewan country alone. Alice was undaunted. How could she, Emma happily-married-Thornton, cry out at the thought of a couple of months on her own? She would give Jack a Euston Station send-off — show her courage not her fear.

"Come on, then," she said slipping her arm through Alice's. "Let's see if we can get Mr. Thornton to teach you the mysteries of the breaking plough. And he'd better make pleasant conversation, by heavens, or I shall make him wish he had."

Alice squeezed her arm. Emma felt proud of her own steadfastness — smug even. Once Jack was in line, she'd see to Alf.

• • •

Despite her brave resolutions, Emma was entirely wretched for the last week of May and the first part of June 1904. The night before Jack's departure, she'd lost her nerve and said they would spend the dowry to get them through the next year. He knew she didn't really mean it and talked her out of it. Even Ostrich moped, but only for a couple of days. Jack's oats sprouted, received an inch of rain, then basked in a long string of warm, sunny days. The sight of his oat field, thirty-five acres this year, all green and thrusting upward, was nearly more than she could bear. She shouted at it sometimes — asking it why Jack wasn't here to watch it grow.

The nights, mercifully short, were the worst. She woke from a blurred dream one moonless night, uneasy and acutely alone. Seized with a half-conscious urge for companionship, she went out and climbed behind the house to the hilltop — looking for light from Alf's window. There was no light, of course. It was probably three in the morning. Her own house, invisible below her, became a frightening cave. She walked slowly down, feeling her way along the dirt wall to the door. Then, one quick look at the stars and she darted inside, fumbling in the darkness to light a candle. This she placed in the window then rushed back outside, breathing heavily. The lit window calmed her. It projected a small, yellow rectangle onto the grass and seemed to welcome her. She walked to the window and looked in, as Jack would have done had he come home tonight. She re-entered the house, started a fire, heated a kettle, and made tea. By the time she finished the drink she knew one thing. She was alone here on this empty ground. She could pine uselessly for Jack and be beaten by the Saskatchewan wilderness. Or, she could harden herself and fight back

"Right! Ostrich, come here, boy."

The dog stumbled sleepily to her.

"From now on, no blubbering over Jack. Be hard!"

He flapped his ears.

She swamped her days with toil. Housework, tending to the oxen and Buttercup, mending the corral fence, smudging the house and barn when the mosquitoes became intolerable, sawing wood, making butter — the line-up of tasks was endless and they at least tired her to the point where she slept well. Watering the vegetable garden once a week was her favourite job because it required some thought. She dug a crisscross of shallow trenches through her garden. Then she took both waterbarrels, loaded them on the stone boat, harnessed One and Two and went to Jordan Lake. Barefoot, skirts tucked up, she loaded the barrels by the pailful from the slough. Then she drove back and poured the water into her trenches. It took several trips and her entire day, but gave her immense satisfaction. There would be potatoes, carrots, and beans to spare this winter because of her irrigation system. But even those days ended badly for she had to stable One and Two and the sight of the empty Clydesdale stalls in the barn hurt. She forced herself to be cheerful whenever Alice visited — her pride would not let her do otherwise. But when Alf came to disk the sod Jack had broken, she couldn't even muster the enthusiasm to try match making.

Alf was the "man" of the cooperative. He would break and disk land on all four homesteads in equal portions until the earth became too hard to plough. He would mow hay to be split four ways, and he would start cutting oats in late August. In return, Jack's, Davie's, Blast's and Damnation's wages would be pooled and split evenly between the Buxtons and the Thorntons. Alice didn't need cash, so she would take Alf's labour and none of the summer money. It was all very sensible and logical and would see them miles ahead of most colonists by the end of the summer. But Emma was wretched, nonetheless, constantly looking for diversion. She and Alice and the girls spent two days with Mrs. Hill, which was pleasant. They picnicked on the banks of the North Saskatchewan River the day after the ice broke up. Huge pieces of grey ice, three and four feet thick, ground and crashed down the torrent.

Several icebergs had beached. A small group of Indians in European clothing industriously sawed these into cubes and packed them in straw on their two-wheeled carts. Anxious to meet her first "red Indian", Emma called to them asking their price. They replied in French and, against Mrs. Hill's advice, she walked down to the shoreline. The price was low and they cheerfully packed two large blocks into her wagon. Her schoolgirl french amused them. One of the women offered her a pipeful of tobacco which she declined and they went on their way.

"Half-breeds," Mrs. Hill said. "Treacherous bunch, always out to skin the settler and the Indian alike. Shouldn't trust them, Mrs. Thornton."

"Ten cents for a half-wagonful of ice," Emma replied. "I wish to heaven the store in Lloydminster would skin me like that."

A few days later, Emma was watering her garden and thinking of the river when the river, in a way, came to her. A serrated dark line, almost like a train, near the southeast horizon caught her eye. She climbed up the hill behind the house and picked out the tiny dark blob that was the Buxton soddie. A caravan, possibly as many as ten or twelve wagons, was proceeding up the trail toward her. Why would a freighter be coming up this trail? She unhooked One and Two, put them in the corral with some hay, and walked out to the trail. A mounted, scarlet dot rode at the head of the train. A police train? It still didn't make sense. The rider waved and spurred his horse into a canter. Constable Roberts, particularly handsome today, reined in and leapt rather theatrically down at her side, sweeping off his Stetson in a low bow.

"Constable," she extended her hand and he shook it, giving her a dazzling smile. She found herself remarking what an attractive specimen he was; then, to her horror, she found an image of her last bath night with Jack had somehow sneaked into her mind. Husband gone three weeks and she was having carnal thoughts in the presence of the first handsome man in sight! Ah, well, better a touch of lively fancy than weepy longings.

"Mrs. Thornton, delighted." He gave her hand a subtle but extra squeeze. "Bearing up well without Mr. Thornton, I hope?"

She blushed, pulled her hand free, then flushed scarlet at his contented, satyr grin. It was the greeting men used to give her after news of her bohemian behaviour leaked out into London society — but only if their own wives were not present — otherwise, there had been no greeting at all.

"Very well, Mr. Roberts. You are bringing company, I see. Freighters, are they?"

"*No!* Freighters indeed, Mrs. Thornton. This is Mr. Barr's —
well, Lloyd's, now, I suppose — second wave! The much-touted
reinforcements."

"Settlers?"

"Precisely. You've got new neighbours. Swept down on us from
Edmonton."

Emma shook her head. "You mean Saskatoon, surely."

"I do not, ma'am. These folk took the train to Edmonton.
Bought their kit, loaded on CPR barges, and came whooshing
down the North Saskatchewan River in the lap of luxury."

"No trek? No Eagle Creek?"

"Scarcely got their teams warmed up!" he cried. "They think
they've been trekking, though." He laughed, unkindly. "It's taken
this lot a day and a half to get here from Lloydminster and they're
nearly ready to quit!"

Emma found this to be quite delightful. "Why, they are green
as grass — no clue of the real hardships we have endured."

"That's the spirit, Missus." Roberts winked at her. "I'm locating
thirteen families in your township and the one east of you. I'll
depend on you to whip 'em into condition. No mollycoddling,
now."

Emma laughed. "If only Jack were here," she said. "He'd love
to see the blank squares on the map filling up. He would be their
teacher, and a good one, too."

Roberts' face betrayed a palpable disappointment at her
mention of Jack's name. Emma wondered how many women did
not blush when the constable galloped gallantly into their lonely
homesteads. How many would be glad of his company, undetected
and alone, on the vast empty land. Roberts would be a very capable
lover, she thought, like Charlie and the old civil servant. She
shivered, all her light-hearted carnality vanished.

"I plan to stop in at the Jordan place on my way back tomorrow. Terrible tragedy — her husband was a fine man."

Emma started at this. Good heavens, the man was bent on seduction. He'd fail, of course, Alice Jordan was well-experienced with men attracted to her beauty. She would see him off, wouldn't she? The policeman swung up into his saddle.

"Bad luck, Constable," she lied. "But Mrs. Jordan and her children are visiting me tomorrow evening. Perhaps we'll plan a welcome dinner for the newcomers." She stroked his horse's neck. "But rest assured that she is coping very well. I'll tell her you asked about her."

"Obliged, ma'am." He tipped his head. "Maybe I ought to take a run up there right now," he mused.

"*No!* I mean, what about your wagon train? Can't leave those green colonists on their own, can we?" She forced a nervous laugh.

"I suppose not." He turned his horse. "I shall make a point of patrolling out here next week — see how things are progressing. Good day, Mrs. Thornton."

Emma set out immediately for the Jordan homestead to inform Alice of their "plans" — just in case the North West Mounted Police decided to investigate her story. Perhaps they really should arrange a welcome feast. It might be a good chance to throw Alf and Alice together. Her depression ebbed. She gazed back at the newcomers — greenhorns.

• • •

Emma's change in mood seemed to inject her with energy. She cornered Alf and made him teach her to plough with One and Two — their old horse collars worn upside down to suit their short necks and wide shoulders. Once she learned to set the beam high enough and make sure the clevis didn't jam crooked after the pin

491

was in, well, breaking was rather good sport. One and Two were very forgiving — in fact, she really didn't have to tell them what to do. Her main task was to keep them moving. They worked so slowly compared to the Clydes that they almost seemed to go backwards. Nevertheless, she managed five hours with them each day. Reciting Jack's old arithmetic, she paced out her progress. Six miles in the five hours — eight miles of furrows was one acre — three-quarters of an acre broken on a good day. She even managed to keep the blade sharp on the old grinder in the barn. The newcomers were, by turns, embarrassed, curious, then delighted to see two English women ploughing. Alice and her horses were making twice the progress that Emma managed with One and Two, but the horses required much more muscle from the ploughman to steer and control the blade. Emma was happy to inch along behind the mild oxen.

The hours on the grassland, creating long, brown ribbons of earth allowed her to mentally organize the Dominion Day picnic and plan out assignments for Alf and Alice. She had convinced Alice that they should host a dinner dance on July first for the new colonists. Then she appealed to Alf for his help hinting, ever so subtly, that it would be a good opportunity for him to resume at least his friendship with Alice and the children. Alf balked, back up and jaw set. Emma took a different tack, one of duty. They ought to mark July first — Dominion Day — with a celebration and use it to showcase the cooperative's success to their, as yet, inept countrymen. He agreed to haul wood, collect canvas, and rig a marquee tent. The dinner dance preparations flowed smoothly, but the subplot — Alf and Alice — stalled. Emma contrived to involve Alf in some of the food preparation — cooking a mountain of bannock with Alice. And she managed to have Alice help Alf sew pieces of old, tent canvas needed for the marquee. But so far no sparks had been struck.

These thoughts preoccupied Emma as she was working her seventh acre. The land was good, only a few stones and those were relatively small. But there were occasional rocks that demanded caution. One such brute protruded just above ground level and Emma's plough tip struck it dead centre. One and Two were working with uncharacteristic speed and their power blew the plough out of the ground, launching its hardwood handles upward. Emma heard the blade clang and, simultaneously, a pop, like a coconut being struck. Her head shot back and the sky described a parabola before her eyes. Horizon, then a huge, blue bowl revolving slowly over her, then the opposite horizon, then her face planted in unploughed grass. She blinked for a long moment.

When she opened her eyes, she was surprised to find green shoots, an old crocus bud, and the petals from a tiger lily plastered to her face. They smelled wonderfully, like perfume, and she was quite content to lie on the grass, although she wasn't sure why, or how, she'd got there. Her neck and back tingled, fuzzy and warm.

Ploughing! Of course. She had been ploughing, then what . . . decided to lie down for a rest? How odd. She sat up, but couldn't. Her mind gave the order but her body was being completely insubordinate. She decided at least to rise up on one elbow. Her right arm obeyed, finally, and twitched under her ribs, but it wasn't sufficiently strong to lift her limp body. She licked a bit of grass off her lips. Ostrich trotted into her field of view and began sniffing her skirt.

"Ostrich." A bright pain shot down her jawbone and zipped like a lightning strike along her neck. She tried to call again but the pain forestalled her. "Ost . . . "

The little hound stuck his nose in her eye and snuffled at her ear. He licked her face until it was thoroughly clean. Then he sat and howled, whining and high. The sky was brassy, dull from a setting sun. It had been near noon when she'd been ploughing. She must have been unconscious — several hours, likely — and no possible explanation came to mind. Her brain was clear now and she tried to fight back an encroaching panic. She couldn't lie out here all night. Ostrich's yowl brought coyotes to mind — they would scavenge her — eat her alive. God, no, stop thinking like that. She moved her head painfully. The sun was low in the west and the day breeze was waning. A mosquito landed on her forehead. She brushed it away with her good hand — the other was still tingling and weak. Mosquitoes would eat her alive — then the coyotes.

The Dominion Day festival was two days off. Alf and Alice were due early tomorrow to make the final preparations. Neither of them would come by tonight — that was almost certain. The idea that Ostrich might somehow be convinced to run for help was quickly rejected. He was, even now, trying to curl up on her belly for a nap. She had two options, then. One, lie here for the mosquitoes and scavengers; two, get up regardless of pain and walk the four hundred yards to the house. Mind now under control, she found all her limbs responded — with varying degrees of pain and efficiency. She rolled onto her stomach, dumping Ostrich — pain, but not agony. She placed her hands under her shoulders like an athlete doing push ups, took a deep breath and heaved up.

Agony.

Pain, like the thick frostbite needle, gouged her back and neck, but she was standing. The ground tilted beneath her. Terrified of going down, she lurched forward into a stumbling run. The deep, fresh-cut furrows slapped her feet. She swayed and jerked, stars bursting before her eyes. Her stomach rebelled at the sawing hurt and it vomited. She fell, unable to avoid landing in her own mess. The pain didn't diminish. Angry now, she threw herself to her feet and ran for the house. Two more falls. Two more runs. Then she passed out on her bed.

It was dark, therefore the middle of the short, summer night. Mosquito bites covered Emma's face like measles, her lips were swollen from them. She sat up stiff, sporting an almighty, great headache, but otherwise fit. She closed the door, started a small fire in the stove, and put green twigs and leaves on it. Smoke billowed from the Aga firedoor while she washed her face and stripped off her stinking blouse. She rooted a piece of ice from the cellar under the floorboards and carefully slid it into her mouth to ease her burning jaw. Then she doused the fire and fell into a deep sleep.

• • •

"Have you checked the house?" Alf's worried voice roused Emma.

"No, I've just this minute arrived," Alice was shouting. "What are you doing out there with One and Two?"

"Found them here!" Alf's voice drew near. "They were harnessed to the plough. It was caught in the poplar brush — they must have dragged it there. No sign of Emma."

"What can have happened?"

"I don't know, but I'm worried, Alice," he checked for a moment, "Mrs. Jordan. Something is gone wrong here."

"She must have been breaking, south of the oat field," Alice's voice began to fade. "Do you suppose she's out there, hurt? I'm going to look for her."

"Wait for me," Alf said.

"Alice! Alf! Here, I'm alive and breathing."

They turned. Alf let the oxen go and they immediately began to lumber toward the young oats.

"Alf!"

He picked up the lines and steered them to the house. Emma slipped back in and threw a wrap over her shoulders. Outside, the chastened oxen stared curiously at her, but no more so than the two humans.

"Cor, it's the bloomin' plague," Alf said, removing his burnt-brim bowler deferentially. Alice elbowed him. Then she drew close and touched her fingertips gently to Emma's chin.

"Whatever have you been up to, Mrs. Thornton?"

"I wish I knew," Emma clawed at the bites around her hairline. "These are mosquitoes — left the door open last night. Not the plague, thank you very much, Alf."

"But your face! It looks like somebody landed you a right good punch on the chops," Alf said.

"I know, hurts to talk. And I haven't any idea how it happened." Emma recited her story. Ploughing one minute, reviving some hours later with a concussion but no explanation for the intervening time. They chivvied her back inside. Alf tended to One and Two, then retrieved the plough. One glance at the dented shareblade and a visit to the field told the story of Emma's injury. They put Emma to bed, prepared tea and toast, and washed her blouse. Alf chipped ice, wrapped it in some oilcloth, and packed it into two of Jack's wool socks. These nestled on either side of her face as she lay propped up in the bed, feeling actually much better than she let on. Alice and Alf bustled about cheerfully, exchanging small talk, working instinctively as a team. Sparks, at last, Emma thought. Now to fan the flames ever so gently.

"You, two, may have to host my party tomorrow. I shan't be up to the mark, fully." She said this gamely, gallantly, but with just enough warble in her voice that she wouldn't lose their sympathy.

"We'll simply cancel," Alice said.

"You're staying in bed for at least another day." Alf felt her forehead. "No fever, thank God."

"Can't cancel." Emma played her trump card. "You'd have to ride all day in every direction to tell the neighbours. Besides, we would waste all that food and Oliver Hill is coming from Lloydminster with another violinist and a man who plays the squeezebox. Can't have them make . . . "

"All right." Alf capitulated with a furtive glance in Alice's direction. "There's no way out."

Alice looked Alf fully in the eye. "We will have to do this together. What say you, Mr. Buxton?"

Alf smiled awkwardly. He did not refute the "we". Aching from stem to crown, jaw hot enough to melt the ice in Jack's socks, and tormented by her itching face, Emma enjoyed a surge of satisfaction. The Newland Cooperative would be restored to working order.

• • •

They began arriving in the late afternoon. The ladies were the best or, at least, the most prominent. Beautiful, wide hats with silk ribbons and flowers. There were velvet dresses of blue, red, and mauve, with lace shoulder caps. The majority wore long skirts with high-neck, pleated blouses and smart, cotton jackets with large puffed shoulders. A few only managed skirt and blouse — but best skirt and blouse of lace with throat brooches and pins. Every man wore a suit of some kind with collar and tie, some wore high boots and breeches. The children were miniatures of the parents, even a couple of little boys in bowler hats. They parked their wagons and buggies near the oat field fence or beside the barn and corral. One and Two watched nervously for a while then, shy of all the company, retreated to the barn. The line of vehicles and animals recalled something to Emma, but she couldn't retrieve a specific memory. The visitors drifted toward the marquee. The old, bell tent canvas cracked in the wind, twitching the ridge pole and guy ropes. Alf had performed a miracle with crooked, poplar logs to form the ridge and main posts. He even had two Union Jacks snapping from either end of the ridge.

Emma's kitchen table held the teapots and cups. Emma was allowed to sit here preparing and dispensing tea. Alf ran her the boiling water as needed. At a right angle to the tea table Alice presided over a long trestle laid on sawhorses. The trestle was, in fact, a door from the Buxton house, scrubbed and covered with a white oilcloth. It was loaded with platters of sliced beef, goose, and bacon. Mounds of sweet bannock and bread lay beside crocks of butter, courtesy of Buttercup and several long, churning sessions. Tinned jam had been ladled into china bowls on the theory that nobody would be rude enough to comment on its freshness if it was served from china. Emma, still battered and bumpy of face, was thrilled with the picnic. Alf had even scythed down a patch of grass near the tent, arranging chairs and smooth logs along two sides for the dance later. Every brown-eyed Susan, wild rose, goldenrod, and tiger lily within a half-mile radius had been picked and tied into bouquets by Alice and her girls. Emma shook hands, memorized names, dispensed tea, explained her face injuries, and found she could not stop smiling. The wind was annoying, but it killed the dreaded mosquito threat and it was a fresh northwest breeze, flying under a blue sky. Alice, dressed to rival the best ladies present, was stunning. Kitty and Mary were perfect as her assistants. Alf, throttled in collar and tie, was master of every crisis, from spilled milk to a wandering team and wagon.

The Davis and Armstrong families were the last to arrive. The Davis parents, in their forties, with two grown boys and a young daughter, had settled on the quarter southwest of the Buxtons, Section Two. Adjacent to them were the Armstrongs, roughly the same age as Emma and Jack, with a boy toddler and a baby girl ten months old. The Davis family spread a blanket on a corner of the grass dance floor, some distance from where most of the families were picnicking. Margie Armstrong pitched camp with the rest of the guests while Len Armstrong fetched two large, wicker baskets to the Davis group. He unpacked dishes and cups, even a small vase, then carried a trayful of cups to the marquee. Emma introduced herself, poured tea, and felt an earlier memory pushing into her mind. Len was just leaving Alice's table when a high voice called him.

"Armstrong! I say Armstrong, don't forget the flowers."

He wheeled back into the marquee but Alice came to his rescue.

"Here, Mary. Take this pitcher of water and that bouquet. Follow Mr. Armstrong."

Len smiled his gratitude and led Mary back to the Davis party.

"Tintern Abbey," Emma said.

"Pardon me?"

"Sorry. A reminiscence has been nagging me since the first guests arrived. This reminds me of a picnic we took to Tintern Abbey. So English and . . . I don't know."

"Sounds lovely." Alice removed her pinny and crossed the empty tent for a cup of tea. "How I miss home at times like this. It must have been a wonderful day for you and Jack, early in your love. Did he recite any of Wordsworth's poetry for you?"

"Yes, he did, but not quite as you're imagining."

"I'm imagining a very romantic and private recitation. What other kind could there be?" Alice smiled quizzically.

"Jack did recite some Wordsworth, but it wasn't really his place to do so. Imagine Armstrong reciting poetry to Mrs. Davis, if you will," Emma said, scratching viciously at her half-healed bites. "Not really a pleasant memory at all, although I never thought much about it at the time. Thornton seemed so natural to me then. He wasn't Jack at all."

"Like Buxton. The major and I referred to Alf and Davie as servants, they referred to us as master and mistress." Alice gazed out over the happy, chattering picnic. "It was normal, natural to all of us. But we have changed this last year. Scarcely know who I was in Essex."

The thought was like a suddenly-ringing alarm clock, waking Emma from a sound sleep. She had changed. Little by little, the tiny insanities she and Alice joked about had altered her. Old England still survived in Lloydminster. Committee — merchants — workers — and the unfortunates scraping by on charity. The descending class structure survived with all the correct titles and normal behaviour. Witness the cold reception in the Christmas choir. But out on the homesteads the wilderness crushed such structure ruthlessly. Those lacking were cast out. The major had been cast out. She looked anew at Alice. Of course Alice would stay on. How could that have been a surprise? Emma remembered her thought that Alice was staying for Alf and Alf alone. How wrong she had been.

"Shall we attend to our duties as hostesses?"

"Yes," Emma said. "Mingle rich man, poor man, beggar man, thief. It's all one now."

"So it is."

Taking teacups they strolled out to their guests. Counting the Hills and Bowens there were ten families in attendance. Of the eight newcomers none, save the Davis clan, had any farming experience — the Davis' having actually left a farm in Devonshire to come to Canada. Alf and Mr. Bowen were the lions of the day — every new man sought their advice on breaking, house construction, well digging, hay, and a thousand other topics. They were stubbornly refusing advice from Canadian or European settlers, but they were eager to hear from Englishmen. "Englishmen of muscle with plenty of hustle," Emma thought. Alice and Emma were nearly as popular with the women, although two of the ladies quickly made it plain that they disapproved of any of their sex actually performing farm labour. Emma's face, grotesquely bruised black and yellow up to her angry red strip of mosquito bites, caused several averted gazes. A slender, Norfolk woman went so far as to imply that it served her right for ploughing. But the others, including Mrs. Davis, seemed heartened by Emma's pluck and success. She motioned Emma and Alice to her side.

"We've come to stay," Mrs. Davis declared proudly. "We've filed on three quarters. Imagine, four hundred and eighty acres, just for showing up — splendid land, too. We've heard the stories, harsh climate, hard work, uncertain return, but we wanted rid of county tax and transport tax and road tax and lease payments and such that were ruinous to gentle farmers at home. The hardships will be acceptable in return, and they are mostly exaggerated, I should think."

"Well, you've come to the right place for hard work and hardship," Emma replied. "My husband is entranced by the idea of free land. I sometimes wonder if he notices the hardship."

Her own words cast a shadow on her enjoyment of the day. Jack should be here. He should be the one lionized by the newcomers. She could not suppress a longing for Jack to see her bruised face and make it better.

"Aye, well," Mrs. Davis nudged her. "You and he have done wonders in a year. It looks almost a proper farm. You've found your house to be comfortable in the bad weather?"

Emma gestured to the soddie. "Yes, that's it, on the hill. It's cool in the summer and warm in the winter and cheap."

Mrs. Davis stared past the marquee. "Hill? I'm sorry, dear, I can't see it. Where is it from that barn there on the rise, beyond the trees?"

Emma and Alice exchanged suppressed grins. Mrs. Davis coloured.

"I say, that is your hill, I suppose. And, oh, I am sorry. The earthen . . . structure, is your house?"

Emma touched her sleeve. "Please, don't worry about it. I thought the exact same thing a year ago. Never realized I was on the top of a hill until Jack told me. And I positively rebelled against the sod house."

"It does take some getting used to," Alice chimed in. "Bumps become hills, sloughs are turned into lakes, yet the truly significant features of this landscape are often understated."

"For example?"

"Well," Alice touched Emma's face, "the mosquitoes can be horrendous. So far we've been relatively lucky this year, a bit drier . . . "

"They can be worse?" Mrs. Davis lost her tearoom composure for a moment.

"Much," Alice said firmly. "And the old Nor'Westers told us funny stories of the winter. We took them to be tall tales but, in fact, they were understated."

"Yes, one hears much about the winter." Mrs. Davis sipped her tea. "The Bowen woman mentioned that two men nearly died walking home from a social. And then she became rather tedious, going on and on, in great, salacious detail, about another colonist — no name — who died not one hundred yards from his own house. Wife somehow complicit, locked the poor fellow out in a blizzard, gone half doolali from the isolation." She sniffed. "Didn't believe half of it myself. Ridiculous, wife locking her husband out."

Emma, stunned with awkward indecision, simply stared at Davis, a smile frozen on her face.

"Some truth in the tales," Alice said calmly. "Mr. Buxton, there, and his brother were the two who nearly perished. The other story, tragically, did end in a blizzard death." Alice gently took Mrs. Davis' cup from her. "But Mrs. Bowen has made free with the details of the death. Nobody knows the full story and we all go a little crazy from the isolation. More tea, ma'am?"

Alice sailed off placidly to the tent without waiting for a reply.

"Lovely woman," Mrs. Davis murmured. "Absolute shame how she bobbed her girls' hair. Don't care how much trouble long hair is, little girls should look like girls, not boys."

"If you'll excuse me," Emma finally unlocked her tongue. "I will just see to the musicians. We shall start the dance at seven, before the light is gone."

"Of course, dear. Could you ask Mr. Buxton to attend me. I want to hear of his narrow escape from the snow."

Emma fled, coward that she was, she couldn't bring herself to tell Mrs. Davis about the major. Alf was more than happy to see the grand lady. He laughed when Emma told him to introduce himself as Mister Buxton.

"But I am Mister Buxton! Alf, the Stepney butcher boy, is gone . . . God knows where to . . . but he's gone. Did I tell you, I'm buying four heifers next week? Found four dandies at Paynton's — two for us, and two for Jack . . . you. The Buxton Land and Cattle Company is about to be born!"

He winked hugely and straightened his tie.

"Orf ve goes now, luvvie. Dasn't kip the guvnor and 'is laydee a vaitin. I don't fink."

Alf and Alice would shed the old disdain as easily as the geese ran slough water off their backs. Emma did not feel as strong yet. But Mrs. Davis' opinion certainly mattered much less to her than the depth of her vegetable cellar, of that Emma was confident. She caught Oliver Hill's eye and motioned like a violinist.

The wind died to a sighing breeze as the sun began its long descent toward the western horizon. The fiddlers and accordionist began with a waltz — which was promptly boycotted by the shy newcomers. As the music began to falter, Alf strode to the centre of the grass "ballroom" and halted. He bowed deeply from the waist and extended one hand toward Alice, standing with a knot of women beside the musicians. Alice glided onto the "floor" and slipped into his arms.

Emma held her breath. Alf Buxton could not waltz to save his life. Yet they did, Alice clearly leading. They whirled, smoothly, down the length of the scythed lawn. Erect, handsome, eyes locked on one another — a striking couple. Slanting sunlight cast their shadows long and elegantly behind them. Mrs. Davis stood up. She spoke a sharp word to her oldest son who leapt to his feet. Then they danced. The floodgates opened and Emma's party was a success. Mosquitoes arrived with the dying wind and threatened disaster, but Constable Roberts galloped up — scarlet and dramatic and an hour late — with Emma's special request. He brought a role of muslin which the ladies cut to wrap around their hats and over their faces. The men lit their pipes and the dance continued despite the onslaught of bugs. The constable was amply rewarded for his dash by being the most sought-after partner. One new colonist, the Norfolk man, even had a brief exchange of hard words with his wife over her unseemly pursuit of the North West Mounted.

A fire was lit in the centre of the dance floor to extend the fading sunlight. Couples polkaed, waltzed, or swept in linked-arm reels around the fire. The men looked comical, puffing their pipes as they leapt and dipped, like overgrown leprechauns from an Irish folktale. The women were eerie, faceless, swathed in white muslin that flashed pink and red in the flames. Emma shivered at the sight, half expecting the major with his frozen white moustaches to arrive, hoarse-voiced and drunk. Then Alf whipped her away to a dangerously athletic polka that shot great pains up her neck and face. She bore it stoically. Concussion or not, she was still an English hostess and she would do her duty. The Saskatchewan Territory couldn't have its way all the time.

After the last possible glimmer of light was danced into darkness the new settlers made their uncertain way home. Emma slept well and dreamed of her husband and two new heifers.

• • •

The hay was mown and some of it stacked. They would rake and retrieve the rest when Jack and Davie came home. But Alf didn't want the animals on it, so the cows were expected to graze elsewhere until winter. The best, uncut grass was on the quarter section south of the Thorntons and today had been Emma's turn to herd them. She made her way home in late afternoon, mindful of the sleek pounds the heifers had gained and of the warm, early September sun on her back. The oat field was high, thick, and silver-headed, drooping with its own weight. Prosperous. Prosperous was the unlikely word in her thoughts. She rounded the barn and called hello to One and Two, resting in the corral. A lean Clydesdale snuffled at her over the fence rail and a second one whinnied loudly at the sight of her.

She stopped, staring at them in wonder.

"Blast and Damnation!" she cried. "It's over! I've made it!"

She ran for the house, burst through the door, and found herself alone. The zinc tub sat before the stove, a few inches of water in it. The kettle and a large saucepan sat atop the stove, heating more water. Footsteps sounded behind her and Jack stepped through the door, a pail in each hand, Ostrich sniffing frantically at his knees. He set the buckets down, took a single stride and tripped, knocking one over, flooding the floor.

"Damn my eyes!"

He bent to retrieve the bucket and hit his head on the corner of the table.

"Double damn my eyes!"

He stood upright, holding a small cut on his forehead. His grin was lopsided, foolish, and his eyes were unblinking, on hers.

"Jack Thornton. Whatever is wrong with you?"

"Chelsea morning room all over again, Holmes." He pointed at her. "Those green rascals still take my breath away."

"Jack." She walked forward and slipped into him. "You do say the loveliest things."

They bathed that night. Emma was shocked at the sight of his ribs sticking through his skin, then warmed by the realization that she would fatten him, like the heifers.

"You've broken eight more acres," Jack said sleepily. "What a wonder you are. We'll get the binder going on the oats in the morning."

Then they both slept. Tomorrow was harvest, with frost perhaps only days away.

CHAPTER 25

Jack chewed the pencil stub thoughtfully, then rose from the table, paced to the window, and looked out at the April rain. It was the first big rain of 1905. A lump of mud the size of tuppence released its last grip on the ceiling pole and fell with a plop on the table, splattering the paper. Emma wiped it clean and pretended to frown as she read it.

"Like Waterloo," Jack said thoughtfully.

"You mean a fierce battle? I should hardly think so . . . "

"No, Em. The Duke of Wellington said about the battle — a near-run thing."

"Did he really say that? I always thought he trounced Bonaparte."

"Near-run thing. Waterloo and the Newland Estate financial position."

He returned to the table, tapping the paper with his finger. "What do you think, Em? Honestly."

She smoothed her cardigan down over her mightily-extended abdomen and rested the paper on it as though it was a small escritoire. Nearly seven months pregnant was awfully difficult to manage in a small, dirt home, but there were compensations.

"Don't sweeten it, now," Jack urged.

How many men wanted their wife's honest opinion on anything — much less a serious money matter? And if they got it — how many would actually take heed of it? She consulted the page again. It was divided in half. On the left was written INcoming and on the right, OUTgoing. Under IN Jack had listed the money left from his railway work last summer, the money still owed from the Davis' for the last of the oats they had bought, and the projected revenue from the sale of eight hundred and twenty-five bushels of wheat to be grown on thirty-three acres this summer at twenty-five bushels to the acre. In parenthesis was noted twenty acres oats equals eight hundred bushels for horses and cattle. On the OUT side he listed their monthly living expenses, farm supplies, payments on equipment, and an estimate for incidentals over the coming year. The difference between IN over OUT was not large, but comfortable. Was it sufficient to construct a house, was the question before her.

"I'd say, *if* the wheat crop is successful, then we can build our house. But I'm not sure we should."

He reached across the table, patted their growing baby and smiled.

"This place will be two years old in October. It's done well, but poles and tarpaper aren't enough anymore. Another blob of watery mud hit the floor. "Can't have a baby in a soddie. Besides, it's two years today since I landed at New Brunswick. We should have a proper house. But a proper house might break us. Damned close this is."

"Let's sleep on it," she said, trying to be serious. "And if we both still feel the same way tomorrow morning — then we should go to Lloydminster and order the lumber."

"Agreed. We can have it framed and roofed before seeding starts, if everyone in the district will give us a couple of days labour."

"Of course, they will. And Davie will supervise to see it's done properly." She had to bite her tongue to suppress a giggle.

"What is it? Got a mosquito in your knickers?"

"Oh, just baby, I expect, broody."

Jack left to do his chores in the barn, Ostrich went along. Emma opened her letter from England, received two weeks prior, without Jack's knowledge. She laughed out loud and carefully tucked it back in the bottom of the trunk. Tomorrow Jack would find his lumber had been ordered long ago, delivery only days off. Wait until he met the delivery agent. She laughed again and hugged herself.

• • •

Eight miles out from Lloydminster they encountered three wagons nearly mired in a spring mudhole. The drivers were just managing forward motion. Each wagon, stripped of its box, had long, two-inch-thick barge planks piled high on their straining frames. A wiry, late middle-aged man walked briskly on the grass at the verge of the muddy trail. He had green written all over him. Tweed trousers and jacket, light boots, puttees, homberg hat, and walking stick. Even a bow tie and collar.

"Jack and Emma Thornton," he called, waving his stick. "Thank God for fine weather. Let us build a house!"

Emma, desperately excited though she was to greet her uncle, kept her eyes on Jack's face. He did not disappoint her.

"Well, damn me to hell and look at that," he said, a croak in his voice. "Vicar — Uncle — Henry Wilson on the Saskatchewan plains. By Christ, the old son of a bitch is a sight to see."

"Jack! Railway language, please!"

"Sorry, Em." He whipped the team up, laughing and wiping a tear from the corner of his eye. Emma blubbered uncontrollably. Must be the baby, her emotions were all over the shop.

• • •

Vicar Henry Wilson was like a perpetually-opened bottle of very fine whiskey. His company was warming, his attitude uplifting, and his zest for the new world was positively intoxicating. He brought letters and news and even photographs from England. Jack's mother and Vi posed amid the flowers at Offa's Rose; Mrs. Toomey displayed a cake; Charlie outside the Ostrich, pipe and pint to hand. Emma felt a homesick yearning tug from the photographs, but it disappeared once they were set upon a shelf along with her one silver bowl. Good things from England, but not home so much anymore. Uncle Henry was more interested in their farming venture than in transporting news. He explored every corner of the one hundred sixty acres. He cast a critical eye over the animals, badgered Davie with a thousand questions on the construction of sod buildings, and continually raved about the soil conditions.

"Not what I expected, niece! Not at all!" he crowed with delight at each new discovery. "Ingenious, Master Davie, devilish clever of you." Davie wallowed in the praise. "Knew you had it in your blood, Jack. I *knew* it from the moment you first picked up a scythe." Jack glowed.

He told everyone who would listen about his adventurous ride down the North Saskatchewan River from Edmonton. On Emma's instruction he'd cashed one-quarter of her dowry and taken boat and train to Edmonton. There he hired a carpenter and bought the very first supply barge of the spring. Dodging ice flows, rocks, and rapids, he'd seen it safe to the landing, hired Lloydminster teams, supervised the dismantling of the barge, and marched on the Thornton homestead. The carpenter, a taciturn man named Cross, brought his own tent for accommodation. Emma suspected he tented alone in order to gain at least a few moments of privacy and peace from Uncle Henry's constant, sometimes shrill, supervision.

The plan for the house was on a much-creased and stained piece of paper, sketched in Hampstead by two excited, young newlyweds. Emma scarcely recalled the couple she and Jack had been, but she had never lost hold of the home they had designed. When Henry showed the paper to Jack and explained about the dowry, Jack turned wordlessly and marched to the barn. Emma and her uncle drank a nervous cup of tea, certain they had offended Jack, but not knowing exactly how. The lack of consultation? Damaged ego — the captain of the Newland Cooperative not even consulted about his own home? None of these fit Jack. A half-hour later the oxen plodded up to the house. They pulled the stoneboat on which rested one very large rock. Jack stood on the boat, reins in hand, grinning like a cat — clearly not offended. Emma, relieved, looked to Uncle Henry. He merely arched his eyebrows and shrugged.

"Surely you recognize it?" Jack said, patting the miniature boulder.

"Recognize it? I should say not," she replied.

"Vicar, look here." Jack ran his hand along a deep gouge in the stone surface. "What do you suppose made that?"

"Crowbar?"

"No. Your niece! She drove a breaking plough into this very piece of granite, at One and Two's top speed, I might add. She nearly split both plough and her jaw in two."

Emma then had to relate the entire story to her uncle who vacillated between laughter and wincing concern over her injuries.

"But I'm still mystified by its sudden presence here." She stroked One's nose. "Why did you force One and Two to haul the beastly thing all the way up the hill?"

"Got it!" Henry snapped his fingers.

Emma shook her head, not with either of the men.

"Cornerstone for the new house. Am I right, Jack?"

Jack nodded.

"Davie and I will dig the foundation and cellar holes, starting tomorrow. This is the first stone in." Jack beamed at her. "If Lady Thornton will grace us with her presence, she can lay the cornerstone. Well, perhaps not lay it, but she can preside over the ceremony at least."

"You men, for heaven's sake." Emma stroked her waistline. "I carry this weight every minute of every day. I'll toss yon pebble in the hole if you like. Just call me when I'm wanted."

Over the next week, Jack and Davie dug holes and hauled stones from the rock pile. The carpenter measured, laid out string guides, and precut the heavy barge planks for the frame. Uncle Henry drove the oxen with the stoneboat, but that scarcely occupied his day. Each afternoon, when she sensed carpenter Cross had suffered all the supervision he could withstand, Emma would insist that she needed her uncle's help with house or barn chores. The former he bore with good grace, the latter he soon laid claim to as his own domain. The animals had never been better tended nor the barn cleaner. On Reverend Lloyd's sufferance, Vicar Wilson conducted Sunday church services in the large Davis home. He charmed the elder Davis' clean out of their socks, and his first Sunday preached on Christ's disciples carrying the Word to foreign lands —religious pioneers. The carpenter had laid out his framing; the foundations were prepared; and the subfloor installed. Davie had been promoted by an impressed Mr. Cross to "second carpenter" on the project, demoting the Vicar. For an uncharacteristic afternoon Henry Wilson moped, then appointed himself chief contractor and cheered up.

On a cold, bright day in late April, the Vicar's congregation turned out at the Thornton Hill. The men, tools slung from their belts like warriors, swarmed over the building site, quickly sorting into platoons commanded by Cross, Davie and the Vicar. Emma and Alice reprised their cooking feat of the previous summer and prepared all the food they could muster — bread — cold and hot beef — bacon — potatoes — pies and an ocean of tea. District wives contributed buns, jam, butter, and sweets.

The framing flew up. Cross was hard pressed to keep up with the rafter crew while the Vicar's team closed the open framing like magic. Davie and his small band of talented men cut and installed door and window frames more slowly, but even they were pitching shingles up to the roofers by mid afternoon. Cross and Davie were fitting windows and doors when the stove and pipe were shifted from the soddie to the new house. The overly enthusiastic crew even tried to move all the furniture from the soddie before an exasperated Mr. Cross made them move it back. He couldn't finish the interior walls with furniture in the way. At this point, the entire gang quit work, gorged themselves on the remaining food, miraculously produced several pails of beer, and packed into the new house. They lit every candle and lamp the Thorntons owned and proceeded to test the new floor. Oliver Hill fiddled, the colonists danced, and Emma, without knowing why, returned to her dark sod house.

She was only twenty-four years old yet she felt like a grandma, rather than an expectant mother. The sounds of laughing, dancing, voices from next door bounced off the sod walls. Emma sat on the bed and ran her hand across the mud-plastered wall. Cool, smooth, and barely cracked. Her wall, only two years old yet already stepping back into her past. A house might stand for a dozen lifetimes in England. Her soddie was a lifetime gone in twenty months. She touched her chin, her scarred ear, and felt the skin of her fingers, permanently roughed and creased from frostbite. A wave of melancholy lapped at her and she was startled by the tears that slid down her cheeks.

"Sod and sticks and tarpaper, Em." Jack stood in the open door. His body blocked the moonlight making the soddie quite black inside. "That's all it is."

"I know, but it was our sod and sticks and tarpaper."

He crossed the room and sat beside her. His arm circled her shoulder. She shifted the baby and leaned against him. He touched her head gently and she laid it on his shoulder.

"Why am I crying over a dirt house when I have a lovely new home built by the best people in the world?"

He stroked her face, carefully winding a loose strand of hair behind her ear.

"Why not? It's where we blazed our trail."

She smiled and sniffed loudly. "Yes. Anyone can live in a warm, spacious house built and finished by a carpenter. But only trailblazers could thrive in a dirt home built with their own hands."

"That's the way I see it. We were first here and this little soddie — awful place that it undoubtedly is — was first. We should be crying like babies at the thought of leaving it."

She laughed and punched him in the ribs.

"Two against one, not fair."

"Let's go watch them dance," she said, anxious now to rid herself of the melancholy. "Uncle Henry waltzes like an angel."

"Cuts hay like an angel, too," Jack said thoughtfully. "I wonder if he can do anything about Alice and Alf?"

• • •

A solid week of sunny, windy days put the homesteaders into their fields. Vicar Wilson immediately lost interest in the house construction, abandoning a much-relieved carpenter Cross to the interior finishing work and the verandah. Jack was relegated to disking with One and Two while his uncle-in-law ploughed behind the Clydes. Henry called to Blast and Damnation like a "man with the bark still on." Despite the best will in the world, his body gave out on the fourth day of ploughing and he was forced to retire to the house with a puffy knee and twitching back.

"If only this had come twenty years ago, niece. Just think of the work I could do here — spiritual and agricultural — if I were a young man."

Emma consoled him while he lamented his bad luck and advancing age. She reminded him of his achievements with the Foresters at home, both spiritually and agriculturally, and he eventually brightened. He was looking forward to summer and harvest, but agreed it was wise that his leave ended before the Canadian winter arrived. Which led to the story of the major's death.

"Tragic," Henry mused. "Him dead and gone, but in a way, so is she. No hope of her actually marrying the wayward Alf Buxton, then?"

"There is hope, Uncle." She shifted herself to the door and spied Mr. Cross measuring an angle on the veranda. "And since we're alone for the moment, I have a proposition for you."

"Not matchmaking, Emma! I'm liberal — more liberal than most — but I'll not discredit my collar by manipulating — "

"No, Uncle Henry, of course not." Emma heaved herself back onto a chair, the baby walloping her for the ups and downs.

"I say! Little squib must be kicking like a donkey — I saw that!" Henry blushed. "Excuse me, dear. I shouldn't be making such intimate comments, but heavens, I've never seen the like before."

Emma breathed deeply and her passenger calmed down. "As I was saying, there is no need, the match is made. It was made two years ago on the trek out here."

"Oh. Like that, was it? Mmmm. I didn't realize there had been impropriety before the major's accident."

"No impropriety." Emma found her patience these days was either endless or extremely brief. Her uncle was treading on the latter. "There was nothing outwardly improper, but they did fall in love while she was still married — against their intentions. Neither acted on it. Now that she is a widow there is no impediment. Last summer, I managed to play a small part in reintroducing them, as it were . . . "

"Matchmaking," Henry allowed a lilt into his voice.

Emma forced a smile. "Out here, I think the practicalities of life are so stark, so pressing on one, that one must behave in a way that would not do in England. So if you like, I threw them together."

"Point taken, no offence intended." Henry fumbled for his pipe self-consciously. Emma leaned across and patted his knee.

"None taken, I'm just a bit prickly these days. But the fact remains, they are at an impasse. They need help. Your help. I believe. The scandal over the major's death has died down — it will never disappear — and neither Alice nor Alf are much governed by the social gossip anymore."

"Gossip, the bane of my existence as a preacher," he puffed his pipe into life. "A man dies in a blizzard — terrible — but the gossip jackals aren't satisfied. Never are. So a story is concocted about cut safety lines and . . . "

"Uncle," Emma forced herself to speak. "My proposition involves you and Alice and Alf and . . . redemption, I suppose, is the word. I couldn't ask your participation in such a serious affair if I thought you were deceived in any way."

"Deceived?"

"About the major's death."

"An accident," he pointed the stem of his pipe at her. "Then a widow racked with guilt because she disliked her departed husband. I have dealt with such things before, you know — people do confess . . . "

"The widow, in fact, may be guilty," she said it quickly to get it out and stop the Vicar's condescension. "The line was broken — perhaps cut — Jack says cut. The light was removed from the window, we think — Mary said so and Alice never denied it."

"Good Lord." Henry put the pipe down. "She confessed to . . . to murder?"

"Just the thing, Uncle, she never confessed." Emma stood and turned her back on the Vicar. "I asked her point blank once if she killed her husband and she may have nodded yes. She may think she killed him because she let him die."

"She doesn't know herself? Is that what you're saying?" Henry was calm. Almost like a police investigator. He retrieved his pipe and sucked on it quietly. "Look at me, Emma." She turned and met his gaze. "Is Alice Jordan, in your opinion, blameless of her husband's death?"

Emma froze.

"I'm not asking for her guilt — I'm not a courtroom judge. I'm asking if she is innocent."

"No, Uncle," Emma's voice was so reluctant it nearly failed. "No," she tried again. "She reached the end of her endurance. She knew one of them would go. It was him. She is not innocent. I can't say guilty — but not blameless, either. She hears his voice in the wind and she cries because of it."

She walked quickly to him, knelt, and took his hands in hers.

"I want you to give them permission to marry. Talk to them, tell them you know the whole story, and then say it is all right. Absolve them, Uncle, redeem them. Tell them . . . I don't know."

He squeezed her hands. "I'd like to tell them what I suppose somebody ought to have told you and Jack in the Forest years ago. They love each other, so they are loved. They have forgiven each other, so they are forgiven. And they have God's grace, if they only ask for it. But I'm not sure I can, Emma. Infidelity, guilty consciences are one thing, but this . . . I'd have to talk to them privately and frankly before I could know where to begin with redemption, as you call it."

Emma exhaled and sat back heavily. The baby shifted and lay with her, contented it seemed. "I am truly sorry to have placed this burden on your plate. But I would be ever so grateful if you'd try."

"Pressing practicalities, indeed," Henry said. "Your friends have dirtied some of the new-world slate, but I suppose that is the way of things."

•••

The first wave of mosquitoes arrived late May. They drove Emma off her cot on the verandah into the house for her afternoon nap. She was up most nights now with sore back, kicking baby, and a multitude of trips to the chamberpot, so she afternoon-napped to get some rest back. But she was not resting, she was dreaming of the heifers and their first calves again. Such a lovely dream to begin, so terrible to end. In the barn, a cold, snowy March day and a calf on its way. The dream was real, no fantasy quality attached to it. It unfolded as the actual events had done. The first of the heifers, bred in Paynton, delivered a fine, bull calf smoothly into Jack and Alf's arms. Slimy and steaming and wobbly but also bawling and full of life. She had helped them wipe it down with straw, convinced she'd never seen anything so wonderful before.

"Herd's just grown by fifty percent," Jack said.

Alf laughed. Emma pushed the calf to its mother and thought of her own baby, inside her these months. It was a happy thought of contentment. Then the dream changed — again real — but two nights later, the second heifer calving. Jack and Alf straining and

518

cursing, heaving mightily on a rope tied to the reluctant newborn. Fluid sluicing onto the barn floor, over the men, steaming and frightening. The new mother bawled, drowning out their human voices. She humped and pushed, but her calf would not come. Emma stood cold and aloof, holding the lantern so its flickering light cast an evil illumination on the painful scene. Finally the calf slid free and landed on the straw, motionless, and utterly limp. Alf tried to revive it but saw it was no good — twisted and strangled, it had died much earlier. The cow seemed to be fine, no prolapse or bleeding. Jack removed the stillborn calf, walking past her without a glance, as though he didn't know she was watching him in her dream. That night the coyotes shrieked and gorged. She wept in her dream and she woke now, cheeks wet. Her back spasmed and a cramp struck her. She lay quietly, the tears running into her hair. Dreams of birth — one good, one bad. Don't let it upset you. It is just a dream. They are cows, not human beings. The spasm gradually eased and she sat up drying her face. She took hold of the edge of the headboard and lurched to her feet. She was seized by a sudden sensation of relief — release. Then she was soaking wet and another spasm hit, but not, she realized, a back pain.

"Uncle Henry!" She sat heavily on the bed, glad her waters had not ruined the bedclothes. "Get Jack to fetch Mrs. Davis."

As luck would have it, Mrs. Hill was stopped at the Davis homestead on her way to Lloydminster. Both women had determined themselves to be the district midwife. Henry had brought Alice in the interim. She quickly ejected the men from the house and made Emma comfortable. She slipped into the background when the older women appeared. The preparations and even the first contractions were rather exciting. The pain wasn't as bad as she had anticipated and when Mrs. Davis "had a peek", the news was encouraging.

"Well done, my girl. You're halfway there, I'd say, and all seems well." She whipped out a pocketwatch. "Contractions seem regular, let's time them."

Mrs. Hill shouldered her way between Emma and Mrs. Davis. "Perhaps that is what they call "halfway" in Devonshire, ma'am, but, in truth, she's only a third open and I'd say the contractions are still quite eeeeregular."

She produced her own watch and shot Emma an ingratiating smile. "No point riding false optimism, eh?"

"False optimism?" Mrs. Davis sniffed. "We shall see."

They both stared expectantly at Emma, who now seemed unable to produce a contraction under the intense scrutiny. Eventually the gripping recommenced. She tried to relax, to float on it, but this one accelerated and took her by surprise. She found herself holding her breath, fighting it.

"Breathe girl, breathe!" both women ordered, consulting their watches. The pain ebbed and Emma gasped for air.

"There, see, eeeeregular."

"Don't be daft woman. Regularity is measured by time between, not during, the contraction," Mrs. Davis said confidently.

"A good midwife can tell from one go," Hill shot back.

"Here she goes again! My, that was quick."

Emma felt as though the plough handle had hit her. The baby must have found room to take a running charge at her, for this time she was bowled over. Her eyes squeezed themselves shut and in the vague distance she heard Mrs. Davis screeching, "Breathe, Mrs. Thornton! Breathe! Don't hold in!"

It was no good; her body seemed intent on self destruction and the baby bent on matricide. Every muscle she owned was hard as rock, a second away from rupturing. Then it slackened and she opened watering eyes, rasping air in and out. The midwives, startled by the change in pace, began calling Alice for their "kit".

Had she washed it? Was it in boiled water? Well, could she hurry up? Then they argued again.

"Thank you, Mrs. Hill, but my instruments will suffice, no need to clean yours."

"There wouldn't be, *if* you were going to deliver this baby, Mrs. Davis, but I'm afraid you really should leave it to me now."

The two women were nose to nose, smiling like gargoyles and extremely polite. Emma felt like she was an intruder when she asked for water.

"No water! It'll only come back up."

"A sip is fine or she'll have trouble breathing."

"Well, at least ensure it's been boiled and cooled."

Emma received her sip of water. Then the next onslaught commenced. Her breath faltered again. She grunted oxygen in and out, ending the contraction with a high, thin cry, like a prairie falcon. It helped. During the next contraction she simply opened her mouth and bellowed — at least it moved air through her lungs. It made her think of the bawling cow in her dream.

"I never uttered so much as a whimper — four children successfully delivered," Mrs. Davis said, wiping Emma's face with a damp cloth.

"Go to hell," Emma said, or at least her voice did, mimicking Jack's railway language. She didn't really seem to care about anyone or anything except this boulder lodged inside her. When would it shift?

"Well said, Mrs. Thornton," Mrs. Hill agreed triumphantly. "I screamed my lungs out. Doctor has since told me it's the best way for both mother and baby."

Emma passed into a series of screamers. It could have been one hour or ten, she lost touch. The planked ceiling pattern was her view now, the small bed enclave was her world. Everything else was the rise and ebb of birthing pain. The midwives continued their duel but she scarce paid them notice until Mrs. Davis' voice cut clear to her.

"Breech? I don't think so."

"Well, she's ready now, you must agree to that!"

Mrs. Davis touched Emma, then nodded. "Yes, agreed."

"And no progress for some time now, I don't see a head, so . . . "

Emma's mind suddenly cleared, as though she was an abstract observer. Breech. The word seized her and shook loose the image of the stillborn calf. There was no contraction, but she screamed nonetheless.

"*Jack! Come quick!*"

Jack must have had his hand on the bedroom door for it flew open and he nearly flattened Mrs. Hill. His face was in an agony of worry.

"Em, my love. I'm here, I'm right here."

"It's breeched, Jack. Just like the calf, it's breeched," she grappled for his hand and clung to it weeping. "And it hurts worse than frostbite."

"That's only one opinion," Mrs. Davis said sternly. "I'm not so certain, Mr. Thornton."

Jack let go of her hand and moved to a position between Emma's legs, reaching for their baby.

"Steady, Mr. Thornton!"

"I say, Mr. Thornton, I really must protest this."

" . . . no place for the husband."

Both women finally agreed on something, Jack was committing an unforgivable intrusion.

"Not breeched, Emma," he said, his voice steady, assured. Emma continued weeping, but with relief. "Baby's a little off kilter, like that Buxton heifer that calved late. Here, let me push this bit down and straighten it out . . . "

"*Mr. Thornton!*"

Emma peered through waterlogged eyes. Jack's sunburned face and bullet-holed cheeks smiled at her just above her belly. A sharp, slicing pain took her groin and a contraction began.

"I'd say it is time," Jack looked up at the outraged women. "Ladies?"

"Of course, push, now that he's meddled," Mrs. Davis allowed.

"Agreed, ma'am," Mrs. Hill said stiffly. "Never seen such behaviour."

The women, now firmly allied against the common foe, threw Jack out and supervised the final, long, screeching push that gave Emma her lustily bawling baby boy. Emma fell back spent, and began crying yet again.

• • •

"The great harvest will signal your final victory over the wilderness." Henry Wilson, red-faced from too much food, too much port, and an exceedingly hot August day, would not concede the point. "That wheat crop will go thirty bushels to the acre . . . "

"Now, Vicar, twenty-five, maybe," Alf puffed the opinion from his pipe.

"As I was saying, thirty bushels to the acre," the Vicar furrowed his brow. "On nearly thirty-five acres is . . . "

"One thousand fifty bushels."

"Thank you, Davie. We'll say one thousand bushels of Red Fife — the best hard-milling wheat in the world. That's eight hundred dollars . . . "

"If the railway gets here. Otherwise, we'll have to haul it and lose a quarter to freight . . . "

"The railway will come, Jack," the Vicar fought like a bear in a pit, surrounded by cautious colonists. "Your costs will drop, your cattle will sell, you'll buy more heifers and you will have double the acres broken and seeded next year. I tell you, this will be known as the "great harvest" that wrought the victory. The turning point. And I haven't even mentioned oats. Twenty acres of the best crop . . ."

"This country always has a surprise, Vicar," Alice entered the debate, "and it's rarely to our advantage. You may be right or the men may be back working the railroad again."

"Mrs. Buxton, not you, too! And to think of the lovely service I performed for you." Henry fanned his beet-root face and laughed. "I pray God will grant me the humility *not* to say 'I told you so' when I'm proved right."

The baby began a wailing cry in the bedroom.

"Oh heavens!" The Vicar reached for the port bottle. "Even William Henry Edmund Thornton is against me. I yield the floor."

Emma went to her son while the others began to clear the dishes. The bedroom was only slightly less stifling than the kitchen, yet Billy was warm, not hot. He seemed to adapt easily for a three-month-old baby. Jack called him the "wee Canadian", said he had the constitution of a coyote and jackrabbit rolled into one. His cot was beneath the window, which was propped open on a bit of screening to let some air move through the room. She sat by the window and took him up. Even when he called in the middle of the night, which he didn't do often anymore, she enjoyed these moments. The warm, little body fitting so well, the sensation when she let down, then the contented flow from mother to child, quieting his impatient demand. It was a sequence of sublime contentment to her. It made her agree with her uncle; it gave her an unreasoning optimism that she simply accepted without introspection.

A flutter of cooler air hissed through the screen, fanning her. Billy lifted his dark, pudgy face to it. She set him over her shoulder and he belched like a Roman senator. By the time she finished the other side, there was a steady, cooling breeze and the voices in the kitchen were moving outside. She put Billy's cap and muslin veil on him, then went onto the verandah. He gurgled happily at the company and Jack leapt to hold him before Davie or the little girls could. The men were lighting pipes, everyone was looking northwestward, into the freshening wind.

"Ten days of ninety degrees or better," the Vicar said, mopping his face. "Thank goodness, looks like it's going to break this evening."

"It was good weather to ripen the wheat, though," Jack said.

"Exactly! Shoulder-high, ripe wheat — at least thirty bushels to the acre — eighty cents a bushel. I tell you it will be the . . . "

"The 'great harvest!'" they all chorused the quote.

"This wind will bring rain. Hope it doesn't lodge the crop too badly," Alf said dourly. As if on cue, thunder rippled in the distance and the breeze picked up, thoroughly cool now, pushing the heat away. Alice and Alf made tea while the others lounged, idly watching westward as a scatter of small, dark clouds rushed in to shade the sunset. Emma smelled rain and looked anxiously to Jack. He was absorbed with Billy, explaining to Davie how the boy was gaining weight faster than a steer on oats. Moments later the crop below them wavered like ocean waves and a feisty squall hit, slanting rain over the hill, angled so that the verandah stayed dry. It lasted but minutes then ran southeast across the prairie, leaving the Thornton wheat swaying and sparkling in a shaft of late-day sunlight. A half-arch rainbow sprang over the field, as though God himself had reached down with a paintbrush. The colonists fell quiet, staring at the beauty.

"Remember this one, Jack?" Vicar Wilson said. Then he began to sing. His choir tenor was not as strong as it once had been, but it was still lovely and clear.

Now the day is over
Night is drawing nigh
Shadows of the Evening
Steal across the sky.

He paused, suddenly self-conscious, looking to Jack, but he and Billy had eyes only for Emma.

"I know it," Emma said. "I know it well. The harvest dinner of 1899. This song, I should say, the singer of this song, saved my life that night."

She began to sing. Jack, then Henry, then Alice Buxton joined her.

Jesus give the weary
Calm and sweet repose
With thy tenderest blessing . . .

They were all very quiet when the last words floated downhill and out onto the prairie. Quiet enough that the far-off whistle of a train was heard clearly.

"Can't be," Jack said.

"It is — a train — I heard it, too," Alf admitted.

A rushing locomotive was drawing near and it stood hair up on the back of Emma's neck. The major. Somehow he was on the verandah in this ghostly train noise. She looked to Alice. She was gripping Alf's hand, her tanned face drained to a sickly-pale hue.

"If that's a train, it's coming at a hundred miles per hour," Alf said. "Davie, cut up the hilltop and scout it for us, eh?"

Davie and Ostrich leaped from the verandah and raced uphill. A moment later his panicked shout reached them.

"Hail, Alf! And a right barstid it is, too!"

Emma recoiled from the words, as though he had shot a gun at her. He pelted back down the hill, Ostrich barking with him.

"Thunderhead two miles high," Davie gasped. "Solid wall of white underneath her. She's a killer."

"Going to hit us?" Jack asked quietly.

"Dead on, I'd say. Should get the animals under cover."

Jack handed Billy to Emma. "Right then, lads, let's be moving ourselves."

Emma suddenly had a clear, real vision of Jack. He wore filthy khaki clothes and sported a bloodstained, foul bandage around his head. He was standing calmly on a garbage-strewn prairie pointing to a distant target. He spoke conversationally to a man perched at the handles of a machine gun. They were in terrible peril, yet seemed oblivious to it. The image flickered and disappeared.

"All right. Em?"

"Yes, of course," she took Billy.

"Too late!" Alice shouted as suddenly the train changed to a roaring avalanche. Thunder cracked simultaneously with lightning flashes that backlit the white curtain sweeping over them. The bedroom window exploded — its tinkling pop just audible over the timpani drumming of the hail. The horses and oxen in the corral crammed themselves into the sod barn, which then disappeared in the opaque white blanket. Mercifully, perhaps, Emma could not see the wheat and oats through the storm. The Vicar was praying loudly, scarce heard above the thudding ice rocks. Fifteen minutes later the sun returned and gave full view of the steaming landscape. The thunderhead with its white flail followed the path of the earlier squall, narrowly missing the Buxton crops.

Alf and Davie exhaled simultaneously — they had been holding their breath. They tried to keep the elation from their faces. Emma felt her own face fall in despair. She looked to Jack who stood stunned, motionless, tiny muscles twitching in his jaw. The bullet scars glowed bright red, otherwise he had himself under control. Billy pushed against her and Emma realized she'd been squeezing him. She looked again for the wheatfield, then for oats. A jagged mess streaked with white was the reality. Their summer's work, therefore their year's work, was gone. It was too much. Hope was leaving — trailing after the thunderhead. She was just able to set her jaw, like Jack, and maintain her peace. Jack was the first one to move. He lit his pipe, set his cap firmly over his brow and led the way down hill.

"Let's see if we can rake some of it up for feed. Maybe now is the perfect opportunity to buy some pigs."

Alice and the girls went with the men, Emma and her uncle paused on the verandah.

"My God, it looks like a battlefield." Henry shook his head slowly, his wispy white fringe of hair fluttered in the breeze. "And to think that not an hour since I was braying like an ass about 'the great harvest'. It's almost like a . . . judgement."

"Don't be silly, Uncle. It was a hailstorm and we were unlucky. Don't try to take it on your conscience," Emma said.

"But Jack must be absolutely shattered. His whole year — his livelihood — destroyed in minutes. He's ruined; you're ruined," the Vicar said despondently. "If that crop was your victory, then surely its destruction must be your defeat."

"Only if he admits it," she said, not entirely convinced that her uncle was wrong. "And Jack is certainly not going to admit defeat. He means to succeed here — no other thought enters his head. He will have his victory. If not this year, then next."

"A Pyrrhic victory, my dear. Not worth the cost." He stepped unsteadily down onto the ground, bent and picked up a hailstone. It nearly filled his palm. He held it up wide-eyed, his mouth in the shape of an O. "I gave Jack a speech before your wedding —

about Canada being new and fresh. I was thrilled to help build your new house, but now . . . well, thank God above, you still have the bulk of your dowry to pay your way home and start over. You can't stay with a baby — you'll starve out on these plains."

"Jack can work the railroad next summer; we won't starve."

"Sorry, my dear, but I don't see how working as a navvie to stave off ruin is a better choice than office work and a decent home in Paddington." He held the hailstone up, squeezing it in his fist. Emma looked away. "I prayed for your success. It sounds cowardly now to suggest retreat but I really think you should consider it — while you still can."

"You are right, Uncle." Billy squirmed, pointing and gurgling at Jack, stooped over in the destroyed wheat. "It seems we are sinking — perhaps time to take to the lifeboat."

"Lifeboat?"

"My dowry," she said turning Billy so he could see Jack. She thought of his IN and OUT sheet. "I've always worried that one day this country would knock us down and we'd have to use it to escape — our last refuge."

"At least you have the option," Henry said, glancing guiltily downhill to the slain fields where the Buxtons squatted with Jack among the wrecked stalks.

"You have achieved much in this land, there is no shame in coming home. Your district is almost one-fourth ploughed — you've broken the back of prairie fire threats. You have cut trails and established villages." He pointed at the Buxton homestead. "But it is still so raw and hard; it may be for others to finish the job."

The new house, the acres of crops, the fences, barn, haystack, all leaped suddenly into focus. Blast, Damnation, One and Two were wandering out of the barn, licking the hail.

"No, Uncle," she murmured. "Trailblazers or quitters. Nothing in between but shame." She gripped Billy under his armpits and swiveled him around. "Survey this godforsaken, beautiful place, wee Canadian. See it new and remember it."

Henry looked at her with a strained expression. "It is a harsh country. I confess I'm a trifle homesick for the softness of England and a decent cup of Mrs. Toomey's tea."

"Excellent," Emma stepped down from the verandah and handed Billy to him. "Because you have business to transact for me in England, and I want it settled before we reach the others."

She took his free hand through her arm and they sloshed their way downhill through the windrows of melting hail.

"Pigs will do it," said Alf. "I can't wait to get a porker properly slaughtered, cut up, and smoked."

"Pigs will do what, Mr. Buxton?" Emma asked, approaching the wheatfield. All their beautiful, strong wheat, high as her shoulder this morning, was smashed and re-smashed into the ground.

"Eat this goddamned pulp." Alf kicked a sodden pile of straw.

"Alf!" Alice nodded towards the children.

"But that sonuvabitch'n' storm . . . " he looked up at the Vicar.

"Oh spit it out man," Henry said.

"Green wheat and straw might kill a horse or cow, but pigs will eat this and shit gold afterwards."

Alice clocked Alf with the back of her hand.

"And the oats?"

"Oats were nearly ripe," Jack said clinically. "If we can rake them up out of the wet and get a bit of a warm breeze, then we can scythe them carefully and save something. Lashburn has a milling grinder — I can chop it into some sort of bait."

"Scythe?" The Vicar's rubbed his hands. "Now there I can help. Might as well salvage something from the ruin."

"So you can, Uncle," Jack clapped him on the shoulder. "But there'll be no cash, especially if we're buying pigs. I'll be all right with my savings and a bit of credit 'til next spring, then I'll go grade for the railway again in the summer, if they're still hiring."

It was said without the tiniest inflection of emotion. Emma glanced at her uncle. She collected Billy and walked to Jack. She took his hand and pressed it to her cheek, and smiled. He grinned at her.

"Blast and Damnation will grade that railway straight past Lloydminster and right to our front door next summer. How d'you like that, Mrs. Thornton?"

"Will you not think again?" Henry interrupted.

"How's that?"

"I have received instructions," he nodded at Emma, "to liquidate her holdings in London and disburse all funds to her account in the Canadian Imperial Bank of Commerce, Battleford. She means to keep you here next summer. But I appeal to you, Jack, think of Emma and Billy. What if you get hail or frost next year after the dowry is gone? How will you return home, then? You will have passed the point of no return."

"I'll climb yon hill." Emma pointed to her new house. "That's how I'll return home."

Jack turned to her. She opened her eyes, and stared at him without blinking. "Really, Watson, come along now, the game is afoot."

ACKNOWLEDGEMENTS

I had the help of many people in writing this book and I would especially like to acknowledge five of them. Cyril Miles of Gloucester wrote me twelve foolscap pages, single spaced, on the old farming practices and customs of the Forest of Dean. Major C.P.T. Rebbeck of The Soldiers of Gloucestershire Museum provided a wealth of detail on the Glosters and soldiering at the time of the Boer War. Kay Hauer provided kind assistance at the Lloydminster archives where several gems in the form of letters and journals of Barr Colonists are located. Stella Richards found and drove most of the old Hudson Bay trail between Saskatoon and Lloydminster so that I could take pictures and notes of it. Seán Virgo rescued several characters in this book through insightful editing.

I relied on many nonfiction works in writing this book and I would like to acknowledge five of them. Winnifred Foley's *A Child of the Forest* (Holt Rinehart Winston, NY, 1975) takes one right into the people and places of the old Forest of Dean. Hart McHarg's *From Quebec to Pretoria With The Royal Canadian Regiment* (William Briggs, Toronto, 1902) marches one from Capetown to Paardeberg in 1900. Lynne Bowen's *Muddling Through* (Douglas & MacIntyre, Vancouver, 1992) tells the whole story of the Barr Colonists, and tells it very well. Mary (Pinder) Hiemstra's *Gully Farm* (Fifth House, Calgary, 1997) and Marjorie Wilkins Campbell's *The Silent Song* (Western Producer Prairie Books, Saskatoon, 1983) tell us what it was like on the homesteads, inside the soddies. Nearly all the personal accounts of homesteading were written by the women, most of who did not want to homestead, but without whom the whole enterprise would have failed. As my Uncle Mac (farmer and son of homesteaders) said: "there should be a statue built for those gallant ladies."

The Forest

The forest farming practices, animals, crops, etc. Jack met were very old by 1898 and did not change much into the twentieth century. Many people alive in the year 2000 have vivid memories of the mining and farming described in this story.

The story of Dilke and his women was, in fact, a widely believed and much repeated piece of gossip at the turn of the century, but it was just gossip, as Emma pointed out. A village in Saskatchewan is named Dilke after Sir Charles, in recognition of his efforts to bring English homesteaders to the Canadian west.

The Boer War

The Glosters and the RCR did serve in adjoining divisions at Paardeberg. Their marches and battles occurred as described here. Lt. Col. Lindsall, his wife, Lt. Wethered, Lt.Col. Otter, and Captain Arnold are not fictional characters. Lindsall did, in fact, survive his lung wound.

The RCR and the Glosters became formally allied regiments in 1925. The enteric fever and conditions of the hospitals at Bloemfontien are not exaggerated here.

London and Canada

Sullivan did conduct the *Absent Minded Beggar* in November 1899 and he died November 1900, but no anniversary show coincided with his death. Lloyd's letter to the *Times* and Barr's pamphlets, posters, recruiting techniques etc. presented in this story are not fiction. The English people's trek and their first years on the land occurred much as described here. The power struggle between Barr and Lloyd still sparked debate among the older generation in

Lloydminster decades after Barr fled. The fires, winter, soddies, hardships, and desperate loneliness are all fact. The story of the man feeding a tree into his stove while he read Shakespeare and starved is based on an NWMP report of the period. Lloyd did serve under Otter in the campaign against Poundmaker's Cree and was badly wounded in the battle.

DAVID RICHARDS' education at the Royal Military College in Kingston and his experience as a member of the Canadian Army for six years provided him with the perfect background to explore his fictional territories. First there was *Soldier Boys* (Thistledown Press, 1993) that transformed the Northwest Rebellion from a "history lesson into a human drama." Next came *Lady at Batoche* (Thistledown Press, 1999) that rewrote the Gabriel Dumont/ Louis Riel mythology and won a Saskatchewan Book Award. Now his historical fiction widens its lens to encompass late nineteenth century England, the Boer War, and Canada's Barr Colonist experience. Throughout it all, David Richards' research, insight and storytelling are impressive.

David Richards lives in Moose Jaw, Saskatchewan, and teaches at SIAST — Palliser Campus.